THE REALT

Tourmaline: Book Two

JAMES BROGDEN

SNOWBOOKS

Proudly Published by Snowbooks in 2015

Copyright © 2015 James Brogden

Snowbooks Ltd.
Tel: 0207 837 6482
email: info@snowbooks.com
www.snowbooks.com

Paperback ISBN 9781909679535
Ebook ISBN 9781909679542

To the Memory of Graham Joyce
Without 'Dreamside', this story wouldn't exist.

BEFORE

Sometimes, when we dream, we dream too deeply, and we find ourselves in the world which lies on the other side of consciousness. The problem is that we take our dreams with us, and they superimpose themselves on the surrounding reality, forcing the inhabitants of that world to act out our most extreme fantasies and nightmares. This phenomenon is called Subornation, and it is the greatest threat their world faces. Specialised branches of their law-enforcement agencies are tasked with finding us and expelling us from their world, overseen by an organisation called The Hegemony.

Sometimes, we bring the inhabitants of that world back with us. They awaken in our bodies like possessing spirits, or secondary personalities, often taking over altogether. Sometimes it isn't people we bring back, but animals – or worse. When that happens, these Exiles find themselves in our world, possessing reality-altering abilities which are the backflow of subornation. Then the Hegemony, which exists in our world too, hunts them down, to exploit their talents for the aim of keeping the two worlds forever apart.

Bobby Jenkins awakens to find himself on Stray, an island-sized raft adrift in the Tourmaline Archipelago. Stray is inhabited by people who, in our world of the Realt, lie trapped in comas, and amongst these is Allie Owens, with whom he falls in love. With no memory of his identity in the Realt, he starts to build a new life with the Strays, who want nothing more than to survive as best they can, and be left alone. Their most immediate threat is the presence of an *araka*, a psychic parasite from the dreaming space between the worlds, which has entered Tourmaline attached to one of the dreamers and lies dormant under Stray.

Stray's position puts it in the middle of a conflict between two of the Archipelago's island states, and in the interests of maintaining regional stability, the nation of Oraille sends a team of agents from their Department of Counter Subornation to eradicate it and its inhabitants. They are led by the zealous and increasingly unhinged Berylin Hooper, who doesn't care that Bobby, Allie and the other Strays aren't hurting anybody – she simply wants them gone. In defending his home, Bobby tricks the *araka* into attacking Berylin's ship; it explodes, catapulting both Berylin and the *araka* into the Realt, fused together into one entity which calls itself Lilivet.

Lilivet sets about completing Berylin's original mission of stopping subornation by infiltrating the Hegemony and using its resources to build an army of Exiles with which to wage war on the Realt. Bobby is the only one who can stop her, having entered Tourmaline physically rather than in a coma, and feeling responsible for her existence in the first place. He accomplishes this, but not before she spawns her monstrous brood in the canals of Birmingham.

Bobby is now trapped in the 'waking' world, with no way to return to Allie – she, in the meantime, is one of only two survivors of the battle which destroyed not just Berylin's ship but Stray too. Berylin's second-in-command, Runce, offers them sanctuary in his homeland of Oraille, and Allie is only too happy to accept the offer, because – despite the fact that it is impossible, and with her real body comatose in the Realt – she discovers that she is pregnant.

CHAPTER ONE

THE BROOD OF LILIVET

1

From underwater, the lights of bars and nightclubs were actually pretty, thought Eddie Toren. The thought quite surprised him – he'd never considered himself to be a poetic soul – but then, he'd never drowned before either. Maybe this was how it went.

The first panicked spasms of choking and thrashing had given way to a dreamy, drifting contentment, and he stared upwards at the lights twisting like neon snakes above him in the darkness. They were so beautiful that Eddie found himself wishing that the guy whose foot was currently bearing down on the middle of his chest would move so that he could see better. Plus, of course, so that he could stop, you know, drowning.

He'd been doing such good business tonight, too. His pockets had been almost empty, and it wasn't even midnight. Maybe it was something to do with the season. Maybe summer put people more in the mood for a little extra buzz in their clubbing. It was easier to party till dawn when dawn came at four o'clock with birdsong rather than the freezing bloody cold. Still, at the end of the day he didn't really care and couldn't be bothered thinking about it too much. He just hustled his little bags of powders and pills in and out of the clubs along Broad Street, easing his way through the perfumed masses of clubbers which he loved, which he just fucking *loved*, man, because there was nothing like the press of other human beings to remind you of how alive you were.

The Russians had caught up with him in an alleyway leading down to the canal at Gas Street Basin. Two of them, big bastards, blocking the exit. Eddie had cursed himself for being a careless prick and curled his fingers tightly around the handle of the knife he kept in his jacket pocket. Just in case.

Rainy had been with him too, sharing the night. His off-sider. His wingman. Rainy, short for Rain Man, on account of him being a fucking retard for everything except numbers. Rainy counted the money and kept the stock-take straight in his head, while Eddie ran his mouth at the punters and made sure everybody had a good time.

But Rainy, prize thickhead that he was, tried throwing money at the problem, waving a fat roll of all their cash at the Russians in the hope that this would make them go away. Eddie had known that was never going to work. The Russians had all the money they wanted from their whores and their gambling outfits – this was about territory. This was about pride. You couldn't argue with the Russians when it came to pride, and you sure as shit couldn't buy your way out of it with them. Everybody knew that, except apparently Rainy – Eddie might have tried to point it out to him but there he was flashing *all their money* at the fuckers. Let them beat it out of him, fine, but don't give it up like a bitch.

Toren had only started to get really scared when he pointed out that he paid his dealer's dues to the Balti Boys and they'd laughed in his face. He'd hoped that they would back down when they realised that they weren't dealing with a pair of unconnected scumbags – because, hard as the Russians doubtless were, you'd have to be actually crazy to take on the Balti Boys on their own turf.

All the same, when one of them had pulled a gun and shot Rainy in the face, it had come as something of a shock.

While Rainy slid slowly down the wall, making godawful wet, gurgling noises, the Russians dragged Toren to the end of the alleyway where the canal ran and the biggest of them stuck a foot in the middle of his chest to keep him underwater while he made gurgling noises of his own.

And then it was now. For a moment, the terror and outrage woke again and he thrashed briefly, feebly. But the foot pushed harder and he sank deeper, away from the pretty lights.

There were things down here.

Crawling things.

Toren felt them in the darkness, exploring up and down his body on dozens of spiky legs like crabs, and somehow this was worse than anything else so far. To die was bad enough, but to be eaten before it happened... he gathered himself for one last, almighty doomed heave, but before he could move, one was crawling up his neck. Its articulated joints curled over his chin, prising his lips open and probing inside, and then (*ohgodohdearsweetjesus*) it forced itself inside like a mouthful of bone shards, sharp and squirming against his tongue, and there was a sudden awful, tearing agony as it bore up through the back of his throat, ripping flesh and ligaments, and he could hear the heavy crunching of it resonating in his skull as the creature chewed its way into his brain, and he thrashed then, screaming the last of his breath in black bubbles and...

He could see.

Plain as day, he could see right through the water and night sky above that, and the heavy boot pressed into the middle of his chest.

See and *breathe*. Well, not exactly breathe – his lungs weren't pumping anything – but the crushing sensation of drowning had disappeared, and the pain in his head had gone with it.

The guy holding him down turned and said something to his mate, and even though Toren didn't speak Russian, he knew that the gangster had just said 'How long does it take an Englishman to just fucking die?'

Toren thought that, interesting though this was, it was about time he got up.

It was surprisingly easy. He couldn't tell where the strength came to him from, but it threaded his muscles like quicksilver, and for a fleeting second it felt like he was in warm, bright shallows rather than a stinking canal. He took hold of the

Russian's heel with one hand and shoved his knee hard with the other, meaning only to topple him backwards, but there was a sickening crunch from the joint like a chicken leg being pulled apart, and it actually flexed backwards just before he collapsed, screaming, on the tow path.

The gunman, already alarmed by the howls of his crippled comrade, turned to see Toren emerge from the black water, caked in the rotting filth of the canal bed. A few of the remaining creatures which had been too slow to inhabit him skittered over his head and around his shoulders before dropping off and seeking safety in the water. Even the dim lights of club-land were too bright for the brood of Lilivet.

The gunman crossed himself, swore, and legged it up the alley. His mate, abandoned, began to drag himself along the tow path, throwing fearful glances behind.

Toren had intended what happened next to be quick and brutal, but necessary. He found instead that once he had the guy sprawled and sobbing at his feet, with his limbs pointing in all the wrong directions, he was reluctant to finish it. He could feel that the thing in his brain was ravenous, being so newly hatched from its father's belly and having consumed nothing more substantial than its weaker siblings. Here, now, was a grown victim in the prime of his conscious, adult terror, and it wanted – demanded – to feed. Toren had heard the phrase "the smell of fear", and now he knew the literal truth of that; it was coming off the dying man in waves, squirting out of the glands in his brain and the pores of his skin like battery acid. When the creature in his own brain showed him what it wanted him to do to the Russian, he shrank from it at first, sickened. Then he remembered: they'd tried to drown him and shot Rainy in the face, and for what? A few little bags of coke? Fuck them.

So he bent to it.

To reward him, the child of Lilivet stoked the arousal centres in his brain, so that the more the guy screamed the harder Toren got, and when his victim finally, gratefully died

Toren came so hard that he nearly passed out for a moment. But he held it together long enough to tip the corpse into the canal and then slumped back, panting, looking at his hands. It looked like he was wearing red rubber gloves right up to the elbow.

'That was all kinds of messed up,' he muttered to himself. And grinned.

As if in reply, something bubbled weakly behind him.

'Rainy?!' Toren scrambled over to him through the litter. 'Are you alive? Can you hear me, mate?'

It didn't seem possible. The whole left side of his head was a bloody mess: his eye was a red hole, his molars gleamed, and there was something that looked like a huge shard of eggshell stuck to his head, which Toren realised was part of his shattered skull, still attached to his scalp, hinged and flapping as he twitched. Automatically Toren fumbled for his mobile phone to call an ambulance, never mind that it was certainly waterlogged and useless, or that what was left of Rainy was probably nothing more than the random jerks of dying nerve endings. He couldn't do *nothing*.

The solution, in the end, came from the same place as the sudden new appetite for torture and murder.

He went back and knelt by the water's edge, reaching a hand below the surface, and he called – not with his voice, but with his mind. He called to the black creatures which had crawled all over him in the darkness, fighting each other to feed in his fear, and he summoned them up by the power of the one which now lived inside him, the first of its kind to win the precious gift of awareness which they all blindly craved. Helpless to prevent themselves, they were drawn to its strength, which was his strength, because he and it were one and the same thing now. He understood that. It wasn't an intruder; it was filling a hole in his soul which had always been there – he'd just never known it, or else he'd patched it with the feeble solace of drugs. The rest of Lilivet's brood clustered in the water beneath his outstretched fingers.

All of you, he promised them. *One day, soon. But for now…*

He fished one out and inspected it. It squirmed, attacking his hand in its hatred for the light and the open air, so he squeezed it until it squealed and fell still.

He took it over to Rainy and clapped it to the splintered and bloody mess of his head. At first the Brood resisted. There was nothing here to nourish it; the host was close to death, if not there already. But Toren insisted, pressing it into the damaged flesh, not allowing it any choice.

'Heal my friend,' he told it. 'Like your sister healed me. Or else die too.'

It burrowed inwards and he watched carefully as the injury closed behind it, trying to see how it was done. There was no such thing as magic – he wasn't a child – but there didn't seem to be any other explanation – except that possibly somebody had spiked the ecstasy he'd taken earlier and he was hallucinating the whole thing. But he'd had bad trips before, and this felt nothing like it. He felt clearer and more sober than he ever had in his entire life. What it came down to, Toren figured, was this: the people that had tried to kill him were dead or fled, and anything responsible for that was alright by him, however it worked.

Rainy twitched again, opened his eyes and bleared at Toren. 'What happened?' he grunted. His head was completely normal, except for the fact that it, and his left shoulder, were covered in gore.

Toren squatted down beside him and brushed the matted hair out of his eyes. 'How do you feel?'

'Bastard of a headache.' Rainy struggled to his feet with help. 'Seriously, what happened? Where'd the Russians go?'

'It doesn't matter. They're gone.'

Rainy focussed on him properly. 'Jesus, Ed. You look like shit.' He wrinkled his nose. 'And you smell like it. Have you been swimming in the fucking canal?'

'Questions later, buddy. Answers too, if you're lucky. Come on, let's get you cleaned up.'

2

Toren dreamt and found himself on a sandbar in the middle of a glaringly blue ocean. He'd never believed such colours could exist, or that the sea could be so bright. The smell of brine stung his nostrils, and his bare feet were sunk an inch deep in hot, dry sand. He wiggled his toes experimentally. His only experience with the seaside had been one rain-soaked day trip to Kings Lynn when he was eight, a doomed attempt by Grannie to get him away from his feckless powder-head of a dad for one day. Wherever this place was, it sure as shit wasn't Norfolk.

The sandbar wasn't much bigger than the footprint of his flat, completely devoid of plant life or anything resembling shelter, but it wasn't unoccupied. The sound of hammering caught his attention.

At the far end of the sandbar a woman was working on the half-built keel of a small boat. Surrounding her, the sand was littered with lengths of wood and tangles of rope. She had her back to Toren; her vest top was damp with sweat, and the muscles in her shoulders gleamed as she hammered.

Toren cleared his throat. 'Uh. Excuse me?'

The woman turned. She had dark hair tied back under a straw hat, but it was the glasses which she wore which Toren recognised instantly.

'Ms DeSalle?' he asked, incredulous.

His old Design and Technology teacher. The only one out of the whole bunch of them that, as far as teenaged Eddie had been concerned, wasn't a smug, dismissive prick.

'No,' said Ms DeSalle. 'But then, since that's how you've dreamed me here, I suppose yes.' She looked down at herself critically — at the flip-flops, the frayed beachcomber shorts, and the figure above them. 'Could be worse,' she grunted and went back to her hammering.

'What do you mean, no?'

Ms DeSalle stopped again. 'I mean no. You know you're dreaming, don't you?'

Toren nodded.

'Well then, I can't be her, can I? I'm just in your head.' She chuckled at that.

'What's so funny?'

Ms DeSalle flip-flopped over, spraying little bits of sand as she did (It was the *details*, Toren thought. This was the most detailed dream he'd ever had.) and tapped him gently in the middle of the forehead with her hammer. 'I am in your head,' she repeated. 'And I don't mean metaphorically, Edward. Metaphors are your job here. I am physically inside your head, cuddled happily around the top of your brain stem, with my feeding limbs plugged into your limbic system, and...'

'Stop!' Toren stumbled away, suddenly nauseous.

'You want me to sugar coat it for you? Piss off – it is what it is. I saved your life, and you've given me awareness. I'd say that's a fair trade. I'll go you one further, though: I'll make you strong, Edward Nigel Toren. I'll give you the power you've craved all your life, power to fuck over the ones who have stepped on you and squashed you since you were a boy. I know you want that. I've seen your school records; I know everything about you. Why else this?' She stepped back and gestured at herself sardonically. 'You've got some serious Oedipal issues that need working out, Edward, did you know that?'

'Stop calling me that.'

'Sure you don't fancy a little wriggle around in the sand?' She blew him a kiss. 'This is just a dream after all, Edw-'

'Stop calling me that!' he yelled.

'Okay, Eddie. Fair enough. I'll make you strong, and in return...' She paused, and smiled.

'In return, what?'

'Well for a start you can help me build that bloody thing,' she answered, pointing her hammer at the boat. 'DT was the only subject you were ever any good at, let's face it, and even then all you did was make bongs and key-rings shaped like dicks.'

Toren laughed. 'Yeah, I remember that.'

'See? I'm on your side. I'm the only one that ever was. That's why you see me like this: deep down, you know you can trust me. We want the same thing.'

Toren looked around, at the empty sandbar and the glittering flatness of the sea, which seemed to merge into the equally featureless sky, without any clear horizon. It was possible that in the haze where they met he could see wavering blurs that might have been distant islands, or else his eyes were just playing tricks on him. 'What is this place?' he asked.

'The Tourmaline Archipelago,' answered Ms DeSalle. 'On the other side of your dreams.' She spat. 'In other words, the middle of pissing nowhere. Come on, boy, we've got a long journey to make.' She held out her hammer.

After a moment's hesitation, Toren took it.

3

Toren woke up feeling ravenous. He was no stranger to hunger – on occasion he'd gone days without food if it had been a choice between that and his next high – but he'd always been able to powder over the problem with a bit of speed. He'd never felt like this straight, and he'd never ever felt it this bad before. His guts were coiling in on themselves like a nest of snakes eating their own tails.

Memories of the previous night immediately crowded his brain, thick and hot, and he tried to push them away.

Nightmare. Bad trip. Drug-induced psychosis. Some dickhead had messed with the E he'd taken, that must be it. He couldn't have done those things. He wasn't a violent man; he'd never been in a fight, not even at school. He was the Happy Man, he was Captain Easy, the one who brought love to the party in little white pills. He didn't even deal the hard stuff. He didn't want to make addicts out of people – he just wanted to make everybody in the world happy, so that they'd all love him.

Because the alternative – that there was something like an armoured spider living at the bottom of his brain, making him hurt and kill and enjoy it…

Push it away.

It was only when he opened the blinds and then checked his phone for confirmation that he realised how insanely early it was: nearly ten in the morning. He swore in disbelief. He couldn't remember the last time he'd seen this side of midday.

He went into the cramped living room, where Rainy was crashed out on the sofa, and shook him awake.

'Come on, twinkle-toes,' he said. 'Arse. Gear. In.'

Rainy muttered something incomprehensible and twisted away.

'Seriously.' Toren shook him again, harder. 'We've got some questions need answering, remember?'

'Fuck off,' replied Rainy, quite distinctly this time. 'My head hurts.'

At this, the morning's frustration boiled over in Toren and Captain Easy disappeared. Something squirmed at the bottom of his brain and sent its strength surging down and out along both arms as he grabbed Rainy and dragged him upright. It was similar to what he'd felt when he'd torn that gangster apart last night – and there was no hiding from it now, nor did he want to – except then he'd been half-drowned and panicking and convinced it was all just a hideous hallucination. Now, part of him watched what he was doing to Rainy with detached fascination. Where was this power coming from? How much of it was there?

He held Rainy up by his blood-stained shirt collar and shook him. 'What did you just say to me?' he demanded. 'Fucking what?'

But it seemed that Rainy – or the thing inside him – was not in the mood to be intimidated. His hands reached up to lock around Toren's throat and he felt that same pulse of energy, only this time it was directed at him. Rainy's hands squeezed with appalling strength.

'Oh no!' Toren laughed, choking at the same time. 'No no no. That's not how it works, buddy. Not in the fucking slightest.'

He roared and bore back down on Rainy with everything he had, until the other man's hands fell away and he hung limply from Toren's grip, mewling. The creature that was in Toren had been the strongest of Lilivet's brood to claim its prey, and that hadn't changed.

'Now I know that something genuinely fucked up is happening with you and me,' he said, 'and we will find out what it is and who is responsible and we will make them pay. But.' He shook Rainy again. 'Are you listening to me? But that is not going to happen unless you accept that I am calling the shots, okay buddy?'

Rainy mumbled something, so Toren shook him a third time, hard enough to make his teeth clack together. '*Okay?*'

'Okay.'

'Good.' Toren dropped him. 'Now go and have a shower. And take one of my t-shirts while you're at it. This one's covered in bits of your brain.'

Something about this made Rainy snigger, and that in turn made Toren snigger, and then the sniggers turned into snorts, and soon the pair of them were laughing like drains.

4

Lee the Chemist lived on the eighteenth floor of a standard high-rise which had been scheduled for demolition for over a decade but never actually put out of anyone's misery because the council lacked the finances to even demolish things these days. He lived behind a reinforced door with two of the Balti Boys' thugs, who seemed alright; they'd never bothered him or even said two words to him, probably because he was too far down the food chain to even step on.

Toren had a feeling that things like that were about to change drastically.

He and Rainy climbed the eighteen flights of stairs (because of course the lift was broken), a lot easier than they ever had in the past, never having been especially fit specimens of humanity. He wondered if they could even call themselves that anymore, strictly speaking.

Like a lot of front doors in this tower block, it was protected by a heavy-duty wrought iron security gate which was as far as anybody usually got when buying stuff from Lee. Toren reached through and knocked on the door, making sure to stand right in view of its fish-eye lens. After a moment, his phone rang.

'Harry's Happy Whorehouse,' he answered brightly.

'You were only here yesterday,' Lee replied, without any pretence of greeting. 'What's going on?'

'Nothing's going on. Business was unexpectedly good, that's all. Really, really unexpectedly good.' He turned to shush Rainy, who had started giggling. 'I've come for some more of your best bikkies.' He knew that Lee was standing just the other side of the door, watching him through the peephole. Toren could feel him, the weight of another human soul shifting like slow clockwork in close proximity to his own. Fear seeped through the steel, and he cranked the smile a notch wider.

'It's early,' said Lee. 'Come back when it's not stupid o'clock in the fucking morning.'

The call was disconnected, and footsteps moved away from the door.

Toren sighed and turned to Rainy. 'I tried to do it the civilised way, didn't I?'

'You did. I saw.'

'Well then, he's responsible for this, not me.'

He turned back to the security gate and considered its lock. Exactly how strong was he? If he could survive drowning and then inflict that much damage on his would-be killers, not to mention his and Rainy's little pecking order dispute earlier… He grasped the lock and twisted, trying to recall the feeling of power which had surged out from him on those occasions.

Backwash, something deep in his mind said. Something which sounded like MsDesalle, and for a moment his dream about the sandbar and the boat was crystal clear in his memory. *It's called backwash.*

Rust bloomed on the lock. The metal's white enamel crazed and flaked away like dried toothpaste, and on the bare metal a lifetime of corrosion ate into the lock casing. It spread up and down the bars either side, which crumbled in moments, while the non-ferrous parts of the mechanism simply fell apart and clattered to the floor. The gate swung open.

'I thought you were going to just, you know,' said Rainy. 'Smack it one.'

'I just want to talk to him. I don't want to wreck his whole place.' Toren placed his hand flat against the middle of Lee's front door. The paint began to blister as the wood beneath bulged with a sudden onset of decay, and the deformations spread from his outstretched fingertips until the whole panel was buckled. When he pushed, the bolts holding it closed tore free from the door frame which had become rotten and soft. He walked in.

Lee was already backing away fearfully down a short hallway. He was tall and cadaverously thin – the result of too many years being his own quality control – and the effect was like looking at clothes peg learning to walk.

'So this is your place,' nodded Toren, looking around. 'Nice. I like it. Very neat. Very professional.'

The flat was bare and sterile; bottles and boxes of chemicals were lined up in the hall, and through the kitchen door behind Lee, he caught a glimpse of industrial-grade glassware. 'Nice to see everything ship-shape and that you haven't been bothered by anybody recently.'

'What the fuck are you talking about?' said Lee, still backing up. 'What the fuck did you do to my door?'

'Nothing that I didn't do to the pair of Russian gangsters that came after me and my accountant last night. You wouldn't happen to know anything about that, would you?'

Lee turned and fled into his kitchen.

Toren sighed.

Rainy was peering into the other rooms which led off the hallway. 'Hey Eddie,' he wondered, 'where are his flatmates?'

'Hey Lee!' Toren called. 'Where are Harvey and Oswald?' Not their real names, of course, but it had always amused him that none of them got the joke. 'Shouldn't they be trying to beat the crap out of us right about now? Or have they been forced to take involuntary redundancy as the result of a hostile foreign takeover bid?' He was almost at the door to the kitchen, and he could hear Lee clattering around in a panic, opening and slamming cupboard doors. 'Because what I'm trying to figure out, Lee, is how your sales personnel – i.e. myself and Rainy here – got forcibly retrenched while it all seems to be business as usual with you.'

He walked into the kitchen – which looked more like a mad scientist's laboratory than a place where food had ever been prepared: all rubber tubes, glass retorts and large metal canisters crusted with chemical precipitate. Lee was backed against the fridge, waving a jar at him.

'Don't fuck with me!' he yelled. 'This is hydrochloric acid! It'll fuck you right up!'

Toren stopped at the threshold and raised his hands to show that he meant no harm. He could smell the terror coming off the man. It was intoxicating.

'Jesus, Lee, calm down, will you? I'm not here to hurt you. If I were I'd have done it by now. Why are you so bloody twitchy? Just tell me, simple yes or no. Russians?'

Lee nodded and seemed to relax a little.

'See? That wasn't so hard. Okay, so, I want you to get a message to them for me.'

Lee nodded and allowed himself a small, nervous smile. 'Sure. What do you want me to say?'

'Say?' Toren blinked at him. 'I don't need you to say anything.'

Sudden horrified comprehension flashed in the chemist's eyes, and the spike of it was finer than a hit of the finest speed. Toren moved far too quickly for him to react, grabbing the wrist of the hand which held the acid. There was a momentary tug of war, during which the liquid slopped out and onto their flesh; where it struck Toren, it simply ran off like water, but Lee's skin blistered immediately. He screamed, and as he did so Toren emptied the rest of the jar over his head.

Rainy came in and together they watched the screaming, staggering figure bounce around his own kitchen until his head connected with the corner of a cupboard unit and he collapsed.

'I thought you said you weren't going to hurt him,' said Rainy.

'I know, it's a real puzzle, that. I've never been a violent man. Can't think what's got into me.'

They both laughed at that, and a third voice joined in, which only Toren could hear.

CHAPTER TWO

THE KARASAND

1

Seb knocked on the door to Allie's cabin and without waiting for a reply stuck his head around it. 'We will be at the scuttlebutt soon,' he grinned and disappeared. In his thick accent it had sounded like *scurtleburt*. Privacy had been non-existent on Stray, and it seemed that old habits died hard.

She put down the copy of the Odsae Clarion which she'd been reading – weeks out of date and half of it in a language she didn't understand, but it was all she could find to give her some kind of clue about what to expect in the wider world beyond the Tourmaline Archipelago. She shrugged into a thick, high-necked pullover and followed him up on deck.

The OAV Karasand's twin cigar-shaped gas nacelles obscured much of the view to either side of the aerostat's superstructure, which was suspended between them by a cradling framework of girders and cables, but this hardly mattered since the world was wreathed in cold, white cloud. She was immediately chilled despite the sweater; never mind having been born and bred next to Lake Superior with its long winters and heavy fogs, the past six months spent drifting on Stray had given her an appetite for tropical heat.

For the first few days after they'd departed Danae, she'd done nothing but stand for hours on end at the rail and stare out at the shifting cloudscape and what it revealed of Tourmaline's glittering, opalescent seas. The prospect of every day taking them further south of the equator didn't exactly thrill her.

For all that the cloud hid, it made sound much clearer: Captain Parmley shouted orders to his men, who clambered around in the ship's cradle preparing the Karasand for landing. The bass thrumming of her electrical engines that powered twin propellers, each as tall as a person, took on a subtle vibration as she decelerated, and was accompanied by the hydraulic whine of hydrogen compressors in the nacelles sucking the gas back into its tanks. Smoothly, the Oraillean airship descended out of the cloud cover.

Grey ocean rolled less than a hundred feet beneath her.

Directly ahead lay the long bulk of a vessel which looked like the bastard offspring of an aircraft carrier, oil-rig and Victorian iron foundry. It was an island of soot-stained and riveted steel, with dozens of chimney stacks belching black smoke and competing for space with bristling masts and 'stat mooring pylons. The fat shapes of airships cast their bloated shadows over the scuttlebutt's multiple decks, stacked haphazardly atop each other like a badly shuffled stack of rusted iron playing cards. Sunset had been lying hidden under the cloud, low on the horizon, and streaked everything with brass. A constellation of satellite vessels ploughed the ocean around it, the largest of which was transferring tons of coal by scow straight into a pair of hangar-sized doors open at the water-line. Crewmen of the Oraillean Aeronautical Corps derisively referred to such floating maintenance and supply stations as 'scuttlebutts', joking that they were little more than floating coal scuttles. The navy had them stationed all over the Antaean Ocean, and the Karasand had already stopped at several since leaving the Tourmaline Archipelago, but this was by far the largest Allie had seen yet.

At the bow, Runce was pointing out features and explaining them to Seb. They made an incongruous pair: William Runceforth, the ageing Counter-Subornation Agent with his bald, pale head, next to the tall, dark-skinned Sebastian, whose other body was comatose in a hospital somewhere in France, on the other side of reality. Buster, the flop-eared beagle, was hanging through the railing as far as he could get, sniffing at the odours which rose from below. The men turned as Allie approached.

'I hear this is the last one before Oraille,' she said. 'Nearly home then.'

'Aye,' nodded Runce, impassive as ever. She couldn't tell whether this was good news for him or not. Nobody really knew how his superiors were likely to react after the debacle of the Spinner's mission. It was one of the reasons she had agreed to come along. One of them. 'How's the morning sickness?' he asked.

'About what you'd expect. Navy food doesn't exactly help.'

'Welcome to my world,' he grunted.

She laughed, which was a rare and welcome thing these days.

He looked puzzled. 'What?'

'It's just, you said... oh never mind.'

With much shouting and ratcheting of windlasses, the Karasand's gas nacelles were winched from the lateral cruising position, up and together above the fuselage, which now hung beneath like a standard gondola. Semaphore flashes from the scuttlebutt guided the Karasand, under Captain Parmley's expert hands, to nudge against one of the mooring pylons. Guy cables were thrown, a gantry swung across, and from the scuttlebutt maintenance hands began scampering to and fro.

'You coming?' Seb asked, heading for the gantry after Runce.

'Thanks, but I'll pass,' she said. 'Noisy. Smelly. Not really my thing.'

'You'll want to get used to that, you having a baby and all.'

'Thanks,' she grimaced. 'But I've been there too. Go, find something disgusting to pickle your French brains.'

He saluted with a grin and followed Runce below. Buster whined after him.

'No chance,' she said, scratching his head. 'I want you where I can see you, troublemaker.' Her guts rolled over queasily again. 'Time for a bit of light evening puking, I think.'

She went back to her cabin. As a diplomatic and courier 'stat, everything about the Karasand was designed to minimise mass and maximise speed, including crew space, with the exception of a few cabins for VIPs. This consisted of little more than space for a narrow bunk, a few bits of furniture and a privy, so at least she didn't have to vomit for the public entertainment of the crew.

Afterwards, she lay on the bunk and reached under the pillow for her treasures; they were in an old tobacco tin, and pitifully few. A piece of liquorice. A plastic Christmas-cracker compass. An empty matchbox. A small pearl-handled pen-knife and an iridescent porcupine quill bracelet, confiscated in the police cell on Timini and returned by a shame-faced Chief Constable Osk under the stern gaze of his wife.

Not enough. Not nearly enough.

'Sorry, Bobby,' she whispered. 'Waiting's not really an option anymore.'

Her hand crept to her lower belly and rested there.

She'd agreed to return with Runce to his country of Oraille, despite all that his people had done to Stray, for the simple reason of the life growing inside her. She was going to need doctors, and if theirs was the most advanced culture in this world, then it wasn't even a debate.

I'll find a way to return, he'd said. *I'll come back to you.*

Across the length and breadth of two worlds? She couldn't allow herself to hope for that. It seemed fitting that the last thought which chased her down to sleep was how badly she wanted a cigarette.

2

She was woken by the sound of Buster whining and scratching to be let out.

'For the love of…' she muttered, knuckling her eyes. 'You couldn't've gone before we left? Alright, alright!' she protested as his scratching became more insistent.

She tugged on the big pullover and let him out, then followed. Buster was clever enough to have learned to do his business over the side, but they were moored half-over another vessel and she didn't think he was clever enough to avoid accidentally doing it on the heads of the people below. 'That ain't why they call it the poop deck, you know,' she said to him as he trotted ahead.

The scuttlebutt was ablaze with lights and raucous with the noise of machinery and men, but with most of the Karasand's crew enjoying the hospitality of the mess deck, up here the world was dim and quiet. She felt secretive, as if she were looking down on a brightly-lit stage from the catwalk of a theatre.

Allie passed a good evening nod with the bridge watch and tried to encourage Buster over to the oceanward side, but at one point he suddenly stopped and stared straight upwards, whining again, and refused to budge.

'What? If it's another damn seagull, I swear...'

He began to growl.

She looked up.

Her view skywards was obscured by the gas nacelles which had been retracted upwards and together in its mooring configuration, but they weren't in direct contact. There was a gap of about six feet, spanned by rigging to allow maintenance workers easy access between them, and as she looked she thought she saw the silhouette of a human figure leap quickly from one to the other. At the same time a savage cramp of nausea twisted her guts, and Buster launched into his alarm bark.

Moments later the bridge watch came running. 'Are you all right, ma'am?' he asked.

'Not really,' she grunted, arms locked tightly over her stomach. 'You might want to get the captain back up here. I think we've got a guest.'

3

A thorough search of the Karasand revealed no stowaways, nor had anyone passed the sentry on duty at the base of the mooring pylon. There were no other 'stats within jumping distance, and – no matter how the intruder had got aboard – if they had escaped by simply jumping overboard, the fall would have been fatal. There was no suggestion that Allie might have imagined it, as an inspection by the ship's engineer discovered that somebody had definitely been tampering with the nacelles.

'Nasty little bit of sabotage, too,' he reported to them later, in the Captain's office. He tossed a tangle of electrical cable onto the table. 'One of the insulator blocks underneath the starboard prop has been smashed, sir, and the overload grid which is supposed to dissipate electrical surges like static build-up or lightning was wired right into the hydrogen inlet collar on cell eight.'

'Meaning what?' asked Runce.

'Meaning "boom", I'm thinking,' said Seb.

'He's right, sir. You start that prop and sooner or later there's bound to be a short, routed straight into the H-cell. They'll be collecting what's left of us out of the water with sieves.'

'I don't suppose the name Hindenburg means anything to you people, does it?' Allie put in.

'Designed to look like an accident?' asked the captain.

'To someone who didn't know what they was looking for, probably, sir, yes. But these are complex systems, sir; this wasn't a quick in-out-bang-it-all-about job. Whoever did this had access to at least three separate areas of the ship, knew exactly what they was doing, and had the tools to do it. I don't see how that could've been done without them getting spotted, never minding how they got on in the first place.'

'So it's either one of our own, which his bad enough,' growled the captain, 'or a foreign power has the specs to one of our most advanced aerostats.'

'Sabotage or espionage,' observed Runce. 'Lovely.'

'Obviously this has something to do with you three,' Captain Parmley continued, overriding their collective indignation with a wave. 'Oh shut up, the three of you. I'm not blaming, just stating the obvious. The Aeronautical Corps will get you safely home, don't you worry about that, and then you'll be somebody else's problem. In the meantime, Chief, a complete check-up for the old girl before we set off again, if you please.'

4

Her time in Stray's little claustrophobic community had given Allie a sharp radar for the nuances of other people's behaviour, and over the next two days she saw the new tension in the way some of the Karasand's crew stepped aside when she passed, or made no eye contact, or too much of it. It was the officers, she noticed, not the deckhands. It gave her the same kind of twitchiness she felt whenever someone was talking about her behind her back. She tried approaching Seb about it, but he just gave one of his exquisitely indifferent Gallic shrugs, and she wasn't sure that she trusted Runce enough yet with her misgivings – for all she knew, he was the one doing the talking. There were all kinds of tall tales with which he could be regaling them about how he'd come across his pair of Strays. So she kept to her cabin as much as possible, and only ventured on deck when the hands began shouting excitedly that land had been spotted.

Oraille.

Her new home.

CHAPTER THREE

THE WORLD SPINS BOTH WAYS

1

Bobby eased the hospital fire escape door open as gently as he could, wincing at the grating sound it made; after years of dereliction, it was warped in its frame, the hinges rusted through disuse. He peered into the darkness beyond. Nothing of the bright June morning in which he stood survived past the threshold – as if the interior existed in an entirely separate world. He smiled. The irony was not lost.

It was brief, that smile. This was a bad idea. It had been a bad idea from the moment the Exile – who called himself simply Chandler – had said that he'd meet Bobby in a decommissioned hospital in the middle of bloody nowhere, on his own, without so much as a wrist-watch, never mind an actual phone. It had continued to be a bad idea on the long drive back up to the Midlands, where he expected every motorway camera to be clocking his number plate, and it had stubbornly remained a bad idea as he'd ducked through a gap in the security fencing and scouted around the hospital's graffiti-scrawled buildings looking for a way in.

'Carmen!' he called softly. 'Are you there?'

There was a ripple in the air like heat-haze, or as if he were viewing the world from underwater, and a woman walked out of it. The fact that she was wearing a towering tutti-frutti hat and a flamenco dress made her sudden appearance even more striking.

He gestured at the outfit. 'Really?'

She rolled her eyes with a sigh. There was another ripple, and the dress was replaced by combat fatigues and a red bandanna. 'Pick your cliché, *señor*,' she pouted.

'You are, as ever, incomparably gorgeous whatever the outfit. Did you find the old MRI room?'

'*Si.*'

'And?'

'Two men. Your date and his chaperone.'

'Are you sure they didn't see you?'

She waved her hand dismissively. 'Pfft!'

'That's very comforting, thanks. Okay, hang back. If I need help, I'll let you know by running away very fast and yelling. And probably being shot at.'

'Same plan as ever, then. You be careful now, Roberto.' She blew him a kiss and rippled away.

For all he knew this was an elaborate Hegemony set-up to find the location of the Exiles who'd been sheltering McBride, Vessa and himself since the catastrophe at Lyncham – and none of them had been particularly pleased that he was jeopardising their safety by doing this. But all, in the end, had agreed that it couldn't be helped. There was no other way anybody could think of to get back to Tourmaline and Allie.

The last sight of her replayed itself in his memory: standing at the edge of Stray, having to be restrained by that old soldier chap Runce from flinging herself into the surging waters between worlds, despite knowing that if she did so she would only awaken in her own crippled body, but prepared to do it anyway to help him.

There must be other ways between our worlds, he'd said to her. *I'll find one, and I'll come back to you.*

Of course it was a bad idea. It was a fucking terrible one, come to that. But just like all the others for as long as he could remember, it was the only one he'd had.

He pushed the door wider and stepped inside.

2

Countless past intrusions by vandals, junkies, thieves and urban explorers had let damp and a mulch of leaf-litter in too; the linoleum floor tiles were mould-black and lifting at the corners, while the walls shed paint and leprous scabs of their own plaster. Broken light fittings and drifts of yellowing paper from ransacked files added to the litter, making any attempt to move quietly futile, so Bobby concentrated on simply trying to navigate through the maze of wards, clinics, offices, and operating theatres.

He'd been told to meet Chandler in the old MRI scanning room; there'd been no explanation of why. He assumed it would be somewhere near Radiology and X-ray, but it was tricky, with many of the signs missing or defaced.

Noise from behind…

He spun. A few yards back, a bin of clinical waste lay overturned, and from it poked the wedge-shaped head of a rat. For a moment it stared at him, eyes glittering, then it shot off down the corridor, trailing a shred of bandage.

Bobby swore and sagged. 'I don't suppose you know where the bloody MRI room is, do you?' But the rat had disappeared with its prize.

He spent some time scrounging through the debris of a storeroom and found a length of wood hefty enough to act as a decent weapon against any of doctor rat's little friends, before carrying on.

Ground or Lower Ground, he figured, for no logical reason other than it seemed to him that that kind of big machine belonged on the ground. He found an operating theatre with its big rosette of lights still angled at a bed, as if waiting for the next patient while the surgeons had nicked out for a fag break. A paediatric unit with cartoon curtains still hanging – one of which, disturbingly, had been slashed to ribbons. An office desk stacked high with crutches.

This must be what the end of the world would look like, he decided.

He'd been forbidden from bringing even a torch, but enough light came through broken windows and skylights for him to make his way to Radiology without scaring himself to death more than a dozen or so times. The former control room was a gutted shell, and through a connecting door he found the main scanning room. It was large, the floor wet with puddles of rainwater and strewn with leaves which had come in through the broken panes of a wide skylight, under which were two plastic chairs. In one sat a young Asian man dressed in urban explorer gear – camo t-shirt, daysack, and combat trousers with about a million pockets and pouches – as casually as if he were enjoying a picnic in a sunny park.

'Mr Jenkins?'

'Chandler, I take it.'

He nodded. 'Hold still.'

A second man – older, bulkier, tattooed – stepped out of the shadowed corners of the room and came towards him with the kind of body-scanning wand he'd only ever seen in airports.

'Hey!' Bobby protested. 'You said alone!'

Chandler looked surprised. 'You didn't think I meant me, did you? This is Joey. Now be a good boy and raise your arms. He's just doing the necessaries, and then he'll be leaving us.'

Bobby did as he was told. 'Joey and Chandler,' he commented. 'Nice.'

'What can I say – I'm a fan of the classics. In answer to your question,' he continued, though Bobby hadn't asked one, 'rooms built to house MRI scanners are designed as Faraday cages, with frameworks of aluminium to stop outside electromagnetic radiation from bollocksing up the image. They also do a good job of blocking phone and radio signals – you know, like the ones used by people who like to eavesdrop on private conversations such as this one.'

'I'm not wearing a wire, if that's what you're getting at.'

'You might not even be aware if you were. They took the equipment, of course, when they closed the hospital. Streamlining the services of Nottinghamshire's Primary Care Trust, they called it, by which I assume they meant a nice extra-streamlined journey of an hour to the nearest accident and emergency. But we're all in it together, so that's okay then.

That,' he added, pointing up at the skylight, 'was so patients could look up at the sky while they were lying on the scanner bed before they went into the machine, which I think is a nice touch, don't you?'

'Depends,' said Bobby. 'If it's the British sky you're looking up at, that might not be such a cheerful sight.'

Chandler gave him a sidelong look. 'Not like the sky above the Tourmaline Archipelago, I suppose. How did you find me?'

'You know a man called Ennias?'

Chandler nodded.

'Well he's dead, sorry to say.'

'That surprises me. He was an extremely paranoid man.'

'A friend of mine rescued the SIM card out of his phone. It took a bit of fiddling but we managed to get the contact details off it, and there you were.'

'I should be worried. That sounds far too easy.'

'Trust me, it wasn't.'

Frisked and found to be mostly harmless, Bobby dropped his arms as 'Joey' gathered his things and left.

'Good,' said Chandler. 'Now we can talk.'

'What – just you, me and a bunch of guys with sniper rifles?'

Chandler produced a thin, patient smile. 'That's a healthy case of paranoia you've got there yourself, Mr Jenkins.'

'Oh?' Bobby called out to the room: 'Blennie! Front and centre!'

The air rippled, and out of it stepped a small, conservatively-suited man. He had protuberant eyes in a round face and a line of permanent worry etched between his brows. 'Yes sir?' He glanced nervously at Chandler, who was rising, startled. 'Is everything alright, sir?'

'For the moment, Blennie, for the moment. Tell me, what's the perimeter guard on this place like?'

'Well sir, there are four marksmen concealed at points covering the main approaches to the building. Their support van is just around the corner, and there's one car parked outside the rear entrance with its engine running and a driver inside. He's playing Angry Birds, sir. I think that's all of them. Is that what you wanted to know?'

'Perfect. Good job.' Blennie's anxious expression broke open into a brief smile. 'Just stick around for a minute, would you?' The smile disappeared. Bobby turned to Chandler again. 'Yes, I knew your men were there, and I walked in anyway. No, you've got no idea where this chap has come from, who he is, what he can do, or how many more of them I have working for me. So why don't we, for the sake of argument, assume that neither of us is a complete idiot and have a civilised conversation, yes?'

He could see that Chandler was obviously weighing up whether or not to walk away. Waving Blennie in his face had been a necessary gamble, but the Exile would never have agreed to this meeting in the first place if there hadn't been something he'd wanted.

'Very well then,' he said presently. With a wave he invited Bobby to take the other chair. Bobby sat. 'Please, tell me about what happened at Lyncham. In return I will tell you everything I know about how to get back to Tourmaline – although I want you to understand from the outset how little that is. If I knew a fool-proof way home, I would have taken it long ago.'

'Fair enough. So. I used to work as a security guard at a gallery, until I got pushed through a painting and into Tourmaline by a woman with strong connections there.'

Chandler nodded, impressed. 'A painting. Never heard that one before. What kind of connections? A twin?'

'No. Apparently there was another personality in her which had gone there, and between them they created some kind of link. I don't really understand how that works. There was a big raft, with half a dozen people living on it – coma patients from this world. While I was there I met someone who I – well, we became close, let's just say that.'

'So why did you come back here?'

'There was also a monster. An *araka*, I think they called it. It somehow bound itself to a Counter Subornation agent who got sent to kick us out, and it ended up in Lyncham, trying to build its own little Bloefelt army of world-ending goons. Again, I don't really understand why. All I knew was that it had to be stopped. So we stopped it at Lyncham – me and my slippery friends you met just now.'

'What was the mechanism?'

'Mechanism?'

'What kind of portal? You say you got in through a painting; how did you get back?'

'A whirlpool in the ocean. A *world*pool, actually.'

'And you assumed that, having got into Tourmaline physically in the first place, you could physically return without ending up trapped in someone else like any other normal Exile.'

'Yes.'

'That was a bold move, Mr Jenkins. You have the soul of a gambler, I believe.'

'My soul is another story entirely.'

'And now you want to get back to your special someone.'

'Yes. Can it be done?'

'Oh it can be done. It absolutely can be done. The question is whether or not you're prepared to make the kinds of sacrifices necessary to do it.'

'You'd be surprised at what I'm prepared to do.'

Chandler leaned forward and inspected him. 'It is something of a boast to claim that you have saved the world, let's be honest, but even so, assuming that you're telling the truth, what would you do with it now, for the sake of the woman you love?' He frowned slightly. 'Man?'

'Woman,' said Bobby. 'Very definitely woman.'

'Can't be too sure these days. After all, the world spins both ways. But still, what would you do with it? Would you burn it, and everything in it, to get back to her?'

Bobby leaned forward and matched his gaze. 'Sir, I would tear it apart with my bare hands.'

'Good. Then maybe you'll see her again. Because the only way that's going to happen is if you get yourself recruited by the Hegemony, and your friends might have a problem with that.'

'Recruited. You can't be serious.'

Chandler stood and glared at him. 'Wake up, Jenkins. You think this is a joke? Yes, there are other ways into Tourmaline, and yes, every single one of them is controlled by the Hegemony. Why do you think it's called that? It does exactly what it says on the tin: total and ubiquitous control over everything. They're the ones who split the world in the first place – do you not think they'd keep some intersections between the two?'

'There has to be another way. Something they've overlooked. Something that's been created since then.'

'Well if your story about the friend with the split personality is true, then I'd say yes, probably, there is the odd random intersection out there, but that's something you can hardly rely on. You could spend the rest of your life looking for them – lots of people do. I don't think you appreciate how rare your experience is, Mr Jenkins – you have seen with waking eyes what those few people who have travelled to Tourmaline experience only in their dreams. Your perspective is unique. I'd very much like to know: what did you see, in the meniscus?'

'You mean the space between the two worlds?'

Chandler nodded. There was undisguised eagerness in his eyes.

Bobby frowned, trying to recall it. 'They were big,' he said eventually. 'No, huge. You know coral? Like coral, but the size of skyscrapers. Massive, massive things. And aware, too. Not really conscious, not really thinking, but they knew when somebody, some dreamer was nearby. I wouldn't want to be caught by one of those things. Do you know what they are?'

Chandler's face closed again. 'No,' he said, and Bobby knew that he was lying. He considered pushing it, quizzing the man for what he knew about the monstrous forms which lurked on the other side of sleep, but his overarching goal was to get back to Allie, and if Chandler was his best shot at that, then Bobby didn't want to scare him off. So he let it lie. 'Well what the hell *do* you know, then?'

'The only thing I know for certain is this: the Hegemony operates under lots of names in lots of places, but the body which oversees and coordinates their operations is called the Interstitial Assembly. They must meet or communicate somehow. Find out how, and you might find your way back.'

Bobby laughed. 'And that's it, is it? That's everything you know? "They must meet somewhere"? What a waste of bloody time.' He stood to go.

Chandler made no move to stop him. 'Mate, you're asking the wrong man the wrong questions. Ennias knew better than to dig too deep, and they caught up with him even so. Still, I hate to see you leave empty-handed.' He reached into one of his innumerable pockets and produced a business card. 'You ever hear of a thing called lucid dreaming?'

'No. What is it?'

'It's what your lady-friend and all her coma-buddies on that raft were doing. Dreaming, but being conscious at the same time. It's a way in, of sorts. Short of finding a magic wardrobe, it's your best shot.' He tossed Bobby the card. 'It's a private clinic, very expensive, but give them my number and you should be right.'

Bobby examined the card. *Redos Sleep Clinic*, it read. *Specialising in all forms of sleep disorder including insomnia and sleep apnoeia, as well as hypnotherapy and lucid dreaming classes.* 'Ennias told my friend that these are exactly the sorts of places that the Hegemony keeps its eye on. Why should I trust this?'

Chandler laughed. 'You shouldn't. Like I said, the clue is in the name; nowhere is safe. But we keep our eye on them too. We have one or two people on the inside – and on the outside, for that matter. You've got to start somewhere, haven't you?'

'Thanks, I think. And what if I do decide, you know, to sleep with the enemy? How do I go about getting myself recruited?'

'Oh that should be easy enough for you,' grinned Chandler. 'Just do something spectacularly stupid.'

'Yeah, I reckon I can just about manage something like that.'

3

Bobby went back to the hopital's deserted car park and stopped by his van to light a cigarette, taking a moment to enjoy the bright open space after the claustrophobic madness inside.

No, Steve McBride's van, he thought, and flicked ash. Inherited from Ennias – Bobby had never met the fellow, but McBride had trusted him well enough. Now McBride was gone too.

After Lyncham, the three of them – Bobby, Steve, and Vessa – had crawled back to Birmingham and the shabby bedsit where Ennias had told Steve to lie low. A week of uneasy cohabitation had followed, during which they had talked themselves around in circles, failing to decide what to do next and growing snappy with each other in the tiny space. It didn't help that McBride kept looking at him as if expecting him to drop the whole 'Bobby Jenkins' act and revert to being Caffrey again – as if he could. As if he *would*. It didn't help, either, that Vessa did her best to avoid him altogether, as if worried that he was expecting her to wave a magic wand and teleport him back to Tourmaline and Allie. That wasn't going to happen, and she obviously thought he resented her for it.

He couldn't truthfully say that he didn't.

Despite his best intentions, he couldn't stop himself from pestering her for everything she knew about the Exiles. He took the train down to London and spent a frustrating day looking for the safe-house where she said Ennias had taken her the first time, but either she'd got the details wrong, or she'd lied, or Ennias had simply been too thorough at cleaning house before everything fell apart, because Bobby couldn't find any trace of it. When he got back to Birmingham, he found McBride and Vessa on the doorstep of the bedsit with their bags packed.

'What's this all about?' he'd asked. 'Going on holiday?'

McBride hadn't cracked so much as a smile. 'Not really. We're getting as far away as we can from all of this. It's still too dangerous, even here.'

'I have a feeling that the Hegemony are the kind of people who find you wherever you try to hide,' Bobby pointed out.

'Maybe. But that's no reason to make it any easier for them.'

Bobby caught the accusation in McBride's tone. 'What's that supposed to mean?'

'Bobby,' said Vessa, intervening. 'We understand, we really do: you have to get back to Allie. But the fact is that we can't help you, and every step closer you get brings the Hegemony a step closer to us. Yes, we're protecting our own skins – but we're also giving you a clear run so that you can do whatever you need to do without having to worry about endangering anybody else.'

Bobby looked at her for a moment, and then burst out laughing. 'Damn, you are good!'

She sketched an ironic little curtsey. 'Seriously though,' she added. 'You saved my life; if the only thing I can do in return is to get out of your way, then okay. But please don't ask us where we're going. You know we can't afford to let you know that.'

'Fair enough,' he conceded. 'To be honest, if I was in your position, I think I'd probably be doing the same thing.'

She hugged him briefly, murmuring a 'thank you' into his shoulder.

McBride tossed him a set of keys. 'It's yours now,' he said. 'The place. The van. This whole vast and glorious empire.' He shifted, looking suddenly uncomfortable. 'And if, you know, Caffrey does come back…'

'He won't,' Bobby said curtly.

McBride nodded. 'Right.'

The last thing Bobby had seen of Steve and Vessa was their heavily-packed rucksacks as they headed towards the city centre, to quickly disappear amongst the traffic and other pedestrians. He had no idea where they were now. It might be possible to find them, if he really wanted; Carmen and Blennie should be able to sniff out the traces of their fellow Fishketeer Igor in Vessa's soul. But he'd promised to leave them alone, and things would have to get pretty desperate for him to break that.

Then Carmen rippled into existence on one side of him and Blennie on the other. She wrinkled her nose in distaste at Bobby's cigarette, plucked it from his mouth and tossed it away.

'Hey!' he protested.

'Hey yourself. You don't smoke, remember?'

'*Caffrey* doesn't smoke,' he corrected her, annoyed. 'Robert Jenkins does.'

'Well you didn't in Tourmaline.'

'Well in case you haven't noticed, this isn't Tourmaline,' he snapped back. He yanked the van door open, climbed in, slammed it shut, and tore out of the car park with a savage grinding of gears.

Blennie and Carmen watched him go. 'The sooner we do something about that, the better, I think,' he said.

CHAPTER FOUR

NEW ORDERS

1

The Karasand put down briefly at the port city of Havenmouth, which straddled the wide estuary of the river Tara with miles of naval and civilian wharves, slipways, docks, and shipyards. Craft of every conceivable size and shape busied both the water and the air. The Captain informed his passengers that ordinarily they would have de-barked here for a rail transfer inland to the capital city of Carden, but that the Karasand had been given orders to proceed directly there – so they followed the Tara's sweeping breadth through a flat green landscape that was patchworked by hedgerows, dikes, earthen banks, and a shining veinwork of canals. They passed over an abrupt escarpment of chalky hills and into a country which was more recognisably traditional farmland, and she realised with surprise that everything they had just flown over had been reclaimed from the ocean. It was an engineering feat to rival anything in her world.

So too, as they approached the brown pall of smog which lay over Carden, was it evident that the capital city of Oraille could easily have given nineteenth century London or New York a run for their money.

It bristled with chimneys and spires, warehouses, foundries and workshops in a sea of soot-blackened redbrick tenements which washed up around the islands of older, more monumental stone structures: cathedrals, domes, halls, palaces. Through it all, the river flung its curves, gleaming and intestinal with the spillage of countless factories, and spanned by everything from soaring stone arches to footbridges of riveted iron. It all clustered, as if piled up by its own accreted weight, at the wide triangular point where the Tara was formed by two tributaries, and Allie – assuming that Runce's bosses in the Department for Counter Subornation would be found here, under the thickest bristling of 'stat pylons – was surprised when the Karasand veered to take a course out towards a much more heavily industrialised part of the city which she overheard one of the crew calling Blackyards.

This also seemed to worry Runce. He caught up with the captain on the bridge.

'Where are we going?' he asked. 'Clatter says we're to be taken straight to Shotton House. DCS orders.'

'I'm aware of that, Mr Runceforth,' replied Parmley, 'but I received fresh orders from the coastal station at Havenmouth. The DCS has arranged a safe landing zone in Blackyards for you and your passengers.'

'I'll see those fresh orders, if you don't mind.'

Parmley produced a folded strip of clatter paper which Runce read with deepening anger and an utter lack of surprise. Everything about it, down to Director Jowett's ministerial code, was legitimate.

Runce didn't bother wasting time on arguing or trying to pull rank – just strode from the bridge and went straight to find Allie and Seb, who were in her cabin poring over maps of this strange new land.

'This could be bad,' he warned them.

'Bad?' demanded Seb. 'Bad how?'

'There's been a change of landing zone. Instead of taking us straight to the Department, we're being picked up in the middle of nowhere. Maybe they're playing it safe, keeping you away from people in case you attempt to suborn anyone, but they told the captain, not me, and that's worrying.'

'Not as worrying as the fact that they seem to know what we are in the first place,' Allie objected. 'How did that happen?'

'I don't know,' Runce grumbled.

Seb unleashed a stream of French obscenities and made a dash for the door. Allie stopped him with a palm on his chest.

'So what can we do?'

'You're the lucid dreamer,' replied Runce. 'You tell me. What can you do?'

It took a few moments for the significance of what he was asking to sink in. During their journey from the ruins of Stray he'd described to her the phenomenon of subornation – by which dreamers from her world of the Realt temporarily overwhelmed the reality of this world with their own fantasies and nightmares – and it explained many things about her experiences in Tourmaline but at the same time sounded too much like magic for her liking. She didn't believe in magic – and even if she had, the idea of twisting the world around her and forcing its inhabitants to obey her will was just plain wrong. As an experiment, and feeling absolutely ridiculous, she'd tried to effect some simple changes in her immediate surroundings, like making her rock-hard mattress a bit damn softer and turning her breakfast biscuits into a stack of pancakes. Of course, nothing had happened. Seb had been similarly unable to do anything remotely resembling a subornation. Runce had been at a loss to explain why.

She gave him a look. 'That's not funny.'

'I know,' he said. 'I wasn't joking. You're telling me that you haven't been able to change anything at all?'

'Nothing.' The familiar terror of returning to her old life – of waking up into a world of pain and crippled dependence on others – seized her again. 'I can't let them send me back,' she insisted. 'I just can't.'

'Fine,' Runce sighed. 'Then we'll have to do this the hard way.'

'What's that?'

'Well we're going to have to rely on my natural bloody charm to talk us out of this, aren't we?'

'Sorry, but that doesn't make me feel a whole lot safer.'

Runce shrugged. 'At the end of the day, the safest you can be is dead.'

2

It was blustery, and the sky was a hurrying tatterwork of shredded cloud; their shadows chased pools of sunset-light over the bristling roofscape, so that Carden looked like it was at the bottom of a shallow golden sea. The Karasand descended through smog towards Blackyards, a district of rail-yards and warehouses whose serrated roofs squeezed together like crippled accordions. Somehow, hearing the sound of freight cars clashing and chuntering along beneath her made this place seem suddenly, frighteningly real.

Presently, in a wide area of rubble-strewn concrete, she saw human figures standing around the perimeter of a large circle formed by fat electrical cables and what looked like high-tech bollards with rotating mirrors.

'To contain you,' explained Runce. 'Theoretically.'

Captain Parmley appeared at the rail. 'What's all this?' he demanded, staring down at the welcoming committee. Closer now, they could see that at least two of the waiting figures carried tezlar rigs. One of them looked up, grinned, and waved.

'Something you weren't told about, lad,' answered Runce. 'Welcome to the club.'

Parmley turned to Runce in baffled outrage. 'What's going on? Why is there a tezzer squad waiting for us down there? Who are you people, really?'

'Take us to Shotton House like you were supposed to do in the first place, and I'll tell you all about it. Those people down there aren't our friends, son, and they're certainly not yours.'

'Sergeant-at-arms!' bellowed Parmley. In moments, Allie, Seb, Runce and a snarling Buster had been marched to the very tip of the Karasand's bow and found themselves staring down the rifles of half a dozen spooked-looking marines.

'We're no danger...' started Allie.

'One thing, Miss Owens,' warned Parmley. 'Say or do one thing, and I'll take my chances with a court martial.'

The airship's gas nacelles locked into their landing configuration while crewmen threw down long mooring lines which were caught by men on the ground who guided her to a landing in the very centre of the mirror stations. The gangway was already being winched out before they'd touched down; Parmley plainly couldn't wait to get them off his ship, and in fairness to the man, Runce couldn't blame him.

The three were marched off, into a circle of weapons aimed at them. Buster was growling continuously, and Allie had to keep a tight hold of his collar. There was a hurried conversation and an exchange of documents between the Captain and the head of the welcoming committee – a man with saturnine brows and a wide, smiling mouth – who carried a rifle cradled over his arm as if he fancied himself as a sporting gentleman. Runce felt the first shiver of real fear when he realised that the tez guns weren't accompanied by any PV detectors. Also, the men facing them were dressed far too casually for agents of the Department for Counter Subornation, and the DCS never ran plain-clothes operations. Worse, he didn't recognise a single one of them, and for such a small, highly specialised department, that was impossible.

This wasn't an investigation; it was a firing squad.

Runce shouldered his way into the conversation. 'Right!' he demanded. 'Who are you buggers, and what's this bloody circus all about? Let's see some warrant cards, for starters.'

The sporting gentleman laughed in his face. 'Officer Runceforth. You've had quite a trip, I'm told. Unfortunately, you also exceeded the remit of your orders quite significantly in bringing these two abominations back with you, and I've been sent to put that right. Sorry, old boy.'

Runce snorted. 'Your little bit of sabotage on the scuttlebutt didn't work quite so well did it? At least this time you have the guts to do it face to face instead of sneaking around like a filthy spy.'

Around the circle, weapons were raised.

Numbly, Allie raised her free hand in surrender.

Seb did too – but he kept going. His arms stretched high above his head, fists clenched, veins and sinews standing proud. His face was clenched too, red and perspiring, and he grunted with effort as if he was trying to tear something out of the very air.

With cries of alarm three of the firing squad started to rise slowly off the ground.

'*Subornation!*' someone yelled.

One of the tez guns fired, and its crackling energy bolt hit Seb square in the torso. For a moment his body seemed to absorb the energy and redirect it outwards through every pore in a blazing purple nimbus, and then it overwhelmed him, burning him away completely and collapsing into the black hole of its own after-image. Buster tore free from Allie's grip and threw himself at the gunman, barking furiously. The sporting gentleman's rifle cracked, and Buster spun away across the ground, motionless.

'No!' Allie screamed. An instant later the second tez was fired at her, and all she could do was throw her arms up to shield herself instinctively, fuelling the gesture with every ounce of outrage and denial in her soul.

Runce gaped as, impossibly, the second bolt glanced away at an angle from her crossed arms, deflected upward and straight at the massive bulk of the Karasand's nearest gas nacelle. Its electrical discharge system, designed to handle static build-up and the occasional atmospheric lightning strike, couldn't begin to cope, and the hydrogen cells in the main envelope exploded in a white-hot fireball.

Allie felt something like a pair of giant hands shove her from behind with brutal, neck-snapping force, and then the world was full of fire and gunshots and screaming. Somewhere in the middle of it, Runce dragged her to her feet and they ran, skirting as close as they dared to the inferno; the fire was racing through each of the gas cells in turn, their flame-retardant material overwhelmed and incinerated in seconds to reveal the glowing, buckling metal framework beneath. The Karasand's crew were running, leaping clear, some helping wounded companions, others on fire themselves. The bullets aimed at Allie and Runce only added to the chaos, and allowed them to disappear into the dark labyrinth of freight cars and warehouses.

3

Major Oliver Crowthorpe (Regimental Surgical Corps, retd.), was on his second muffin of a late evening supper when Mrs Buckley returned to announce that a most peculiar looking young woman and an old man were at the front door claiming to know him, but that not to worry, she'd have Mansell see them off the premises straight away.

'Just a moment, Mrs B,' he said, pausing mid-butter, 'what do they want?'

Damien raised eyebrows at him from the other side of the fireplace. 'My dear Oliver, taking house calls from strange young women? What a very, very dark horse you are.' He turned his own muffin on its toasting fork to brown the other side.

'It might interest you to know,' Crowthorpe responded, wiping his fingers on a napkin, 'that I have recently offered my retired services to a charitable foundation for the health and welfare of the poor. It may well be in connection with that. In the meantime, you young oaf, make yourself useful and finish buttering my muffin.'

Damien smiled archly. 'As always, it will be an exquisite pleasure.'

Crowthorpe found Mrs Buckley scowling at a man and a woman who did indeed look like little more than beggars: ragged, leaning on each other as if drunk, and smelling strangely burned. Their breath plumed between chattering teeth; it was late Autumn, and chilly.

'Ollie,' croaked the old man. 'For Reason's sake, let us in.'

Crowthorpe recognised the voice first, and the face soon followed.

'Bill? Bill Runce?! What on earth has happened to you, man? And who is this?'

'I've been bloody shot, haven't I! This is my niece, Alison. Alison, Oliver. Old army pal. Long story. Now are you going to let us in, or am I going to have to bleed all over your front doorstep?' Crowthorpe saw now that the young woman had a wad of filthy, blood-stained cloth pressed to his shoulder.

'Mrs Buckley!' he barked. 'Bring me my bag at once! And have two of the guest rooms made up!' He stepped in to take Runce's weight off Allie and together they eased him, cursing and grimacing, over the threshold. 'I'm assuming that you have a good reason for showing up here dressed like a tramp and in the company of a woman who is not your wife, when you should be in hospital? Eh?'

'An excellent reason,' grunted Runce.

'Does it involve thugs and plots and high-level bastardry?'

'It's starting to look that way,' said Allie.

Crowthorpe's eyes lit up. 'Splendid. Very pleased to meet you, my dear.' He shook her hand, somewhat awkwardly, given that Runce was staggering between them. Allie liked him instantly. Though the two men were of similar ages, Crowthorpe was tall and expansive, with a luxurious mane of silver hair, while everything about Runce was sober and cropped.

They were halfway down the hall when an extremely handsome and much younger man appeared from a side doorway, holding a muffin. He saw the three of them, stopped, and blinked. 'I'm eating this, you know, if you're not,' he said to Crowthorpe, waving the muffin defiantly, and disappeared back into the sitting room.

4

Crowthorpe steadfastly refused to let Allie assist him in any way as he went about the business of extracting the bullet from Runce's shoulder, despite her protestations that this was exactly what she was trained to do. It was for the best, because she wasn't really in much of a fit state. He seemed competent enough, but stealing a look at his surgical instruments she was dismayed. They were gorgeously made, with elaborately engraved steel and pearl-inlaid handles, but they were antiques – at least by the standards of her world. Would these people be able to look after her properly?

She kept her misgivings to herself and afterwards he tended to her own wounds, which were mostly cuts, abrasions, and minor burns.

'How long have you known Runce?' she asked, as he applied a piece of sticking plaster to the side of her neck.

'Oh, I've been patching him up for years – him and a lot of the old boys in the regiment, even after we've all been put out to grass. They don't trust the public hospitals, and they can't afford private care on the army's retirement stipend,' he shrugged. 'So I help them for old times' sake, and they repay me when and how they can.'

'It sounds very civilised.'

'Oh, one makes do, one makes do. How long have you known him? I take it that none of us believes this absurd fiction of you being his niece, by the way, do we?' And as she started to protest he added: 'Oh do stop. You're amongst friends here, in case you haven't realised it.'

She relaxed slightly. 'Almost two weeks. And in a purely professional capacity. In case you were wondering.'

He raised an eyebrow.

'Oh, no! Not *that* kind of profession!'

'I don't know what you mean,' he replied, all wounded innocence. 'I simply assumed that it was Department business, what with all the running around and being shot at. He was working up until recently with a most peculiar young lady. Very brusque. I like you much better; I can tell we're going to get along splendidly.'

She shifted, uncomfortable at the mention of Hooper, and changed the subject. 'Do you treat the soldiers' wives too?'

'Sometimes,' he nodded. 'A female practitioner would be more appropriate, but I think they know I'm, ah, no threat to them, shall we say.'

'In that case I wonder if you could check something for me.'

'Of course.'

She hesitated, fidgeting with the plasters on her hands. 'I'm pretty sure I'm pregnant.'

Crowthorpe's expression contorted dramatically as a series of possibilities, each more alarming than the next, occurred to him. 'It's not...' he whispered, and rolled his eyes in the direction of the room where Runce lay, bandaged and sedated.

'God no!' she cried, horrified, then burst out laughing. 'Please, no. Ugh. I don't even want to think about it.'

He subsided in relief. 'Thank Reason for that. Well in that case, please allow me to offer my congratulations – assuming that they are in order. I simply observe that you aren't wearing a wedding locket.'

'It's... complicated.' Complicated enough without raising the subject of what her options might be if she chose not to keep it; for all she knew, this culture might burn her at the stake.

'It generally is. May I ask how far along you are?'

'Four weeks – maybe six. I'd just like to know if everything is healthy, you know, as far as you can tell.'

'I will need to call someone – a midwife I know. She's very good. Very discreet. But it will have to wait until morning, I'm afraid, after Bill has told me exactly what's going on here and I can decide how much danger I might be exposing her to.'

'I understand.'

He ordered a highly disapproving Mrs Buckley to draw her a bath, and then kindly left her alone, deciding that the remainder of his questions could wait until the morning.

5

In front of a bright fireplace, a full copper bath steamed. Two baths in as many weeks – Allie might have felt like a princess, if she didn't currently feel like the wrong end of a game of whack-a-mole. Making sure the door was firmly locked, she stripped and examined her reflection critically in the long wardrobe mirror. Lean from life on Stray, scorched and scraped in a dozen places, but basically intact.

'Not bad for an old chick,' she told it. She ran a hand over her belly. Not the stomach she'd had in her twenties, that was for sure, but childbirth had been kind to her, and there weren't too many stretch marks. She tried to imagine it swelling now.

'I can't do this again,' she whispered.

Then she climbed into the bath.

CHAPTER FIVE

DREAMS OF WAR, DREAMS OF LIARS

1

When he'd read the word 'clinic' on the card that Chandler had given him, Bobby had imagined white-coated orderlies escorting shuffling patients through antiseptic wards. Not a garden party.

His first group session at Redos was held outdoors on a warm May evening, under the rustling canopy of an immense willow tree. The surrounding grounds of the clinic, itself in the leafy southern suburbs of Birmingham, were more like the manicured gardens of a stately home than a medical establishment. This, Bobby supposed, was what private health insurance bought you. There were eight of them, himself and Doctor Sapna Nandhra included, seated comfortably in wicker chairs around a table glowing with candles and glasses of wine. If it was true that most of the people around him were suffering from various forms of anxiety, depression, and mental illness, then the easy smiles and laughter belied it.

'The thing to bear in mind,' said Doctor Nandhra, 'is that lucid dreaming is not the same thing as dream control. I know you'll all have read plenty on the internet about manipulating what happens in your dreams, and lord knows *Inception* has got a lot to answer for...' she paused while they laughed at this '...but very often there can be measurable therapeutic effects from simply being aware of what is happening in your mind while you sleep.'

She had an easy-going manner for someone so young, Bobby thought. In his experience, young women in authority tended to overcompensate for the prejudice of their male colleagues by being overly formal and stiff-necked. But he'd done his research on her, downloaded one of the books she'd written and pretended to himself that he understood half of it, and sat in her office for his orientation chat and seen all her qualifications on the walls; she had nothing to prove. Then with a sudden pang he remembered that Allie had been a doctor too, and he realised he didn't know what her specialty was.

'So for the moment,' Dr Nandhra continued, 'all you need to try and do is remember what you dreamed the previous night. From recall afterwards we can progress to awareness during the dream, which can then proceed to standard therapy – and maybe even control for those of you who want to meet Leonardo DiCaprio.'

More laughter at that.

2

'It says here,' said Blennie, reading from the doctor's guidance notes, 'that often the simplest way to remember your dreams is to repeat to yourself "I will remember my dreams" over and over again as you fall asleep.' He tutted sceptically. 'It can't really be that easy, can it?'

'Bah!' snorted Carmen through a mouthful of rice. She was sitting on Bobby's bed, eating a Chinese takeaway out of the box and watching Jeremy Kyle on the suite's plasma screen. 'Human brains are nowhere near as complicated as they'd like you to think. See? Look at these stupid *pingas*. Get a job!' she yelled and threw a sweet-and-sour chicken ball at the screen. 'Fucking bottom feeders.'

'Oi!' Bobby walked through from the bathroom, towelling his hair. 'A little less of the rock-star-in-a-hotel behaviour, please. We're here on somebody else's tab, remember?'

'Ah, *si*, and speaking of which,' added Carmen, waving a chopstick at him. 'You know you are being followed by this Chandler and his men since we left the hospital, yes?'

'Yeah, very probably. Let's hope it's just out of curiosity. Keep an eye on them for me and let me know if it turns out to be anything more, okay?'

'You got it, boss.'

As with everything else about the Redos Clinic, it seemed more like a five-star hotel than a medical establishment. After the events at Lyncham, he'd gone with Vessa and McBride back to the Exile house in Milton Keynes, which had been so crowded that he'd had to sleep on a roll of old carpet in the garage; after that he'd crashed at Ennias' stinking bedsit on the Hagley Road while he checked out Chandler's information, and both had seemed luxurious compared to conditions aboard Stray. This suite was palatial to the point of being intimidating. He'd been afraid to touch anything at first. Until, that was, he discovered the shower.

'Anyway,' he added to Blennie, 'if you read on, you'll find she says that it can take weeks or even months, and sometimes never at all.'

'Ha!' laughed Carmen. 'Somehow I don't think it will be so long for you.'

'Really?' he said, amused. 'Why's that?'

'Because you're already doing it, that's why.'

'I know, this place is unreal…'

'No, I mean you are actually dreaming. Right here, right now.'

'Carmen, if this is you trying to develop a sense of humour, now really isn't the time.'

'Oh, you think I don't have a sense of humour?' she bridled. 'Okay, you want to hear a joke? Here's a joke for you, Roberto. What do you call a stupid-ass *gringo* who can't tell the difference between when he's asleep and when he's awake?' She turned back to glare at the TV screen, which was now showing *Aliens*. He hadn't noticed anybody change channels.

'Wait…'

'She's right, sir,' added Blennie. 'You're not here at all – not physically, I mean. Your body's back at the bedsit. You've

54

been asleep for about fifteen minutes. I'm afraid you've been drooling a bit.' He frowned in concern. 'Is everything quite all right, sir?' He put down the doctor's notes and came towards Bobby, brushing through the dangling tendrils of willow leaves which hung from where the ceiling used to be, except that now they weren't hanging down but drifting upward, and they weren't willow but a forest of kelp, and Bobby was under Stray again, looking up through shifting prisms of light towards the ocean's surface, and there was something in the darkness below his floating feet – something which was rising with long, toothed limbs to take him…

…and he jerked awake, gasping, in the narrow, lumpy bed of Ennias' bedsit. Reality slowly reassembled itself around him like pieces of broken crockery in his head.

Carmen got up from where she'd been sitting at the foot of his bed and looked around with a heavy sigh at the peeling walls. 'Personally I preferred the other place,' she said and took the rest of her takeaway out onto the fire escape.

'What just happened?' he asked, his voice as fuzzy as his head. He looked at the time on his phone. It was still only just past nine o'clock.

'I believe you've just had your first lucid dream, sir,' said Blennie.

'But I didn't even know I was having it! I thought it was supposed to take weeks of practice!'

'For ordinary people, sir. You have already lived for a month in a place most dreamers only ever visit by accident, if at all, and I imagine that your unique, um, perspective on such matters has given you something of a head start.'

'No kidding.' Bobby knuckled sleep out of his eyes. 'It didn't help that you two are exactly the same there as you are here.'

'Well sir, we are such stuff as dreams are made on, after all,' Blennie replied with an expectant little smile. When Bobby didn't reply, it wilted. 'That was Shakespeare, sir,' he added.

'Yes, I get it.'

'Oh.'

'Sorry. Little distracted here. I was thinking about what Carmen just said. How do I know if I'm really awake now, or still asleep and dreaming lucidly? I don't want to end up in one of those waking-up-over-and-over-again things.'

Blennie brightened again. 'Oh that's an easy one. You simply need to perform a reality check. Write something down – if it changes when you look at it again, you're still dreaming. If it stays the same, you're awake. Or, try holding your nose closed and see if you can still breathe through it. That works too.'

Bobby tried it. 'Good,' he said. 'Plus my sinuses are clear, which is nice.'

3

In his next lucid dream, Bobby, Blennie and Carmen wandered the smoking ruins of a distressingly vivid World-War-Two era Singapore. Whole streets – in some cases whole neighbourhoods – were nothing more than mounds of rubble punctuated by the occasional disembowelled shell of a building, with beams and rafters jutting like splintered bone. The destruction caused by Japanese bombers had been left to fester during their three-year occupation, with only the crudest exceptions: hovels and shanties scraped together out of the debris, inhabited by the gaunt and shambling human wreckage of the city's brutalised population. Smoke rose in shrouds from both the cooking fires of refugees and the smouldering ruins of their homes. Stinking lagoons of stagnant water in the streets bred cholera and plagues of mosquitoes while big-bellied children dipped buckets of it to drink. Singapore was a city of ghosts.

'Why this?' wondered Bobby.

Carmen shrugged. 'Don't ask me, *señor*. This is your mind.' She was dressed in a 40's WAF uniform with a rifle slung over one shoulder, glaring at everyone they passed, daring them to try something.

'Yeah, but it isn't. I was never here. These are old Robert Jenkins' memories, not mine. How am I supposed to find

Adriana in all this?'

'You mean Allie,' Blennie corrected him. In contrast to Carmen, he was in a civilian suit and sweating in the heat. He mopped the sweat off his neck with a handkerchief. 'Adriana was the girl he never went back for, remember?'

'Shit! Yes, Allie, of course. I hate this.'

Carmen was unsympathetic. 'Your mind basically got hijacked by an old man dreaming of what he should have been like when he was young – what's not to hate?'

'I love it when you try to reassure me like this.'

'Look, you want a nice pretty lucid dream, that's fine. We can ditch this place and go find some flying unicorns or something. I mean, I wouldn't mind; these nylons are killing me. You want to get to Tourmaline, on the other hand, well that's different. You got to go deep, way down right to the bottom, and then out the other side. That's what dreaming is, lover boy – it's a tunnel under the wall into the other place.'

Occasionally they passed groups of nervous-looking Japanese soldiers who looked more like they were huddling together for protection than patrolling an occupied city. Three days ago Hiroshima and Nagasaki had been bombed, and their generals had issued an unconditional surrender, but the Allies wouldn't arrive to take over for another six days. These were the ones who hadn't committed an honourable suicide and were adrift now in a place where they were neither masters nor prisoners. Bobby and his companions had seen one soldier, who had obviously been caught out on his own, hanging from a lamppost with his entrails around his knees.

The looks Bobby was given by the locals were not much friendlier. Those who could spare the energy glared, and some spat. The Allies had abandoned them to three years of atrocity, and now they were coming back in triumph? Fuck them.

The trio walked on, past the shabby grandeur of colonial buildings pockmarked with bullet holes and inhabited by the walking skeletons of prisoners-of-war too newly released to do much more than stare after them with sunken eyes. These in turn gave way to the burnt-out shells of warehouses and docks, and finally the wreck-littered waters of the Port of Singapore.

'I know this place,' Bobby said to himself. 'I *remember* this place. This is Keppel Harbour. They evacuated from here in forty-two. They could see the smoke and hear the bombs from the north, just clambering onto any ship brave enough to come. Thousands of civilians – families, children. Soldiers, too – Churchill had ordered them to fight to the last man, even though he knew it was a waste of time. That's how you run an Empire, ladies and gentlemen.'

'*Si, si,*' Carmen yawned. 'War is heck. Come on.'

Despite evident attempts to clear a channel for the occupying forces, the harbour remained choked with half-sunk ships. The jagged remains of their prows, sterns and superstructures reached from the water like broken tombstones.

'What?' Bobby pointed. 'Down there?'

'Right to the bottom and…'

'…yes, yes, out the other side. I remember.'

His two Fishketeers led him along quays which in places were nothing more than tangles of splintered timber. In the gaps he saw corpses floating amongst the pilings. They reminded him of the dreamwreck he had harvested on Stray.

His destination was a partially submerged steel-hulled fishing vessel, her arse high in the air and her bow under water – the opposite to the last time he'd seen her, just before she'd exploded.

The Spinner. Berylin Hooper's ship.

'No!' he whispered, backing away. 'No, I can't go in there. Not again.'

Memories flew at him, blinding him with their wings. Darkness and the sound of tortured metal mixed with human screams, a madwoman and the toothed tentacle around her waist, and her final plea – *help me!* – before being taken by the monster in the hold.

'Suit yourself,' said Carmen and sat on a pier piling to examine her nails. 'Blennie, you bring your flying unicorn saddle?'

'Oh, now that's not fair,' protested Blennie.

'What?' she snorted. 'He's being a pussy.'

'There's no call for…'

'She's right,' Bobby interrupted. 'Of course I'm going in there. What choice do I have? It just took me a bit by surprise, that's all, seeing it here. You're sure this is the way through?'

Carmen stopped buffing her nails and looked at him soberly. 'Not the only way, no. But is *your* way, yes.'

'Right then.'

As they boarded the ghost of the Spinner amidships, she groaned and shifted under their weight. Her deck was slimy with weed, her plating flaking with rust. She looked and smelled like she'd spent several months at the bottom of the ocean; Bobby thought it was likely they'd go straight through. They picked their way carefully along the side of her superstructure towards the open door of the engine room.

'I bloody hate déjà vu,' he commented.

'Still, look on the bright side,' said Blennie. 'The last time you did this was with both hands tied and people shooting at you.'

They edged cautiously down the steps and into the engine room. The darkness was absolute and filled with the ship's groans.

'I don't suppose anybody brought a torch with them, did they?' Bobby whispered.

A sudden cone of light sprang from a large-barrelled torch that Blennie was holding.

'Good planning, that man.'

Carmen rolled her eyes. 'You think that was planning? You are lucid dreaming, remember? As in, under your control? *Ai! Stupido!*'

'I'm never going to get the hang of this,' he muttered.

They picked their way between the shapes of broken piping and control valves towards the far end of the engine room, where steps led further down towards the boilers. The floor sloped down ahead of them. There was water down here; he could feel its weight and hear it shifting things around deeper inside. It was from this direction that the araka had come, tearing its way through the hull and the crew and in the process flooding the boilers which had exploded so catastrophically.

Bobby stopped dead. 'Wait a minute.'

'What is it?' Blennie's eyes were wide and fearful. 'Did you hear something?'

'No, I've just had a thought. This ship blew up, but it's here because I'm dreaming it, right?'

'*Si*,' said Carmen. 'So what?'

'So what if I've dreamed the araka back here too?'

Blennie emitted a small whimper.

'Then you dream it the fuck out of here!' she hissed. 'Just like you made the torch appear, *comprende*?'

'I really hope it's that simple.'

Soon they were in the boiler room and up to their knees in scum-covered water. Yet another doorway led ahead, this time into the forward cargo holds, but it seemed that there was some kind of light down there – a shifting, iridescent glow exactly like the one he'd seen when he'd torn a hole in the world at Lyncham. What had Sophie called it? The meniscus.

His skin prickled at its nearness, and he sloshed eagerly towards the doorway.

'Stop there!' barked a voice in clear English.

A dishevelled figure appeared in the opening, framed against the glow. It was pointing a rifle at them. Carmen cursed and swung her own upwards.

'No!' shouted Bobby, slapping hers down with one hand while at the same time turning his other in surrender. 'Wait! We're Allies! Allies!'

Blennie's torch picked out the stranger's face, and Bobby gaped in astonishment.

'You're nobody's ally but your own, Mr Jenkins,' said Denton Harcourt. 'And you're certainly not mine.'

4

Bobby had only met the Oraillean scientist once, and that was briefly, when he'd been brought aboard the Spinner and Harcourt had spotted that he'd unbandaged his wounds so that the araka would be attracted to his blood and attack the ship. The young man was scarlet and peeling with sunburn, and his multi-pocketed overalls were completely drenched. He was also plainly terrified; his hands were shaking, and the aim of his rifle swung wildly between the three of them.

'Listen,' said Bobby. 'Harcourt, isn't it? Why don't we all just calm down and…'

'No!' Harcourt shrieked. 'You set that monstrosity on us!'

'Do you see a monster? Look around. Do you see any of the crew? Do you recognise where you are?'

Harcourt glanced left, then right. 'Nooo…'

'What happened to you? What's the last thing you remember?'

Harcourt frowned. 'It attacked the ship. I ran below. I'm a, well, I'm rubbish in a fight. The ship was shaking, I lost my footing and I think I must have banged my head…' One hand left the rifle to rub at his temple. Carmen twitched but Bobby motioned her back. '…and then I was here. What happened?'

'The ship blew up. At almost the same moment someone in the Realt opened a hole in the meniscus. Wackiness ensued. Your guess is as good as mine; actually, your guess is probably better than mine. You're the savant.'

'But if the ship exploded…'

'Dream. All of this.' Bobby waved at their surroundings.

Sudden realisation dawned on Harcourt's face. 'Dear Reason, you've suborned me!' His grip tightened on the rifle again, and then all of a sudden he wasn't holding it at all. Bobby was. Harcourt wilted.

'Sorry man,' said Bobby. 'My dream, my gun.' He flicked the safety catch off and with unexpected venom aimed it directly at Harcourt's face. 'I should kill you now for what your people did. And don't give me that "I was only obeying orders" bullshit, either.'

Harcourt flinched but, to his credit, met Bobby's glare with an intensity which was almost bravery.

'We didn't know what you were,' he protested. 'We were trying to protect our world. Tell me you'd have acted differently.'

'I wouldn't have shot at women and children, you bastard.'

'No, just made them food for a monster. Or what did you think it would do when it was finished with us? Toddle off back to the depths, smacking its lips?'

'You left us with no choice!'

'And I *was* only obeying orders!' shot back Harcourt. 'If you're going to shoot me, just go ahead and do it, or else get that thing out of my face.' He closed his eyes.

Slowly, Bobby lowered the rifle. 'You know, for someone who claims not to be a fighter, you've got a lot of guts.'

Harcourt put his head in his hands. 'Those two things aren't even remotely similar,' he whispered. 'Only killers confuse the two.'

'Bobby, this is a waste of time,' objected Carmen. 'He's not even real! He's just a part of your dream like everything else here.'

'As far as I can tell, I'm the only real thing about this place,' said Harcourt.

'Well you would say that, wouldn't you?' pointed out Blennie, from a safe distance.

'There's an easy way to find out,' said Bobby. What we need is a reality check. Harcourt, have you got anything to write with?'

'Oh, only slightly.' Harcourt produced a small notebook and pencil from one of his many pockets.

'Write something.'

'Like what?'

'Anything. Doesn't matter.'

Harcourt thought for a moment, scribbled, and then showed it to Bobby, who laughed and passed it to Blennie.

'"To be or not to be",' read Blennie. 'I don't get it.'

'The point is, it says the same thing for all three of us – meaning that either this really isn't a dream at all, which is impossible, or that somehow savant Harcourt here is a real person trapped in the middle of my dream. Which is also impossible.'

'Maybe not,' mused Harcourt. 'A large explosion – a breach opened between the Flats and the Realt – plus my own unconscious state at the time – it might have trapped me momentarily in some kind of interstitial space between the worlds...'

Bobby jerked as if electrocuted. 'What did you just say?'

'It's just a theory. Barely even that. I was just thinking aloud.'

'No, that word you used just then. Interstitial.'

'It's just a word. It means relating to the space between things.'

'Yes, I know that. Have you ever heard of a thing called the Interstitial Assembly?'

'No, why?'

'But you're a specialist in this kind of thing, aren't you? The connections between your world and mine.'

'Mr Jenkins, there are no specialists in this kind of thing. The notion of a second world – your world – being the source of subornations is a ridiculous fringe theory. Nobody in the Collegium who wants to be taken seriously subscribes to it. I didn't believe it, and I still wouldn't were it not for, well, all of this.' He gestured at their surroundings.

'In that case, savant Harcourt, I am about to do you a very great favour. I'm going to send you home, having made one of the greatest scientific discoveries of your Collegium, with your own self as living proof. I'm going to make your career.'

Surprise and suspicion chased each other across Harcourt's face like clouds at sea. 'In return for what?'

'Believe it or not, I am not some kind of nightmare-manipulating monster hell-bent on destroying your world. The last thing I want is for more people to get hurt on my behalf. All I want is to get back to the woman I love. I was on my way to see her, and I'm going to take you along so that you can make up your own mind. I think you're a good man, Denton; I think your heart's in the right place. If I'm wrong,' he shrugged. 'Put it this way, I have nothing to lose by taking a chance on you. The only thing I ask is that if I do get you back, you help her. You help Allie. You were one of the people who destroyed our home – you put that right.'

Harcourt nodded.

The ship gave another loud groan and shifted around them.

'I think you're running out of dream,' warned Carmen.

They went forward into the next hold, where the water both deepened to mid-thigh and brightened towards the centre. It had the shifting rainbow sheen of soap bubbles or oil-covered puddles, which Bobby had seen in the Ops Room of the Park Royal Hotel when the waters of the Tourmaline Archipelago had spilled into the air. It set his teeth on edge and raised gooseflesh on his arms.

'I suppose we just dive straight in,' he said, and then to Blennie and Carmen: 'How can I be sure I'll end up in the right place?'

'Is your dream,' replied Carmen. 'It will take you where you dream you want to go.'

'Probably,' said Blennie. 'We, ah, we can't come with you though. Sorry.'

'Why not?'

'If we go back to *where* we were,' said Carmen, 'we go back to *what* we were.'

'Probably,' Blennie repeated.

She hit him.

Bobby waved them back. 'Okay, fine. Whatever. This is just a bit of a look-see, anyway. I'll be fine. You ready?' he asked Harcourt.

'No.'

'Good.'

Together, they dived into the brightness.

CHAPTER 6

SHIPS THAT PASS

1

Bobby prepared himself for the crushing agony which had accompanied his trip from Tourmaline back to the Realt, but, surprisingly, there was no pain – nor any sensation of crushing or drowning. There was just a brightening and a lightening of whatever was around him. He couldn't see Harcourt anywhere. If he *was* in water, it was of a kind that his body knew how to breathe, and he had just enough time to wonder if it was because this time he wasn't taking the journey physically, but asleep and dreaming.

Then he was aware that he wasn't swimming but walking, and the formless light around him was resolving into gauzy, wavering shapes, deepening as it did so into the warmth of gaslight. Something like a room with the morning sunlight pouring in through tall windows, and a dressing table with a large mirror that gleamed, reflecting the face of the woman who sat at it with her back towards him.

Allie.

'Allie!' he called, but his voice made no sound.

He reached towards her, to touch her, to let her know in some way that he was here, right here beside her. She was doing something to her head. Metal gleamed in her hands. Scissors. She was cutting her hair, and not just trimming it – cropping it short like some medieval woman in mourning. She didn't think he was dead, did she?

'Allie! What are you doing? Allie, I'm here!'

She must have heard something, because she spun around quickly to look behind her. Her gaze explored the room and her lips moved as she asked questions of the empty air; she obviously couldn't see him. She got up from the dressing table and walked over to check the window – walking *straight through him*. For a maddening second he caught her scent, and then it was gone.

She couldn't feel him either. He had to catch her attention somehow, but in his dream he weighed less than a thought. That gave him an idea: he needed to try something lighter. He went over to the stool and tried to pick some scraps of her hair up from the floor, but his fingers passed right through them. Nevertheless, they did seem to flutter a little, though it might have been nothing more than a draught.

'Bobby!?'

He turned in joy, and she was running towards him, and he wanted to say 'You know you really shouldn't run with scissors,' and as he reached out to her his hand grazed against her wrist – the most maddening of feather-light contacts with the iridescent porcupine-quill bracelet which he'd bought for her in the port town of Timini. He remembered that he'd been buying it when he'd heard her being attacked by the Spinner's crew, and the intensity of the fear it evoked twisted the dream around itself and he found himself losing his tenuous grip on this reality, being hauled away by a rip-tide of association beyond his conscious control.

'No!' he screamed soundlessly, but even as he fought against it, his frustration simply fuelled the distortion until Allie and the room slipped away, and he found himself somewhere else altogether.

2

Properly clean for the first time in days, Allie awoke and found herself in a large and well-appointed bedchamber, with an actual four-poster bed, a massive wardrobe stuffed with clothes, and an ornate dressing table neatly laid with brushes, combs, and dozens of cosmetics, most of which she had no clue what to do with. Mrs Buckley had already been in to light the fire, and had left a tray with a pot of tea and some toast by the bed.

She sat at the mirror and regarded her reflection, realising that it was the first time she'd seen it properly since the illness which had stranded her here nearly a year ago.

'Looks like you've been in the wars, honey,' she said to herself. The worst of it was her hair – grown long on Stray, it had suffered a nasty crisping at the back when the Karasand had caught fire. She took up a pair of scissors reluctantly; she'd never had short hair, not even as a girl. With a sigh, she started to cut. Dark blonde sheaves fell about her bare feet.

Something moved in the reflection behind her.

She spun on her stool.

Nothing in the room. It might have been a draught stirring the long drapes, but when she checked she found that the window was closed quite securely and there was nothing outside but a bright autumn morning and the roof-scape of a foreign city.

Movement behind her again, this time in the window's reflection.

Heart beating, she whirled around, holding the scissors out protectively.

'Who's there?' she demanded.

A haze was forming in the air around the dressing-table stool, reminding her of the shimmering meniscus between worlds which Bobby had torn open when he'd left her to save the victims of that insane Hooper woman.

Bobby.

As if in response to her thoughts, the haze thickened, became more substantial. There was movement in it; she saw it stirring the cuttings of her hair which lay on the floor, like a breeze playing with autumn leaves. Briefly, a face swam out of the empty air. His face.

'Bobby!?'

She ran forward, fingers outstretched, but even as she did so the face and the swirling haze scattered in shreds, as if she'd destroyed it with the very strength of her yearning, or else it had never been there in the first place and was only the product of her overwrought mind.

Nothing there – possibly, there never had been. She knew enough about shock to know that it could do strange things to the mind. Reluctantly, she settled back on the stool to finish the job. There would be breakfast, then questions – both asked and answered.

Then the door of her wardrobe burst open, spilling clothes all over the floor as a young man in ragged overalls fell out of it, dripping wet, and she screamed the house down.

3

Moments later there was a hammering at her door and Crowthorpe calling in concern. The stranger thrashed, getting tangled in sleeves and pants-legs, and falling over again. She leapt for the lock and Crowthorpe stormed in, brandishing a fire poker.

'You sir!' he thundered. 'What the devil do you mean by this? I'll beat you hollow, you swine!'

The whole household seemed to have crowded behind him in the doorway. Mrs Buckley was gripping Damien's arm as if she was about to pick him up and use him as a club. At the back came Runce, bleary-eyed and tottering, but not so doped that he didn't recognise the half-drowned intruder.

'*Harcourt?*'

The dripping savant waved feebly from the floor. 'Hallo Mister Runce,' he croaked.

Crowthorpe stared from one to the other. 'You *know* him?' he demanded.

'Yes, I bloody do,' Runce scowled. 'He's a colleague. A shipmate. From the Spinner,' he added to Allie.

'Well I must say, you don't sound terribly pleased to see him.'

'That's because he's supposed to be dead.'

'And just how exactly did he get in? You!' Crowthorpe brandished the poker at Harcourt again, who cringed. 'How did you get into this woman's chamber?'

'Oliver, please.' Runce laid a hand on Crowthorpe's and pushed the weapon aside gently. 'I'm as confused as you are, but he may have answers about who it was that attacked us. Give us until after breakfast, and I'll have answers for you, I promise.'

Crowthorpe pinched the bridge of his nose. 'Bill,' he replied wearily, 'you know that as your friend I will do anything you ask.' He gestured at Allie and Harcourt. 'But please, for the sake of that friendship have a care that you do not ask too much. Your back-from-the-dead shipmate here will be given one of the empty servants' rooms in the attic. It's the best I can do, I'm afraid; this house is filling up quite rapidly.' Shouting down the protests of his household staff, he shooed them out as Runce shut the door after them all and locked it.

Then he sat down with a grunt in the armchair beside Allie's bed and rubbed his shoulder. 'I saw someone perform a miracle once,' he said to Harcourt. 'At Bles Gabril. Remember that place?' From the pocket of his dressing gown Runce took out his revolver. 'I ended up having to shoot the bastard. Take that any way you want, just so long as you start talking. Now.'

As it turned out, Allie did most of the questioning. She interrogated Harcourt ruthlessly about every detail of his meeting with Bobby, but the little he could tell her frustrated her more than no news at all.

'He's learning how to dream lucidly, that's all I know,' Harcourt repeated. He was wrapped in a blanket by the fire, demolishing her toast.

'Well what the hell use is dreaming?' she demanded. 'Why isn't he trying to find another rip and come here properly, like last time?'

'I'm afraid we didn't quite get around to that,' he said. 'It wasn't quite the comfy fireside chat you seem to be imagining. He said he'd get me home if I agreed to help you, and that's what I'm doing, but I can't help you with information which I simply *do not possess*. Now can somebody please explain to me why I can't go and see my mother and father? They must think I'm dead. They'll be beside themselves.'

'Think how much happier they'll be to see you carted off to Beldam,' said Runce. 'That's what will happen the moment our sporting gentleman and his friends get wind that you've resurfaced. Assuming that they don't just kill you outright.'

'But why? What have we done? We only did what we were told, didn't we?'

'That's what you're going to find out for us.'

Harcourt stopped chewing and stared at him. 'What do you mean?'

'Time to strap on your cloak and dagger, lad – you've been promoted to Military Intelligence.'

'Me?!'

'Yes. That was the agreement, wasn't it: making yourself useful? Plus, you're always going on about how intelligent you are.'

'That's not funny.'

'Really? Shame. I thought I might be developing a sense of humour in my old age.'

'But I'm not a spy! I'd be useless!'

'Ordinarily I'd agree with you there. But the fact is, every plod in Carden will have my description and Ms Owens' here; we won't get as far as the nearest bus stop before we're picked up. You, on the other hand, are missing, presumed heroically dead in the service of King and country. You can speak to quite a few people before anyone cottons on. But don't fret, lad. There's only one person you need to see.'

'Who's that, then? The bloody King?'

'Oh no, somebody far more useful than that. Miss Angela Fortescue, personal secretary to Timothy Jowett, the Director of the Department for Counter Subornation. Your boss and mine. Everything that comes out of his office goes over her desk. If he's been handling tezzer squads off the books, she'll know about it.'

'And just why in the name of all that's rational would she tell me anything?'

'You're a resourceful young bloke. You've just returned from the dreaming space between worlds, haven't you? I'm sure you'll think of something.' Harcourt's scepticism was etched in every furrow of his brow. Runce leaned in. 'Because if you can't, they'll come for you just as hard as they come for me and Miss Owens, and then your dear old ma and pa really will have a dead son to mourn.'

4

At first Bobby thought he'd found his way back to the dream of Singapore. There were cobbles under his feet and the heavy stench of bougainvillea mixed with smoke, and the sound of a bell in a high tower clattering out a panicky, arrhythmic alarm. But the buildings were all wrong – narrow and tall, with steeply-pitched terra cotta roofs – and the sky between them a shade of azure he'd never seen in his own world.

He was in Timini.

The sound of the bell mingled with screams and a deep, percussive rattling which he knew so well that his reaction bypassed conscious though completely; he flung himself into the cover of the nearest doorway. Automatic weapons fire? In the Archipelago?

'I really hope this just a nightmare,' he said and went to see what was going on.

Darting from doorway to alley, he made his careful way down through the town's steeply switch-backed roads towards the harbour against a stream of townsfolk fleeing in the opposite direction. Most carried armfuls of belongings; some supported wounded, their faces simultaneously blank and terrified. The standard expression for refugees in a warzone in any world, he supposed.

He collared the nearest one – an old man struggling under the weight of an antique sewing machine. 'Who is it?' Bobby demanded. 'Who's attacking?'

The tailor gaped at him. 'You gone wampy, boy? Elbaite, of course! Who else?' He pushed past Bobby and was gone.

He was less than halfway to the waterfront when he saw the first airship. Its bulk blotted out the sky above the narrow street, armour-grey and as implacable as an eclipse, emblazoned with an insignia he didn't recognise: green and blue concentric circles overlaid by a four-pointed star like the points of a compass. The airship was spitting fire from its gondola, and the weapon's recoil was actually making the craft drift sideways. He saw its crew scampering in the rigging, fighting to keep her on a level course.

'Jesus,' he wondered, 'what are you firing?'

A jingling rain of very shiny, modern-looking brass bullet-casings fell to the cobblestones. He snatched one up, dancing it from hand to hand because of the heat. This was all kinds of wrong. The guns which Berylin's men had fired at him from the Spinner had looked no more sophisticated than World-War-One-era rifles, five rounds to a magazine, and Oraille was supposedly the most technologically advanced culture in this world. Whatever was up there in that gondola was being fired full auto, hundreds of rounds a second.

He ducked into the open doorway of a house which had been hurriedly abandoned – the family's belongings were scattered everywhere – and upstairs through a ransacked bedroom to the balcony which he knew would be there. He stopped, and his hands, where they gripped the rail, turned white-knuckled with fury at what he saw below.

The great curving arc of Moon and Sixpence Bay was full of Elbaite warships, and the air above equally thick with the fat shapes of their armoured dirigibles. They gleamed as if on fire in the westering sunlight behind the town. Every fishing vessel in Timini's harbour was either burning or reduced to wreckage, along with many of the harbour buildings. The combination of smoke from this and the invading ships' funnels cast a poisonous yellow pall across the sky. Danae had nothing which could hope to answer this, yet the Elbaite airships continued to pour fire into the defenceless town, their heavy-calibre rounds tearing chunks out of the stone quayside and virtually demolishing entire buildings. Bodies floated in little red smudges in the harbour or lay smeared across the cobbles.

Then the wind shifted and the smoke began to drift his way, quickly obscuring his view of the carnage and everything else besides, filling his throat and stinging his eyes, and…

5

…he awoke coughing, in Ennias' bedsit. Bright morning light flooded through open curtains; Carmen was sitting in the open fire-escape door smoking a cigarette. While he was fumbling his way into full consciousness, she plonked herself on the edge of his bed.

'So,' she smiled archly. 'How was your romantic reunion?'

'Rough,' he grunted, sitting up. 'It's a war zone.'

'Meh,' she flapped at him. 'Every relationship has its up and downs, *si*?'

'No, I mean it literally is a war zone. The Archipelago. An Elbaite fleet has attacked Danae, and I think somebody in our world is arming them.'

She hopped off the bed. 'I'd better get some coffee going, then. Looks like is going to be a long day.'

It was only when Bobby rolled over and climbed out that he found a wisp of blonde hair in the sheets. He gathered it up carefully and put it to his nose. Was it ridiculous to imagine that he could detect a trace of her scent? Probably. He went to find something in which to keep it safe.

CHAPTER 7

TEA AND NIGHTMARES

1

Later that morning, Allie saw her first subornation.

It started, appropriately enough, with a blazing argument between her and Runce. She was at the front door, bundled up in her thick naval coat from the Karasand, when he accosted her.

'Where do you think you're going?' he scowled.

She looked him up and down: the sling around his arm, the dark circles under his eyes. 'I think I'm going to kick your ass if you try pulling this bullshit on me,' she replied, all sweetness and reason. She pulled the door open.

He pushed it closed and held it.

'We agreed,' he reminded her. 'Keep our heads down. Let Harcourt find out what he can.'

'You mean you and sleeping beauty back there?' Harcourt had crashed soon after their early conference and not yet stirred. '*You* agreed. Between you. The menfolk. I, on the other hand, have been cooped up in that bedroom after six months living on a goddam *raft*. And now I finally get a chance to see something of your world you expect me to just sit quietly indoors and wait for you all to figure out what's to be done with me? Bobby had a saying for that: fuck this for a game of tiddlywinks.'

'Stupid woman! You've got no idea the kind of people we're dealing with!'

'No.' She put out all her strength – more than she thought she possessed, or should have possessed – and opened the door easily against him. '*They* haven't. I'm the monster under the bed, remember? I'm the suborning agent from another reality that none of you have any clue about. And right now, I'm going shopping.'

Runce, plainly having no choice in the matter, relented. 'Just wait five bloody minutes then while I get my coat on.'

'I don't need a bodyguard, Runce.'

He laughed shortly. 'You think I'm in any fit state to guard anyone's body, my own included? No. If you insist on seeing the sights then you might as well have a decent guide, that's all.'

2

It amazed Allie how easy it was to convince herself that she was walking around any large European city, despite how much there was to marvel at. Somehow it was easier to overlook the obvious things – the bloated-wasp shapes of aerostats bullying the air over a roof-scape bristling with mooring spires, and the fact that everybody was dressed as if they were extras in a costume drama, all hats and high collars, coats and mufflers against the autumn chill. The cobbled streets were choked with belching steam-trucks between which zigzagged small electric carriages; *pernes*, Runce called them. Because for all that, she simply saw people going about the business of their daily lives as they would in the morning of any large city. They commuted to work reading the paper, they bought food from sidewalk stands, they cursed the traffic and the weather, they held their children's hands on the way to school. It was the little things which reminded her that she was in an alien world – the things caught out of the corner of her eye and dismissed as ordinary by everyone else.

Like the milk-man's cart pulled by something which looked like a horse except that it had huge tufted ears, which it was cleaning with a long, blue, whip-like tongue.

'That?' said Runce, surprised. 'It's just a sollet. You don't have those?'

Or the man stopping to light his cigar with a tiny, fire-breathing salamander which he produced from a silver case in his jacket, fed with a peanut, and then put away again as casually as if replacing a box of matches. Or the things she glimpsed leaping across alley rooftops on leathery wings, like sugar-gliders. Or the tall arrays which looked like lamp-posts lining the wide boulevard of Bertram Street, except that each was wreathed with a purple nimbus of crackling energy which reminded her of Runce's tezlar gun.

'Ah, now those *are* interesting,' he said, when she pointed them out. 'They're subornation detectors – a bit like our PV rigs only more sensitive and with a longer range.'

'You realise that I have no idea what you're talking about, don't you?'

'Right then. When a dreamer from your world causes a subornation event, it plays silly buggers with the laws of nature here – air pressure, temperature, gravity, that sort of thing. We call it the event's Protean Vector, or PV for short. The worse the event, the bigger the PV. Those are basically big PV detectors. Usually we rely on someone calling the local plod whenever there's an event, but the DCS has started setting these up as an experimental early warning system – at least, in the city's central districts to start with.'

'The plebs in the suburbs can look after themselves, is that it?'

'No that's not it. Stop twisting my words. If it turns out to be successful of course it'll be rolled out across all of Carden, and then other cities and towns.'

'Of course.'

Her scepticism obviously nettled him, because he took her by the elbow and said: 'Let me show you something.'

They caught a river taxi across the Ulver, the larger of the Tara's two tributaries, and Runce pointed out a massive, many-storeyed granite building which rose sheer like a cliff from the waterline. Here, the river lapped at wide-arched tunnels protected by rusted iron grates, hinting at a labyrinth of catacombs, cellars, and sewers. Higher, walls and wings rose to towers, gables and garrets which scratched at the overcast sky, all punctuated with hundreds of deep-set windows brooding from the stone. This, he told her, was the asylum of La Belle Dame de Merci, Beldam for short, Carden's great hospital for the rehabilitation of the worst-affected subornation victims – or else their permanent incarceration.

'Berylin used to work here,' he said, 'before she joined the DCS. The tales she told of the things she saw, well, let's just say they'd put some war stories to shame. It's not just the physical injuries, you understand, it's the mental trauma too. That there building is the safest place from subornations. They've got multiple cordons of mirror stations, guards with tez guns everywhere – even tez grids built into the actual walls of the newest parts. My point is, we protect the most vulnerable as well as we can, but there's only so much you can do when the whole bloody population is vulnerable.'

It was only a short while afterwards that she witnessed a subornation event for herself.

Its appearance had none of the subtlety or tentativeness of Bobby's attempt to reach her last night; this was like one of the worldpools around Stray – a brutal slap in the face of reality, happening in the bright light of mid-morning on a busy public thoroughfare.

A tree materialised in the middle of the pavement. It had a face, formed out of knot-holes in the trunk: twisted, stretched wide and screaming silently. It tottered for a moment, grasping at the paving stones with writhing roots, but even as it did so the pavement became a circle of weed-snarled earth which spread with the speed of a spotlight being switched on – much too fast to escape, even for the pedestrians who saw it in time. Those too close to avoid it were snared and instantly suborned to the event's dream narrative, becoming screaming trees themselves and adding to the tortured grove, which grew in a few seconds to reach its limit at half the width of the street. Panicking trucks and pernes swerved around it, into the path of oncoming traffic and onto the opposite pavement, their collisions with each other and unlucky pedestrians adding to the chaos. Stuck in the middle of this – literally – lay a screaming man in work coveralls, one of a team of navvies who had been repairing a section of the street's drains. He'd been half caught by the subornation zone: flesh and blood from the waist up, but lumpen bark and moss below. From the noises he was making, the partial transformation was agonising. He was reaching out to his work-mates, pleading for their help, but their terror was too great for them to do anything but scramble away from him.

Allie's astonishment at the event disappeared. In the face of human pain, the possibility of not helping didn't even cross her mind. She started forward.

'No!' ordered Runce. 'You are not – '

She pulled free without even sparing the energy to answer back.

When she reached the navvy she saw that he'd already ripped the ends of his fingers to bloody shreds trying to claw himself out of the subornation zone. She hunkered down in front of him and clasped his hands in both of hers. 'Hey, none of that,' she said. 'It's going to be all right. We're going to get you out of there, okay? Just you hang on.'

'Please! It hurts!' His voice was a clenched howl. 'I can feel it… it's moving… inside, moving *up inside*…' and he screamed again.

Bystanders were shouting at her not to touch him, themselves too frightened to come any closer. She ignored them and carefully started to explore the region where his flesh and clothes became wood and bark. At the precise point where one became the other it seemed that there was a faint rainbow shimmer which she was learning to associate with all things related to the interaction between her world and this, but it was gone even as she saw. The transformation retreated before her hand, his suborned flesh becoming human again. Cautiously, she moved her hand along his body, and the subornation zone shrank from her presence, further and further, until his thighs were free of it, then his shins, and finally his feet, and he was scrambling on all fours towards his friends.

But they backed away even further. The bystanders' warning shouts had changed into murmuring – an awed, scared noise. The sound of a mob revving its engine.

'What did you just do to him?' one of the other navvies demanded.

'What did I – ?' Allie couldn't believe what she was hearing. At the same time, though, the question rang true: what exactly had she just done? Was this what Runce called a protean effect? The kind of thing that Seb had tried to do when he'd been tezzed?

Hands grasped her shoulders – the first of what she feared would be many – and she tried to flinch away, but it wasn't just out of fear for herself. She didn't know what else she might be capable of. It might not be such a jump from making a subornation retreat to calling one up.

'Please – ' she started.

'Shut up, nightmare bitch,' a voice growled.

More hands. A fist in her hair. In response, she felt heat building behind her ribs – part fear, part anger, part something else altogether. 'Oh Jesus, you assholes, don't make me do this…'

Then there were blue uniforms everywhere and truncheons swinging, driving the mob back and her along with it as the Carden constabulary enforced a perimeter around the screaming grove by simply shoving everybody back as hard and fast as they could. In the face of a subornation event they didn't care what the unaffected civilians were doing, just so long as they remained unaffected.

Allie slammed up hard against a brick wall and saw stars. She barely noticed Runce grabbing her by the arm and steering her into an alley until his face was in hers and he was growling 'I should've bloody let them have you.'

'I was just trying to help that man.'

'Help? Look out there! Berylin was right. You and your world are the problem. How can you possibly help?'

Chastened, she watched from hiding as a tezzer squad arrived and set up an inner cordon of mirror stations around the grove. In contrast to the barely controlled hysteria of the regular police, the DCS agents moved with calm discipline, suiting up like deep-sea divers and unloading crate after crate of equipment. Night seemed to have fallen inside the event; it was blurred and indistinct with shadow despite the daylight in the street around it. Dim shapes moved furtively between the trunks. Something leathery and bat-like flew out from the darkness, turning back into a perfectly ordinary pigeon as soon as it crossed the perimeter; it was scooped up quickly with nets and taken away in a cage for dissection by men who Runce identified as savants of the Collegium.

'Boffins,' he snorted. 'That's enough. Time to go.' He took her by the elbow again.

'No chance.' She shook free. 'I want to see what happens. I need to know. If people from my world are causing this kind of damage, I need to know.'

'Why? So that you can put a stop to it? That's just what Berylin wanted. You can't stop people dreaming, Allie. But all right, let me tell you what's going to happen in the next few minutes. The friends of that chap you helped just now, well they're about to convince the local plod that a woman from that event somehow got loose and is hiding in the crowd right now.'

Allie saw that this was indeed the case: the navvies were deep in agitated conversation with a group of uniformed police. 'I think you're right.'

'Then whistles are going to blow and everybody in this crowd will get herded up and sprayed with salvol until…'

'Okay! I said you're right! Let's get out of here.'

'Good. I'm gasping for a brew.'

They found a quiet tea-shop away from the main thoroughfares, where they calmed their nerves by sipping fragrant tea from glass tumblers held in ornately worked metal holders.

'What I don't understand,' said Runce eventually, 'is why wait until we got here? If Jowett meant to do for us, why not have that tez squad on board the Karasand when it came for us on Danae? Or if not that, then when we got here why take us all the way out to the Blackyards to do it and not straight to Shotton House, where there was no chance we could do a runner?'

'Maybe he's trying to hide something,' she suggested. 'Cover his tracks so there's nothing official linking him to us.'

'Or it could be that someone else is pulling a few strings of their own.'

'Jeez, I hope not. I remember what Serjeant Osk said back on Danae about not wanting to get involved in anything political.'

Runce hmphed. 'Frankly, I'd prefer it.'

'Why? And don't call me Frankly.'

'Beg pardon?'

'Never mind. Why would you prefer it if we were stuck in the middle of something political?'

'Because that would mean there was somebody in this whole bloody mess that I might still be able to trust.'

'You're thinking about Berylin, aren't you?'

Runce didn't answer, just scowled and fidgeted with his arm sling, but the haunted expression in his eyes was answer enough.

'Granddad on my mother's side,' he said eventually, 'he grew up during the Great Mechanisation. Bit of history for you, this; things you'll need to know if you're going to get by in our world. There was a war. The ins and outs of it don't matter, except to say that we were a very religious people back then, and most of the men of my granddad's generation went off with the Hegemonic Church telling them how glorious it all was to be fighting in the Lord's name. Standing at the pulpit telling them how noble they were, and that every man should do his duty, and any man that didn't was sure to burn in hell as a white-ribbon coward.' He snorted. 'Like any of them had a sodding clue.

'So off they all went, whistling *The Fields of Maronne*, and they all died. In their millions. In mud and pain. 'Course, it wasn't only the Church's fault, you understand, but afterwards there was this big movement of the mothers and sisters and wives of the dead for the Church to be held accountable. Called the Lace Crusade, it was. There were a lot of strikes and riots and whatnot, couple of bishops got assassinated by radical secularists, and at the end of it the King and Court passed a load of laws to take the Church out of the way the country was run. It probably helped that there was also a lot of money to be made out of encouraging people to adopt a more worldly view of things and look to Reason rather than God. There's a saying: "Hands that pray don't pay". We had one in the army: "Men are born killers; gods should know better". That's the clean version.

'Anyway, you'd probably be thinking that by becoming all secular and scientific we changed overnight into a fair society where people got treated equal and there were free kittens for all.'

'And I'd be wrong?'

He tipped his tea-glass to her. 'Dead wrong. There are people – not just men, it has to be said – in the Department who will never accept that a woman can do a tezzer's job, no matter how good she proves herself to be. Don't get me wrong, I'm just as narrow-minded as the rest; as far as I'm concerned every human being on the face of the earth is a dangerous moron until proven otherwise. It's just that,' he shrugged. 'Berylin proved herself to be otherwise. Well, I thought so. There was something broken in her, I just couldn't see it until it was too late.'

'It makes you think what else you haven't seen, doesn't it?'

'It does that. But listen, it weren't because she was a woman; I've seen men get just as crazy broken too.'

She thought, despite her brief acquaintance with the man, that this was probably the longest speech Runce had ever made in his life. 'I think I might have liked your Officer Hooper if it hadn't been for the whole, you know, trying to kill me thing,' she admitted.

'Not kill. Wake.'

'It's the same thing as far as I'm concerned. Still. It sounds like she had balls.'

Runce stared at her and then burst out into a great rolling peal of laughter. Allie smiled; that was probably a first too. She looked at his dour, craggy features as he poured another cup of tea and wondered at what point she had begun to trust him. It wasn't so very long ago that he had been pointing a gun at her. 'Runce,' she said slowly, picking at her fingers, 'I realise you may be the last person to ask this, but what does a woman do in your country if she thinks she's pregnant?'

Runce's eyes widened fractionally, which was as close as he got to an expression of surprise, and he shifted in his seat. 'You mean if she's a stranger and on the run, with no money or family to take her in?'

'Yeah, something like that.'

'You're right. I'm the last person to ask.'

She gave a hollow little laugh and gestured around them, at the well-dressed couples drinking tea and eating small cakes politely together. 'I don't seem to have many alternatives.'

'Fair enough. Most cases, unless she was in danger of it actually killing her, she'd have it. There's plenty of hospices for unwed mothers and orphanages for their babies.'

'And if it wasn't life or death? If she just simply… couldn't?'

Runce's face set coldly. 'That's not a question a civilised person asks. Or answers. When I said we took religion out of the way we run our affairs, don't be thinking that it's anything goes, with folks living three to a bed and everybody marrying their cousins and whatnot like in the Islands. If you cut a man's leg off, you give him a crutch; we cured ourselves of superstition, but there's still rules and lines which you do not cross, and they're stronger because of it.'

'And the mothers and the unwanted children have to suffer for that, do they?'

'Plenty of those children have decent lives. Lots of them join the army, for example,' he added pointedly.

She coloured. 'I'm sorry. I didn't mean – '

He waved it away. 'As I say. The last person to ask about it.'

They sat in silence and watched the street a while longer. Eventually Runce said 'I don't see how this would be a thing you'd be fretting over, in any case. It's not like you don't have the power to do something about it yourself.'

'You mean as in my so-called "protean" ability to shape the very fabric of reality around me?' she replied, weaving the air in front of her with theatrical hands.

'Yes.'

'Well, I can't.'

'Well, I've seen you.'

'Bullshit. Pardon my French, but seriously, don't you think if there was something I could do, I'd've already done it? I've been trying to make something happen ever since Stray, but there's been absolutely nothing. That man I helped, if I did anything at all it was to make the PV effect or whatever *go away*.'

'I'm not talking about that. Back at Blackyards, when that sporting gentleman and his pals tried to tez you. It should have taken your head off and sent you back to your own world, but you spanked it away like a kiddie's water pistol. That's what blew up the Karasand. What did you think happened?'

Allie stared at him. 'I thought...' She tried again; her voice had dried up. 'I thought they missed, that was all.'

'People like that – people trained like me – don't miss.'

It was too big, this knowledge. It filled her up, inflating

her head like a balloon, making it impossible to collect her thoughts. Either that or the tea shop had suddenly shrunk, crowding in on her from all sides. She stood and knocked her chair over with a clatter. People turned to stare.

'I need to, um,' she said. 'Think about this for, yeah, uh, a bit. Excuse me.'

'Right-oh.' Runce tossed some coins onto the table and followed her out to where she stood on the pavement, blinking like a lost child. 'About time we got back, anyway. Harcourt's had more than enough beauty sleep by now.'

CHAPTER 8

CHESTNUTS

1

Miss Fortescue heard the Exterior Minister approaching long before he actually appeared. His cheery voice boomed along the corridors of Shotton House like the bow-wave of an approaching freighter, giving her enough time to shoo the young man who was trying to make an appointment out into the waiting room.

'Yes, I know,' she said, in the face of his half-spoken protests. 'It does sound quite important. But that is Lord Terence Ashby approaching to see Director Jowett, and you would be better off standing in front of an omnibus than getting in his way. I suggest you take a seat over there and wait until the Exterior Minister concludes his appointment.'

Lord Ashby swung around the corner at the end of the corridor, escorted by a flotilla of aides and secretaries. He was grinning from ear to ear, and she felt a twinge of sympathy for her boss; it was a commonly known fact that the Exterior Minister was only ever happy when he was savaging a rival. It was also a long-standing joke – at least in the privacy of the Secretaries' Lounge – that the main reason he was Minister for the Exterior was because his own was so very expansive.

He sailed past her with a grin like a steam locomotive's cow-catcher. 'Good afternoon, Angela!' he boomed. 'Timothy not in the middle of anything important, I hope?'

'Of course not, sir. Do go in.' As if it would have made any difference.

'Oh I shall, my dear, I shall.' He paused by her desk for a moment, peering down at her over his belly. 'After which, maybe you and I can get together over dinner and discuss the possibility of your transfer to a department which isn't about to have its head shoved up its own arse.' He chuckled and tipped her a heavy-lidded wink. 'I'm sure I can find a number of interesting positions for you.'

'My lord is, as ever, too kind.'

When he'd passed through into Director Jowett's office – leaving his flunkies to hover aimlessly outside – she shuddered, sighed and crossed out the next entry in his appointment book. Then, when the shouting started, she crossed out the next two as well.

2

Timothy Jowett, Director of His Majesty King Alexander VII's Department for Counter Subornation, glanced at the fistful of papers which Lord Ashby had slammed on his desk, with an air of mild curiosity calculated to infuriate the man as much as possible.

'Mmmyes,' he drawled, sitting back and steepling his fingers. 'I've read those reports too. War in the Tourmaline Archipelago, it seems. Damn shame, if you ask me; I was planning on taking some leave there soon. Nevertheless, my Lord, I'm not a hundred percent sure what exactly it is you'd like me to do about it.'

'Do?' Ashby grinned savagely. 'I'd say you've done just about bloody enough, wouldn't you?'

Jowett blinked slowly. 'I'm sorry, you're going to have to be a bit more spec – '

'A simple job!' spat the minister. 'Get one of your teams out there, stabilise the subornation which was keeping everybody nice and tidily away from each other's bloody throats, and back home in time for tea. What in the name of the Queen Mother's left tit did your people *do* out there?'

'Far be it from me to stoop to I-told-you-so's, my lord, but it was you who insisted on sending agent Hooper, remember?'

'That's completely irrelevant! You are the director of this Department. Responsibility stops with you. It seems, however, that your leadership leaves something to be desired, and that I'm going to be forced to oversee this godawful mess.'

'Well I'm flattered by the attention, obviously, though I am curious as to why the sudden passionate urgency. Elbaite and the Amity have been at this particular tug-of-war for years; they are thousands of miles away, and even if Elbaite were able to dominate the Archipelago, they still couldn't hope to mount a serious challenge to the Southern Alliance.'

'Promises were made, Director Jowett. Personal assurances based on long-standing friendship and a sense of honour – none of which you, with your background, would appreciate. I'll make it very simple for you: I demand to see the reports of your debriefing of the Spinner's crew this instant.'

Jowett spread his hands apologetically. 'Alas, I am unable to furnish you with such, as they have not yet returned.' This was not, technically speaking, a lie. Runce had sent his reports by clatter but had not been personally debriefed – Jowett had no idea where the man was, and as worrying as this was, it was nowhere near as disturbing as the other reports which Jowett had received about the kinds of weaponry which Elbaite was deploying in the Archipelago. He wondered what colour Ashby's face would go if he could read those too.

'Horsecocks!' Ashby was grinning so hard it seemed that his eyeballs might pop out and roll away across the floor along with the rest of his marbles. 'You and I both know that three survivors of the incident have arrived recently on Oraillean shores. Do you seriously expect me to believe that you haven't spoken to them or that you don't know where they are at this very moment? That the subornation on Bertram Street this morning is a complete coincidence?'

Jowett's serene smile belied his deepening dismay. The fact that Ashby had spies and informants in many departments including his own wasn't surprising, but his sudden and vehement interest in Jowett's was. This was much more than a case of honour and friendship – if Ashby even possessed such qualities in the first place. All he could do was play for time. 'Ultimately, my lord, there is room for all manner of beliefs in an infinite universe,' he said sagely.

Ashby cut him off with a contemptuous snort. 'Oh don't be so bollock-achingly smug, Timothy. Just get me that report, or you leave me no alternative but to raise the matter of your incompetence with His Majesty personally.'

The Exterior Minister slammed out of his office as unceremoniously as he'd entered, collected his milling swarm of assistants and departed, humming to himself with gleeful animosity.

Jowett went straight to his drinks cabinet and poured himself a large whiskey, which he knocked back quickly, and a second, which he sipped as he stared out of his window down at the busy streets.

A postal 'stat took off from its mooring spire atop a nearby building. Crowds of pedestrians went about their businesses, umbrellas raised against the drizzle, sheltering beneath shop awnings or weaving their way between pernes and steam-lorries which chuntered along the cobbled streets. Directly across from the doors of Shotton House, a chestnut vendor was filling cones of waxed paper, ha'penny a time. Nothing but normal, preciously dull Carden life; a veneer of reality which never seemed so thin as it did right now. Someone in the Realt was arming Elbaite; he had a very good idea who that was, but nothing which came close to evidence. At the moment, they seemed content to inflame a foreign war, which was not necessarily his concern, except that foreign wars had a tendency to spread if left unchecked. Suddenly Jowett desperately needed a cone of roast chestnuts. He gathered his overcoat from the back of his office door and went out.

'Angela,' he started, 'please would you reschedule my – ' and then stopped as he saw the young man seated in the waiting area. 'Harcourt?'

The savant shot to his feet. 'Yes, sir!'

'I have a clatter report on my desk from Sergeant Runceforth stating that you are dead. That you were, to be precise, blown to smithereens.'

'Ah well, yes, sir, that's really what I've come to talk to you about, sir. I know where he is, sir. Mister Runce, that is. And the woman he brought back from the Archipelago. They wanted me to do a bit of, er – ' he darted a nervous, sidelong look at Miss Fortescue ' – snooping around, so to speak, but I can't, sir. I just can't. It's not me.'

'I'm sure they did. And do you mean to tell me that you've been sitting there all this time?'

'Yes, sir.'

'You saw the Exterior Minister come past you both times, and he never so much as looked at you?'

'No, sir. Should I have said something?'

'Should you have – ?' Jowett stared and then burst into laughter. He laughed so hard that Miss Fortescue began to wonder if she shouldn't call someone in the psyrgical division, but in the end he subsided, wiping his eyes.

'Angela,' he said, 'I need you to please cancel all of my appointments for the rest of the day, would you? Savant Harcourt and I have a lot to talk about, and we're off to get some chestnuts.'

'Of course, sir,' she replied, and when they were gone she tore the entire page out of his diary and threw it in the bin.

4

Allie and Runce returned to Crowthorpe's house late in the day by a wandering route which took in the feeding of pigeons in Alexander Park and watching the Royal Guard drilling at Hythe Battery, whose towers, battlements and naval wharves filled the wide triangular point of the Royal Quarter, where Carden's tributary rivers met to form the Tara. From the high point of Sutter's Keep, she could see along its wide, sluggish waters, which were busy with scows and barges and spanned by dozens of bridges nestling one behind the other into the sepia haze of smog and autumn sunlight. She explained to him that it wasn't just claustrophobia and boredom which had driven her from the safety of hiding; if this was going to be her home, then she needed to see it as being real, not just some dream place, and that meant seeing as much of it as possible, the big and the small – the garbage floating on the water and the wide arches of the bridges over it. He seemed to understand and took her by perne-trolley out into the red brick tenements where children scuffled in back-to-back yards between lines of laundry, and rag-and-bone men drove their sollet-drawn carts through the cobbled streets, calling for scrap.

By the time they returned, she hadn't exactly processed the whole of what had happened during the subornation, but bits of it were slotting into place in her head – enough to make her think that maybe she could work her condition to some kind of advantage.

The usually grim-faced Mrs Buckley met them at the door with a small smile, and, while Allie was wondering what that little mystery was all about, ushered them into the drawing room where Crowthorpe and a second man – evidently a guest – rose the greet them. He wore a neat goatee and glasses and looked like an insurance salesman.

Runce cursed when he saw who it was. 'Harcourt,' he spat. 'That cockless little pencil-licker. I'll rip his shrivelled bloody…'

'I'm sorry, Bill,' said Crowthorpe. 'He came with a warrant.'

'Yes, Officer Runceforth,' confirmed his guest. 'Along with a dozen agents in the streets around the house in case you try to do something even more outrageously stupid than you have already. Please don't, I beg you.' He turned to Allie and added 'I'm so sorry – I'm forgetting my manners. I'm afraid that Officer Runceforth's reports were a little sketchy on details of your name, so forgive my familiarity if I simply call you Alison for now. I am Timothy Jowett, Director of His Majesty's Department for Counter Subornation. I'd like to ask you a few questions.'

CHAPTER 9

HOUSE ARREST

1

The pain in Runce's shoulder was keeping him awake, so he went in search of a medicinal brandy in Crowthorpe's study, easing his way out of his bedchamber as quietly as possible to avoid drawing the attention of that bloody Buckley woman. The panelled landing was adrift in midnight silence, with each slow tick of the hall grandfather clock falling muffled into the carpet. The landing window overlooked the street at the front of the house, and he paused to peer through a crack in the curtains.

To the right, in the sifting cone of drizzle under a street-corner gas lamp, a man in a derby hat stood with the collar of his long coat turned up against the damp. To the left, two similarly dressed men passed out of sight behind a tall hedge. Those were only the three he could see – the few that any would-be intruder was *meant* to see. There would be others much more carefully hidden. Jowett's men. DCS agents set to keep watch over the house and make sure that nobody got in – or out.

"'All for our safety" my hairy old arse,' he whispered.

Then he noticed that there was a light shining from underneath Allie's door.

He hesitated, not wanting to disturb her, but then reasoned that if her light was still on at this hour she was probably disturbed enough already, and knocked quietly.

Bedclothes rustled, bare footsteps padded across the floor, and the door opened. She was wearing the same old threadbare navy pullover, like a child with a security blanket, and he felt a sudden pang of terrible sympathy for her. 'What is it?' she asked. 'Is everything okay?'

'Fine, lass, fine. I was just heading downstairs to plunder Oliver's drinks cabinet. Wondered if you wanted anything.'

She gave him a tired smile. 'No, I'm good, thanks.'

'Right then.' He paused for a moment, with no idea how to express the concern he felt for her; the imperative to simply wrap her up and make her safe. 'Busy day, then,' was all he said and turned to go.

'It was good of him,' she said, catching him back again. 'Your Director Jowett. To let us stay here, I mean. He could have arrested us and dragged us off anywhere. At least this place is familiar.'

'Hmm. It'd be nice to think he was being kind. More than likely it's because he doesn't have to explain us to the top-brass while we're nicely hidden out of the way.'

'You really are a very paranoid man, do you know that?'

'I'll take that as a compliment,' he said and really left that time.

Turning at the landing, he glanced up to where the servants' quarters were and saw that there was also a light glowing under Harcourt's door. 'Bloody insomnia central, this place,' he muttered and carried on downstairs. Harcourt could get his own damn nightcap.

2

Harcourt was completely oblivious to the lateness of the hour. He sat at the room's washstand – as he had done for the last several hours, with only a few reluctant breaks to take food – scribbling in a fresh notebook which he'd begged from Crowthorpe, in the light of an old paraffin lamp. With Jowett having told him that a message had been sent to his parents to let them know that he was alive and well, Harcourt's mind had been given the liberty to turn back to the incredible things he had witnessed in the Spinner's last days, and he was frantic to get as much of it down on paper as he could while it was still fresh in his memory. The araka, the breach of the meniscus into Lyncham, the dreaming limbo in the place that Bobby had called Singapore, and even Bobby himself – any of one of these things on their own was enough to overturn conventional theories regarding the nature of subornation. Taken together, they promised a fundamental paradigm shift in almost every one of the Collegium's scientific disciplines. Assuming that he could support any of it with hard evidence, this was going to make his career. He was so engrossed in this that he barely even noticed the presence of another human being in the room – and certainly not that it had managed to get in without the use of door or window – until it ahemmed politely.

Harcourt looked up.

The sporting gentleman waited patiently while Harcourt struggled to form a response.

'Who are?' he managed. 'You're not supposed to be here.'

Everything about him was strange, not least his being here: he wore a high-necked garment of some black material which clung tightly like a second skin, trousers which looked like bib-overalls cut off at the waist, and heavy boots fastened with metal clasps. He was also holding a strange-looking pistol with a long barrel – not pointed at Harcourt directly, but in a casual way which suggested that it very easily could be.

'To be fair, neither are you,' smiled the intruder. 'Runceforth's report said that you were lost on the Spinner. Of course, he could have been lying to protect you for some reason, but then he doesn't strike me as being that imaginative.' The smile widened. 'Imagine my curiosity when you popped up on my radar.'

'Your what?'

'Never mind. Why don't you tell me how it is you're not dead, and we'll take it from there.' He sat on the edge of Harcourt's bed and crossed his legs neatly, the pistol cradled across them, and pointed at him directly now. Harcourt couldn't take his eyes off it. Nevertheless, with the initial shock wearing off slightly, the clinical, scientific part of his brain was making observations and deductions. The paraffin lamp threw flickering shadows around the room, but not of the man with the gun; the wall behind him was as clearly lit as if he wasn't there at all.

'You're from the Realt, aren't you?' he asked.

The sporting gentleman considered this for a moment. 'Yes, I suppose I am.'

Harcourt indicated his notebook. 'Will you give me just a moment to write down one more thing? Then I'm all yours.'

'Very well, but make it quick.'

Harcourt wrote four words, and as he finished he swept his hand away violently, knocking aside the paraffin lamp. Glass smashed, fuel spilled, ignited, and a sheet of flame spread across the floor.

The assassin from the Realt leapt to his feet, but Harcourt kept his seat. 'You'll have to put that out if you want the time to torture me,' he said. 'Because I am telling you nothing.'

The assassin sighed in disappointment. 'You stupid little shit,' he said, and shot Harcourt twice in the chest. The gun was very quiet, Harcourt noted; it only made a kind of dry coughing noise. Much like the noises he was making himself, ironically. He slid to the floor, watching the blood spread across his shirt. The assassin stood over him, and that gun's wide-open barrel stared him straight in the face. 'It won't stop me finding out what I need to know from the old man, or the woman. Or any of you, for that matter.'

Harcourt tried to reply, but he had no breath with which to do it.

Then there was a third coughing shot, which he didn't hear.

Out of curiosity, the assassin took a quick look at Harcourt's last scribbled message: *Love you, Mum, Dad.* Sneering, he tossed it into the flames and went to deal with the others.

3

Runce was choosing between a bottle of Moss Bay Gin and a nice Coronsay single malt when he heard the first door being kicked open and the sounds of screaming, coming from upstairs. He ran for the front door, cursed at the bolts and locks as he fumbled at them one-handed, yanked it open and bellowed into the night: 'Inside! He's already inside!'

4

Allie stared around at her doorway in shock as the assassin raised his gun.

'No dreaming mojo now,' he said. 'This time we do things the old-fashioned way.'

There was a yell, and someone body-charged him from the hallway outside. Damien, dressed only in a long nightshirt which flapped below his knees, straightened up, circling his fists before his face like an old-fashioned pugilist.

'Come on then, you swine!' he roared. 'Attack a woman, would you?'

The assassin's counter-attack was almost too fast to follow. There was a brief tangle of limbs and then Damien was on his back, clutching his throat and choking. Still, the distraction gave Allie time to throw herself to the floor on the other side of her bed. Two shots, and the bedclothes jumped as if someone was kicking at them from inside.

Then there were footsteps thundering up the staircase, more shouts, a scream of pain, and the violent purple-white eruption of tez-fire which silenced everything.

5

'Where are we going?' Allie asked Jowett, as their perne sped them through the empty streets, escorted in front and behind by others carrying armed DCS agents.

'Where I should have taken you the moment I saw you,' he responded curtly. 'Where you would both now be safe, if you had come to me in the first place – instead of which you have put innocent people at risk with your ridiculous suspicions, and I'm just as much to blame for trying to accommodate them.' The shouting and the recriminations had continued long after the bodies of Harcourt and the dead DCS agents had been removed, and Jowett had stood them stoically, but it had already been a long and stressful day and his nerves were fraying.

'He's taking us to Beldam,' said Runce.

CHAPTER 10

LA BELLE DAME DE MERCI

1

Bobby found that it was not so easy to get back to the same kind of lucid dreaming state as he'd hoped. He tried to exhaust himself with dozens of laps of the Redos clinic's indoor pool, stuffed himself with huge meals in the hope that they would make him fat and sleepy, then tried to bore himself into a coma with daytime television and endless hands of solitaire – but all any of it achieved was to send him into a dreamless sleep from which he awoke frustrated and snappy. Carmen and Blennie disappeared and left him to it.

He got to the point where he found himself in his nearest pharmacy reading the packets of medication for anything which May Cause Drowsiness and wondering if you could overdose on antihistamines. In the process he saw a stand selling the kind of medical information bracelets and necklaces used by travellers with rare blood types and allergies, and bought one in the shape of a medallion which unscrewed to reveal a shallow circular recess just large enough to fit the wisp of Allie's hair which he'd been carrying around in his pocket. When he got back to the clinic, Carmen looked at the thing hanging around his neck and snorted. 'You going to wear your shirt open to the waist and start singing Bee Gees songs now?' she mocked.

He attended the post-supper dream discussion groups at Redos more out of boredom than anything else, though quickly found himself becoming irrationally annoyed by some of the other 'delegates' – in particular, one middle-aged woman in a bottle-green velvet dress who gave the impression of having unresolved Bronte-related issues. She dominated the session with a loud and pornographically detailed report of having dreamed one of her past lives as a courtesan to King Charles the Second.

'Why is it,' he said, 'that whenever somebody claims to have dreamt a past life it's always as someone fabulously exciting or famous, instead of just some poor ordinary sod working his farm and dying of TB before he's forty? I mean what are the odds?'

'Oh really?' The woman gave him a withering glare. 'And what do you dream about, Mr Jenkins?'

He wanted to say *Disembowelled soldiers hanging from lampposts and six-year olds with dysentery and airships firing on unarmed villagers. You know, just the World*, but he'd already overstepped the mark and didn't want to make things worse, so he backed down and had another beer.

'I think there's a possibility that you are both being a bit literal about it,' Dr Nandhra suggested, trying to offer a conciliatory position. 'The contents of dreams are very often symbolic. Yes, we dream about what we have done during the day, and there are aspects of the unconscious mind which function purely for sorting memories and information, but there is also the part which seeks to express the aspects of ourselves which are hidden or repressed. The people, the objects, the places and the landscapes in our dreams represent parts of ourselves which our brains are telling us we need to acknowledge. Of course,' she added, seeing Bronte-woman start to object, 'that doesn't preclude the possibility of those figures being the echoes of past lives, if you believe in such things, but that doesn't stop them being symbolic too.' She took a rose from the table's centrepiece. 'This rose, for example, is simultaneously a physical object and a representation of romance. There is no reason why dreams can't be both literal and figurative.'

Bobby found his anger rising as he listened to this. There had been nothing symbolic about the bodies floating in

Timini's harbour. 'What if they're real, though?' he asked. 'I mean really real, not just echoes or wish fulfilments. Actual people in actual places, actually getting hurt.'

'I think in that case, Robert, you're moving into the realms of telepathy and clairvoyance, which is a bit out of my professional scope, I'm afraid.' Dr Nandhra laughed, and the others joined in, and Bobby smiled politely as he put his beer down, unfinished. It had made him careless, and he excused himself soon afterwards, before he opened his big mouth any further.

2

'One of the group said something interesting tonight,' said Dr Nandhra, and she passed her tablet across to the man sitting opposite her in the doctors' lounge. He was neither a doctor nor a patient. If he had existed in the clinic's records as anything at all, it would have been as 'external consultant'.

'Define interesting,' he responded, reading it with a notable lack of enthusiasm.

Mr Croft's most recent excursion to Carden had not gone well, and even though the details were confidential, of course, it told in the haggard look on his face. He had shadows under eyes which were dark enough already. She thought about asking him if he wanted her to prescribe him something but decided against it. The man was not predictable.

'He asked what would happen if the people and places in dreams were actually real.'

'That's pretty vague. He didn't mention any names?'

'No. He shut up quite quickly after that – almost as if he was afraid he'd said too much.'

'Robert Jenkins. Hm. Well, obviously he's not an Exile, or the buoys would have detected him by now. More likely he's just some ordinary idiot who discovered how to get through by accident, and that's why he signed up for the LD classes. It'd be worth keeping an eye on him. If he doesn't get himself stuck with a Passenger, we might be able to recruit him. Authorise a deep check; I don't want any surprises from this bloke.' Croft passed the tablet back to her, stood, and stretched his crackling spine. 'I have to crash. No disturbances for thirty-six hours at least.'

'Certainly, sir. Do you want me to prep the room?'

He offered her a tired smile. 'No. I just need to sleep; this one's recreational, not business.'

3

Either the beer or the argument had been exactly what Bobby's brain needed, because as soon as he got back to the bedsit his eyes began to grow heavy, and he threw himself onto the bed fully clothed. When he opened his eyes again, he found that he was back in his chair at the table under the willow tree, and there was a peculiar sensation of warmth and brightness coming from under his shirt.

The SOS talisman containing Allie's hair was glowing.

Then he saw that the people around him had been replaced by Carmen and Blennie dressed in the white uniforms of the clinic staff, while the willow tree above the table was doing its upside-down seaweed trick again, and he realised that he was dreaming after all.

He pulled the capsule out and examined it; its glow was pulsing with a heartbeat which didn't match his own. *Allie*, he thought. *Something to do with her hair.*

'Either of you two have a clue about what's going on with this thing?' he asked the Fishketeers. 'And while we're at it, where exactly have the pair of you been?'

'Nice to see you too, *Señor* Bobby,' replied Carmen and knocked back a glass of someone's wine. 'We have our own stuff going on, you know, as exciting as your life of shopping and television is. As for that – ' she waggled her glass at the glowing medallion.

'We know as much about this as you do,' Blennie finished for her. 'Probably less. Maybe you should try following it.'

'Following it?'

'It might point towards where Miss Owens is.'

'Why would it do that?'

Carmen threw her glass at him in exasperation. '*Stupido*! And you wonder why your dreaming is not working! In this place, if you want it to be a thing, it is a thing, get it? If you want it be a beacon back to... Ai! I give up!' She began hunting around for another glass.

With a bit of experimentation, Bobby discovered that the medallion glowed more brightly when he faced in one particular direction, and based on nothing more than the spurious logic that Allie's hair was somehow homing in on its origin, he set off that way – into a dreamscape which was already beginning to twist like a hall of funfair mirrors.

Fortunately there was no war zone this time, past or present, in either world. At first he thought he was back in the ruins of Corvedale Hospital where he'd met the man who called himself Chandler. It had the same institutional feel: long corridors and high ceilings filled with the echoes of countless unseen footsteps. Except here the walls were rose-coloured rather than white, and instead of overhead strip lighting, the place was illuminated by what looked like old-fashioned wall-mounted gas lamps.

He followed the medallion's glow along halls and through doors, passing right through them, as insubstantial in his dream as a ghost. As his focus sharpened, he became aware of others around him, vaporous presences passing by and through him, and the closer he got to Allie the more solid they became, until he could make out voices and faces. They were definitely doctors and nurses, though their robes were an odd lilac. Often the patients wore padded restraints as they shuffled along, escorted by orderlies in violet waistcoats and derby hats. Sometimes they were struggling, and being propelled along forcefully. What was this place? Something must have gone wrong – Allie couldn't be here. What had happened to the bedroom in the big house?

It was one of the strugglers who saw him first. An outstretched finger pointed straight at him, and a drooling mouth shrieked 'It's here! It's back! Help! Heeeelp! It's come back for me! *It's here!*'

Faces turned to look, and other eyes saw. Bobby realised that he was neither as insubstantial nor as invisible as he'd been a moment ago. Also, that this wasn't a dream. He was somewhere in Oraille. Somewhere *real*.

'Oh crap.'

He ran.

Alarm bells began ringing.

People mostly just got out of his way as he sprinted past, flattening themselves wide-eyed against the walls or diving through doorways, obviously terrified. Vaguely it occurred to him that there must be a way to use his lucid dreaming ability to make escape easier, but for the moment he was acting on instinct, and anyway, he reckoned the way things were going nobody was going to accost him before he could find somewhere to hide until all the fuss died down.

Then he skidded around a corner and straight into a trio of large orderlies carrying rubber truncheons, who surrounded and proceeded to accost the living shit out of him.

They let up on him just long enough for Bobby to see a fourth man approach, armed with a peculiar Flash-Gordon-style pistol wired into a heavy battery pack at his belt. Bobby recognised the tez rig only too well. 'Suborning bastard,' snarled the DCS agent, and flicked off the gun's safety. There was a rising whine of charging capacitors.

Bobby's mind raced to remember anything which he could use from those few conversations with Runce aboard Stray, and came up with precious little. 'Runce! Officer Runceforth!' he babbled. 'He'll vouch for me! I'm not a fucking subornation!'

'Shut up, nightmare, and get off the skin of this world.' The gun was levelled at his face.

'Think, man! If I'm a subornation, how can we be having this conversation? *How can I know what I am?*'

The gun lowered fractionally. The DCS agent frowned. For a frozen moment even the alarm bell seemed to be holding its breath. Finally, the agent turned to one of the orderlies. 'Go and get your superior,' he ordered. 'And be quick about it. As for *you*,' he jabbed the tez gun so close to Bobby's face that he could smell the copper of its contact relays, like freshly spilled blood. 'One twitch and I'll burn you black, understood?'

'Understood, officer.' Bobby sagged to the floor and waited.

4

The room that they put him in looked like a police interrogation room – as far as he could tell, having only ever seen one on TV – with one major difference, which was that instead of there being a large two-way mirror there were four of them, one on each wall. It meant that there wasn't a place where he could hide from multiple reflections of himself marching into infinity, and after a while the experience became so disconcerting that he kept his eyes on the table or the floor. It reminded him of when he'd first arrived in the Flats, and the featureless blue void of the horizon had threatened to suck his mind away from any sense of itself. By the time a door in the corner opened and Director Jowett came in, it was a relief simply to have something different to focus on.

'Good morning, Mr Jenkins,' he said, taking a seat opposite and placing a thick manilla folder on the table. 'My name is Jowett. I'd like to start by thanking you for your forbearance. I understand that you could have left at any point by simply waking yourself up, and I'm grateful that you have chosen to remain; it is an encouraging sign to me that we will be able to work together. Yes, Mr Jenkins,' he added, in response to Bobby's look of astonishment, 'I know what you are. You are aware already that I know your name. I know a fair amount about you, but by no means everything. I am, for example, extremely interested in anything you can tell me about what happened in Lyncham, and I'm prepared to reward you handsomely for the information. One thing, which I suspect

I already know that answer to, is this: would you like to see Miss Owens?'

Bobby jumped to his feet. 'Allie? She's here?' He ran to the door and found it locked. He tried to summon up the dreaming sense of insubstantiality which had allowed him to walk through doors and walls on his way here, but nothing happened. He remained stubbornly solid. Reluctantly, he sat back down.

'One of the fundamental limitations of a suborning phantasm,' said Jowett, as if Bobby hadn't moved in the first place, 'is the fact that they cannot abide the sight of their own reflections. It is how we are able to control the range of their protean effects; we think that being forced to confront their own reality is actively debilitating to them. Of course, you are somewhat different, being lucid in your presence here, but we suspect that the effect is much the same. I'll take your reaction as a yes, by the way. Miss Owens and I have been having some very interesting discussions recently. I know that she is most eager to see you.'

'Discussions, right,' Bobby sneered. 'Mate, if you've hurt her…'

Jowett sighed, got up, and went to the door. 'Officer,' he said, to someone on the other side, 'please would you allow Miss Owens to come in, before this conversation becomes more absurd than necessary?' He turned to Bobby. 'She will confirm what I'm about to tell you, which is that you're both currently being held in protective custody of the DCS, in a secure wing of La Belle Dame de Merci Hospital for psychologically traumatised victims of subornation. She is here because there have so far been two attempts to kill her, or at least dispel her from this world, which I understand she considers to be even worse, and this is the safest place I can find for her. I'm not unsympathetic to your situation, and I will try to help you as much as I can.'

'That's not saying much, given that you sent a boatload of soldiers led by a madwoman to attack me and my people.'

Jowett's face darkened. 'We will discuss Officer Hooper presently.'

A few moments later Allie came in. Their manner of greeting at the door – her hand briefly on his shoulder, Jowett's brief nod – was all the confirmation that Bobby needed that the Director of the DCS might just be telling him the truth after all. And then she was in Bobby's arms, or he was in hers, neither could tell which, only that it was impossible that it had been little over a fortnight since they'd been together on Stray. A hundred years must have passed, at least.

She traced the smooth line of his jaw with those long, clever fingers. 'You've shaved,' she said. 'I like it. It makes you look younger.'

He stroked the fuzz at the nape of her neck. 'You cut your hair,' he replied. 'You look like that chat-show woman. Whatserface – Ellen Thingy.'

'Whatever floats your boat, sailor boy,' she laughed.

He fished out the SOS medallion, which burst into life like a naked light bulb. 'I put some of your hair in this,' he explained. 'It helped me find you. What happened?'

'It sort of got a bit scorched,' she said, and told him everything that had happened since boarding the Karasand – almost. He, in turn, gave her an account of his attempts to contact her by lucid dreaming. All the while their hands were busy touching, stroking, and intertwining as they reassured themselves of the physical reality of the other. The irony of this wasn't lost on Allie.

'This is nuts,' she said, shaking her head. 'I'm hooked up to a ventilator in Minneapolis and you're asleep in a dream lab somewhere in England and we're both here playing touchy-feelie like a couple of teenagers. I don't know what good Jowett thinks we can be to him.'

'I don't plan on being any good to him at all,' Bobby replied. 'Not after what happened to Stray.'

'He says he didn't know what we were when he ordered that, and I think I believe him. Bobby, these people are just trying to protect their own world. Can you blame them?'

'The bottom line for me is simply, do you trust him?'

'Do we have a choice?'

'Of course we do! We're not prisoners in this place – we're here by choice. Both of us could wake up any time we wanted.'

'That's not an option for me. You know that.'

'You woke up and then came back once before – what's to stop you doing it again? What's to stop both of us getting out of here and then coming back somewhere else and just laying low? If we don't cause a subornation or whatever they call it, they can't find us, can they?'

'You know they're listening through the mirrors, don't you?'

'Who cares? What can they do? Zap us out of here? Great! Bring it on!' He flourished the medallion at her triumphantly. 'Now that I've got this I can find you wherever you are!'

She shook her head, trying not to lose her patience with him. 'You don't understand. It's not that simple.' This was certainly not the time and place to tell him that she thought she might be pregnant with his child, that she had no idea what she wanted to do about it if she was, or what would happen to it if she got tezzed back into her old, broken body. But typically, Bobby wasn't taking no for an answer.

'Then make it simple for me,' he insisted. 'Tell me what I'm missing here. In a moment, Jowett is going to come back in with some bullshit carrot-and-stick deal and I need to know all the angles before I can decide how to play this.'

Her patience evaporated then. 'Oh, *you're* going to decide, are you?' she retorted. 'While I do what? Sit in the corner and wait for the two of you to thrash it out? Bobby, do you know what I've been doing with my day? I've been out exploring this city, because this is my new home. It's all right for you; you can have your waking life and come and visit me every night like some kind of freaking dream vampire, but *this is where I am*. I saw a subornation this morning and I was able to stop it. Bobby, I think I can help these people somehow; I think I can make a life here, at least for a while. If you want to be any part of the decision making process regarding what I do with that, then I suggest you get yourself back here physically, like you did the last time.'

The hurt in his eyes was too much for her to look at. 'That's not even remotely fair.'

'Nothing about this is fair, Bobby. Nothing.'

Jowett returned, shuffling handfuls of paperwork self-consciously, and ahemmed loudly into the frosty silence. 'There's something I'd like to show the pair of you,' he said.

'I thought you wanted me to tell you everything about what happened at Lyncham,' Bobby replied.

'Oh I do, I just need you to appreciate the magnitude of why I need to know. I wouldn't want you to be under the impression that this is something like a common plea bargain or some – what was it? – "bullshit carrot-and-stick deal". But yes, I am going to offer you a way to be together permanently, just in case you were wondering. This is a place which I could be executed for even telling you about, but then since I've already broken several capital laws by allowing you to exist here at all when I should have had you both tezzed immediately I don't suppose it really matters. In for a penny, eh?' He smiled brightly.

'What place?'

'The meeting chamber of the Hegemony's Interstitial Assembly, which exists neither in your world nor in mine but in the dreaming space between. Come on, there's a taxi-perne waiting.'

CHAPTER 11

THE INTERSTITIAL CHAMBER

1

Bobby stared out of the perne's windows as it drove them through Carden, taking in its sights properly for the first time, and Allie felt very smug in being able to name some of them for him.

'One thing I don't understand, though,' he said. 'It's the middle of the night at home, but it's, what – eleven in the morning here?'

'You're nearly halfway around the globe from the Archipelago,' explained Jowett. 'Geography and time zones still exist.'

Shotton House's red brick façade was just as ornately decorated as Beldam, with turrets, bay windows, arches and capped towers, but it somehow managed to feel less like a medieval fortress. Over the door was the DCS' heraldic device of a quartered wheel crossed by a lightning bolt, which Bobby had seen emblazoned on the uniforms and weapons of the guards at the asylum. The sentries let Jowett in without so much as a sideways glance at his strange companions, and the Director led them to his office, locking the door behind them. He went behind his desk to a smaller door which looked as if it belonged to nothing more remarkable than a stationery cupboard, and took out another key – a wooden one.

'The wood from which both this door and its key are made,' he explained, 'are from an ash tree which grew at a time when there was no distinction between my world and yours. There was in fact only one world. Historical records are non-existent, but a good estimate for this would be five to six thousand years ago.'

'That's incredible,' said Bobby.

'Yes. Polishing it is a nightmare. The place which it opens onto, therefore, has also existed since that time, and in those millennia it has had many names: the Great Temple of Atlantis, the Shrine of Mammonanda, the Omphalos, the Hidden Cathedral of the Hegemonic Church… those are just a handful. Best if you see it for yourself, I think. It is, at present, empty.'

He opened the door.

The space beyond was vast and circular, like a theatre in the round, with a high, domed ceiling supported by concentric colonnades of ancient stone pillars, between which rows of tiered seating descended to the chamber floor. They had entered high up, at a level where many more doors, all closed, lead in from every direction. At the same time, it gave the impression of being two very different semi-circular halves joined uncomfortably together. On the Oraillean side, the chamber was lit by brass gas lamps set in walls panelled with dark wood, and the chairs of creaking maroon leather smelled of wood polish. In contrast, the other half looked like a modern corporate conference room, completed in pastel shades, blandly ergonomic furniture, and fluorescent strip lighting.

'The Interstitial Assembly,' explained Jowett, 'comprises representatives from every – well, most – major nation states, religious and corporate entities in both realms. It has a governing council, and its day-to-day operations are overseen by a system of committees and sub-committees with budgets and quarterly reports and special monogrammed stationery.'

'My God,' said Bobby. 'So middle management really does rule the world.'

'Seriously,' added Allie, pointing. 'Is that a flip chart?'

'You would prefer robed priests chanting and sacrificing virgins during solar eclipses? That has been done too. Everything moves with the times, even universe-spanning super-conspiracies. We find the current arrangements to be more humane, not to mention much less messy.'

Bobby couldn't quite believe that they had so far avoided being accosted by anybody. 'Why aren't there any guards?' he wondered. 'For as important a place as this?'

'To whom would they answer?' Jowett replied. 'The members of this Assembly control, one way or another, all of the most clandestine and far-reaching intelligence-gathering communities in two worlds. Who could they possibly trust? Behind each of those doors – my own included – are armed soldiers from their own forces, who are not just there to stop intruders getting in. Only a madman or someone with absolutely nothing to lose would attempt to violate the neutrality of the Assembly – they'd find themselves on the sharp end of armies from every corner of reality; collectively we simply have too much at stake. You could see it as a form of anarchist self-governance, which, when you think about the number of authoritarian regimes we're currently propping up…' He shook his head and laughed. 'I swear, some days I think that if the monsters don't get me, the irony will.'

'Have you got any idea what he's on about?' whispered Bobby to Allie as they followed him inside.

She shook her head. 'He lost me at Atlantis.'

Jowett led them down through the tiered seating, towards the centre of the chamber, where the open floor was dominated by a heavily engraved circular altar the size of a pool table, but what made them catch their breath and falter back a step was the air between the two halves of the room. Down here they could see that it shimmered like a curtain of rainbow heat haze, bisecting the Interstitial Chamber completely. It made no noise, but Bobby could feel its presence as a tingling of his scalp and pimpling of goose flesh down his arms. Allie felt something flutter in her womb, almost too light and brief for her to be sure it was there at all.

'I've seen this before,' said Bobby. 'Twice.'

Jowett looked at him sharply. 'That's twice more than most lay people see and remain sane, or alive. It's called the meniscus; the skin between our worlds. On this side we are in Oraille.

On the other, your world, which we call the Realt. At least, this is how it appears to our limited three-dimensional senses. It looks like you could simply step through and be in the other side in a moment, but that is just an illusion. It's actually more of a transitional dreaming zone – an oneirocline, to give it its ugly scientific name. This is what is damaged every time you dream yourselves into our world. This is what the Hegemony, or whatever you want to call it, is pledged to preserve.'

'Brilliant!' Bobby took hold of Allie's wrist and strode across the chamber floor towards the shifting haze. 'Cheers for showing us the way home, Timothy, old bean.'

'Wait – ' protested Allie, pulling free.

'Yes, wait,' advised Jowett, though with a marked lack of urgency. He had taken a seat and was polishing his spectacles.

'Wait for what? We are *gone*, right, Allie?'

'I think in all the excitement, you may have forgotten where you are,' Jowett observed.

'I can tell you where we're going to be in about ten seconds, mate, and that's in the glorious land of flip-charts and swivel chairs.'

'No, I'm afraid not, Mr Jenkins. Remember, you are currently lying asleep in the Realt, while Miss Owens is, of course, still in her coma in Minneapolis. All either of you would achieve by passing through the meniscus now would be to wake up in your respective beds, which as I understand it is not a pleasant prospect for at least one of you.'

'You're lying.'

A note of irritation crept into Jowett's voice. 'Why, exactly? If I'm so duplicitous as you seem to think, why would I possibly bring you to a place from which you could so easily escape?'

'Bobby,' murmured Allie, 'listen to him. He makes sense. I don't want to risk it.'

'Neither of you can return to the Realt from here and remain together. I can, however, offer you one possibility whereby you, Mr Jenkins, may return to this world physically, as you did before.'

'And what is that, exactly?'

Jowett waved around at the doors which led in from all sides in both halves of the chamber. 'Each of these doors leads to an office like mine, owned by another member of the Interstitial Assembly. Quite simply, I am going to help you find one of them on your side so that you may cross through as a waking, physical entity – in flagrant breach of our highest law, by the way.'

'The catch being?' Bobby asked.

'You are going to help me apprehend whoever is responsible for arming the Elbaite navy with guns from the Realt. You are going to be my agent in your world.'

2

'When humans first began to dream,' said Jowett, 'there were so few of us and we were so barely human that it didn't really matter. The things which were born from our sleeping minds were weak and short-lived, indistinguishable from the wild creatures that hunted us. These were the evolutionary antecedents of every god that has ever existed. We call them the Aions.

'As our imaginations became more powerful and our numbers increased, living in animal-skin tents as the ice retreated, the Aions grew correspondingly stronger, and began to take the forms not just of concrete threats to our physical survival, but personifications of our fears and anxieties, hopes and dreams. They became gods and monsters and walked the world.

'But as our populations continued to grow – especially once we'd invented farming and cities – the stronger the Aions became, threatening our civilisations with their demands for worship and the wars which men fought on their behalf. So at some point, the wisest of our holy leaders decided that enough was enough, and that for the good of humanity the Aions should be banished.'

Bobby laughed. 'Just like that.'

'Just like that. The exact details of the ritual are long forgotten, of course, but that doesn't really matter. The main thing is that they created a Schism, a process by which the world was split in two, with the Aions trapped in the dreaming space between.

'Understand this, though: the Schism was not a single, cataclysmic event. It was a time of chaos and instability as parts of reality dissociated from each other. Imagine two combs with their teeth meshed together being slowly pulled apart. Families, villages, whole regions of geography and consciousness became separated from themselves by shimmering rainbow clouds of fog and mist.'

'The meniscus,' said Allie.

'Yes. At first, people were able to travel between these fragments through weak spots in the meniscus, but as time went on it grew stronger, until the worlds were entirely separate and people on both sides began to forget that there was any other world than their own – except in myths or fairy tales.'

'Or dreams,' she added.

'Quite.'

'I still don't understand why crossing this barrier is such a problem,' said Bobby, 'or why you people have to go to such extreme lengths to prevent it from happening.'

'The Aions currently exist in a vegetative state in the dreaming limbo of the oneirocline, as they have done for millennia. They achieve a brief existence and a kind of consciousness through people's dreams, and human dreamwrack in turn nourishes them, but mercifully that is the extent of it. Any influence they have is through the actions of certain powerful individuals who from time to time are able to tap into their sleeping power: politicians, artists, religious leaders and the like. They are contained easily enough.

'The problem is that every passage through the meniscus weakens it, and if our worlds grew sufficiently close enough for it to fail altogether, then the Aions would awaken and walk the earth again – and in case you are thinking that this might be a long-overdue return to some charming pre-lapsarian Golden Age of magic and wonder, consider this: at the time when our forebears created the Schism, when human dreaming gave the Aions enough power to wage war with each other on a scale which caused the ancient Greeks to call them Titans, the earth's population is estimated to have been only twenty to thirty million people. That's roughly the size of your state of Florida. In your world alone, there are now seven *billion*. Nine, if you add mine. Can you imagine how powerful the Aions would be, fed by so many? Humanity would be annihilated.'

'But the Aions would be destroying themselves in the process, surely,' Bobby protested.

'Yes, they would. And like any other ecosystem, everything would die back to a more manageable level, which I'm sure will be a great comfort to the pitiable few thousand of our species left to survive in the shattered ruins.'

Allie watched the shifting iridescence of the meniscus, finding it hard to believe either that something so thin could hide something so huge, or that something so beautiful could contain something so horrific. 'I understand why you think it's so important to tell us this,' she said. 'If everything you say is true. You have to admit, though, it's a bit much to take in all at once. Right, Bobby?'

Bobby was frowning. 'No,' he said slowly. 'Sorry, but it's actually very easy.'

'Really?'

'Yes. Because I've seen them. The Aions. And I believe every word of it.'

Jowett patted the seat next to him. 'I think it's your turn, Mr Jenkins.'

Bobby agreed, and began to tell him everything.

3

When Bobby finished telling Jowett about what had happened to him after Stray, the Director led them back to his office, where he questioned Bobby more closely on every aspect of his encounters with the araka and then the demon Lilivet.

'You'll have noticed,' he added, 'stark differences between the way the two halves of the chamber are appointed. This is precisely to do with the policy of minimising breaches of the meniscus. It is feared that even conceptual cross-contamination such as the sharing of scientific and technological knowledge would bring our worlds dangerously close, and so the prevailing eschatology for centuries has been to permit each reality its own separate evolution.

'There is, however, a dissenting Symmetrist faction which believes that the best interests of both worlds are served by as close cooperation as possible. Predominantly they are on our side of the meniscus, from poorer nations disgruntled that you have mobile telephones and they don't, and they can generally be placated with the newest Oraillean toys. Some of them may have less self-serving, less *sane* interests. I fear that they are the ones who have been trying to stop you from talking to me, Allie. I fear also that they may be behind infecting that poor young woman Sophie with an araka in the first place. Somebody somewhere is tinkering with ways of building connections between the worlds.'

'I think they're doing more than just tinkering, if the guns I saw being used on Danae are anything to go by,' said Bobby.

'But why would these Symmetrists do all that if they knew it was endangering the whole of humanity?' asked Allie.

'Because they disagree with us. They have statistics and studies which prove, they claim, that their efforts actually strengthen the barrier. They're wrong, obviously.'

'Hang on,' said Bobby. 'So what makes the rest of you right, then?'

'We have studies of our own which prove the opposite.'

'*That's it?* Statistics? You're policing reality itself and all you've got to go on is a bunch of bloody pie charts?'

'And once again I ask: you would prefer that we slaughter a virgin and study the pattern of her entrails? This is reality, Bobby, not magic. What do you think people use to forecast the weather with – crystal balls?

'You understand that this is not a thing I can investigate using my resources. The sabotage is obviously occurring in the Realt, and I have a very good idea whose hand is behind it. Find him, find what's going on, and tell me so that I can put a stop to it; the closer you get to him, the closer you get to that door into my world and the arms of your lovely lady here.'

'Sounds straightforward enough,' said Bobby, with heavy sarcasm. 'Who's the sorry sod I'm looking for?'

'He is Regional Supervisor for the United Kingdom, and his name is Martin Foulkes, MBE.'

'And how exactly do you propose I do this? If this Foulkes chap is one of your lot, then I'm not going to get within a mile of him without getting caught, am I?'

Jowett smiled a mirthless little smile. 'Ah, but that is precisely how you are going to get close to him – you are going to get yourself caught. The name of Neil Caffrey is very high on certain watch-lists in the Realt now. He was the friend of Sophie Marchant's lover, and disappeared around the same time that Marchant did, and Foulkes would dearly love to get his hands on her. Get the attention of any law-enforcement agency in your world and Foulkes will bring you to him himself. He'll be dying to prod around in that head of yours and find out who Caffrey is and what he knows.'

'Yeah,' said Bobby. 'It's the dying bit that worries me.'

4

'Pregnant.'

The weight of it had hung silently between them during the perne ride back to Beldam but now lay before them in the open, to be reckoned with.

The main quadrangle of the asylum surrounded a large garden where, during the day, patients were encouraged to take exercise and fresh air. Allie and Bobby sat on one of its wide benches. Everything that Bobby had just learned about the Interstitial Assembly, its laws and powers and factions, was nothing more than smoke in the wind compared to the bombshell she had just dropped on him. Allie let him process it for as long as he needed; she could almost hear the gears in his brain crunching, tracking backward, working out how and where and when, and then grinding forwards, stumbling over the implications.

'But I thought you said – that night when it rained – we couldn't – '

'I did,' she shrugged. 'I was wrong.'

Back on Stray, in the central chamber where poor, damaged Sophie kept her monster leashed, she had tasted the blood from his cut hand and said: 'You're all here. How can you be all here?' His blood, which had dropped through the ocean in ruby pearls to be gobbled up by fish – Blennie and Carmen and Igor – because he was physically present in a world of dreams and it was solid and nourishing. Life-giving.

'Oh shit.'

'Yep,' she said. 'That's pretty much the reaction I was going for.'

'But your body's in…'

'Yes. And the answer to your next several thousand questions is "I don't know". Nobody here does. All I know is that Jowett and his people are the best qualified to help me work out what's going on and what my options are.'

'What do you mean, options?'

'Bobby, I'm forty-one years old. Even under the best of normal circumstances that would come with a great big grab bag of complications, and this is about as far from normal as I can imagine. Quite apart from, you know, me already having kids waiting for me in the Realt. It might be better, all things considered, to simply not have it at all.'

Bobby leaned forward as if he was either trying to throw up or stop himself fainting, running both hands backward and forward over his skull. 'And do I get any say in this?' he asked bleakly.

'Of course you do! That's why we're having this conversation at all.'

'I don't know what I'm supposed to say. I don't know if there is anything I *can* say. This is – you've had a bit longer than me to get your head around it.'

'Yeah, a whole fortnight, big whoop. Just – ' she laid a hand on his arm, wanting him to look at her, not lock himself away in his own confusion. 'Tell me how you *feel*.'

'Feel? I feel fucking terrified! How do you think I feel?'

'Well that makes two of us, then, doesn't it?'

Eventually their arms found each other, and they sat that way for a long while.

'You know what?' he said softly.

'What?'

'I think if it's a boy we should call him Lachlan.'

She hugged him tighter and lovingly whispered 'Shut up, Bobby.'

'Yes, ma'am.'

CHAPTER 12

THE OBMENEK

1

It took three days for the Russians to come at Toren and Rainy. He could imagine what they'd been up to in the meantime – surveilling the pair of them, hacking their emails, and generally pussying around, trying to figure out how two small-time dealers with absolutely no record of being able to do damage to anything more substantial than a wet paper bag had managed to kill two of their muscle and put a third man in intensive care. If Toren had been in their position, he wouldn't have believed it either. They were afraid of him, and that felt good.

He and Rainy did nothing out of the ordinary for those three days; they got on with business, selling the gear that they'd taken from Lee's flat to the usual people in the usual places. Rainy had continued to crash on his sofa during that time to make it harder for them to be picked off individually. He did sort of wonder what the Russians made of their trip back to the canal carrying a bucket with a big lock-down lid, but he contented himself with knowing that they'd find out soon enough.

'Soon' came when he looked out of his flat window in the broad light of midmorning and saw a silver-grey Jaguar XF completely failing to look inconspicuous parked in the street outside.

'Oi, Ezzio,' he called, interrupting Rainy in the middle of playing *Assassin's Creed*. 'Game over, man. It's reality time.'

From between half-closed blinds, he watched two men get out of the car. Large men, hoodies up, carrying sports holdalls. No driver left in the car. They must have convinced themselves that he and Rainy didn't have any hard friends after all. They were wrong, of course, but not in a way they could have possibly imagined. Toren knew he should be bricking himself right now – if this had been happening to him less than a week ago, he'd be out there on his knees with his hands in the air, blubbering for them to leave him alone. But he didn't even feel nervous, and he supposed he had Ms DeSalle to thank for that.

If anything, he felt hungry.

The two men disappeared from view under the angle of the building, and then he heard a heavy crash.

'There goes the front door,' said Rainy.

Toren just nodded. 'You got our new recruit?'

Rainy went into the bathroom and collected the plastic cleaner's bucket which contained several litres of canal water and one very agitated inhabitant. He held it up and peered into it. 'I think it knows.'

'Of course it does. It's just like us, so take good care of it.'

Boots tramped up the stairwell, and with the new senses that Ms DeSalle had given him, Toren could feel them: twin vortices of adrenalised hostility echoing in the enclosed space like miniature tornadoes. The boots stopped outside his flat door, and for a moment there was silence. Toren gestured Rainy back into the bathroom, while he hid in his bedroom across the hallway.

A single savage kick smashed the door open. Toren could have strengthened it beyond their ability to harm it with anything smaller than a bulldozer, but he hadn't even locked it. He wanted to see what they were going to do.

A milk bottle, sloshing with petrol and capped with a flaming rag, tumbled past him and straight into his living room, where it smashed and ignited with a dull coughing sound. Then, nothing. Just fire blazing in his home.

Across from him, in the bathroom, Rainy's eyes widened in alarm.

I know, he thought. *They're not coming in. Expecting us to run out in a panic, and then do us in the corridor.*

So what do we do? Rainy thought back at him.

Toren blinked. *Did you just...?*

Shit! I think I just did! Can you hear...?

Never mind that. What we do is we sit tight. They'll have to come in sooner or later to make sure we're properly dead, especially after last time.

Something exploded in the living room, and billowing smoke began to fill the hall.

Eddie, what about the smoke?

We can't suffocate, remember?

Yeah, but we can still fucking burn to death!

A moment later, the smoke alarm went off in a shrieking din. The flat's door had bounced halfway closed again after it had been kicked open, and Toren broke cover, pressing himself flat against the hinge-side wall and sneaking quickly forwards. He reached out with his foot and slowly pushed the door all the way shut.

Are you fucking crazy? yelped Rainy in his head. Smoke hung in a thick brown blanket a foot below the ceiling, and flames were curling over the top of the living room doorframe.

Yeah, they're pissing themselves now, all right.

As if in response, a shotgun blast tore a ragged hole through the door. The main blast missed him, but he was struck with splinters and stray shot all the same. He shrugged it off and grinned.

See? Told you.

The door was kicked open again, and this time the kicker followed. The squat nostrils of a sawn-off shotgun came first, then the hands holding it, then the arms attached to the hands. Toren grabbed and pulled as hard as he could – which was extremely hard indeed – bracing his back against the wall and pivoting so that he flung the man past him and deep into the hall, where he sprawled on the floor by the bathroom, dazed.

'Rainy!' he yelled. 'Monsterize the bastard!'

123

Rainy stepped forward and upended the bucket over the gunman's head. Something black and multi-legged was left clinging to his collar, and it scrambled for his ear while he tried to bat it away in horror. Toren didn't stop to watch but turned his attention to the one still outside; if he had a gun too, they were probably fucked.

He didn't. He was only just starting to react to his colleague's sudden disappearance when Toren grabbed him by the throat and lifted him into the burning flat. The gangster struck at him, savage blows to his elbows, neck and knees which would have crippled a normal human being, but Toren shrugged these off as he had the gunshot. He propelled the struggling man backwards towards the inferno which was now all that was left of his living room, past where his partner was writhing on the floor, clutching the side of his head and screaming, blood squirting from between his fingers. The heat beat at Toren but, again, didn't affect him; the man he carried was not so fortunate. Toren didn't have to hold him in the actual flames – just being within half a dozen yards was enough. He smelled the hair on the back of the man's head burning, and the first rush of his pain was like inhaling a line of the finest, smoothest coke.

Hey Rainy, you getting this?

Jesus, yes! Any way we can get that in a pill? We'd make a fortune!

The burning man was babbling now, pleading and crying something in Russian, but that only made it better. Then the smell of burning hair was replaced by that of burning flesh, and he began to thrash in Toren's grip, his words lost in a high-pitched animal keening. It almost drowned out the sound of sirens.

'Shit!' He'd allowed himself to become distracted – sloppy. Angry with himself, he tossed the man into the inferno and turned back to the shooter on the floor, who had given up the hardest of the struggle and was now just twitching, his eyes rolled up to the whites and a bloody hole where his ear had been. It was already closing, from the inside.

Toren and Rainy picked up their new brother and carried him out of the burning flat. In the panic of people escaping down the stairwell, nobody saw anything unusual in two men supporting a third between them (nobody offered to help, either, but that was just human nature, and just as well, thought Toren), and they were able to get him out to the Jag just as the first fire appliance arrived.

2

He lay on the back seat, drooling, while they sat in the front and waited for his passenger to settle in, watching the emergency services in the meantime. Toren drummed the steering wheel – half-impatient, half still jazzed on the high from the other guy's death. They were going to have to move soon, before they got noticed. He wished the Lilivet-spawn would hurry the fuck up.

'This car is sick,' crooned Rainy, examining the dashboard in admiration. 'Shame we stink of smoke. The upholstery's going to be fucked.'

'That's right, man,' he muttered. 'Priorities, priorities.'

'What? What'd I say?'

A groan from the back seat brought him around. The Russian struggled to sit up.

Toren looked back. 'You all right, mate?'

The man put a hand to his ear. Beneath a bristling military-style cut the flesh of his newly-healed wound was pink and shining, like a burn scar. Prison tattoos crowded his collar and wrists. 'You speak Russian?' he asked.

'No,' Toren replied. 'You speak English?'

'No.'

'Too weird,' said Rainy.

'What's going on? What's happening to me?'

'This,' said Toren, and grabbed his wrist.

Ms DeSalle had grown and comprehensively infiltrated his body during the last few days, threading tendrils of her own semi-corporeal tissue throughout Toren's muscles and central nervous system. They uncoiled from the flesh of his fingertips like the stinging tentacles of a jellyfish and invaded the other man's arm, and he screamed as if electrocuted. 'What's your name?' Toren demanded.

The man continued to scream and struggle.

What's your fucking name?' Toren held fast, harder.

'M- Makarov! Denis Makarov!'

'Well, Denis, what's happening is that you work for me now, understand?' He pushed harder still, forcing the poison deeper, talking not just to the man but the creature which now lived inside him. It, like the others, had been chosen for its compliance to his authority, but all the same he felt it was prudent to reinforce the point just in case it began to feel ambitious in its new incarnation. He took Makarov's agonised spasming as a good sign. 'Are you good with that? No stupid noble sense of loyalty for your ex-boss, I hope?'

'N-no! Please…'

'I don't know what it's like in a Russian prison or the military or wherever it is you've come from; I suppose it's pretty grim. But the things I'll do to you if you fuck with me… have a good deep look into that black pit that's just opened up in the middle of your soul, Denis, and tell me I'm lying.' He leaned in close so that Makarov could see the black things writhing around his bared teeth. 'Because I will rip the nerve strings from your flesh one by one and floss my fucking teeth with them, are we clear?'

'Yes! I believe! Please… my arm…'

Toren let him go, and Makarov collapsed. 'Good. Then get your shit together quickly and drive us out of here before the boys in uniforms come to move us on.'

Makarov managed to pull himself together enough such that once they'd changed seats he could get them away from the scrutiny of onlookers and emergency services. It was understandable that all three of them had so much on their minds that they failed to notice a second and much more discreet car which pulled out of a side street and followed them at a safe distance.

In its previous incarnation as a Royal Mail depot, the Mail Box had been the largest sorting office in the country, and after a multi-million pound conversion into high-end restaurants, department stores and apartments, it cut an even more impressive shape into the Birmingham city skyline: squat, blocky and blood red. Toren, Rainy and Makarov walked up its broad steps and into the echoing space of its central mall, riding escalators up past gleaming shop fronts inhabited by people – smiling and easy in their wealth and each other. These were the same respectably-suited executives who bought Toren's merchandise when they went slumming it on Friday nights, swigging it back with alcopops or snorting it in lines from the seats of nightclub lavatories as if butter wouldn't melt. He'd thought he was free before – Captain Easy, a colourful wandering mountebank dispensing nostrums and nosegays to the muddy masses – but now he knew that he'd been nothing more than a parasite. A lamprey feeding off their fat bellies.

Now, though… oh now he was so much more. He wanted to grab each and every one of them and show it to them: grin the black pit of his soul into their faces and see how long their colours lasted while they drowned in his abyss. He despised them for it, recognising that hatred for the simple jealousy that it was and despising them all the more for making him feel something so petty.

Makarov led them through to the concierge's lobby, with its flawlessly polished desk and equally flawless young woman guarding access to the residents' lifts. If she was at all unnerved by their scruffy appearance, she was far too professional to show it.

'Good afternoon, sir. Can I help you?' There was just a trace of ice under her voice – a crackle which said *I doubt it; look at the state of you*. Her too, Toren thought. Her and everybody like her.

'Sixteen oh seven,' responded Makarov curtly, giving his name. Now that he was speaking English, Toren could hear how thick his accent was. 'I am here to see Mr Voluschek. Please tell him I am here.'

'One moment, sir.' She queried an intercom and then turned her bright and utterly weightless smile on them again. 'That will be fine, sir. Please find the lifts through and to your left.'

'Why does it feel like this is too easy?' murmured Toren as they passed her desk. 'Honestly, it can't be this simple.'

Makarov raised an eyebrow at him as they waited by the lift. 'You think today has been easy? I'd hate to be with you when things are difficult.'

'Oh you will be, my friend. You'll be right there on the front line.'

'Front line of what? What war are you fighting? Toren,' Makarov looked at him squarely. 'I spent fourteen years in the army. I know how to take orders. But it would help me to do a better job for you if I knew where you are going with this.'

It was a long moment before Toren admitted: 'I don't know. For now it's just survival – you know, big fish little fish stuff. If it gets any bigger than that, you'll be the first to know.'

The lift arrived, a gleaming capsule which whispered them aloft.

It got them as far as another lobby on fourteen, after which it was two flights of stairs to the topmost floor.

'Of course it would have to be a penthouse suite, wouldn't it?' Toren observed with a wry smile. 'Oi, Rainy, end of level boss.'

Rainy grinned and cracked his knuckles.

They stood close to either side of the richly patterned wooden door to suite 1607, out of the security lens' sightline, while Makarov knocked. There was a muted conversation with someone on the other side, a rattle of the door chain, and it opened.

And they were in.

Toren had the door guard up against the wall in a heartbeat, his feet a yard off the floor. The black energy of Ms DeSalle was burning in his muscles. 'Voluschek?' he snarled.

In reply, the guard spat at him and reached inside his jacket. Toren slammed him against the wall hard enough for his skull to cave a curved dent in the plasterboard and then dropped him bonelessly to the carpet.

'I'm here,' called a voice from further inside, quite calmly, and in perfectly good English.

Toren followed it to a huge sitting room with floor-to-ceiling windows overlooking the city. In an armchair by this panorama – just in the process of putting down a book as if having been interrupted by nothing more dramatic than a neighbour calling by for tea – was the man who had ordered his death. Voluschek was not the grizzled, big-bellied patriarch he'd imagined; he was tidily dressed in a linen suit which had that look of being so unassuming that it probably cost more than most of his men made in a month. His receding hairline was compensated for by the wildest eyebrows Toren had ever seen. It looked like his face was trying to grow wings – which was a good idea, he thought, because in a few seconds it was going to find itself flying out of that window.

'Mr Toren,' he said, rising. 'You appear to have been misinformed.'

That was when the guy Toren had missed stepped through from an adjoining room and tasered him.

The shock was like being hit by an iron bar, everywhere, simultaneously. His limbs locked, his jaws clacked together, and he crashed to the floor, unable to even put his arms out to cushion the fall. He raged inwardly. If it had just been pain he could have overcome it, but this was actually stopping his muscles obeying his brain. His entire body had become one huge funny bone, whanged on the edge of a table the size of the universe. He felt warm around the crotch, and knew that he'd just pissed himself.

Voluschek approached to a safe distance and looked down at him in distaste. 'Yes,' he added. 'Somehow you've been given the impression that I'm a complete moron.'

Then a second taser hit him and the world went away.

4

'So that went well, then,' said Ms DeSalle.

She was sitting at the stern of the boat, one hand on the tiller, the other controlling the boom rig.

'Oh shut up,' groaned Toren, struggling up from where he found himself lying: in a puddle of briny water in the bottom of the boat. He looked around.

There was no sign of the sandbar. They were surrounded by a glittering, horizonless blue void. The sun beat down from directly overhead, and the most imperceptible of breezes brushed his face and toyed with the sail. 'When did you get her finished?'

'While you were busy being an arrogant, cock-sure idiot,' Ms DeSalle replied casually.

'Jeez,' he muttered. 'Who rattled your cage?'

'I give you a little bit of grunt for you to defend yourself with, and what do you do with it? You have to go full-on Dirty Harry. Did it never occur to you that there might be people out there who know exactly what you are and are more than capable of dealing with you?'

'Well then why didn't you warn me?'

'Because in your world I'm not the me that's here, am I? I'm you.'

Toren sat up a little straighter in the boat. 'You know what? Now that you mention it, I still don't have a bloody clue what you're on about,' he finished sourly and slumped back.

Ms DeSalle chewed her bottom lip, mulling something over. 'Okay then,' she said eventually. 'I suppose we're going to have to raise the stakes. Let's start with this. Can we assume that you know you're dreaming?'

'Dreaming? Is that supposed to be a joke? The bastards tasered me!'

'Maybe something a little deeper than dreaming as you ordinarily understand it. So deep, in fact, that you've popped out the other side.'

'Other side? Other side of what?'

'Everything.'

'Every – ' His face dropped. 'Shit, I'm not…'

Ms DeSalle laughed. 'No, you're not dead. If you were, we wouldn't be having this or any other kind of conversation. There's no afterlife. Dead is dead. That's why they call it dead, boy. You're in the Tourmaline Archipelago.'

'Yeah, you mentioned something like that last time. So where's Tourmaline then?'

'On the other side. And before you start shouting at me again,' she went on, as Toren opened his mouth to retort, 'just tell me if you want this conversation to keep going around in circles, because I can do this all day.'

Toren shut it again. 'No.'

'All right then. This is how it is. Two worlds and the dreaming space between. That's what makes you strong.'

'The dreaming space between.'

'Yes.' Ms DeSalle leaned forward and there was a fierce, avid light in her eyes. 'Would you like to see it?'

'Go on then, I'm game.'

She took a hold of the tiller and began hauling in the boom rig. 'Good,' she said. 'In which case, grab that line. We've still got a fair way to go.'

They sailed for the better part of the afternoon, though without any landmarks it was impossible to even guess how far they'd travelled. He still couldn't quite shake the impression that they weren't moving at all, but as the relentless sun began to dip towards dusk he saw what he took to be a cloud shadow on the water ahead of them, coming closer. Except that there were no clouds in the sky.

'This is the place where our mother was born,' said Ms DeSalle, as the shadow grew larger. 'Of humankind and a creature from the Between which had been trapped here.

There used to be a great raft here up until very recently, but the people who lived on it couldn't control the powers they possessed and caused *that*.' She pointed.

The boat was close enough for Toren to see that the shadow was in fact a hole in the ocean – a whirlpool wider than their craft was long. He could hear it now: its endless, churning roar as it sucked the very fabric of itself into a funnelling pit of green-black water so deep that the bottom was lost in darkness. Ms DeSalle was piloting their craft right at it.

'What are you doing?' he protested. 'That thing's going to kill us!'

'On the contrary. That thing's going to save our life.'

'This is no time to get all zen on me. Turn this thing around!'

'Listen.' The boat began to pick up speed. 'Our body is currently at the mercy of men who, probably by sheer luck, have found a way to incapacitate us. If they're curious about the powers we've demonstrated against them, they'll tear you apart until they find me. Or they might simply decide to torture us to death for pissing them off. Either way, we're screwed. Our only hope is to go Between and beg for help from the powers that exist there.'

'What powers?' Toren had to raise his voice over the noise of the approaching maelstrom.

'The Aions.'

'What are – ' But the rest of his question was lost in the roar of water and the sound of his own screaming.

5

Understand this first: the gods did not create us. We made them. We spoke them into being.

The creature's voice spoke directly in his head. No longer Ms DeSalle; she was just a mask spun by his subconscious. He was alone, drifting in an immensity without form or colour.

We told each other the stories of our hunts as we sat around fires on the savannah, working our flint tools, or else we painted them on the walls of caves while the ice buried the land kilometres deep, or else we sang the landmarks of our migrations across the desert in threads of melody — all so that those who came after would know what we knew, and so know us.

And as we spoke, so we dreamed. And as we dreamed, so the dreamwrack which was left collected in the shapes of the figures with whom we populated our dreams — hero, goddess, trickster, shadow — until so much had collected that, like an unborn star which collects hydrogen until it spontaneously ignites under its own density, they acquired life of their own.

He became aware of shapes moving below him, vast and ponderous, like boulders the size of city blocks. But his mind intuited more than his eyes told him, and reeled under the implications of scale which were suggested, because it seemed that these massive forms were themselves nothing more than the very tips of the hairs on the heads of creatures more colossal still.

They are the Aions. They are the distillation of everything we are, and they are as ancient as the memory of existence itself.

This must be what it felt like to be a microscopic organism, he thought, floating through a forest of anemones. He tried to move back, to widen his field of view so that he could see them better.

Don't. Don't try to see them in their entirety.

'Why not?'

Because you'll go insane.

He laughed at that. 'You mean I'm not already?'

Quite the opposite. You are currently experiencing a dangerous level of clarity. You have passed through the meniscus. This is the oneirocline. This is Between.

'This is one belter of an acid trip, I'll give you that.'

Don't! The voice was stern, and it stung. *Don't make the mistake of thinking that this isn't real, that you're dreaming or hallucinating, and that any minute now you'll wake up. You won't. See those little flecks?*

Toren focussed, and saw them. Drifting clouds of particles which he'd overlooked as nothing more than the usual underwater junk. 'So?'

Look closer.

He did so. 'Oh my fucking god,' he breathed.

They were bubbles, much bigger and further away than they'd seemed, shifting and pulsing with colour like pearls, or Christmas tree baubles. Within each one a human figure floated, curled foetus-like with its eyes closed.

Each one of those is a dreaming sleeper, quite literally in their own little world.

'Can I see inside one of them?'

If you must. But be quick about it. There is still such a thing as time here, and you are running out of it.

He approached one of the dream-bubbles, and found that he could see through its opalescent surface. Inside looked like a Vegas casino, except that it was snowing as the gamblers laughed and collected their chips. Intrigued, he reached out to touch the surface, and as his finger dimpled it the colours rushed towards the source of the disturbance and the whole thing exploded soundlessly, leaving nothing but a few scraps drifting up towards the surface. He shook his head, dazed.

The voice in his head laughed. *Someone just woke up with a shock. It takes a lot of practice to get inside a dream without breaking it like that. A lot of stealth. You don't have the leisure to practise – at least not yet – so pay attention. The Aions seed themselves in our dreams, where they can take form, for a while, and achieve a sort of consciousness.*

The bubbles shrank and grew randomly, some coruscating with colour, others gnarled globes of darkness. They drifted amongst the Aions' gigantic limbs like plankton – where they touched, the Aions' surface swelled slightly, budding up and puffing out spores of itself into the dream-bubble, which carried them away again.

'What do they want?'

What does any living thing want? To exist. To be aware of itself as existing. If you mean what are their plans, well – they're beyond petty concerns of ambition or desire. But they are powerful. They are the source of all human creativity and endeavour. The most influential people in history – artists, geniuses, saints, dictators – have all in one way or another tapped into the power of these things, and for a brief moment become gods incarnate. Now it's your turn.

'How?'

Come with me.

He drifted closer, and even though there was neither light nor the absence of light, it nevertheless felt colder. Darker. Lonelier. The Aion's bulk rose around him in canyons, like streets lined with crumbling, deserted skyscrapers built of black coral. There were fewer dream-bubbles in this region, and those which brushed against the jagged surfaces recoiled as if stung by something venomous.

'Are you sure this is such a good idea?'

Of course it isn't – this is the Shadow. It is what spawned me and my kind; it will protect us. It will make us much stronger than we are now.

Still, Toren hesitated. 'What am I supposed to do with it?'

Let it into you, as you let me.

He laughed; a short hard bark of derision. 'Not likely!'

It is your only hope to defend yourself against the man who wants to kill you.

'No way. This is fucking insane.' He kicked upwards, but as he did so he passed close enough to the monolithic creature that it was able to extend a pseudopod of itself which grazed the sole of his foot, and his head was suddenly filled with

...BONE-MOUNTAINS RAPE-ENGINES FLESH-SMOKE BELCHING FROM CHIMNEYS SCREAMING TORTURED BABIES JUNK NEEDLES IN PLAYGROUNDS BLOOD-RUSTED IRON LEER-JET-BLACK DEAD-SMILE NO GOD PLEASE-NOT-THAT I-THOUGHT-YOU-LOVED-ME I'LL-DO-ANYTHING...

and then the contact broke, but it left him sobbing as he thrashed his way back into the waking world, moaning 'That's not me, that's not me, that's not me...'

6

The charge of a defibrillator punched Toren back into full consciousness.

He was sitting, prevented from pitching forward by something across his chest. His head lolled. Leather. Leather strap. Electrodes attached to his chest trailing wires to a trolley with surgical equipment and instruments. Breathing hurt. His shoulders hurt too, stretched back behind him and his wrists handcuffed, but neither hurt as much as the crushing, liquid agony in his groin. Lots of blood down there. And why was he naked?

Toren moaned. *Oh Jesus, what have they done to me down there?*

His face was slapped, and his head jerked up by the hair. Something was being waved in his face. He tried to focus.

Voluschek stood over him, holding that something pinched between thumb and forefinger a few inches from Toren's sweat-stinging eyes. It looked like a Chinese dumpling covered in sweet-and-sour sauce. His hands wore purple surgical gloves.

'No dying,' Voluschek admonished. 'Not until I say so. You work for me now, okay? I own you – every last little bit of you. Just like this little bit.' He waved the gristly lump.

Toren muttered a response, then twisted in agony. Even just using the muscles it took to speak made it feel like a red-hot spike was being hammered up into his lower abdomen.

'Yes, very good, I have cut off a part of you.' Voluschek retreated to where a huge black dog sat obediently at his side. 'You are actually more resourceful than I gave you credit for, and I hate to see anything good go to waste, so I have decided that you will work for me.'

'Didn't say cut,' Toren managed.

'I beg your pardon?'

'Said, I didn't say you cut me. Called you a cunt.'

Voluschek considered this dispassionately and then continued as if Toren hadn't spoken at all. 'There are many capacities in which you can make yourself useful. However, if you will not learn that you belong to me…' He snapped his fingers at the dog, which sat up with an alert little whine. Voluschek dangled Toren's testicle above its expectant jaws for a moment, teasing it, then let go. A snap, a gulp, and it was gone. 'Then I will take the other one. And then your cock. And then your hands, until finally your usefulness will be limited to your mouth and your asshole, which would be a shame, after all I am doing to invest in you.'

Dimly, from a room somewhere beyond this, came the sound of screaming. Voluschek smiled. 'Yes, I am also investing in your friends.'

Toren felt his araka flesh rise at that, finally, and tensed his muscles to snap free so that he could feed Voluschek in bite-sized chunks to his own animal, but it never happened. As soon as his wrists strained at the handcuffs, Voluschek flicked a switch and ten thousand volts crashed through them, turning his limbs to spaghetti. He screamed and collapsed.

From a steel, kidney-shaped bowl on the trolley Voluschek produced a syringe; the smack inside it looked a bit like iced tea, thought Toren, and laughed. It was an ugly, tearing sound. He could do nothing but moan impotent denials as the Russian put a rubber-tube tourniquet around his arm to raise a vein.

Then he noticed that Ms DeSalle was in the room too, and he knew that he was finally losing his mind. His Technology teacher was marking papers at an old-fashioned wooden school desk in the corner of the room.

'Help me,' Toren croaked.

Ms DeSalle looked up, and frowned. 'Help you? Haven't you been paying attention, Edward? I told you, I've helped you all I can. I'm a fragment of a nightmare wrapped up in a scrap of flesh nestling at the bottom of your brain, and that's it. Any strength I've got comes from what you saw Between. You're just talking to the messenger, here.' She returned to her papers.

'All right! I'll do it!'

Ms DeSalle looked sharply back at him. 'Really?'

The needle's tip dimpled his flesh. 'Of course you will,' said Voluschek, thinking Toren's plea was meant for him. 'But we're going to do this anyway. You see, it's a very simple equation. I make the pain come, I make it go. I'm the closest thing you will get to a god.'

It hurt so much to speak that all Toren could do was plead with his eyes. Ms DeSalle disappeared, and the needle slid in. As he drew the plunger back, Voluschek thought that the little bit of Toren's blood which came with it looked black, but this was impossible, and he pressed the plunger home.

7

Voluschek watched the broken figure in the chair slump, a boneless sack of flesh held up only by its chains. ECG readings showed that both heartbeat and blood pressure had dropped right down but not life-threateningly so. A thin line of drool ran from one corner of his mouth and over his chin. Voluschek snapped the gloves off. Let the little *mudak* enjoy himself while he could. He tossed the gloves down and called Borya to heel.

But Borya didn't heel. He began to growl at the human in the chair, hackles raised and lips curled back from his teeth.

Voluschek drew his gun and sidled towards the door; he trusted the dog as much for its instincts as for the physical protection it provided, and if Borya said there was something fucked up going on, he didn't intend to get himself killed by ignoring them. He made it three paces when Toren spoke:

'Grisha, where do you think you're going?'

Voluschek froze. It wasn't so much that Toren should have been too smacked up to say anything at all, nor that it was said in the perfect Russian of Voluschek's home town – it was his grandfather's voice. It was that particular nickname which his *dedushka* had only ever used, and in that particular tone of icy rage which made Voluschek want to cover his head and curl up in a corner of the room. It was a name which had inevitably been accompanied by the heavy whistling crack of his grandfather's walking stick on his arms, legs, and buttocks. "Grisha, why are your school marks so low?" *Whack!* "Grisha, why are your chores not finished?" *Whack!* "Grisha, why are you such a weak, snivelling little piss-ant? *Whack!*

Grandfather: a psychotic Soviet-era relic whose desperation to keep his Red Army glory days alive had driven his son to alcoholism and suicide before turning its watery, zombie gaze on his grandson. When the old bastard had finally lay dying in a bed of his own filth on a Moscow public cancer ward, he'd reached for that walking stick like a Viking determined to die with a sword in his hand, but Voluschek had kept it from him and enjoyed hearing his *dedushka* beg for something for the only time in his life. After the funeral he'd burned it and cut the ashes into a quarter kilo of cocaine which he sold to the junkies that Grandfather had so despised. Voluschek didn't believe in ghosts, but the part of him that was still little Grisha definitely did.

'I asked you a question, boy.'

Toren's face, but Grandfather's voice – and Grandfather's glittering, weasel malice in his eyes. A thin trickle of blood and smack wept from the hole in his arm, and the wound in his groin seemed to be knitting over with something black and gleaming.

'You're dead!' he whispered.

'Nothing dies for the Aions, Grisha. You think you know what power is? Toren-Grandfather spat a laugh. 'You have no clue. Pain, no pain; life, death. Simple binaries for a simple mind. Power is knowing that it wasn't the cancer that got your dear old *dedushka* in the end, but the smack you addicted him to and then denied him. Power is knowing all the shitty lies and evasions that you deceive yourself with. It's knowing about all that money you stole from your mother. It's knowing how you charged the other boys in primary school ten roubles apiece to see your eight-year-old cousin Katya's pussy and then beat her up for being a whore.'

The figure in the chair was still glaring at him, but it was different now – no hatred or defiance, more a weary contempt, as if it had seen this kind of thing a million times before and even though it was disgusted by him, at the same time he was utterly common and predictable. Insignificant. That hurt worse than a lifetime of Grandfather's walking stick.

Voluschek screamed and fired, emptying the clip. Its crash was deafening in the small room. Toren jerked, hit in half a dozen places, and was still. Borya was barking continuously now.

But the glare remained, glittering. The wounds closed, a web of sinewy black tissue pulling them shut and leaving little puckered scars.

'Yeah,' said Toren. 'It's that too. But that's just flesh. Flesh passes.' He got up from the chair as if the manacles had never been there in the first place. The light fled from him, repelled to the edges of the room, and left him in a pool of darkness at its centre. He pushed the shadows into the corner of the room where the door was and wrapped them firmly around the handle, as there came shouts and thumps from Voluschek's men.

The dog launched itself at him, and Toren batted it away with a backhand swipe which crushed its skull against the wall, killing it instantly. 'I'm sorry to have to do that,' he said. 'It was only doing its job, I know. Still, a dog can't have two masters, can it? I know all of that about you because you've pushed it into the Shadow, Grigori, and the Shadow is in me. The Shadow *is* me.'

A heavier *crack-crack-crack* hammered the door as the guards tried to shoot out the lock, but Toren's shadows held it firm.

'I can see into every filthy, cockroach-infested corner of your soul,' he continued. 'Do you want to know what I see? Shall I show it to you?'

'No…' Voluschek pleaded. 'Please…'

Toren showed him anyway, pushing the darkness into his brain, right behind the eyes. He let the man shriek and sob for a while on the floor, clawing at his eyes, while he looked outward, to discover where they'd taken him.

He was in a disused storeroom off the old post-office tunnel leading from the basement level of the Mailbox to

New Street Station – abandoned and all-but-forgotten in the building's reincarnation. He saw other tunnels, a complex of abandoned sub-basements and empty bunkers underneath the city – places where creatures of the dark could hide and grow strong. He knew this because Voluschek knew this; the information was leaking incontinently from his nightmare-torn mind. Makarov had been executed immediately as a traitor, which was a shame. Rainy was in the next storeroom along, beaten and held by the same electrified-handcuffs setup. How had Voluschek known the way to incapacitate them? That information was there also – that and much more besides – but Voluschek was going to have to host one of the Brood himself now if he was to be of any use. His mind was going to need some reassembling. Toren finally laid a consoling hand on his shoulder, and Voluschek recoiled like an animal.

'What you need to understand, Grigori, is that it is like this for everyone, and that you are nothing special. We are all shit, all monsters in the Shadow. Knowing this truth is a freedom. It frees you from the shackles of conscience and the lies of morality. It frees you from the pretensions of humanity, or loyalty, or faith. It frees you to pursue the purest of callings, and that is this: to bring all people into an absolute knowledge of themselves and their own darknesses. To this I am a living testament: the Shadow made flesh. You, little Grisha, with all your knowledge and contacts, are a hollow man, headpiece filled with straw, alas – but I will fill you, and you will be a valuable disciple.'

The door burst open, and two of Voluschek's bodyguards swept in. They saw their employer sobbing, curled in a foetal position, at the feet of a naked and blood-streaked figure rendered indistinct by the shifting veils of shadow which it wore.

'You, on the other hand,' Toren said to them, 'are simply food.'

'How do you feel?' asked Toren. He was sitting in what had been Voluschek's wide-backed armchair, gazing out at the city from his penthouse picture window. The slow twilight of a summer's evening was stretching itself out to the horizon in elongated shadows, and lights were beginning to pinprick the dusk. Immediately below him – fifteen storeys down – the waters of the Gas Street Basin trembled with the coloured lights of pleasure boats, bars and nightclubs, but the water was still black for all that, and he felt the Brood of Lilivet clustered there, eager and hungry. The armchair was his now, along with everything he saw from it, and most especially the man hovering nervously to one side.

'Odd,' replied Voluschek. 'I feel like I should have the mother of all migraines, but I don't.' He massaged the bridge of his nose, through which his Brood had entered. Toren had given his new disciple the remainder of the day to recuperate while he and Rainy had settled into their new accommodation too, but downtime was over. Answers were required.

'Sit down.' Toren indicated the sofa opposite, and Voluschek obeyed. He moved a little awkwardly, like a drunk man trying to appear sober; the Brood adjusting to its new motor controls. Rainy brought him a drink, which he accepted gratefully, gulping it down. Toren watched, smiling. 'Sort of takes it out of you a bit, doesn't it?'

'I had no idea,' said Voluschek, blinking slowly around at what had been his home, as if seeing it for the first time. Which, in a sense, he was.

'You knew we were coming, didn't you? And you knew exactly what to do with us when we arrived. I'd like to know how that works. This has happened before, hasn't it? This, or something like it?'

'I don't know, and that's God's own truth. But probably, yes. A year ago I was sent here to expand the business of my *bratva* – nothing special, a bit of powder, some girls – but also to keep an eye out for strange people.'

'Strange as in…?'

'Able to do things that people shouldn't be able to do. I was shown videos of people like that, changing things and themselves. Sometimes like animals, or angels, or devils. They took me to one of the old Soviet labour camps and I saw them in the flesh. *Obmenek*, they were called. Changelings. I was told that sometimes I would get instructions that there might be such a creature in the city and that I should find it, and I was shown how to keep it under control until arrangements could be made to have it taken somewhere safe. But the *obmenek* are cunning and very good at not being found, so every now and then we are told to run a little sewer-flushing operation – kick the shit around at the bottom of the pile and see what crawls out.'

'And then me and Rainy crawled out. But you weren't going to have us shipped neatly off to a Siberian gulag though, were you? You were going to slave us up to work for you instead.'

Voluschek shrugged.

Toren chuckled. 'Well isn't that just poetic fucking justice. Who gives these instructions and makes these arrangements?'

'Again, I don't know. I have a number, I call it, a car arrives to pick up… whatever, and money appears in my account. I have one name, but it's not a person. It sounds like an organisation, probably some leftover Soviet thing. *Hegemonya*.'

Toren grinned. 'Now that's more like it.'

CHAPTER 13

SOMETHING STUPID

1

Chandler was sitting on his chair in the wreckage of Corvedale Hospital's old MRI room, in exactly the same position as Bobby remembered; as far as he could tell, the man might not have moved from that spot since then.

'No little extra-corporeal friends with you this time?' Chandler asked.

'Not this time. No hidden snipers?'

'Not this time. I like to think that by now we've built up a relationship of trust.' He gave a sardonic laugh. 'At least you haven't tried to sell me out to the Hegemony, which is something.'

Bobby walked over to the window that looked into the MRI control room, his shoes scuffing aside dead leaves which had drifted in through the skylight. The window was made of toughened glass and unbroken, but it was almost opaque with grime and algae. On the other side he could just about see the blocky shapes of consoles and benches, stripped of their equipment. 'The last time we spoke,' he said, 'you told me something about their Interstitial Assembly.'

'I told you that it was a rumour,' Chandler corrected him.

'Well, I've seen it.'

Chandler got up from his chair and brushed his hands together. 'It's a shame you had to come all this way just to take the piss,' he said. 'I'll be making my goodbyes…'

'The room, at least. Where they meet. Massive, circular, lots of tiered seating, dozens and dozens of doors leading to the offices of the people who run it, in both worlds, and the meniscus running right across the middle like a huge curtain.' Chandler had stopped, listening. 'I saw it from the other side in a dream. I'm going to find one of the ways in from this side, and I just thought that might be of some interest to you.'

Chandler sighed. 'You don't think we haven't already tried? You don't think that people just as brave and stupid and committed to their loved ones as you haven't tried? You will be caught and tortured and used as a vessel for something abominable. Sorry, Mr Jenkins, I've seen it happen far too many times before. What makes you think you're different?'

Bobby thought about this for a moment. 'Nothing, I suppose. But I'm going to do it anyway. I just thought I'd give you a heads-up so you can get out of the firing line – or maybe I'm hoping that you'll choose to throw a bit of weight my way.'

Chandler paused at the exit and looked back. 'I'm not promising anything,' he said. 'Let's see how far you get.'

2

Let's see how far you get.

Now, Bobby sat at a window table of the Bull Ring Tavern, looking out at the market across the road and nerving himself up to do, in the words of his mysterious contact, "something spectacularly stupid". Carmen and Blennie were drinking with him; Blennie nursing half a pint of mild, Carmen sipping something which was all primary colours and umbrellas. When he'd asked them why they were bothering, since they didn't need to eat or drink, she'd replied that they were simply trying to blend in. Looking at the sweep of her hat and the outrageous plunge of her dress, he wondered what it was exactly she was trying to blend into; a thirties Havana gin-joint, possibly. Not an inner city watering hole of market traders, which looked like it hadn't seen the business end of a paintbrush for forty years.

Then it hit him again: Allie was pregnant.

'Come on, let's do this,' he said, suddenly resolved. He drained the rest of his pint and stood. 'Remember, I'm panicking, okay? Just trying to get away, not hurt anyone. So make it obvious but don't put anyone in hospital.' He looked pointedly at Carmen. She pouted, blew him a kiss, and rippled away into the thin air.

Bobby winced. 'Maybe not quite that obvious.' He glanced around, but none of the other drinkers seemed to have noticed – at least, nobody was jumping up and down waggling a finger and yelling "Jesus Christ, where did that refugee from a Pedro Almodovar movie suddenly disappear to?!" He and Blennie left more conventionally, but anyone watching from outside would only have seen Bobby emerge onto the crowded pavement.

I'm getting desperate, he reminded himself, going over his cover story again. *Surfaced in this body a month ago and starting to run out of options. I've been sleeping rough, and I'm starving. I don't know anything about supermarkets, but I do know markets. There's a market place in Timini (or there was until you bastards shot it up with your airships and your guns, and by Christ you'll pay for that), and I don't want to steal, but needs must when the Devil spits in your piña colada, or something like that.*

The Open Market occupied a hundred or so covered stalls between the ancient spire of St Martin's church and the sprawling warehouse complex of the wholesale markets south of the city centre. It was busy even at midweek; unlike suburban farmers' markets where the middle classes went once a month to buy their boutique olives, people here were shopping for their everyday groceries from stalls piled high with fruits and vegetables from every conceivable country and culture.

Bobby counted at least three sets of CCTV cameras. It was harder to spot the Hegemony's wake-sensing buoys which Jowett had told him would be there, since they wore the shape of people, but even if there weren't any, the cameras would be good enough. He wasn't planning to do anything subtle.

Looking for something which offered a good escape route

with a decent run, Bobby settled on a salami merchant's, with sausages, wursts and hams stacked like firewood. He stood in line behind a woman with an enormous shopping bag printed with multi-coloured grapefruit, and while she haggled with the stall-holder – an extraordinarily thin man who looked as dry and tough as his products – he slid one of the wursts off the counter under cover of her bag and walked away.

Fast, but not too fast. You want to run, but you're trying not to draw attention.

It was never going to work. It wasn't *supposed* to work. He felt Carmen and Blennie tensing themselves invisibly around him like a blanket of static electricity.

'Oi!' someone yelled.

Good. He quickened into a run.

'Oi! Tosser! Come back with that!' And then, much louder, not meant for him but a call-to-arms for the rest of the stall-holders: '*Thief!*'

The shoppers who heard him coming shrank out of his way, and he shoulder-barged through the rest. Not so the other stall holders; although the market had its own security guards, they were few and far between, and their role was mostly as a visible deterrent or to pick up the pieces of any idiot who tried to nick something and had to face getting tackled by the traders themselves. Which was exactly what happened.

A big-bellied Indian grocer stepped in from the stall opposite to block Bobby's way, yelling, fists raised – and then appeared to smack himself in the face, blood spraying from his nose. *Easy, Carmen,* Bobby prayed. *I just want to get done for theft, not grievous bodily harm.*

Then the surrounding stalls seemed to explode as their merchandise began flying in every direction. Aubergines, tomatoes, plantains, t-shirts, cucumbers, jeans, lettuces, yams, and trainers; all aimed at the salami guy and his mates who were giving chase, until the passage behind Bobby was chaotic with traders and shoppers tangled in vegetable-splattered clothes and slipping on the pulverised remains.

Yeah, that'll probably do it, he thought. *Nice one, Fishketeers.* He legged it away from the market, down a side street beside the Wholesale Market and then slowed to a stroll. All he had to do was wander about like a culture-shocked exile from a parallel reality and hope that the CCTV operators were doing their job properly.

It seemed they were, because a few minutes later the fluorescent harlequin paintjob of a West Midlands Police patrol car cruised past him and slowed.

He made a token stab at running but let them bale him up by some dumpsters behind a fried chicken shop and surrendered his stolen sausage meekly, before they cuffed him and took him away.

3

To the cops processing his arrest for shoplifting, he gave his name as Archin Foronda, his profession as a fisherman, and his home address as Timini on the Island of Danae, part of the Union of Amicable Island States, in the Tourmaline Archipelago. The cop filling in the form stopped at this point.

'Foronda,' he frowned. 'Is that a Romanian name?'

'Told you,' called one of his colleagues in passing. 'Did I not tell you? Romanians, Bulgarians, the whole bloody lot of them.'

Things became even more interesting when they printed him and discovered that his name was really Neil Caffrey and that he'd been on Missing Persons for well over a month after having walked out of his job as a gallery security guard for absolutely no reason that anybody could determine.

'Looks like Mr Caffrey had some kind of mental breakdown,' said the duty sergeant to his superintendent. 'At least he hasn't come back claiming to be David Beckham, or something.'

'What'd this criminal mastermind nick, anyway?'

'Er, a sausage, sir.'

The super looked at him. 'Get out of my office,' he said wearily, 'before I do something very unprofessional to you with it.'

4

Bobby had some idea of what to expect from whomever the Hegemony sent for him; Steve McBride had told him about the Swarm and the Hradix, and there was his own experience of the demon goddess Lilivet. Knowledge was scant comfort, however, and he could feel Blennie fretting invisibly in the air around him, imagining all manner of horrors.

None of it prepared Robert Andrew Michael Jenkins in the slightest to deal with the people who eventually came through the cell door to collect him.

It was his parents.

5

Neil Caffrey's mother and father crowded through the doorway with tearful hugs and kisses and cries of 'Oh my boy! My poor boy where have you been?' He was a plump, middle-aged man in an oil-stained fleece, with a shining dome of baldness and a thick ginger moustache as if to compensate; she was slightly younger, with a heart-shaped face and dressed in a smart-casual blouse and pants as if she'd just rushed straight out of a school reception office. Before Bobby could protest or pull away, she (*Rhona*, he thought, *her name is Rhona*), folded him in her arms while he (*Edward Ed Teddy Ted the Head all his mates call him*), stood a little off, nodding and blinking back manly tears.

How did he know their names? That was easy: because he was Neil. Or he had been Neil, before his physical translation into Tourmaline had nearly destroyed his mind and the dream-fish of the Flats had healed him with the dreamwrack of another man. Except maybe there was a lot more of Neil left than he'd suspected, and that idea terrified him.

'Whoever I was before I got here,' he'd said to Allie before leaving Stray, 'what if he comes back and doesn't give a damn?'

'You are a good, brave man, whoever you are,' had been her reply. 'You will remember.'

But his brain was fogging. The smell of Rhona's (*Mom's*) perfume was instantly familiar. It was Clinique's 'Happy'; he'd bought it for countless birthdays and Christmases. It mingled with his Dad's smell of cigarettes and engine oil, the way he'd smelled since forever, into an olfactory shorthand for every car trip as a kid to the supermarket, to school, to family holidays in Norfolk, lunch in Burger King at the services for a treat, he and his brother Roger fighting in the back over some stupid bloody Top Trumps game all the way across country until Mom lost her rag and reached over and walloped the pair of them and then that would be that – for about five seconds. He grinned at the memory.

Blennie? He called silently. *Carmen? A little help here, chaps? I think I'm going under for the third time.*

But of his Fishketeers there was no sign.

His what? His fishke-fucking-what-now?

Neil looked at his parents with confusion. 'Hi Mom, hi Dad,' he said. Then he noticed the police cell. 'Oh Christ, what have I done now?'

CHAPTER 14

CAFFREY COMES HOME

1

The police let him off with a caution, since the offence was so minor and obviously the result of a mental breakdown of some kind, and they let him go into the care of his parents on the understanding that he present himself back at the station within three days to make arrangements for a proper psychiatric evaluation. Still in a daze, Caffrey let everybody else sort things out for him, and Mom and Dad took him home. Not to his flat – Dad told him that it had been mothballed for the past fortnight, besides which there was no way he could be trusted to be there on his own. They took him to the family home.

It was a perfectly ordinary semi of the kind built by the hundreds in Longbridge during the thirties for workers in the car factory, itself long since gone to rubble. It had a broad sloping roof and one of those funny circular windows halfway up the staircase, and it couldn't have been more than a month or so since he'd last gone round for Sunday dinner, but all of a sudden it seemed to Caffrey that it had been years since he'd seen it.

They led him upstairs to his old room and left him alone to get changed, and he drifted slowly around the familiar-yet-strange relics of his boyhood: the Prodigy posters (Music for the Jilted Generation), a pair of battered old high-top Reeboks in the bottom of the wardrobe, the sports certificates and photos of him at one Tae Kwon Do tournament or another, his hair centre parted in long curtains on either side of his face; Jesus, the nineties had been an ugly decade.

He opened a drawer and found an old ACDC t-shirt which would probably still fit, though to judge from the mirror he'd lost a few pounds. He put it on and squinted at his reflection sceptically, then grinned.

'I'm back in black, baby,' he said.

Acting on a flash of memory, he knelt by the skirting board and prised up a corner of the carpet, and the section of loose floorboard underneath, and triumphantly drew out an ancient girlie magazine. Nothing hardcore – mostly just tits and ass. He must have been – what? Twelve? He put it back; let some kid in the future find this and have a crafty retro-wank over some pre-internet porn. Then he went to have a shower.

2

'I told you,' said Caffrey through a mouth full of food, 'the last thing I remember is smacking my head against the wall next to that painting. It must have given me a concussion or something.' There was no way he was telling them that it had been a girl who had bounced his head off the wall.

'That's one mother of a concussion,' remarked Dad, reaching across the table for more special fried rice. After an afternoon sleeping off the strangeness of the day, Caffrey had wanted to go out to the Green Man for a pint, but Mom had refused absolutely – afraid, maybe, that if she let him out of the safe confines of the house he'd disappear off to God-knew-where again like an untethered balloon – and instead done the next best thing: ordered comfort food from the Ruby Chinese Takeaway down the road. From the amount she'd ordered, Mom had noticed how much thinner he was and obviously decided he needed feeding up.

'Well first thing in the morning, I'm booking you an appointment at the doctor's to get you checked up properly,' she announced.

There was no use in protesting – and anyway, all he really wanted to do was find out if he still had a job by some miracle and get back to normality. Ideally starting with chicken in black bean sauce.

'By the way, thanks for looking after the flat,' he said.

'I cleaned out your fridge,' said Mom. 'The things that were going manky in there, ew!'

'Dunno how I'm going to afford it now. I don't reckon I've got much of a job to go back to.'

'Eh, you'll come and work for me at the garage,' said Dad, in that tone which told him it was already settled. 'At least until you get back on your feet.'

Caffrey smiled. 'I really…'

There was a knock at the front door.

'Who now?' Dad got up to answer it, and Caffrey was seized with a sudden and gut-churning terror of who would be on the other side. He almost said something, then realised how it would sound and kept his mouth shut.

His father's cry of alarm told him how wrong that decision was.

Ted Caffrey had opened the door on a quite small, quite pretty but otherwise unremarkable young woman dressed in a smart coat and holding a clipboard; she looked like a Council census-taker. She glanced down at her clipboard. 'Are you Mr Edward Charles Caffrey, father of Neil?' she asked.

'Who wants to know?' Hostility and suspicion did as much to block the doorway as his body.

She gave the kind of reassuring smile which was taught in corporate seminars and held up an ID lanyard. 'My name is Pelassis Corle, Mr Caffrey. I'm a senior case officer from Birmingham Social Care Services. I'm afraid there's been a terrible misunderstanding regarding your son's situation. May I please come in so that we can discuss it?'

'No you may not, Miss Whatever Your Bloody Name Is. If you want to speak to my son, you can bugger off and get a warrant.'

Her smile thinned. 'What I have, Mr Caffrey, is an order to detain your son under Section Two of the Mental Health Act…'

He barked a laugh of disbelief. 'You're *sectioning* him?'

'... under which it is an offence in law to interfere with the court-designated officer in the pursuance of her duties. I really would much rather come in and discuss this more sensibly...'

'Sensibly be fucked!' he snapped and slammed the door.

At least, he tried to.

Pelassis casually placed her hand into the closing gap. The door should have broken her wrist, or bruised it severely – left her howling, at any rate – but it bounced off and opened again as if the limb were made of stone. As Ted Caffrey gaped at this, the door of the car parked in the street behind her opened, and someone dressed in a full-face hoodie got out and began walking up the path. It moved past her and through the doorway, expressionless and silent, shouldering him aside and ignoring his objections as if he were no more an obstacle than a child. He could hear wet snuffling noises coming from inside the zipped-up hood.

Back at the dinner table, Caffrey and his mom both looked up in alarm.

'What's that?' she gasped.

'Stay here,' Caffrey ordered, rising, still with a tight grip on his fork. 'Call the police.'

'No! Neil! For God's sake, be careful!' She fumbled for her phone as he ran into the hall.

The hooded figure grabbed him by the shoulders and kicked his legs out from underneath him; he slammed onto his back, winded, black stars flaring in his vision.

It knelt over him, unzipped its hood, and a nest of writhing tentacles fell out.

The skull was elongated backward and curved under itself like a nautilus shell, and a forest of gelatinous, anemone-like tendrils covered the front from brow to chin. They waved and quested the air as if grazing on dust motes, forming ripples and patterns like tall grass in the wind. He knew it wasn't doing anything as passive as feeding, though – maybe that was what it did in its natural state, whatever that was. It was sniffing. At him. He could smell it in turn – a sweaty, peanut smell of crusted dead skin. Its tentacles trailed and tickled over his face while he lay there paralysed with disbelief, then back again, seemingly unable to find what it was looking for. It turned back to its controller and signed something with its hands.

'What do you mean there's no Passenger?' she demanded and knelt beside Caffrey. From this angle he could see the blunt shape of a pistol holstered at her armpit, but all the same there was something like sympathy in her eyes. 'Mr Foronda,' she said, 'I know that you are hiding inside this man somewhere, and I understand that you are having second thoughts. Myself, I'm originally from Dauncette, in Carax, and I really I do understand that all you want to do is run and hide and try to make sense of what's happening to you. But you're only going to cause more damage, and these people, Mr Caffrey's parents, don't deserve to be on the receiving end of it. They don't know what's going on any more than you do; they can't help you. I can.' She laid a cool hand on his forehead, and he flinched from the touch. 'Please, Mr Foronda, let me help you.'

'I don't know what you're talking about,' Caffrey whispered. 'Don't hurt... my folks. I'll come with you... just leave them... alone.'

Pelassis sighed, disappointed, and rose to address her companion. 'Never mind, we can sort it out later. Lloyd, parcel him up. We're to take him straight to the Wardrobe.'

The creature's anemone-face returned to Caffrey's, with more violent intent. Dozens of venom-loaded cnidocytes tipped with microscopic barbs latched onto his face in an obscene kiss. The only comfort to be had from the agony which roared into his head was that it was mercifully brief.

Mr and Mrs Caffrey huddled on their lounge rug with their arms clasped around each other, weeping as they watched their son's legs drum spastically in the hall for a moment and then stop. She buried her face in his shoulder. 'They've killed him!' she sobbed. 'They've killed my little boy!'

Mr Caffrey, white-faced and breathing hard as if to stop himself from screaming, just stared at the woman who was most definitely not from Social Care, whatever she claimed.

'No,' Pelassis smiled indulgently, hunkering down in front of them, the clipboard hugged to her chest. 'Nobody dies here tonight. But you really should learn to co-operate with the authorities. It does save an awful lot of fuss and bother. Now, this part is for you.' She scribbled at a form, tore it off and tucked it into the front of the father's sweater. 'Please keep it for your records. And as a gesture of goodwill to show that there are no hard feelings on our part, let's see if we can't arrange a nice, long, all-expenses break somewhere hot and very far away, shall we?'

She beamed at them as, behind her, their son was dragged out of the house by his ankles.

3

'Eddie!' called Rainy, sounding in somewhat of a panic. 'You need to come and see this!'

'What the fuck is it now?' Toren snapped the bedroom light on and rubbed his eyes. He was tired and out of sorts. He'd been practising the trick of sneaking into people's dreams; it was a lot harder than he'd expected, and on the rare occasion when it did work, the banality of human fantasies was just plain depressing.

'Something weird. One of the vessels.'

'Let's have a look, then.'

The penthouse living room was now dominated by a twenty-foot long aquarium tank full of murky canal water within which tentacled shapes lurked and darted – quite a lot fewer than there had been two days ago. Rainy and Voluschek had been busy. The owners of the neighbouring apartments were the first to be hosts to the Brood, in order that they could provide accommodation for the rest, culled from the homeless, stragglers, and loners in the canal-side area who wouldn't be missed.

One of these, an old woman, was now standing slack-jawed and vacant-eyed in front of the tank. Usually by this stage, they were having second thoughts about whatever they'd been promised to get them up here and were demanding to know what was going on, if not actually screaming, but she looked as placid and uninterested as a sacrificial cow.

'What's wrong with her?' he asked.

'Dunno.' Rainy scratched his head. 'The Brood that we tried to give her to wasn't interested. Just sort of crawled all over her head and then dropped off, and she didn't bat an eyelid. It's like there's nothing even in there – no mind. Nothing that the Brood wanted, anyway.'

'And this didn't register with you when you picked her up off the street at all?'

'Hey, look, a lot of them are stoned off their tits and not much different, you know.'

'Hmm.' Toren peered closely into the woman's eyes. They didn't flicker in the slightest; not even the irises contracted. Up close, the rank smell of neglect was nauseating, and the last thing he wanted to do was touch her, but his curiosity was awake now. He placed the palm of his hand on her forehead. The shadowflesh crawled out of his pores and into hers, through the bone wall of her skull and into the brain behind as he probed for any sign of consciousness.

Nothing.

He poked and prodded, deeper and harder, doing things which would have had a normal person shrieking and pissing themselves in agony, until something flinched, far below the level of anything remotely human. The fingers of the woman's right hand spasmed.

'You're right,' he said, withdrawing. 'Weird.'

'What?'

'Well there is something in there, but it's not a person. It's barely even animal; more like a plant. Some kind of big old jelly fish just floating around in there.' He turned back to Rainy. 'What did she have on her?'

'Just a phone. Shit one, too. Only calls one number, and that disconnects after three rings.'

'Give it here a minute.'

Rainy handed the phone over: one of the cheapest pay-as-you-go models he'd ever seen. Toren took the battery out and put the phone back in the woman's pocket. Then he reached into her brain and goosed it again. With jerky, robotic movements, she took out the phone, rang a number on autodial, hung up without saying a word, and put the phone away. Toren did it again, with the same result. Then he moved a little distance away and gestured at the ceiling light, temporarily dimming it. The woman made another disconnected call exactly as before, and all the while, she remained staring with empty eyes at the tank of dark water.

Toren grinned. 'That's brilliant.'

'What?'

'Clever, clever buggers. It's a warning system! Like a watchdog, but without a bark or bite. More like a sniffer dog. It senses when something like us is nearby and sends an alert.'

'Who to?'

'Well, these Hegemony people, I'm guessing. They must have thousands of the bloody things, everywhere, wandering around like zombies and reporting in whenever anything sets them off. I think I'm going to like our new friends, when we finally meet them. We could compare notes.'

'I'd advise against it,' said Voluschek, from the other side of the room. He'd observed Toren's experiments without comment, but Toren could feel the disapproval radiating from him all the same. 'The next time they come for you, it will be on a geographical scale. They run governments, Toren. Annoy them badly enough, and they might decide to simply throw a cruise missile or two at you, and you won't even know it's happening until your ass is sitting on a cloud playing a harp and wondering what that loud noise was. I don't think you realise the kind of people you're dealing with.'

'Maybe not,' said Toren. 'But I'm positive as fuck that they have no idea the kind of people we are.'

'Hang on!' Rainy suddenly started in alarm. 'How many more of these things have we set off by accident?'

'Exactamundo, Rainy, old chum. As fascinating as this is, we can't have that, can we? Get some of the new people together and sweep the area. Find every single one of these sniffer things you can and get rid of them.'

'They will notice that even more,' said Voluschek. 'A whole section of their network going dark like that.'

'You may have a point.' Toren mulled it over, drumming his fingers on the glass, and the Brood scrabbled at them from the other side. 'What to do, what to do. Oh well!' He threw his arms up in a cheerful shrug. 'Guess we'll just have to face the music, won't we? If they're going to find us, I want it to be on my terms. Grisha,' he said and was rewarded with a cringe from Voluschek. 'I need you to make that phone call. Tell whoever you tell that your flush team has caught something and that they should send one of their pick-up teams. We'll make them part of the family and start working up the food chain. Rainy?'

'Yes, Eddie?'

Toren gestured with distaste at the old woman. 'What do you think this is, a fucking nursing home? Start with this one.'

'Yes, Eddie.'

Rainy led the shell of a human being from the room. When he'd gone, Toren laid his hand on the side of the aquarium tank, and from out of the murk the half dozen or so which were all that was left of Lilivet's Brood emerged and congregated on the other side of the glass from his fingers. He felt the hungry pricklings of their infant consciousnesses and tried to soothe them. *Better than that,* he promised. *Much better.* He'd find them strong hosts with quick minds and positions of influence soon enough, when the Hegemony came calling.

CHAPTER 15

FOULKES

1

Martin Foulkes stared at the two reports sitting side by side on the screen of his laptop and scowled. CCTV images crowded alongside police autopsy reports and local newsfeed grabs of a burning block of flats. There were so many red flags all over everything it looked like Chinese fucking New Year.

He believed absolutely in coincidences, which might have seemed ironic given his position as a moderately large cog in a worlds-spanning machine of manipulation and subterfuge, but that was precisely the point: he believed in them because he made the damn things. He wasn't supposed to be on the receiving end of them. When that happened, the only meaningful conclusion he could draw was that someone or something – the universe, possibly – was fucking with him.

For a start, that simple flush job in Birmingham had gone inexplicably, hideously tits up.

It was one thing to sit and wait passively for Passengers to pop up and then collect them when they inevitably succumbed to reality shock and went on a psychokinesis-powered bender, but there were times when something a little more proactive was called for. The spawning of cephalopodic monstrosities from one of his own men into the Birmingham canal system had most definitely been one of those times.

The East European assets were usually best: brutal and efficient, and great for plausible deniability. Usually. Two of the flush team had been found, not just killed but butchered, and with bare hands by the look of things. In addition to this, the escalation team which had been sent in by whatever incompetent jackass was controlling them (and when Foulkes found out who that moron was he'd be lucky to find himself in charge of anything more important than a fucking cabbage-pickling factory), had either burned to a crisp or else disappeared completely.

Several buoys around the city's central canal basin had gone dark, and nobody was picking up their phones; Birmingham was a communications black hole. No change there, he thought sourly. The situation wasn't unrecoverable, but he would have to choose his preferred scorched earth instrument soon. A gas explosion, maybe, or an outbreak of something highly contagious. He had absolutely no intention of letting things get out of hand like in Lyncham.

And on the other side of the screen, ladies and gentlemen, we have this: Neil Caffrey – ex-colleague of one Steven McBride, who had waltzed off with the rather important araka-carrying young lady, Sophie Marchant – had popped up again almost a month after disappearing off the face of the earth (*this* face of it, at least), apparently carrying a Passenger of his own, some fisherman called Foronda. The report was all in order, i's dotted and t's crossed by the very reliable Miss Corle, and Foulkes didn't believe a word of it. There was so much about this which offended him, not least of which was the way these people seemed to think they could just swan back and forth over the borders of reality – borders of which he was the passing guard. So why turn up now? Did Caffrey know something about what had happened to the Russians?

'Does the Pope shit Catholics, Miss Corle?' he said, typing out a redirect order. He wanted Caffrey here, where he could keep an eye on the tricky little bastard. 'I rather think he does.'

It was while he was doing so that he received a high-priority alert from Wardrobe Control. The nameless button-pusher who answered to his terse 'Yes, what is it?' stammered a bit before spitting it out.

'Sir, the Legate from Elbaite demands to speak with you.'

And then there was that. What had Shakespeare said? When troubles come, they come not single spies but in hundred-and-twenty-eight-bit encrypted data packages. Or something.

Foulkes sighed, screen-locked his computer and left the office to see what this latest display of histrionics was all about.

2

The nickname 'Wardrobe Control' had started as a joke made by some anonymous wit who'd read too much Narnia as a child, but in the way of such things, the name had stuck so well that now nobody – Foulkes included – referred to it as anything else. It was funny, because he couldn't think of anything less appropriate.

Officially, Ketterley was a classified-access radar installation. In reality, a geodesic dome rose over a hundred-and-fifty feet above the surrounding Herefordshire countryside and enclosed nearly three acres of it like a gigantic compound eye, glaring at the heavens. Its panels were hexagonal and constructed of a fluorine-based thermoplastic which was much lighter and more durable than glass, not to mention being an excellent insulator and providing a totally climate-controlled environment for the precious organism which it protected.

Inside the dome, at the centre of a circle of meadowland which had seen neither plow nor pesticide since the Reformation, grew a massive and ancient oak tree. The Ketterley Oak – probably the oldest sessile oak in the British Isles – was certainly well over a thousand years old. The story went that it had passed as an acorn across the Interstitial Chamber between two Symmetrists, hidden in a roll of manuscript, and been planted to form a bridge across the meniscus. Completely heretical, of course; the monks responsible, had they been discovered, would have been immediately executed and their order disbanded. Foulkes found their bravery, and their foresight in planting something which couldn't have come to fruition even in their great-great-grandchildren's time, quite inspirational.

It was not an attractive specimen, however. Parts of it were dead, its canopy patchy and its trunk swollen, and its base yawned open in a gap tall enough for a man to walk right through without bending – though the tell-tale rainbow haze of the meniscus which filled it promised that wherever he ended up wouldn't be in this world. To reach it, Foulkes passed through decontamination and security checkpoints and stopped by the control room, where every aspect of the biome's ecosystem was monitored and controlled, from the humidity in the air to the fungal spores in the soil. The Ketterley Oak had better security and health than a monarch, which was just as well; it had outlived every one of them since William the Conqueror.

Close by the tree were the stone ruins of a priory. They still existed only because it was feared that excavating them would damage the oak's root web, and ordinarily they served no function, but for several months now they had been a convenient collection point for dozens of crates of automatic weapons, ammunition, body armour – anything small enough to fit through the gap and into Elbaite. A number of hand-trolleys stood nearby, idle. No shipments were going out today.

Finally he stood in the shallow wooden cave of its archway, standing on the same patch of dry earth where countless generations of Hegemony priests had communed secretly with their counterparts on the other side of the meniscus, free from the petty interference and bureaucracy of the Interstitial Assembly. The barrier was within touching distance, but he had never touched it. Through its iridescent swirls, he could make out a high-walled courtyard somewhere in the Protectorate of Elbaite – it was the only sight he'd ever had of that world with waking eyes.

Then a man was there: Lord Geiran, Legate to the Assembly. He wore a grey, high-collared uniform with many brass buttons, and beneath his thinning hair, the rear of his skull was elongated in a way which proclaimed his status; only high-born Elbaite families were permitted to continue to ancient practice of skull-shaping. He also looked royally pissed off.

'Ah, Martin,' he said. 'You deign to show yourself as last, I see.'

Foulkes let it pass. He wasn't in the mood to play. 'Let's have it, Geiran,' he sighed. 'Then you can save face with your Admiralty, and I can get on with something actually important.'

'The armaments you sent us are running low. We require more.'

'And you shall have more. At the allotted time.'

'Unacceptable. The Amity forces are proving to be more resilient than anticipated. If we are to maintain our momentum and subdue the Archipelago without getting bogged down, we must be resupplied now.'

'Then listen to me carefully. One,' Foulkes ticked them off on his fingers, 'the shortcomings of your intelligence assets are no concern of mine. Two, neither is the fact that your Admiralty can't hold its collective wad long enough to avoid over-extending itself. You should have stockpiled as I originally advised. And three, you know as well as I do the dangers of stressing this breach; you can't just jump backward and forward through it like some cosmic bloody Hokey Cokey – not unless you want an eruption of the oneirocline on your hands. I doubt even you're that stupid.' He hadn't meant to be so undiplomatic, but the Birmingham situation was preying on his mind. This was a waste of time. 'Besides, I'm sure your boffins are hard at work reverse-engineering their new toys. You'll be able to make your own soon enough.'

Geiran's face coloured with fury. 'Yes,' he responded tightly. 'And then we shall have no need of you or your abominable disrespect.'

'Oh Geiran,' Foulkes laughed. 'You'll always have need of me. I'm the one who will keep Oraille off your back while you enjoy your little war.'

Foulkes turned and left without waiting for the other man's reply.

Back in his office, he cleared his desk and stacked the files neatly in his pending tray, but it didn't help. Despite his reassurances to Legate Geiran, he still felt like he was being handed pieces of a jigsaw which didn't fit, with no picture to tell him what they should look like or any certainty that they were even part of the same puzzle. He still couldn't fully comprehend how Maddox could have gone so completely off the rails so quickly, and without any warning signs; it made Foulkes wonder how many more of his staff might be unravelling quietly behind the scenes. He decided to make one last call – there was no real need to, but there was no harm in a healthy sense of paranoia, either.

The face which answered his skype both shocked and vindicated him in equal measure. 'Croft, what in God's name?'

His lucid agent looked terrible – he was pale, and the eyes which usually gleamed with dark merriment were shadowed by dark circles. 'This is not a good time,' Croft muttered, rubbing his face.

'Spare me. What's going on? Is the situation in Carden under control?'

'Partially. I located Runceforth; Jowett had him under protection in some kind of safe house, along with one of the other crew, Harcourt, who was listed as missing. Had a bugger of a job getting in. DCS agents everywhere. I managed to scratch the kid, but the bastards tezzed me. Those things fucking *hurt*. I think it's safe to assume that whatever Runce was going to tell your pal Jowett about what happened in the Archipelago, he'll have done it by now.'

Foulkes bit back the urge to tear into Croft for his failure – his third, counting the unsuccessful attempt to sabotage the Karasand and the fugitives' escape at Blackyards. Recriminations were evidence of failed management, and the man was doubtless doing the best job he could, given the limitations of the remit Foulkes had given him.

'Well then,' he said, 'I don't see any point in keeping the gloves on. We need to escalate this. It's time to remove Jowett from the picture completely. Don't kill him – he's no use to me dead – just let him know how short his leash really is.'

3

When Jowett returned from his office he absently asked Miss Fortescue to get him a fresh pot of tea and some of those nice biscuits they had in the Committee Rooms – the crunchy ones with the ginger and filchnuts – and settled down with a sigh to the mountain of paperwork which had heaved itself up tectonically from his desk while he'd been out.

When he looked up, there was a man sitting in the chair across from him. Runce's description of the impossible assassin who had killed Harcourt was quite accurate.

Jowett's hand went for the panic button on the underside of his desk.

Nothing happened.

Croft grinned and swallowed painfully. 'Tricky, that,' he said, and coughed. 'Electrical signals. Always prickly in the back of the throat.'

'I'll admit I'm impressed,' said Jowett. 'It must take a lot of control, lucid dreaming your way in here without setting off the detectors. Foulkes trains his people well.'

The assassin inclined his head, accepting the compliment.

'Not that well, obviously,' Jowett continued. 'Killing Harcourt was a waste of time. You must have known that by now my people would have told me everything they saw in the Archipelago. I know about the araka and the guns. So what now? Please don't tell me that Foulkes is stupid enough to think that killing me is the solution to his problems. The IA investigation into my disappearance will – '

'Stop. Right there. Please. Mr Jowett, with all due respect, you're babbling. Of course you're not going to disappear.'

'Then why are you here?'

'To deliver a message, that's all. You're not going to die. You're not going to do anything. Whatever information Runceforth and the Stray woman might have given you, you're going to do precisely nothing with it. No reports, no follow-up investigations. Zip. You've already done your part and cleared the way for the Elbaite fleet; if I were you, I'd invest in some arms shares, put my feet up and keep my nose out of other people's business. Because here's what's going to happen if you don't, Mr Jowett. Two things. One, the IA will hear all about the Strays your team brought back from the Archipelago, at which point you can kiss your career goodbye.'

'And two?'

Croft blurred, disappeared, and was suddenly at Jowett's side, snarling in his ear. 'Your detectors and your tez guns are useless against me. *Useless*. Finding someone in a dream is a piece of piss.' He waved an army medal in front of Jowett's face. 'Runceforth,' he said. He waved a brass pen nib. 'The young savant. I've got something from every member of the Spinner's crew – it's a just a pity they're already dead.' He waved a handkerchief. 'Hooper.' Then he held up a brooch, which Jowett recognised with a jolt. It was fashioned in the shape of a leaping unicorn and was all he had by which to remember his mother; he had been heartbroken to lose it, as he'd thought, months ago. '*You.*'

Another blur, and the assassin was stalking back and forth across the other side of the room. 'I could kill any one of you any time I want! I choose not to, but don't push your luck.'

'Thank you,' said Jowett and picked up the pen from his desk.

'Oh, you're very welcome!' Croft laughed.

'No, I don't think you understand,' Jowett replied, lifting his feet off the floor. 'Thank you for telling me what I needed to know. Please inform Martin next time you see him that I look forward to raising a petition against him in the Assembly for those guns he's been selling to Elbaite. Now, do be a good chap and get out of my bloody office.'

He placed his pen back into the holder – the second one, the one which he had never used nor expected to, except in the worst possible emergency, which this most definitely was. Its nib connected with the copper contacts hidden inside and completed a circuit which activated the tezlar grid that had been built into the fabric of the room. Purple-white energy scrawled across walls, floor and ceiling, and arced through the air in bolts which earthed themselves in the assassin, who screamed for a second before collapsing to an infinitely dense point and disappearing from existence utterly. The tezlar field discharged, and for a long moment the office was filled only with silence, smoke, and a few fragments of scorched paper see-sawing lazily floorwards.

Then the door opened, and Miss Fortescue was there with a tray of tea and biscuits. She surveyed the mess and pursed her lips. 'If you had wanted something toasted, you need only have asked,' she said. 'Would this be a bad time...?'

'No, Angela,' he said, slumping back in his chair. 'This would be a very good time.' As she busied about with the tea things, his mind raced, trying to find a way out of this – anywhere that they might possibly be safe from an assassin who could dream himself literally anywhere, past any security measure. 'Angela,' he said at length, 'I want you to arrange for a perne to pick up Officer Runceforth and Miss Owens from Beldam, immediately. They are to have a full tez-squad escort at all times.'

'Certainly, sir. For what destination?'

When he told her, she was so surprised that she had to ask him to repeat it, but it didn't make any more sense the second time.

4

Croft lurched awake, screaming. For a moment it seemed that crawling purple fire had followed him back through the dream, and he thrashed, batting at himself. Somewhere, a medical monitor was shrilling.

'Turn that fucking thing off!' he barked.

A nurse hurried to obey.

He lay back, rubbing his aching head. That sneaky little fucker Jowett; Foulkes had warned him to be careful. More medical technicians were fussing around him, checking the electrodes on his scalp and the cannula in his arm. Behind them, Doctor Nandhra watched with concern.

'Get me back over there,' he ordered.

'Certainly, sir,' she said. 'Just as soon as we have your check-phrase.' A whiteboard and pen was presented to him.

'Fine. Which one?'

'Number five, sir.'

Quickly he scrawled check-phrase five: *Who looks outside, dreams; who looks inside, awakes.* It was a security protocol designed to guard against the danger of him accidentally catching a Passenger while on an LD excursion. The phrase itself was less important than the time it took him to recall it; Passengers tended to have slower access to complex information in their host personalities' brains. If he hesitated – or, God forbid, got it wrong – there were guards outside the room with tasers and electrified handcuffs who would drag him away to a gulag quicker than you could say 'psycho-linguistic repression'.

'Thank you, sir.' The board was taken away.

Dr Nandhra checked his brain-wave readings. 'We'll programme a course of inhibitors and with a couple of hours' rest you'll…'

'Hours be bollocksed. I need to get over there *now*, before they've got a chance to use Christ-knows what else.'

'But sir, your beta trace is spiking. And after your last excursion there's just no way…'

'Listen.' He grabbed a handful of Doctor Nandhra's jacket and hauled her close enough for the spittle of his fury to hit her in the face. 'You push whatever it takes to get me back over there. I don't care. Don't worry about me; worry about you. Because if I'm still conscious in three minutes, you won't be, got that?'

She disentangled herself with frosty dignity. 'Yes, sir. We will put you under, but I can't guarantee how long it will take your beta trace to even out.'

'You just leave the dreaming to me.' While the nurses were busying themselves with dosages and drips, Croft swigged from a pint of water by the bedside and hastily chewed down a mouthful of fruit and nuts. Prolonged LD excursions were a nightmare on the body, sometimes literally. In his other hand he clutched Jowett's unicorn brooch. There was no guarantee how quickly he'd be able to catch up with them, but…

Ah, there. Iciness crept up his arm from the cannula, where the nurse was pushing a large-bore syringe of barbiturates into his bloodstream.

'Cheers,' he grunted, already becoming drowsy. *Right, you sneaky bastard*, he thought. *Let's see how fast you can run.*

CHAPTER 16

THE GRAND SKY PAVILION

1

The coastal town of Samphort Wells had been a resort since long before the Great Mechanisation. When Oraille had been nothing more than an island of warring fiefdoms, its briny waters had been famed to possess health-giving properties, and the canny sisters of the Priory of Saan Tamara the Gentle had built a politically neutral and, more importantly, prosperous community by encouraging the great and the good to pray for miracles as they enjoyed the spas and springs. Even after the Great Mechanisation had relegated such superstition to little more than a quaint sideshow, the town remained a favourite place of relaxation for the King, and thus most figures of the court. But it wasn't until affordable steam travel and a train line carved through the Stonebrow Range to the east coast that the raucous crowds of the new middle class arrived with money to splash around and an appetite for entertainment. Both were satisfied by the construction of the wonder of aerostatic engineering which was the Samphort Wells Grand Sky Pavilion.

'My God,' breathed Allie, gazing upward. Her head was tilted so far back she was afraid it might fall off. 'How can that possibly stay up there?'

A silver castle was floating in the sky, the sunlight glittering like water from baroque confections of battlements, spires, minarets, turrets, and towers. It was tethered to a second, larger, but much less ostentatious platform – the First Class Sky Pier – held aloft by perfectly ordinary 'stat envelopes, and this mezzanine level in turn hung above the end of a quarter-mile long pleasure pier stretching out into Samphort Bay.

Jowett considered it and scratched his head, perplexed. 'Judicious application of some very ordinary physical laws,' he suggested. 'Granted, some may be slightly different from those in the Realt, but I assure you that it is really up there. Miss Owens, you are looking at literally the pinnacle of Oraillean aerostatic engineering.'

Runce grunted, unimpressed. 'Not to mention a total lack of taste and common sense when it comes to tourist destinations.'

'Honey, remind me to take you to Disneyland some time,' she said vaguely, still staring at the impossible thing.

'The main reach is just a standard pleasure pier,' Jowett explained. 'The mezzanine level is all theatres and restaurants for the great and the good. The Royal Pavilion itself is actually a lot smaller than it looks. Most of what you can see – the walls and battlements and whatnot – are actually a series of completely hollow helium envelopes shaped out of paraluminium.'

The main pier – crammed with booths, bandstands, cafés and kiosks, arcades and pagodas – marched out to sea on high wrought-iron arches from a promenade crowded with tall, many-windowed hotels and guesthouses. The perne had dropped them at the pier's massive, ornate entrance gates. Beyond them, she could see that all of the concession stands and attractions were shuttered closed or covered with tarpaulins against the coming winter, but even in this season a few couples were strolling the boardwalk in hats and coats.

As they passed through the gates, she pulled in a deep lungful of sea air. It was nothing like on Stray – instead of the Archipelago's humidity, it was brinier and had a biting edge which reminded her with a sudden pang of homesickness of family vacations on Lake Superior. Abruptly, her stomach roiled with morning sickness, and before she could utter an apology to Jowett and Runce, she bent over the rail and vomited into the grey sea below. They waited a little way off, embarrassed and fidgeting, while she finished.

'Gotta love that sea air,' she croaked, giving a wan smile as they continued.

A small electric tram took them to the end of the pier and a fairground whose rides were all covered and silent, at which point they were almost directly beneath the leading edge of the First Class Sky Pier. Hawsers and steel cables the thickness of trees held it in place, and the air was full of the twitchy song of high-tension cables. Jowett waved some papers at a pair of sentries in the umber and turquoise uniforms of the Royal Guard, who let them through to an elaborately gilded cage elevator.

'Can't see how this place is supposed to protect us from that assassin chap,' observed Runce. 'Unless we're planning to outrun him on the dodgems.'

Jowett slid back the concertina door of the elevator and beckoned them inside. 'Ladies first,' he said. Hydraulics whined as mechanisms within the elevator housing calculated their combined weight and pumped additional helium to the 'stat envelopes on the mezzanine level to compensate, and they were carried aloft.

'You'll have no doubt asked yourself by now,' he continued, as the cage rattled and creaked, 'why subornation events only occur in this world.'

'Well yes, now that you mention it,' Allie replied. 'People here must dream too, so why don't you haunt us?'

'Hegemonic Church records from around two hundred years ago indicate a small but distinct elevation in the frequency of subornation events around the same time as your Industrial Revolution. The effect has been increasing – slowly, but steadily, as your world rockets ahead and has far too many more babies than it can sustain while ours just sort of plods along. We think it has something to do with the difference in population sizes between the two worlds; the higher psychic density of more dreaming minds on your side of the meniscus, pushing through in one direction, like any pressure system. The nightmare scenario for which we do not have an adequate response is this: what happens when that pressure crosses a certain threshold? How much can the meniscus take before it simply bursts under the strain?'

'It's the first I've heard of this,' growled Runce, glaring at Jowett. 'Why haven't we been told?'

'We have,' said Jowett, 'at an appropriate level of seniority.'

'Appropriate level of my arse, more like.'

As the implications of what Jowett was saying dawned on Allie, she had to hold onto the side of the elevator cage to steady herself. 'You're talking about multiple subornations. Hundreds, thousands, every day.'

'An epidemic of nightmares which would almost certainly destroy our civilisation.'

'Jesus.'

They arrived, and Jowett opened the cage door. The First Class Sky Pier was much grander, designed to look like a square in one of Carden's high-class districts such as Tenorbridge or Chervil Hill – with cast-iron lampposts, marble fountains and gilded porticos. Jowett pointed out that it was all constructed of cunningly decorated balsa wood, papier mache and aluminium, but the artistry was such that Allie couldn't help expecting the whole thing to plummet into the sea at any moment. But he hurried them past here too, to a larger and grander elevator which carried them towards the shining edifice hanging impossibly above them.

'The point is,' he continued, 'plans were obviously laid as soon as possible to protect the Royal Family.'

'Naturally,' said Runce, with heavy sarcasm.

'A location was found and strengthened using state-of-the-art technology, not just against unconscious subornation but also lucid dreaming incursion, one which is capable of being self-sufficient for months.'

'Wait a minute,' said Allie, 'are you saying that this is the equivalent of the Presidential nuclear bunker?'

'Miss Owens, the Hegemony puts Presidents and Kings into power and takes them out of it all the time. And other than the fact that this is the literal opposite of an underground bunker, yes, that's precisely where we're going.'

They ascended towards the underside of the Royal Pavilion and were soon in its shadow. Up close, she saw that its outer surface was nowhere near as gleaming and burnished as it had appeared from below. Rivets and welding scars were evident where the sheets of paraluminium alloy had been joined to clad the helium envelopes contained within. Most were tarnished and streaked with seagull shit. She thought it was a brave or unfortunate soul who was given the job of keeping those clean.

They were met at the top by the Royal Pavilion's Chief Steward, an elderly woman in an immaculately pressed suit, ramrod-straight and nearly a head taller than any of them. She shook hands with Jowett. 'Director, always a pleasure to welcome a member of court.' She took in Allie's and Runce's appearances with a disdainful eye. 'And their, ah, companions.'

'You are too kind,' he replied. 'I hate to be brusque, but I'm afraid I'm going to have to ask you and your housekeeping team to vacate the Pavilion.'

She blinked. 'I apologise, Director, my sense of humour isn't what it was.'

'This is no joke, Madame.' He handed her an envelope. 'You'll find the necessary authority from the Privy Secretary is all in order.'

She broke the seal and perused the envelope's contents. Even though her impassive expression remained unchanged, every line of her bearing radiated intense disapproval. 'Very good, sir,' she responded curtly, turned on her heel, and marched away. Within minutes the handful of liveried staff had descended with her to the mezzanine sky pier, leaving Allie, Runce and Jowett alone in the floating castle.

'Brusque isn't the word,' she commented.

'They'll still be alive by lunch-time,' he replied. 'Which is more than I'm confident about saying for the rest of us.'

The Royal Pavilion, as Jowett had said, really was smaller than its ornate exterior suggested, but not by much. He and Runce disappeared, deep in discussion about DCS business while she stood transfixed at a huge window, gazing out at the tightly-clustered streets of Samphort Wells far below, and the flat, grey sweep of the coastline to either side. She explored, and found parlours, drawing rooms, dining rooms, and suites of bedchambers which would have done a Beverly Hills mansion proud – especially if the interior designer also had a thing for kitsch Victoriana. There was only the faintest perceptible sideways drift which betrayed the fact that they were at the mercy of the wind hundreds of feet up; otherwise it was remarkably steady underfoot.

As if to contradict her, there was a sudden lurch, like a small earthquake. At the same time, the exterior surface of the pavilion crawled briefly with a web-work of purple fire.

Jowett returned, brushing his hands. 'That's better, the tezlar grid is up and running. We should be safe for a little bit. Who's for a cup of tea?'

2

'To be honest, I'm amazed we made it this far unmolested,' said Jowett, sipping his tea. 'My little surprise back at the office must have disorientated our enemy more than I'd hoped. With luck, it may be quite a while before he is able to reach us again.'

'Why take the risk, though?' Allie asked. 'Why come all the way out here?'

They were taking tea on one of the Pavilion's many balconies, overlooking the wide sweep of the Gulf of Kurra and the grey-green haze of the Jassit coastline far on the eastern horizon.

Runce tipped something from a small bottle into his tea and swirled it. 'Keeping the public safe, for one,' he said. 'Am I right?'

Jowett nodded.

'Also, once the lift is locked there's no way of getting up here except by a protean ability like flying, and that will register on any PV detector. But mostly because the skin of this thing is carrying one hell of a wallop.'

'Almost no way,' corrected Jowett.

'Aye, I hate that word.' He swallowed his tea and grimaced.

'Our lucid-dreaming stalker,' Jowett explained, 'has been able to bypass all of our defences because he's somehow obtained personal possessions of his targets, which he uses while dreaming to home in on them – in exactly the same way as Bobby found you,' he added to Allie.

'But he hasn't got anything of mine because I'm not from here.'

'Yes, but he has got something of mine and Runce's.'

'If it were me,' put in Runce, 'I'd more than likely just make myself invisible, fly up to window level and take us out with a hunting rifle from a safe distance before we knew anything about it.'

'Fuck,' she breathed. 'That is nasty.'

'It's not quite that easy for him,' said Jowett. 'Proximity is an issue. We're not talking about homing as in a homing pigeon, or stalking someone from a distance. The link caused by possession of a personal item is associative, not physical; it is based on emotional connections to the object in question. One cannot choose how geographically far one appears from the owner. One is either there or not. He did it on the Karasand, when he tried to sabotage it, and he did it at Crowthorpe's house, when he killed Harcourt.'

'Great! So he could just suddenly pop into existence right next to you and kill you any time he liked? This is better how, exactly? What's the point of electrifying the walls if he can just appear inside them?'

'Because we want him to appear inside them,' said Runce. 'They're a trap.' He tossed back the rest of the tea with a shudder. 'Horrible aftertaste, that has.' He got up and unstrapped the tez gun from around his waist, placing it and its bulky battery unit on the table in front of Jowett. 'You sure you're going to be able to use that, sir?' he asked and yawned massively.

Jowett took the weapon, and checked the charge indicator. 'Don't you worry about me.' He stood, and the two men shook hands. Jowett held Runce's gaze as unflinchingly as his hand. 'Thank you, William,' he added.

'Pleasure, sir.' Runce yawned again, went in from the balcony to a long sofa with many silver cushions, and lay down.

'What?' asked Allie. 'Wait, what's going on here?' She hurried over to where Runce was lying.

''S a trap,' he slurred. 'But only if there's a sleeping body inside it. Only way, I'm afraid.' He raised a hand to her cheek and stroked it clumsily. 'Rock and a hard place, Allie.' His eyes were drooping and his head lolled like a car crash victim. 'I'm the hard place.'

'You're the…'

'It's the place that Berry went to; I'd like to see it. *Need* to see it – your world, what it's like, and what it's doing to ours. Something else too, more important. Shut up and listen, lass. *You.* You're not safe where you are. Thought I might pop over there, y'know, and keep an eye on you. Couldn't help Berry, but I maybe I can help you…'

And then he was unconscious. She checked; he was breathing perfectly normally. Then she wheeled on Jowett. 'What the fuck have you done to him?'

'It was his idea as much as mine…'

The rest of Jowett's reply was interrupted by an incoherent howl of rage which erupted from across the room. Croft, Martin Foulkes' lucid dreaming assassin, blurred into existence on the run, his face twisted in fury.

3

'Get behind me!' Jowett ordered. 'Now!'

She moved to obey as he fired the tez deliberately short, scorching the marble veneer and setting fire to the plywood at the feet of Croft, who flinched, skidded, backpedalled.

'Don't move!' Jowett roared, and in that moment Allie realised how wrong she'd been in dismissing him as just some faceless bureaucrat. 'One more step, and you burn, here! Flee, and you burn at the perimeter. Stand fast and listen!'

'Fuck you!' spat Croft. But he stayed where he was all the same.

'Why isn't he using his special dreaming mojo?' she asked Jowett. 'You know, hiding and flying and all that?'

'Because of you.'

'Yes, you stupid bitch!' snarled the assassin. 'Because of you!'

Jowett fired again, the purple energy bolt burning a long trench in the floor to Croft's left. 'A little civility, if you don't mind.'

'Fuck your civility. You want something, or you'd have fried me already.'

Because of you. Because she'd spent nearly a year of her life living on Stray and trying to keep a low profile, trying to tread lightly in this world to avoid drawing attention to herself. Because she'd stopped the spread of the nightmare grove on Bertram Street. Because, above everything else, *this* was the real world to her. It had to be; the alternative was her own crippled body back in the Realt, and that was unthinkable. Because this world could not be a dream. It was not allowed to be a dream.

'Protean effects don't work around me,' she realised.

Croft applauded sarcastically.

'And you can't escape by waking up...' she started.

'...because, like any other subornation, he'll drag anybody unconscious back with him,' finished Jowett, nodding at Runce's sleeping figure. 'As a Passenger.'

Now she understood the magnitude of the sacrifice Runce was prepared to make. 'My god – he'd really do that?'

'If not, our friend here would eventually have killed him, and me, and many more besides. I have no doubt that as well as items belonging to us, he also has the personal effects of senior members of Court – maybe even the King himself. I'm guessing not just in Oraille, either. He must not be allowed to escape. Here.' He held out Runce's large revolver to her.

She stared at it. 'What in hell do you expect me to do with that?'

'You're an American, aren't you?'

'We're not all gun-toting rednecks, you know!'

'You don't have to be. You just have to be another variable for him.'

She took the gun gingerly, as if afraid it might go off at the simple act of touching it.

'What,' snapped Croft. 'Do. You. Fucking. Want.'

'Oh,' replied Jowett, as casually as if it was something which had momentarily slipped his mind. 'I want you to tell me everything you know about Foulkes' operation over there, starting with how many lucid agents he has, names, passwords, the usual. Then we'll move on to my end of things: your contacts over here, the people you've blackmailed, how you managed to forge re-direction orders to the Karasand – that sort of thing.'

'Right. And then you'll fry me anyway.'

'Don't be obtuse, of course I won't. You and I both know that if I remove you there'll only be another assassin sent to replace you. On the other hand, he,' Jowett indicated Runce, 'I would rather not lose him just to neutralise a petty thug like you, if I can possibly help it. Give me enough information to prevent you from being a threat to my world, and I'll switch off the tez field and let you leave here with your own mind. Face it, I'm going to get the information from you anyway. Either you're going to tell me willingly and take the chance that I'm a man of my word, or I just tez you where you stand and wait for my man to wake up in your body, whereupon he tells me everything you know anyway.'

'So why not do it?' asked Allie. 'It's too dangerous to have him around a second more than we have to, surely.'

The assassin nodded at her approvingly. 'I'd listen to her, mate.'

Jowett ignored him, and for the first time sounded to Allie like he might really be on the verge of losing his patience. 'Because,' he said to her, 'I need you to trust me.'

Croft cocked his head to one side and considered Jowett through narrowed eyes. 'You and Foulkes,' he sneered. 'What a right fucking pair. You think you can negotiate and bargain your way out of anything. Think everyone has their price. You want to watch yourself with him,' he told Allie. 'To people like him, everybody's just an *asset*. Well, fuck you all. I'm not playing.' And he turned on his heel and walked away.

'You can't walk out of here!' called Jowett. 'Stop, or I'll...'

But the assassin was already diving to one side, rolling, coming up behind an armchair as Jowett cursed and fired, missing, the tez blast punching straight through the wall behind. Croft broke cover and sprinted around the edge of the large room back towards them, Jowett tracking him just a little too slowly, firing and missing again, because at the end of the day was not a trained marksman, and his target was fast enough even without his protean abilities. Allie had just enough time to swing Runce's big pistol in his general direction before he vaulted over the sofa on which Runce was lying and threw himself at her. He bore her to the floor easily and locked his arms around her throat from behind, rolling on his back so that she was on top of him, staring at the ceiling in terror, while he hissed in her ear: 'Darling, you were never even a variable.'

She couldn't breathe. His right forearm was an iron bar across her throat, his left hand pressing hard on the back of her head. She struggled, flailing, missing, making ugly, panicked grunting noises as her lungs lurched for air.

'You're an *asset*, like me. Right now your boss is weighing up whether it's worth the risk of tezzing us both and having sleeping beauty over there wake up in you instead of me. How'd you like an old man inside you, eh? Bet it wouldn't be the first time. Now be a good girl and pass the fuck out so I can get my mojo back.'

He squeezed harder. Her heels drummed the floor. She reached back and clawed at whatever of him she could reach, raking his face, feeling blood under her fingernails. He grunted but didn't let go. 'That's it, darling. You fight me.'

Big black flowers were blooming in her vision, obscuring the sight of Jowett, who was wide-eyed with indecision, the tez gun wavering in his hand.

Don't, she begged him silently. *Please don't do this. You want me to trust you? Don't send me back.*

If he was somehow able to understand her unspoken plea, it obviously didn't make any difference.

He pulled the trigger.

4

Purple fire tore through and around Allie and her attacker, binding them in crawling loops of barbed wire tighter than his strangling arms, burning a hole through the skin of reality. They fell, screaming and tearing at each other like dying lovers, into the dreaming space between worlds.

And yet.

Something deep in her belly snagged, caught, and held.

For a moment they both hung there and gazed in awe at the abyss, where huge, dimly-seen shapes rolled and shifted. These must be what Jowett had referred to as the Aions, she realised. The things that Bobby had seen on both of his waking trips through the meniscus – the things from which fragile human minds shielded themselves with dreams. The assassin screamed and clawed at her in his desperation to prevent being sent anywhere near them.

She could so easily let go. Knowing that Runce was doomed either way, she could at least make sure that when he was exiled in the Realt it would be in her body, not this killer's. Would that be a kindness, she wondered, for him to wake up sharing the body of a crippled woman?

But the tiny knot of purpose in her womb refused to relinquish its grip. There was nothing she could do to help

Runce. Despair made her savage, and she kicked the assassin free, watching him tumble away as she fought to clear her head of the purple fire.

<h2 style="text-align:center">5</h2>

When sensation returned, touch came first, and she found herself lying on something yielding but firm which reminded her of a hospital bed. Hands were on her: feeling her brow, taking her pulse. She expected to hear the beep of a cardiac monitor and the hiss of a respirator – repetitive, moronic noises of mindless machines incapable of understanding how badly she wanted them to just *stop*.

Instead, she heard Jowett's voice. 'Alison! *Alison! Allie!*'

He was bending over her, pale and sweating with panic, but when her eyelids flickered open he fell back with a huge sigh of relief which seemed to empty him from the toes upwards.

'You shot me,' she croaked.

He was using the heels of his palms to wipe sweat, or possibly tears, from his eyes. 'I said to trust me,' he replied. His voice didn't sound much better than her own.

'Huh. Well *that* didn't work.'

'How do you feel?'

'Gimme that gun and I'll show you.' She was lying on the sofa where Runce had been. Of her friend there was no sign.

He had gone into Exile.

CHAPTER 17

1

Runce's prey fled from him through the undergrowth, and the stink of its terror intoxicated him. There was pain in the shoulder of his right foreleg where it had wounded him earlier, but the anger at that only spurred him on faster. It kept glancing back with fearful eyes and stumbling on its clumsy two legs – as well it might, for he was a rannul, and a creature to be feared.

He knew he was dreaming, but also that this was a dream on only the most superficial of levels. In a very important sense it was quite real.

The rannul could not be domesticated, but the rainforest clans of Pirogue had managed to find a way to use them against his regiment all the same. The garrison's cook, himself a native, had prepared the soldiers a stew of rannul pup, which they had devoured, though anything which wasn't corned beef would have been just as welcome. What the Orailleans hadn't known – couldn't have known – was that the rannul mother's method of disposing of a dead pup was to eat the remains herself, and that its instinct to do so was utterly implacable. It chewed through two palisade walls of bamboo poles as thick as trees, and then through the stomachs of eight men to get at the half-digested remains of its infant, and had taken virtually an entire drum of ammunition from one of the Edwards guns to bring down.

Runce was not as large as a nesting female. He did not have the scythe-like thumb-claws or the armoured spine ridge, but as a male he was smaller, faster, more agile. His body, low-slung and sinuous like an elongated badger's, wove through tangle of undergrowth that his prey caught on and fell, again and again.

Admittedly, he was toying with the prey, but he had good reason.

He brought it to bay before a wide, vine-choked hole in the ground. The man turned then, defiant in the manner of every doomed creature determined to fight until it was torn apart, and screamed at him in desperation: 'Come on then, old man! Fucking have it!'

Runce howled and threw himself at his prey's belly, the juices of his mouth running free at the thought of unspooling the packed viscera in steaming piles, but the momentum of his charge carried the pair of them over the lip of the abyss and they fell, tearing and biting at each other. Tumbling into an eternity of darkness, each rended great clumps of substance from the other until neither retained the shape that they had worn in the dream, but were reduced to flayed, screaming rags possessed only of the intent to consume and destroy the other utterly.

No you fucking don't, old man. You think it's that easy? Think I'll roll over and just give it up like some witless wet-dreaming little bitch? I am Hegemony, and I will crush your soul to sand!

'No you won't, lad,' said Runce. 'I'm an officer in the Department of Counter Subornation. You're dealing with the professionals now.'

There was no subtlety in his awakening, no gradual fading in of sensory input. He crashed into consciousness like falling through a pane of glass, and the violence of it lashed out into the room, tearing chunks of plaster from the walls and blowing every light bulb and electrical component except for the ones which set off alarms. Something close by his head was making a shrill sound; he thrashed in his panic, knocking it over with a heavy crash. Bedclothes tangled him, though he was lying on them, not inside them, and he seemed to be fully dressed. Something snagged deep in the flesh of his right fore-arm with steel-bright pain, and he saw a tube sticking out of it. He was plucking at it in horror when the door burst open and two nurses in blue tunics ran in. The man stood gaping at the damage done to the room while the woman laid what were supposed to be reassuring hands on Runce's shoulders.

'Mr Croft? Can you hear me?' she asked. 'Everything is fine. You're fine. Please, calm down.' Up close he could see that the badge on her uniform gave her name as Denise, and underneath that, *Redos Sleep Clinic*.

'I'm...' *Calm*, he tried to say, but it wasn't his voice. It felt lighter in his throat, like he'd been breathing that gas they used at funfairs. He coughed. 'Fine, I'm fine. It's okay,' he finished. *I sound like a boy,* he thought, shocked.

The male nurse was picking up the monitor. 'Are you sure, sir?' he replied. 'That wake intrusion was the biggest one so far. Perhaps a quick reality check will help to settle your nerves.'

'Yes,' said nurse Denise of the Redos Sleep Clinic. She took a small whiteboard and marker from one of the bedside tables. 'Maybe you should write your check-phrase, sir, just to make sure that...'

'No,' Runce grunted. He had no idea what they were talking about. 'No tests. I'm fine, I said. Get out.'

'But, sir...'

He fixed them with a glare, hoping that it was the kind of thing that Croft would have done. 'You heard me.'

Reluctantly, the two nurses left, talking to themselves in hushed tones. They weren't going to be satisfied with that for very long. He closed his eyes, struggling to remember what it was that Jowett had said he should do next. It was hard; his mind was still full of shreds of dream, fragmented images of running, fighting, screaming. Not all of that screaming was memory, he realised. Some of it was coming from far, far down, like the sound of tinnitus. That must be Croft, he thought, or what was left of him. Then it hit him clearly for the first time: *I'm a Passenger in the body of a man in the Realt.*

Sudden nausea clenched his stomach, and he leaned over the side of the bed and vomited. This was wrong. Whatever species of bastard this Croft man was, stealing his body – anyone's body – was just plain wrong. This was the world where Berylin had ended up, and it had turned her into a monster. Was this the way he wanted to honour her memory – by becoming as bad as her? He should go back to sleep, go back to Oraille, and find another way of…

He stopped. 'Oh, you tricky bugger,' he said, almost with admiration. 'You're good. But you're not that good.'

A momentary blinding pain stabbed him between the eyes, and then even that faint screaming was gone. He didn't know if it was permanent, but he'd cross that bridge if and when he came to it. He flexed his right shoulder. No bullet wound, at least there was that.

Through a combination of exploration and digging through his stolen memories, Runce found that he was in a private suite, with its own bedroom, reception room, and bathroom. Croft wasn't employed by the Redos Sleep Clinic in any formal capacity, but he had unrestricted access to its facilities – using the services of its staff to monitor and support him in his lucid dreaming excursions – but otherwise able to come and go as he pleased, unquestioned. He cleaned himself up in the bathroom and paused to look in the mirror, seeing the face of the man who had killed Harcourt staring back at him. It smiled when he smiled and frowned when he frowned.

'A mask,' he said to it. Its mouth moved when his moved. 'Just think of it as a mask.' He knew that he had access to a weak form of the power to suborn reality, which here they called the 'wake' or sometimes 'backwash', and that with a bit of practice he could probably change that face into his own, but it would take more time than he could currently afford.

Then the headache was back.

They're coming for you, old man. Those nurses weren't fooled in the slightest; what did you think that 'check-phrase' stuff was all about? Did you think we wouldn't have planned for exactly this kind of thing? They're coming for you with tasers and guns, and if they can't take you alive and find a way of getting you out of my head, they'll put a fucking bullet in it instead, because there's no way on God's green earth the Hegemony are going to allow an Exile to walk around free with all of my dirty little secrets. Give it up and go back to sleep, Runce. Professionals? Christ, you're so far out of your league it's a fucking joke...

With a yell, Runce punched the mirror. Glass shattered and fell, ringing, into the sink along with a patter of blood (his blood? Croft's?), but the pain eclipsed his headache and silenced the voice.

He'd traded one shot-up shoulder for a cut-up hand. That hadn't lasted long.

He hurriedly wrapped a towel around his wounded hand and explored his options. He didn't have many. There would be security people inside and out, but those in the grounds would be less overt since Redos was, for the most part, exactly the ordinary sleep clinic that it claimed to be, and patients generally didn't find armed guards patrolling the walls all that relaxing. That might make them slower to react, and hopefully less lethal. Runce booted the catch on the bathroom window and peered into the night, thankful that he was on the ground floor. He climbed out, a little amazed at how athletic this body was compared to his own old bones, ran across a lamp-lit gravel path, and ducked into the bushes on the other side.

The boundary wall didn't look much to those who weren't trying to escape over it, but Croft's memories told him that the picturesque Virginia creeper which featured in Redos' glossy brochures hid coils of razor wire and motion sensors. Croft hadn't been able to resist working out how he would escape the clinic himself, purely as a thought experiment, but one which Runce was now more than happy to put into practice. The headache returned as the assassin raged impotently at his own thoughts being turned against him. *See how you like it,* thought Runce with savage glee.

As the big willow at the end of the terrace came into view, he heard the first shouts of alarm and started to run.

Reaching the tree, he jumped as high and far as he could, his new backwash power giving him extra strength without him even intending it, and at the top of the leap he grabbed a double handful of the rope-like willow fronds. His weight carried him back down, but the elastic nature of the wood sprang back, dragging him into the air, to which he added the pull of his own arms, and the combined energy was enough to carry him over the wall. Letting go, he fell, hit a sloping bank on the other side, and rolled through bushes, trash and leaf-litter until he slammed down hard on the pavement of a busy dual carriageway.

He lay for a moment, stunned. Then he was off, running across the road between pernes (*cars*, they were called *cars* here) which sounded their horns angrily at him, but he ignored them and disappeared into the night.

2

The first phone number which Runce tried didn't work – but Jowett had warned him that it might not, so it wasn't a surprise, even though it meant that the job of contacting him was going to be much harder. That was where the second number came in. It worked fine.

'Who is this?' said the voice on the other end. 'How did you get this number?'

'Chandler,' said Runce. 'That is the name you're using, isn't it?'

'Who the hell are you?'

'You gave this number to a mutual friend of ours, Bobby Jenkins. He gave it to my boss, and my boss gave it to me. I am Officer William Runceforth, of the Oraillean Department of Counter Subornation, and I've come to take you home, old son.' Runce chuckled. 'You've just got to help me with one or two small things first.'

It took quite a while for Runce to satisfy Chandler's suspicions – they were many, and extensive. In the bar of the Woodman pub he quizzed Runce on so many details that in the end Runce realised he was doing it more to hear news from home: the politics of Carden, the troubles of the wider world, and even sports results. Runce, in turn, demolished a large steak and kidney pie and made grudging compliments about the quality of the beer in this world. Chandler had chosen the Woodman deliberately due to its protected status as a listed building; despite the glamorous architectural projects soaring around it in this part of town, it kept much of its original Victorian décor and so was somewhere a bit more familiar and comforting for Passengers to base themselves when adjusting to their new existences. It helped to forestall the reality shock which so often led them to panic and draw the Hegemony's attention.

'Things must be pretty desperate if Director Jowett's prepared to offer amnesty to any old sod over here,' Chandler observed. 'He doesn't know who I am, does he?'

'Desperate,' said Runce, nodding. 'I would definitely say so, yes. But I don't see why it should be a problem repatriating you or any other Exile.'

'Ah, well, you see there's Exiles and there's Exiles. Some of us may not be as welcome as others.'

'I don't follow.'

'It's a transitive verb, Officer Runceforth. To be exiled to somewhere, by someone. For a reason. Why do you think we call ourselves that, instead of something romantic like…' he made a dramatic gesture. '*Castaways?*'

'Spare me the grammar lesson, son.'

'All right, let me put it this way: giving someone a dose from a bottle of poppy liquor and then waiting for the next subornation to carry them away to the Realt is a very effective way of getting rid of certain troublesome political enemies without having to worry about a body popping up in the Tara the next morning.'

'Ha! And she says *I'm* paranoid. Take it from someone that works for the man: Jowett's a cagey sort, but he's not corrupt, not like that.'

'Really? I know at least one Exiled trade union leader, and a nephew to King Alexander who had a penchant for doing horrible things to Carden streetwalkers. He's currently a Passenger in a fourteen-year-old girl from Doncaster, ironically enough. Would you like to meet them?'

'No thanks,' said Runce, frowning; he didn't like this man's cheerful cynicism, but then maybe it was the only way to cope with being exiled for so long. 'I'll take your word for it. My round, I think.'

'Good man. Just don't go using any credit cards.'

Runce headed toward the bar, examining a handful of their strange paper money and tiny coins. Everything was so small, like the phone; he felt like a giant living in a land of little people.

'So,' said Chandler, sitting back and accepting his pint as Runce returned. 'What does the glorious and morally unimpeachable Director of Counter Subornation require of you and I?'

'This person,' Runce said, gesturing at himself, 'whose body I am temporarily borrowing, was employed by a representative of the Hegemony's Interstitial Assembly in this world, a man called Foulkes, to lucid dream his way into our world as a spy and assassin.'

Chandler gave a low whistle. 'Now that *is* impressively bad.'

'I have access to everything he knows about that operation, and more besides. In a nutshell, we're going to put Foulkes on trial before the Assembly and give him the bum's rush.'

'And liberty and justice for all. Hurrah. What precisely do you need me for?'

'Well, as of this moment, Jowett has no idea whether or not I've made it here with my mind intact. Some might say he'd be hard-pressed to notice the difference, but be that as it may. I need to get word to him that I'm here safe and sound before he moves on anything; he needs to know what evidence he's got to work with. Up until now, him and Foulkes have been operating a nice little communications back-channel…'

Chandler tutted. 'Passing notes at the back of the classroom. Naughty.'

'It's a pair of twins from Carden. One is an Exile in this world, the other one's still at home, both linked by their thoughts.'

'Telepathy.'

'That too. Give a message to one, and it passes between the worlds to the other. Sounds simple enough.'

Chandler leaned in. 'And you don't wonder how that twin got over here? You don't think, just perhaps, that Jowett and Foulkes might have engineered it for their own convenience?'

Runce ignored his annoying innuendo and ploughed on. 'The problem is that the telephone calling number on this side isn't working; it's been changed. Seems Foulkes isn't interested in passing any more notes to Jowett, which leaves only one option.'

'Give up, go home, put the kettle on and have a nice cup of tea with your feet up in front of the telly?'

'Locate the twin over here and deliver the message personally. Do you know how to find a place called Wales?'

Chandler sighed heavily and rubbed his face with both hands. 'I think I can probably manage it.'

'Good. There's only one other thing – a small personal job. Off the books, so to speak.'

'That being?'

'Somebody very important over there is vulnerable over here. Don't ask, because it don't make much sense to me either. All I know is I need your help so that she's looked after. I'm going to need you to use one of your computer machines to help me find her, for a start, then a passport and a 'stat ticket to somewhere called Minneapolis.'

'Those I can do.'

Runce went outside and took in the night air while he waited for Chandler to find the information he needed. With nothing to do, he even walked a little way towards the city centre, just to see what this world was like. So clean, but unbelievably ugly. Carden, he realised, was a city of barely-controlled filth; her streets, skies and water were rank with traders' rubbish, rotting food, animal manure, coal smuts, the sewage from slum tenements, and industrial pollution from countless factories washing into the Tara. Here the pavements were broad and clean-swept, there were no ranks of smoke-belching chimneys, and gleaming cars whispered along the roads. The people seemed no more or less friendly than at home – in the sense that passers-by ignored him completely – but the buildings were awful, bland things which looked like they'd been slapped together out of the cheapest materials available in the fastest time possible, with no thought to artistry or any pride that the inhabitants might feel living in such places. There was also something indefinably hazy about the air, some quality of the light peculiar to this world. The whole thing made his head swim with vertigo, and when Chandler texted him to say that he'd found something that Runce really needed to see, he was only too glad.

Chandler was lurking in the shadows thrown by the massive columns of an old Station building across from the pub. He handed Runce his phone. 'This,' he said.

Runce squinted at the bright screen, reading carefully. 'This must be wrong,' he said eventually. 'You must have got the wrong Alison Owens.'

'It's not exactly a common name,' said Chandler. 'Looks like someone's in for a nasty shock.'

Runce's vertigo was mutating into another head-spike of a migraine. He read the information again, and for the first time since he was a child found himself praying to something – anything – that it was wrong.

'...which is why everybody hates caravans,' said Chandler.

'Eh? What?' Runce shook himself. The car was twisting through narrow country lanes in the pre-dawn light, stuck in a slow-moving convoy of vans and farm vehicles. Chandler had been explaining to him how the traffic system in this country worked, and he'd missed half of it. 'Sorry,' he grunted. 'Drifted off for a minute there.'

Chandler looked at him sharply. 'Drifted off how, exactly? As in I'm just boring you senseless or something more? What's the last thing you remember?'

Runce thought back through it. 'Something more,' he said finally. 'You were going on about 'centre-lane hogs', whatever they are.'

'That was a little while ago. Is this the first time it's happened – you drifting away like that?'

'Yes.'

'Anything else? Dizziness? Headaches?'

'Hell, yes. Whopping great things. When I get them I think I can hear the voice of this Croft chap, deep down inside.'

'What does it say?'

'Nothing useful, that's for bloody sure. Shouting. Insults. Trying to put me off, cloud my thinking. Is this serious, do you think?'

'Potentially. It's hard to say. No two Passengers' experiences of inhabiting a body in the Realt are identical. There's a spectrum of possession; for some of us at one end, control is total, without any sign of the original personality.'

'What happens to them? Do they die?'

'I don't know. I try not to think about it too much. At the other end, presumably some poor buggers from our side don't make it through at all and just disappear in the transition. In between, there's a range of partial control. Some share nicely with the original personalities, some fight, some are just ghost voices at the back of someone else's mind. It would make sense that the stronger the original personality, the more control they retain. Croft was a lucid dreaming assassin, you say?'

'Oh yes.'

'I can't imagine someone like that being a pushover. Don't take this the wrong way, Officer Runce, but you must be one stubborn son of a bitch.'

'It has been observed on occasion.'

'Yeah, well I'm sure Croft is just as stubborn. I think you've got a fight on your hands, there.'

Runce watched the vehicles curving away ahead and behind, chafing at the delay, wondering how much longer it would take them to get to the farmhouse which was their destination and whether Croft would keep getting stronger in the meantime.

Abruptly, the spike in his brain was back, along with the revelation – either stolen from Croft's memories or, more likely, sent to taunt him – that this was not the first time Croft had taken a Passenger. The first time had been an accident, when he'd got sloppy, and recovery from that had been down to luck as much as willpower. The second time he'd done it deliberately, just to see what would happen and work out how to shake off a possessing personality, like a poisoner taking doses of his own medicine to build up a tolerance. *Enjoy being me while you can,* the voice jeered. *By now my people will have cut off my access to every asset and information source, my credit cards will be tagged, and my photo will be issued to every police force in the country. There will be rooms full of people scanning through CCTV footage of every fucking petrol station and stop light...*

SHUT UP! Runce squeezed his cut hand and pain silenced the voice.

Chandler glanced at him sideways. 'Happen again?'

Runce nodded wearily. 'Do you have a gun?' he asked.

'Possibly. Why?'

'If Croft comes back, or I start acting funny and you even think he might be coming back, you put a bullet to me straight away. Got that?'

'Don't worry, I'm way ahead of you there.'

Country lanes dwindled into mountain roads, and eventually Chandler pulled over, seemingly at random, in a wide, empty landscape of moorland.

'Their surveillance will be twitchy for anything parked up within a mile of the place, I'd guess,' he said. 'But even that's too close for my liking. I hope you don't mind a bit of a walk.'

He produced a compass from one of his many pockets, consulted it for a moment, and they set off across springy turf, threading their way through heather and clumps of rushes. Bracken was uncoiling itself from the ground like miniature groves of green violin heads, its scent already thick in the air. The weather had been dry for weeks, so they were able to avoid boggy areas quite easily, and they made rapid progress into a tumbled terrain of granite outcrops.

'We need to have a talk about what you can do as a Passenger,' Chandler said after a while. 'Especially before you decide to go leaping boulders with a single bound or anything like that, because they'll have other surveillance too. The protean nature of a subornation, by which it changes the reality around it, has what we call a backwash effect here. Long story short: you have super powers. It'll take you quite a while to get to grips with them, so my advice is: for the moment, *don't*. Manipulating the backwash causes ripples and disturbances in the meniscus, like the wake of a ship. The Hegemony makes use of certain entities who are capable of sensing these wakes, which is how they find us. The more outrageous a thing you do, the bigger the wake.'

'So if we can't use these powers without alerting the guards at the farm,' said Runce, 'how are we supposed to get in? As soon as they realise they've been found, they'll kill the twin. It's how Foulkes works: destroy everything rather than let it fall into the hands of the enemy.'

'We, which is to say *you*, can't. I can. I can make us invisible, or as good as dammit, so that we can walk straight past all their goons without anybody getting hurt. Just make sure you stay close to me.'

'How can you do that without causing a wake?'

'Because I have been here a very, very long time indeed, and I've learned a few tricks.'

'Oh aye. How long is "very, very long", then?' Obviously there was no reason for the personality to be remotely like the body, but nevertheless Runce found it hard to imagine that he was talking to anything other than a young Asian man in his early twenties. He was only just starting to think through the implications of his new existence – what if this backwash power allowed a Passenger to halt the aging process, for example? How old could a body be? Was immortality itself within reach?

Chandler saw him looking and just laughed. 'Long enough, young man,' was all he said and strode on ahead.

6

At the end of an unpaved track sat the farmhouse: a single, whitewashed building with a few derelict outbuildings, surrounded by tumbled dry-stone walls and overgrown trees designed to provide a break against the wind which blew across the otherwise empty landscape. It seemed that the inhabitants were content to let the isolation be their main line of defence – that and the fact that anything larger than a sheep could be seen coming from miles away. The only thing which might have appeared incongruous to a lost hiker was the forty foot high aerial, bristling with vanes and a satellite dish, which was guyed by steel cables next to the house – but even then, it could simply have been the expensive toy of a farmer who liked a bit of ham radio on the side. Runce and Chandler saw a Land Rover parked out front and watched long enough to see that every fifteen minutes a single figure would take a stroll around the perimeter.

'There'll be two,' said Chandler. 'That's how they work. Human and animal, controller and muscle.'

'Seems straightforward enough,' observed Runce.

'It's anything but, soldier. Remember, the guards are Passengers, just like you and me, which means they're inside people who are just as much victims as anybody caught up in a subornation. Granted, you seem to have ended up in someone who is actually a Grade A arsehole, but that tends to be the exception. Everyone in this situation is a hostage, captors included, so don't go killing anyone unless it's absolutely life or death. These, on the other hand,' he added, holding up a taser and grinning, 'these are just fine. The charge overloads the brain's ability to control the body, so it doesn't matter how strong the target is. Know how to use one?'

Runce took one, inspecting it. It seemed terribly flimsy compared to even a normal pistol, never mind a tezlar gun. 'Croft knows about these. So, yes, I do.'

'Superb. Let's go.'

They set off downhill and were about halfway to the house when Runce whispered, 'So when are you going to do your little trick, then?'

'Doing it. Shut up,' Chandler replied tightly, his face set with concentration.

Closer up, the farmhouse looked like it had seen better days. The whitewash was flaking, and the ancient sash window frames were cracked and warped. They waited by the kitchen door, in a yard littered with old tyres, scraps of timber, and the stinking ashes of a bonfire on which the owners had been burning their rubbish. A moment later, the door opened. The guard who came out was dressed simply, in cords and a sweater, but with a pistol at her belt. It was her eyes, though, which made Runce catch his breath – they were the bright green compound orbs of some insect like a dragonfly, and they blinked sideways as the guard looked around in the open air. Ignoring Runce and Chandler, she sniffed, lit up a cigarette, and ambled away on patrol, tugging the door shut behind her.

Chandler darted forward and stuck his foot in the gap, so that rather than shutting, the door slammed on his shoe and bounced ajar with very little noise. They waited a moment more to see if either the guard or anybody left inside had noticed that the door hadn't shut properly, but nobody came. Easing it open slowly, they crept in.

Inside, it was as dim and cluttered as its exterior had suggested. Piles of hoarded newspapers and unidentifiable junk in supermarket carrier bags teetered next to unwashed dishes and a scree slope of microwave meal debris. A choked fireplace was letting more smoke back into the room than out of the chimney. The only exception was one area of the living room, which had been cleared for an elaborate communications set-up. Chandler made a beeline for it, sitting down in front of an open laptop and cracking his knuckles eagerly.

'What are you doing?' hissed Runce.

'Hacking the fuck out of these people.' He waved Runce in the direction of the hallway and the stairs. 'I'll watch the door for Little Miss Bug-Eyes. Go. Deliver your message.'

'You said stick with you or they'll see me!'

'Then stick with me. But I'm doing this first. This is a goldmine!' He was tapping away at the keyboard and humming.

Cursing silently, Runce headed for the stairs.

The murmuring of a female voice in a distant room drifted down to him, but he couldn't make out the words. The staircase was as uncared-for as everything else, protected only by a threadbare carpet, and he winced at every creaking step, which was most of them. It was impossible that he hadn't been heard – and yet nobody appeared. He passed yellowing family daguerreotypes (*photographs*, they were called here) hanging on the walls, thick with dust; everything was rank with mildew and the sulphurous tang of coal-smoke.

Then a privy flushed, and its door opened in the upstairs hall, and before Runce could decide whether to back down and hide or rush up and attack, a young man – curly hair, glasses – passed along the landing, zipping up his fly.

He saw Runce and stopped, open-mouthed.

Runce raised the taser, then hesitated, suddenly realising that he didn't know whether this was the messenger or the controller.

The young man dived for a doorway.

'Bollocks.' Runce leapt up the rest of the stairs, threw himself through the door and top of the man, who fell, scrabbling for something which he'd dragged off a table: a holstered gun. Runce jammed the square end of the taser cartridge into the side of his neck just under the ear, and growled 'This thing is meant to be non-lethal, son, but I shudder to think what it'll do to you point blank.' The controller went very still as Runce collected the gun he'd been reaching for. 'And just so you know, before you try any of that backwash silliness, I'm in the club, so to speak.'

'What's going on? Who are you?' called a fearful voice; the accent had a sing-song quality which he suddenly knew was called Welsh.

Runce looked up. An old woman was half-rising from a chair. She had a tiny paintbrush in one hand and a small piece of plastic in the other. Then he noticed that everywhere around this bedroom – on shelves, bookcases, hanging from the ceiling – were dozens, possibly even hundreds, of model sailing ships: frigates, sloops, galleons, cutters, caravels… some were in bottles and some on stands, some were in piles, half-finished, and in stacks around the room were boxes of more to be built. He stared around, trying to make sense of this, then dragged his attention back. 'I need to speak to the twin from Carden,' he said. 'It's very urgent.'

The figure of the old woman shifted, seeming to melt and reform, and he found himself looking at another young man – taller and thinner than the one he had pinned to the floor, with great dark circles under his eyes as if he was chronically sleep-deprived. 'I'm Noben,' he said. 'She asked you a question.'

'Right then, Noben, I'm a DCS officer from Carden. I need you to deliver a message to Director Jowett for me. I know you know who that is. I know what you do here.'

Noben crossed his arms. 'I'm not doing anything for you until you get off Michael there.'

'I'd do what he says,' replied the Hegemony agent.

Runce pressed the end of the taser harder into his neck. 'And you can shut it, for a start.' To Noben, he added, 'Son, I don't care what kind of happy families set-up you've got here, or what they've bribed or threatened you with to make you work for them. One question: do you want to go home? Yes or no?'

Without warning, the head-spike came back, screaming with Croft's voice as it rammed between his eyes and blinded him with its fury. There was nothing but the blackness of the hole from his dream, down which he had fallen, fighting with the man whose body he possessed – down which he was *still* falling, had *always been* falling, because he'd never really stopped, not as long as Croft was still alive in here with him. He tried to find the ferocity of the rannul he had been in the dream with which to beat his enemy back, but the strain of coping with this alien world had taken its toll on him while Croft had done nothing but rest and bide his time, waiting for the perfect opportunity for this ambush.

He felt the agent beneath him suddenly lurch with inhuman strength, and he was flung backward through the air to slam against the wall. The blow made him see stars, but it also cleared his vision somewhat as his attacker charged at him, shifting as he did so, becoming hugely muscled and covered in thick plates of hide. Runce brought the taser up and fired as Croft renewed his mental attack, and he howled at the pain. Two slim metal darts attached to wires hit the Hegemony agent square in the torso, making a *krak-krak-krak* noise as ten-thousand volts overrode his motor controls. His momentum carried him like a falling tree straight at Runce. Through the blotches that eddied across his vision, Runce could see enough to get his other hand up, and as the agent fell against him he planted it in the space between the two darts, sharing the voltage. It seared the voice of Croft from his brain instantaneously in a white-hot flash, and they collapsed together.

The other man rolled away, suddenly human-shaped again, and the contact was broken. Runce dragged himself upright, panting.

'That's. The second time. In two days. I've been electrocuted,' he gasped. 'It's not funny any more.' He pulled the trigger again, sending another charge into the twitching body for good measure. Turning to Noben, he said, 'Whatever you do next, you can't stay here. As soon as they realise we've found you, they'll kill you – even if you are idiotic enough to try and stay loyal to them.'

Noben backed away, up against the table where he'd been sitting. Runce saw that it was covered in the bits of another kit boat under construction. They must have been keeping him sweet by buying him toys; it was pathetically simple. He looked around at the huge number of completed models. How long had they kept him here?

'Are you really from Carden?' the boy asked, with fearful hope in his eyes.

'Aye, Lewhead Hill, born and bred. If you count a foundling house, that is. And yes, I can really get you home, but you have to leave with me *now*.'

Noben looked down at the man he'd called Michael, who was making grunting noises and not just twitching but flickering between the shape he'd worn when attacked and something a lot bigger. His fingers were clawing at the carpet, actually becoming claws in the process. Whether Noben had seen this before or not – what kinds of threats or violence had also been used on him as well as bribes – Runce didn't know, but it seemed to decide him. He nodded quickly and followed Runce out of the room.

Halfway down the stairs he heard the rattle of automatic weapons fire coming from outside.

'Runceforth!' barked Chandler from downstairs.

'Here,' he said, dragging Noben the rest of the way and into the cluttered lounge. 'Who's shooting?'

'We are.' Chandler yanked a USB stick out of the laptop.

'Got it. Let's go.'

'What do you mean "we are"?'

But Chandler was already heading outside. Runce followed, towing Noben, and saw Chandler shaking hands with a complete stranger armed with some kind of squat (*that's an L85A2*) rifle. They were standing over the body of the guard. There was something terribly misshapen about its head, which had little to do with bullet damage. It looked like it had been in the process of changing into something with large, toothed mandibles.

'Runce,' said Chandler, 'meet Joey.'

The heavy-set man with tattoos sleeving both forearms simply nodded a greeting.

'How long has he been following us?' Runce demanded.

'Oh, pretty much all of the way,' replied Chandler. 'What? You didn't think I actually *trusted* you, did you?'

CHAPTER 18

DEBRIEFING MR CAFFREY

1

Neil Caffrey woke up in a large, comfortable bed, which was some compensation for the fact that his face felt like it had been mashed with stinging nettles, but not much. He groaned and sat up.

The blue glow from an alarm clock hinted at the shapes of a bedroom which wasn't his. He fumbled for a bedside lamp and switched it on; its light showed him a pleasantly furnished bedroom: wardrobe, dressing table, chest of drawers. It was all plain but solid, English cottage style. Not his bedroom at all. He had no idea where it was or how he'd got here, just a memory of –

'Shit! Mom! Dad!'

He tried to jump out of the bed, but his legs wouldn't cooperate, and he sank in a heap on the bedside rug. Dazed, he dragged himself back up by the counterpane and transferred his clutching hands to the curtains, yanking them open.

Night greeted him. He saw illuminated pathways through a manicured garden of wide lawns and tall hedges, all dominated by the massive floodlit shape of a geodesic dome erupting from it like a blister the size of a football stadium. Small electric cars hummed to and fro, and armed men with dogs were patrolling.

'What the fuck?'

Then the draft up his backside registered, and he looked down to see that he'd been dressed in an old-fashioned, rear-opening hospital gown. An even colder draft whiskered across his scalp, and he discovered with real terror that his head had been shaved. On the verge of panic now, he checked his bare arms for plasters, needles, puncture marks – anything to indicate that he might have been drugged – but found nothing. His discovered that his clothes had been neatly folded on a chair by the door, and quickly pulled them on.

Then he closed the curtains on that ridiculous Bond-movie hallucination, which couldn't possibly be real.

He tried the door, unsurprised to find it locked. Someone must have heard him thumping around and realised that he'd awoken, because a moment later a key rattled in the lock and the door opened.

The woman from last night was smiling at him. 'Good evening, Mr Foronda. I trust you slept well? Supper is waiting for you downstairs.'

'What? What the fuck do you mean supper? What the fuck is this place? Why have you shaved my fucking head? What have you done with my parents?'

Pelassis Corle's smile thinned just a little. 'Mr Foronda, are you hungry or not? We can debrief you just as well without.'

'That's not my name!' he yelled. 'It's Neil!' He peered past her into the hall. Wood-panelled and carpeted like a stately home, with a broad staircase leading down, and presumably out – and straight into the arms of those guards he'd seen. At this point, his stomach weighed into the conversation with a loud growl, and Caffrey slumped in defeat. 'Last meal, is it? Go on, then,' he said, and followed her downstairs.

2

He ate at a table set for one with an immaculate white cloth and gleaming silverware, in a room with French windows wide open on the summer evening. It must have been on the other side of whatever building this was, because there was no sign of that freakish dome thing. At first he decided that despite his stomach he wasn't going to touch a bit, because fuck Them, whoever They were, but his misgivings were soon assuaged by a plate of cold-cuts and fruit. He ate grudgingly, as Pelassis sat across from him, tapping at a tablet. They could have been a couple on holiday.

'To answer your question,' she said, 'Mr and Mrs Caffrey are perfectly unharmed, despite being obviously shaken up by what they have witnessed.'

'Ya think?' he grunted, chewing.

'Honestly, there is nothing to be gained by harming them, except unnecessary complications. If they choose to make a fuss, nobody will possibly believe anything other than that their son Neil went funny in the head and ran away again. I understand that the manner by which we recovered you must have been traumatic, but it was sadly necessary to bring you in quickly before you hurt anybody else, them included.'

'I haven't hurt anyone,' he insisted.

'I have Accident and Emergency reports about three concussions and a broken arm from the market where you ran amok that say different.'

'I did not run amok!'

She offered him the tablet. 'Would you like to see the CCTV footage?'

He subsided. 'No,' he murmured and ate in subdued silence. Presently, an alert burbled, and Pelassis stood. 'If you'll please follow me, Supervisor Foulkes is ready for your debriefing now.'

He squinted at her. 'Is "debriefing" military jargon for "torture with electrodes to the bollocks" by any chance?'

She simply stepped aside slightly to reveal a short hallway – all gleaming oak panelling – with another door at the end. The invitation was clear as a cutlass point in the back of a man walking the plank. Caffrey did as he was told – but he took a last piece of bread and munched it with as much insolence as he could muster.

The office to which he was led was lined with books from floor to ceiling, the shelves punctuated by cabinets, trophy heads, and glass cases displaying peculiar (and probably illegal) objects. Behind a desk which looked big enough to dine a workhouse of Victorian orphans sat an angular man with a widow's peak of iron grey hair and rimless glasses, dressed in a suit which managed to look crustily old-fashioned in a way which suggested it was tailored by some outrageously expensive designer. Two chairs were arranged before the desk, one of which was occupied by the nautilus-headed thing from last night.

Caffrey recoiled and found his retreat blocked by Pelassis. He remembered the concealed pistol he'd also seen and stopped.

'I see you've already met Miss Corle and Lloyd,' commented the man behind the desk. 'My name is Foulkes. You...' he considered the documents spread across his desk with a little gesture of helplessness. '...for the sake of argument, I am going to refer to as Mr Caffrey. I trust that is unobjectionable to you. It's the name on your birth certificate, at any rate, so it will do for a start. The picture as a whole is somewhat more complicated, but that's why we're here, isn't it?' He smiled and gestured at the vacant chair. 'Please, have a seat.'

When Caffrey gave no hint of moving, the smile evaporated. 'The please was rhetorical. If I wanted to be unpleasant about it, we'd be having this conversation with you strapped to a hospital bed being fed through one tube and shitting out of another. Trust me, the chair is more comfortable.'

Reluctantly, slowly, Caffrey obeyed, trying to keep as far away as possible from 'Lloyd', whose facial tentacles were waving absently; Caffrey couldn't shake the absurd impression that this was his version of humming to himself or inspecting his fingernails. Foulkes gave Pelassis a nod, and she left, closing the door softly behind her.

'So is this my debriefing, then?' he asked.

'If you like,' Foulkes replied. 'Please, take those.' He indicated three small white pills on a silver tray next to a glass of water. 'And before you ask, they are nothing more than ferrous sulphate; a simple, harmless, off-the-shelf anti-anaemia medication. Check the label if you like.'

'But I'm not anaemic.'

'No, but it will temporarily elevate the oxygen levels in your blood, which will in turn make it easier for Lloyd to see what's going on in that shiny little head of yours. Lying, Mr Caffrey, like all human actions, is ultimately traceable as a chemical process – in this case, hyperactivity in the pre-frontal cortex. Right here.' He leaned across the desk and tapped Caffrey right between the eyes with the end of his biro. 'I'm going to ask you a series of questions, and you're going to answer them. Truthfully, I very much hope, as that will make things quicker for me and less unpleasant for you.' He regarded the different piles of paper with distaste. 'Then possibly we might be able to sort this bloody mess out.'

'Is that why you shaved my head? You're going to stick me in a machine or something?'

'Yes,' Foulkes said. 'Or something.' He gestured to Lloyd, who got up and moved to stand behind Caffrey's chair.

'Hey – what – wait…!' Neil twisted in alarm, half-rising.

'Mr Caffrey!' Foulkes' voice was a hook, yanking him backwards. 'Tubes, remember? Eating. Shitting. Contrary to what you may believe, I am not the Bad Guy, and I do not want to hurt you, both because I am a human being and because – call me an old romantic – treating people nicely actually works, most of the time. However, I am considerably pressed for time, which I do not have to spare on babying you through this. It's either this, or you let me talk to Archin Foronda, the fisherman from the Tourmaline Archipelago who is currently passengered inside you.'

'I keep telling you people,' insisted Caffrey miserably, 'I have no idea what the hell you're on about.'

'Very well then.' Foulkes waved Lloyd forward. 'Just think of them as electrodes, if it helps.'

Lloyd's hands settled on Caffrey's shoulders, which were rock-hard with tension, holding him still. It was as well they did, because despite Foulkes' words, Caffrey would have leapt up screaming as Lloyd lowered his face to Caffrey's bare scalp, and the tentacles of his nautiloid anatomy slithered wetly over the sensitive, freshly-shaven skin. Feeling them slip down behind his ears and over his brow like a slow spillage of warm, questing spaghetti was the single most disgusting sensation Caffrey had ever experienced, and he couldn't prevent hoarse, panting little whimpers of panic from squirting out of his nose.

'In its natural environment, Lloyd's passenger possesses a hunting sensorium which has evolved to detect the infinitesimally tiny bioelectric signals of its prey,' explained Foulkes. 'For our purposes that makes him quite adept at sniffing out the electrical signals in the human brain. Now, reaction time is a factor in this, so please pay attention.' He might have been smiling that tight little smile again, but Caffrey couldn't tell – he had his eyes screwed tightly shut. 'While he cannot read your thoughts as such, lying or over-thinking your responses will make your pre-frontal cortex light up like Christmas, and then he will do this.'

Sudden white-hot agony shot from the base of Caffrey's skull all the way down his spine, branching out into his limbs like forked lightning, and he screamed.

'Understand?'

'Yes! Yes! God, yes, I understand! I understand!'

'Good.' Foulkes shuffled his papers together and clicked the end of his pen. 'Let's begin, shall we? I want you to tell me everything you can about your colleague, Mr Steven McBride.'

3

'It's the damndest thing,' said Foulkes, watching as a pair of button-pushers carried Neil Caffrey's unconscious form out of his office.

'I know,' said Pelassis. 'Frustrating isn't the word.'

'What am I missing, here? A month ago he gets taken by a Passenger, this Foronda chap, just like we've seen a million times before, and manages to stay off our radar for a month.'

'Which means that the Exiles must have got to him first,' she added.

'Well, possibly. Then he pops up again and as good as throws himself into our arms, throwing backwash around like there's no tomorrow, and yet when we get him here, there's nothing. Absolutely nothing. No Foronda. No Passenger of any description. Even if he'd gone under in Caffrey's mind, there'd still be some residual overspill, but Lloyd couldn't find anything except one boringly ordinary little human soul in there.'

'Lloyd is very cross, sir.'

'I can't say I blame him. Caffrey admits that he was friends with Steven McBride, but claims no knowledge of McBride's girlfriend Sophie Marchant. I for one simply refuse to accept that his disappearance right before all this Stray business kicked off is a coincidence. Nothing about this man adds up. Nothing. I don't like it.'

'Sir, why not simply kill him and have done with it?'

'It's tempting. It's very tempting.' Foulkes drummed his fingers for a moment. 'No, there's something odd about this Caffrey fellow, and I want to know what it is. But not now. There are too many other pressing things. Let's put him on ice and come back to him once the whole Stray business has finished playing itself out. Speaking of which, I hear you have news from Birmingham?'

'Yes, sir. The flush team report that they have the entity responsible for the comms blackout ready for collection. I was going to take care of that first thing tomorrow morning.'

'You've worked with them before?'

'Yes, sir. Voluschek's people have always been reliable.'

'Good, well hopefully that'll be one loose end tied up. Assess and acquire, then bring it back here, too.' He called up the image of Maddox's floating corpse and its constellation of black stars.

She leaned closer. 'What are those things?'

'Assess, acquire, and return. Then maybe we'll be able to find out.' He smiled grimly. 'We can put it in the cell next to Caffrey – it'll be nice for him to have someone to talk to.'

CHAPTER 19

UNEXPECTED DELIVERIES

1

Lloyd started getting twitchy as soon as Pelassis took the car down into the Mailbox's underground car park. She pulled up and turned to him. 'You okay?'

He unzipped the full-face hoodie and his facial tentacles quested the air. *Something*, he signed. *Close.*

'Our pick-up?'

Maybe. Strong, to be felt so far.

She thought of the black spider-shapes in Supervisor Foulkes' photograph and grimaced. 'Right then. According to Voluschek, they've got the Passenger subdued and ready to transport, but I suggest we let muggle rules apply anyway.'

Assume everybody else is a useless cockbrain.

'That's the one.'

He zipped up and they drove on, to the residential spaces at the very back of the car park. She killed the engine, texted Voluschek's number, and received a reply saying that somebody would be down to collect them in a moment. They checked their kit one final time – tasers, cuffs, and enough sedative to tranquilise a rhino – and got out to wait by the lifts.

Did you hear about that bird that was killed? he signed.

'What bird?'

White-throated needletail. Very rare. Not seen for twenty years – only eight sightings since the nineteenth century. Suddenly turns up in the Hebrides. Dozens of twitchers go racing there with their binoculars. All very exciting.

She looked at him, amused. 'I didn't take you for a twitcher. So what happened?'

While they were stood there watching, all spaffing themselves over one stupid bird, it flew into a wind turbine and was killed instantly. He began laughing – a strange gurgling noise.

She shook her head. 'You are a sick puppy.'

Then the lift doors opened and Lloyd went completely crazy. He backpedalled, grabbing for his taser, and even though he didn't have a mouth, animal noises of panic came from the remains of his human vocal cords.

Pelassis, who hadn't been expecting things to go pear-shaped until they'd met their Passenger, if at all, was slower to react. As far as she could tell, the two men in the lift were perfectly ordinary – one in a suit, the other in jeans and a football top.

But by that time Voluschek and Rainy had seen Lloyd's reaction to them and were charging in response. Black whiplash tentacles unfurled from Rainy's outstretched fingers to envelop Lloyd's head, while Voluschek simply body-charged Pelassis as his arms turned into serpents, wrapping around her in a crushing embrace and bearing her backwards.

She head-butted him. These days she rarely used the backwash power which had come with her from home – most pick-ups, like Caffrey, were easy enough to handle with the help of local law enforcement and maybe a quick taze – but it came to her now, triggered and fuelled by panic adrenalin. The front of Voluschek's skull caved in like a deflated football, and he released her, staggering back, a muffled screaming coming from the crater where his face used to be. Not falling, as she'd hoped. Not spouting blood and bits of bone and brain as he should. The crater was filling with something black and fibrous like a supporting mesh which began knitting his ruined face together and squeezing it back into its original shape. But by that time she was running.

Her head rang with a high-pitched keening which was Lloyd screaming telepathically, but she couldn't do anything about that. Voluschek's operation was compromised – by what or whom, she had no idea. Her priority was to alert Foulkes;

Lloyd would have to look after himself. With the backwash's strength, she was soon running faster than the car, and the bright slot of the car park's exit grew quickly.

Her speed betrayed her when a foot appeared very casually from behind a pillar and tripped her up. She flew a dozen yards and collided with the side of a car, caving it in and folding to a stunned heap on the concrete.

A small part of her mind was screaming *Get up, Pelassis! Get up, you stupid bitch, and run!* but it was very far away and buried under an avalanche of broken thoughts.

The figure who had brought her down with such a depressingly easy schoolyard trick loomed above. He reached for her belt and found the taser.

'I fucking hate these things,' said Toren, examining it with distaste. 'Want to see why?'

And he shot her. Again and again and again.

2

Toren came out of the interrogation room, wiping his hands on a towel. It never ceased to surprise him how far blood would spread.

'We're going to have to move fast,' he said to Voluschek. 'They're supposed to deliver their prisoner by the end of the day. I've already had to fake one message to their boss, but there's only so long we can do that before we slip up on one of their protocols and he realises what's going on.'

'It's a shame neither of them could take one of our brothers or sisters,' said Voluschek. 'They'd have been valuable additions to the Brood.'

'It would definitely have made getting the information out of them a lot easier,' Toren nodded. 'My arms are killing me. Seriously though, listen to me, both of you. You're going to love this.' He drew Rainy and Voluschek to him, the Shadow brimming close beneath his skin. 'For a while now I've been worried about how slowly our mission has been progressing, and how far it could go. I mean, once each of the Brood has a host, what then? I had thought that maybe we would split up and spread across the world, seed churches, grow our congregations, grab a few movie stars and politicians, get some nice little tax breaks and build our power base that way. But it's just too slow; we've got momentum here, and I don't want to lose that. How do we spread the Shadow's Gospel further, quicker?

'It's all about the Aions, the Sleeping Ones. It always has been, and it turns out that these Hegemony fuckers have been keeping them trapped – they've been preventing people from communing with the divine darkness that is their birth-right. I mean to put a stop to that. You're going to ask me how, aren't you?'

Rainy nodded and shut his mouth.

'Every prison has gates, buddy. And I've just found out where one of them is.'

Voluschek's scepticism stank from him like terror sweat. 'If you're thinking about trying to accomplish anything by force…' he said and shook his head, '…forget it. Strong as we are, these people control *armies*, Toren.'

'And I control fucking *nightmares!*' he shot back, sudden fury burning his teeth black. The next second he was wreathed in beatific smiles again. 'But no, I take your point. There's no reason why we can't try to negotiate peacefully, at least to begin with. Give them a chance to see we can be reasonable about things, eh? Still, Voluschek, best get everyone together somewhere safe and put together a strike contingency. Just in case.'

Rainy didn't look convinced. 'Just in case of what?'

'I'm trying to take the moral high-ground here and do the civilised thing, but it's likely the Hegemony simply won't listen, and then they are going to start looking this way like a big flaming eye of fucking Sauron. Worse, this Foulkes bloke will go to ground, and we'll lose any chance of finding out what that gate is and how to open it. I want to be ready to move quickly if it all goes pear-shaped.' He grinned ferociously and clapped his hands together. 'Come on, everybody, chop chop.'

As Voluschek left to make arrangements for disposing of the bodies and gathering the Brood together, Toren clapped an arm around Rainy's shoulders. 'Don't worry, mate,' he said. 'I know how it sounds, but it's still the same old business underneath. We are the dream-dealers. You and I are going to open the prison doors of eternity and bring true magic and wonder back into people's lives.'

3

Foulkes was surveying the morning's police and MI5 reports when his phone rang; he glanced at the incoming number and took the call.

'Miss Corle,' he said. 'How are the delights of the West Midlands?'

'Sorry mate,' replied Toren. 'She's a bit indisposed. Kind of permanently, I'm afraid.'

Foulkes sat back from the paperwork on his desk, fully and immediately focussed. In the pause which he knew the other man was expecting, he keyed a tracer app on his phone. 'Who am I talking to, please?'

The next voice which came out of the handset sent barbs of pain jagging into his head and blooming like black flowers across his vision. '*I am the Shadow made flesh,*' it rasped, fraying at the edges with the echoes of screams. '*I am the clown at the funeral; I am the darkness that dances behind your eyelids; the reptile tail you drag behind you as you walk, pretending to be a man.*' Then it changed, and it was human again. 'But you can call me Toren. Martin, isn't it?'

Foulkes swallowed, trying to regain his composure. 'What do you want?'

Toren sighed. 'Okay. I have recently become aware that you control access to Between.'

'I'm sorry – between? Between what?'

'*Do not fuck with me!*' the voice of screams howled; Foulkes felt something burst inside his nose, and blood sprayed over his desk. While he scrabbled for a box of tissues, Toren continued as mildly as before: 'Your team are both dead, and your operation in this city is mine, and you need to understand that I am not bluffing here, Martin. But there's no need for this to be unpleasant. What I am doing is asking, simply, politely, to share. I want physical access to Between, in return for which I can offer you the talents of me and my people. As I hope I've demonstrated, they can pack quite a kick.'

'Mr Toren,' Foulkes' voice was nasal and muffled through the wad of tissues pressed to his face. 'I believe there may be some grounds on which we can come to an arrangement. Give me twenty-four hours to talk to my people, and I'll be happy to get back to you with a proposal.'

'That would be just spiffing. I look forward to your call.'

4

Toren hung up, tossed the phone onto the table and turned to Voluschek. 'How long?' he asked.

'Fifteen minutes, maybe half an hour, depending.'

'I really hope you're wrong.' Toren looked around the penthouse, now empty and stripped of anything remotely useful. Rainy had taken the tank with the remaining Brood to their fall-back location. 'If you're not, well, sorry about this place. It had a nice view.'

Voluschek shrugged. 'You should see my boat.'

5

Foulkes hung up and checked to see where this Toren person had called him from. The result came as absolutely no surprise. He scrolled through his list of options again. He would have preferred subtle, but subtle was slow, and this situation needed to be dealt with immediately; it had gone beyond a joke. The cover-up might stretch his creativity a bit, but Toren and his 'people' had already helped him by choosing as their base the Mailbox, which also housed the main offices and studios for BBC Midlands – and there was no terrorist target quite like a major national broadcaster.

6

From the safety of a pub across town, Toren and his disciples watched along with a room full of horror-struck drinkers as developments unfolded on television. Behind a witlessly babbling reporter, the red box of the building where he'd been not ten minutes ago stood torn open on one side, black smoke billowing into the sky like blood in water. Its surroundings were chaotic with shredded metal, staggering pedestrians, and the strobing lights of emergency vehicles. It could be heard outside: the distant cacophony of sirens and the thudding of helicopters.

Terrorist attack in Birmingham! the ticker-text screamed. *Jihadists target the BBC in Mailbox bombing!*

'What did they use, man?' whimpered Rainy. 'What did they fucking *use?*'

Death-toll feared to be hundreds!

'Cruise missile, like I said,' suggested Voluschek. 'Maybe a hellfire from an unmanned drone. Who knows, they probably have guys with backpacks full of homemade nitro-glycerine stationed in lots of different places, just on the off-chance...'

Outside, an ambulance screamed past. Somewhere amongst the drinkers, someone was crying quietly.

I don't give a fuck what they used! barked Toren in their heads. *I tried to be reasonable, didn't I? You all heard me. I tried to negotiate. It's just so fucking disappointing, you know? You'd expect someone like that to have a little more self-control. Get everyone together — we're going to show these Hegemony bastards what it means to declare war on the Gods.*

CHAPTER 20

THE LAST OF THE FISHKETEERS

1

Two indistinct figures stood looking down at Caffrey, who was supine on a narrow bed. In contrast to his earlier accommodation, this room was small and bare, with an empty chest of drawers, a narrow window which wouldn't open and a reinforced door. A security camera's lens gleamed high in a corner, but it couldn't see them. They could barely see themselves.

What's wrong with him?

I don't know. He looks – broken.

Caffrey's glazed eyes stared sightlessly at the ceiling. He'd been that way since Foulkes' orderlies had dumped him here.

You don't look too much better yourself, you know.

Which one am I?

I can't tell any more.

We're fading, aren't we?

I think so.

This hasn't gone at all according to plan, has it?

What else did you expect?

Shit.

There was a long pause while they continued to watch and wait for the man to do something, and he continued to stare at nothing. A small trickle of drool had run down one cheek and made a coin-sized damp patch by his ear.

There must be something of Bobby left in there or we'd have disappeared completely by now, wouldn't we?

I don't think anybody has the faintest idea how any of this works.

Well, we're going to have to do something.

I've got an idea, but you're not going to like it.

Show me.

The two figures moved together, their blurred shapes overlapping briefly, and then apart again.

Oh. Oh, I see.

Look, if we fade away completely, it won't make any difference what little we've kept of him, will it? If it's all gone, that is.

But do we have the right? This man — this Caffrey — he's not a bad man. He's just another victim. What about his parents and the people that love him?

Do you think any of them are going to see him again, now that he's in this place? Anyway, it's not about what we have the "right" to do. It's about what we can do, in the hope that it somehow makes things better.

I suppose so. Okay then. Which of us shall it be?

Rock-paper-scissors you for it.

I can't help thinking there must be a more, well, grown-up way of deciding which of us gives up their existence.

Can you think of a better alternative?

There was a moment of consideration and then a resigned sigh.

No.

Okay then. One... two... three...

They looked at each other's hands.

Shit. Best of three?

Give it up, fish-boy.

The entity which had once been a fish living off dreamwrack in the Tourmaline Archipelago, who had eaten the blood of a man physically present in a place his kind only ever visited in their dreams, who had then briefly been a man called Blennie, stepped closer to the bed. He raised the disintegrating remnant of his hand up to his mouth and bit at the fleshy pad below his little finger. The blood, when it came, was shockingly red, and its thick smell filled the tiny room. With his other hand he opened Caffrey's mouth and pressed the wound to his lips, to give back that which had given life and mind and a fragment of something resembling a soul.

The effect of its taste was sudden and violent. The body came to life with a scream – a long-drawn wail of denial – and the head whipped back and forth, refusing what was offered. 'No! No, I don't want it! It's not me! *It's not me!*'

'Yes.' Blennie was gentle but insistent, holding the head steady and forcing the mouth to his hand, like a puppy being forced to recognise the smell of its own mess. 'It's you. It always was – the better part of you.'

Gradually the struggles subsided, and the body resumed its blank stare.

They watched anxiously.

'Did it – '

'Jesus, Blennie!' yelled Bobby in disgust, lurching into a sitting position. 'What the hell?' He wiped his mouth with the back of his hand, smearing blood across one cheek like half a clown's smile, and stared around in confusion.

'*Hola*, boss!' grinned Carmen. She'd snapped back into clarity in full Miranda mode: an emerald samba dress resplendent with ruffles and a towering hat of peacock feathers and fruit. Bobby hardly noticed, however, because Blennie was disappearing.

Like young Jophiel back on Stray, who'd shrugged off his human shape when the woman who'd dreamed him into existence had gone, and Igor after him, who had given up his borrowed and all-too brief life to bring Vessa back from death – Blennie was unravelling. Clots and streamers of his flesh broke free and dissolved brightly in the air, as if without Bobby's blood he didn't have the strength to hold the substance of himself together any more.

'Blennie, you prat,' Bobby groaned. 'What have you done?'

Worry furrowed Blennie's evaporating face. 'Um, sorry, did I do the wrong thing?' His voice was feather-thin, almost inaudible.

'No.' There were tears in Bobby's eyes, but he was smiling. 'No, you did just fine.'

'Oh.' The last things to disappear were his large eyes – usually so anxious, relaxed now for the first time. 'Oh, that's a re–'

And he was gone into the air.

2

'Bobby!' Carmen was bouncing up and down with excitement. 'We found it! We found the way through!'

Bobby tore his gaze away from the patch of brightness where Blennie had been. 'Through?' he asked. 'Back to Tourmaline?'

'*Sí*. When we were looking for you! We found it! It's here, right in this complex.'

'That can't be right. Foulkes'd never be stupid enough to keep prisoners in the same place as his door to the Assembly Chamber.'

'It's not a door – it's a tree! In a big-ass dome!'

'A tree?'

'*Sí*, you deaf *gringo*, a tree! How many times you want me to say it? Tree-tree-tree-tree-tree! Now are you going to come and see for yourself or just sit here asking stupid questions?' She pointed to the CCTV camera in the corner. 'You better get a move on, too, because they can't see me, but they sure as shit are going to wonder why you've suddenly woken up and started yelling at thin air.'

At that point, as if to agree with her, a distant alarm began braying.

'Carmen, why are you doing this?'

'No offence, boss, but that is the dumbest question you've asked yet. Now I'm going to see if I can...'

'No, wait up.' He put a hand on her arm – not restraining, not ordering. 'Please. Blennie just gave up his... whatever it was he had that I gave him, for me. Same as Igor did before. I didn't want either of them to do that, and I don't want you to go risking your life just because you think you owe me something. You don't.'

She shook his hand off. 'You finished now? Conscience all clear?' She closed her eyes, took a deep breath, held it, and then let it out slowly, composing herself. 'Okay, Roberto, listen. You think I can't think for myself? That I'm following you around like some crazy-ass religious nutcase after her guru? That was Blennie's take on things, not mine. But that's a blennie for you.' She drew herself up proudly. 'Before you, I was a *betta*. A fighting fish. The araka under Stray was a thing of evil, and worthy to be fought – same with the people who put it there. This Hegemony. So I fight them – for you, with you, it makes no difference to me. Blennie and Igor might have been ready to give it up for you, but if you want your blood back from me, you're going to have to kill me for it, *comprende*?'

'*Comprende*,' he said. 'Can you get this door open?'

Carmen rippled, and her forties nightclub glam was replaced by fatigue pants, a khaki vest top, and a red bandanna. 'Watch me,' she said and disappeared.

CHAPTER 21

GATE CRASHERS

1

The alarms were a lot louder in Wardrobe Control, where Foulkes was leaning over the shoulder of his Senior Response Coordinator and staring at her screen in disbelief.

'Sir, it means they've breached the hard perimeter...' began the ResCo.

'I know what it bloody means!' Foulkes snapped. 'Who are they, what are they using, and how do we kill it?' A sick coldness twisting in his guts told him that he probably already knew the answer to the first question at least. Not the Exiles, that was for sure. Not even they were this insane.

The ResCo was clicking through images from half a dozen security cams: a shredded chain-link fence whose ten-thousand volt charge had made no difference; the smoking wreckage of a MARTY unit which wasn't looking very Mobile, Armed or Responsive; finally, an image of eleven human figures – six men, five women – walking strung out in a loose line, as if they were out for nothing more dramatic than a Sunday afternoon ramble across the Herefordshire countryside. They weren't armed, and didn't even seem particularly well equipped for ramblers – no bags or boots, just t-shirts, blouses and trainers. One fellow was even in a suit. Ramblers would have turned back at the Ministry of Defence 'Danger: Live Fire Zone' notices. Which reminded him: 'What's happening with RAF Valley?' he asked the ResCo.

'They were already in the air, sir, scrambled automatically in response to the Mailbox,' she replied. 'Two Typhoons were re-directed as soon as the hostiles penetrated our soft perimeter;

Platinum Command are treating this as a co-ordinated terrorist incident. We'll have wings over in four minutes.'

'Let's hope we're all still here in another four,' he muttered, and she shot him an alarmed glance. 'Have ground response assets hold until the Typhoons get here; let's see how our unexpected guests handle a couple of Brimstone missiles. In the meantime get facial reck on that lot; I want to know who it is that thinks they can just walk in through my front door.'

For the moment, there was nothing to do but chew the inside of his cheek and watch those casually strolling figures.

2

Toren was a city boy by birth and breeding; this was his first serious day trip into the Great Outdoors, and he was enjoying himself immensely. The air was clear and the sky an eye-stretching blue, the hedgerows were alive with birds and blossom, and even the grass underfoot seemed to be joyfully bouncing him along. He had his brothers and sisters of the Brood with him – not as many as there should have been, but all the more tightly knit for that. They were bound as one by, through, and in the Shadow; it webbed them together, and they amplified it in turn, using it to defend themselves and to destroy the minds and machines sent out to stop them. But when they tore through the final gate and saw the Hegemony installation, with its manor house and outbuildings clustered around a huge geodesic dome, he stopped in surprise. Something in there was awake.

He felt it, trembling in the fibres of his shadowborn nerves. He heard it, roaring with the voice of the maelstrom which Ms DeSalle had shown him in Tourmaline: the black funnel which led to the dreaming space where the Aions slept, imprisoned.

Then the roaring in his head became a roaring in the world, and a pair of gleaming fighter jets swooped low over the head of the valley and banked straight towards them. Their undercarriages gleamed with missiles.

'Circle!' he shouted to the others, and they ran to obey.

The Brood linked hands, and their shadowflesh emerged from fingers and palms, weaving together and thickening like vines so that they were bound into a single, giant, multi-bodied organism. The strength of it attracted more darkness out of the air itself, shadows flocking and swooping about them – it was Toren's gospel that darkness was the resting state of existence, the heat death of the universe rippling backwards through time like an undertow so that it lay beneath the surface of the world from one end of creation to another. Now it erupted outwards and upwards from the circle of joined hands in twisting, gut-like streamers of entropy given substance – an unconscious homage to their araka ancestor. They searched for the war planes and the glimmers of consciousness riding inside which screamed low overhead in a first reconnaissance pass.

The pilots banked in an attempt to avoid what could only be interpreted as some kind of surface-to-air weapon, shredding through the streamers, though some scraps and ribbons stuck.

Where they stuck, they ate.

Veins of corruption infected wings and fuselages at lightning speed, making the carbon-fibre composites of their air-frames brittle, like old bones. Mechanical leprosy killed electronics and made servo-mechanisms arthritic. One plane simply exploded as its fuel tanks ruptured. The other pilot was able to eject while his Typhoon crumpled beneath him, but he was snatched out of the air by the Brood's shadow limbs and shrieked as they ate his mind and mutated his flesh so utterly that what hit the ground resembled something hosed from the floor of an abattoir more than a human being. An instant later, the six Brimstone missiles detonated spasmodically; one of them destroying the access road and the remainder tearing craters in the green countryside.

3

Foulkes and the horrified ResCo watched this unfold on the screen.

'What do we do now, sir?'

Foulkes continued to stare at the smoking wreckage and the twisting serpents which were even now coiling back down to lick at the carnage. But he was also seeing the last moments of Lyncham. Maddox had been compromised because he'd been weak and sloppy in allowing that araka-human hybrid to get too close, and Foulkes had felt no sympathy at all as he'd given the scuttling order and watched it all slide into the ocean. *This*, though, this was just senseless. He thought about the Ketterley Oak, and felt a sick, helpless rage. The idea that these people – if indeed they were people – could just waltz straight past every defence and endanger the existence of a miraculous organism which had lived for a thousand years was offensive to him on every level. He knew he should be evacuating right now and ordering the Wardrobe to be scuttled just like Lyncham (two in less than a month; how was he going to explain that to the Assembly?), but to escape and never know the reason why was more offensive still. He chewed the inside of his cheek, staring, staring.

'Sir?'

Staring.

'*Sir?*'

'Get me down to the tree with a team and as many demolition charges as they can carry. Full evacuation for everyone else.'

4

The shockwave of the exploding Typhoon shook Bobby's room.

'What the hell?'

He peered out of the narrow window, but all he could see was a rising column of smoke and running shapes. *Good*, he thought. Whatever was fucking with Foulkes' programme was just fine by him.

Then keys rattled in the lock and his door opened, and Carmen was there, armed with a pistol.

'Let's rock,' she said.

'Put that thing down,' he ordered, as they crept into the corridor outside.

'Not likely!' She laughed.

He stopped. 'Carmen, if it gets to the point of guns, how long do you think we'll last against this lot?'

Carmen jerked her head at the distant noise of screams, subsidiary explosions, and the rattle of automatic weapons fire. 'I think it's already got to that point, don't you?'

The corridor was lined with a row of doors exactly like his own, ending at a heavy security door standing half-open.

'Come on!' she urged. 'It's safe. I took care of it.' Carmen led him through and into a guard station for that wing of the building; metal desk, lockers, and a second security door leading to a flight of stairs. The guard was slumped forward over his desk, his pistol holster empty.

'Your work?' Bobby asked.

She just grinned and buffed her nails on her vest.

'Stop right there!' bellowed a voice from the stairs.

They threw themselves behind the desk as a shotgun blast tore into the wall above them. A second shot slammed into the desk itself right next to Bobby's head, and the metal dented as if it had been hit with a sledgehammer. He clutched his ear. Hearing on that side had been replaced by a dull roaring whine; tinnitus of rock-concert-feedback proportions.

Carmen popped up with the pistol and ducked back down again. She turned wide eyes to him and plucked at his elbow. 'Bobby…' she faltered.

His eyes were streaming. He blinked, trying to focus on her. 'What?'

'There's something…' She shook her head, unable to finish.

They both peered over the top of the desk.

The soldier who had shot at them wasn't shooting any more, and his shouts had become animal shrieks. Something impossible, mostly human-shaped, had him up against the wall with black whiplash limbs which emerged from the places where its human limbs met its torso – his boots a clear yard off the floor and kicking impotently as it tore him open with the eager glee of a child at Christmas.

'It can't be her,' whispered Bobby. 'She's dead. I saw her die.'

'Not her,' said Carmen, 'but *of* her, yes. It shares her blood – I can smell it – same as me. *Your* blood.' Her face was livid with disgust at the thought of having any kind of kinship with that abomination.

It dropped the soldier's eviscerated remains and turned in their direction. 'I know you,' said Voluschek, puzzled. 'Why do I know you?'

Carmen popped up with the nine-mil again, screamed '*Muere, hijo de puta!*' and unloaded the clip at it. Voluschek's shadowflesh reknit itself with each impact almost instantaneously, so that it hardly slowed him at all, and before Bobby could stop her she launched herself over the desk with a full-throated war cry. Voluschek swatted her aside, and she connected with the corner of the locker unit, too quickly to make herself incorporeal and soften the blow. She lay, twisting.

Voluschek picked her up and inspected her. 'I say again: what are you? Why do you seem familiar to me?' He wrapped tentacles around her from throat to knee and allowed his jaws to lengthen as he reared above her. 'I know one sure way to find out,' he grinned, and licked her face with a tongue that bit as it moved.

Then she was gone. There was a brief trembling in the air where she'd been, as if he was suddenly looking through water, and then he was grasping nothing. He stumbled, caught off-balance.

'She's the last of the Three Fishketeers,' said Bobby, and hit him as hard as he could.

It was Bobby's flesh and blood which had awoken the araka from its deathless sleep beneath Stray; more had given it the strength to attack Berylin Hooper's ship and ultimately merge with her to become Lilivet. It had given her the physical anchor to exist in the Realt, just as it had done Carmen and her brothers, just as in turn it had done Lilivet's Brood. And it hit Voluschek like a freight train.

He flew back through the doorway and sprawled at the foot of the stairs in a tangle of human and shadowborn limbs.

Bobby pursued. 'Sorry,' he said, sounding anything but. 'I don't think we've been properly introduced. Robert Jenkins. Charmed.' He picked Voluschek, who was still stunned, up off the floor and threw him back into the guard station, where he crashed into the janitor's cupboard and fell, surrounded by mop handles and bottles of detergent.

'How...' Voluschek shook his head, dazed. 'How are you doing this?'

'Pilates. Never underestimate good core strength.' Bobby advanced again, but the Brood's responses were quicker than he'd expected. It seemed to turn itself inside out in an eye-twisting contortion of flesh and darkness and then was standing again. It lashed at him, wrapping a tentacle around the forearm he flung up in defence – squeezing, biting.

'It does not matter,' said Voluschek. 'When you die, your secrets will go into the Shadow, and we will know everything about you.'

We? Dear Christ, there were more of them? Another limb wrapped itself around his throat. Instinctively, he pulled back. Something slipped out of the creature, and it grunted in pain.

Desperate to seize on any sign of vulnerability, Bobby wrapped the armoured tentacle around his arm a few more turns and yanked hard. This time the Brood screamed in abject torture as six inches of araka flesh slid out of the human. It looked soft and raw, like naked nerve tissue. He yanked again and more emerged, spasming. Voluschek, panicking, tried to pull away, but this only made the situation worse. He slipped, fell, and Bobby planted a foot in his chest and continued to haul, now with both hands. Once, as a boy (he couldn't remember whether this was Caffrey's childhood or his own, not that it mattered any more), he'd earned some extra pocket money clearing blanket-weed out of an overgrown fish pond, and the damn stuff had just kept coming – handfuls and handfuls of alien-looking, fibrous green slime which couldn't be seen in the water but had obviously permeated every cubic inch. This was exactly the same. The black stuff which came out of the screaming man did so at first in great clotted ropes from his joints, major organs, navel, mouth, and anus, but it started to come in thinner strands from his very pores. It seemed to be a secondary nervous system made of araka tissue which had spread like cancer throughout the host's body.

If the Brood had surrendered, or even pleaded for Bobby to stop, he might have done so, but it didn't. Maybe that simply wasn't in its nature, for a creature incapable of giving mercy to ask for it. Something in it awoke in his own nature an atavistic hatred, as if his blood recognised the trace of itself which had been corrupted and now felt an absolute compulsion to destroy the taint. So he didn't stop. It squirmed in his fists, but he kept going until the last of it came out of Voluschek's mouth, nose, ears and eyes, biting and spitting at him even as it died. It was accompanied by a gush of bright arterial blood, and Voluschek was still.

5

Everywhere across the Ketterley complex, the Brood stopped and howled, seized with agony at the death of their brother. Rainy paused over the dripping remains of a soldier and threw a panicked, questioning look at Toren.

No idea, he thought. *Let's find out, shall we?*

6

Carmen reappeared as Bobby stood shaking with adrenalin, his arms slicked to the elbows with black gore. She was armed with the dead soldier's assault rifle.

'How you doing there, *combatista*?' he panted.

'You know that's not a word, don't you?'

'Hey.' He waved it away as if it had been an apology. 'I don't blame you. This guy was just...' he gestured at the mess on the floor. 'I don't even know what this guy was.'

'Still,' she said. 'You took him. You can take the others too.'

'I have no intention of getting anywhere near any of his mates. I'm more than happy to let them and Foulkes' men kill each other. Just get me to that magic bloody tree.'

They crept up the staircase, though with the alarms and weapons fire it was unlikely that anybody would have heard them, and into a labyrinth of corridors. Bobby would quickly have become lost or caught had Carmen not been guiding him away from trouble by disappearing ahead now and then to scout corners and junctions. Just once were they taken by surprise, when a guardsman ran past them, screaming, taking no notice of them at all as he beat at the black shapes which crawled all over his head and back. In this way they made it to a maintenance door at the end of a narrow service corridor filled with hissing pipes and electrical conduits.

'It's here,' she said.

He eased the door open and blinked at the sudden daylight which flooded through the crack.

'I know you said a tree,' he replied, 'but honestly.'

He was looking at an indoor field. Instead of sky, there was a high dome made up of hexagonal panels, as if he was trapped under a sheet of bubble wrap of gargantuan proportions. In one spot, the dome had been smashed, and wreckage littered the grass. What with that, the acres of meadowland and the ruins of a church which were also enclosed, it took him a moment to notice the twisted oak with its bifurcated trunk like two out-splayed legs, or the small group of armed people busying themselves about it.

'Now would be a really good time for Chandler and some of his mates to turn up. How am I supposed to get to it?'

Carmen scowled. 'I'm sorry, I'll just go see where I put your red carpet and your brass marching band, *Señor* Roberto, eh?' and disappeared.

'Carmen! Wait! Look, I'm sorry about the *combatista* thing, okay?' But he was calling into an empty corridor. 'Shit.'

He turned back to the door, looking for any sign of a way he could make it across several hundred yards of open meadow in full sunlight without being seen. The two soldiers who weren't standing at high alert were busying themselves with attaching small box-like somethings to the oak's trunk. When Bobby realised that they were explosives and that Foulkes was going to blow the tree up rather than let a portal through the meniscus fall into hostile hands, that decided it for him. He shoved the door open and strode forward, hands in the air.

'Hello?' he called. 'Supervisor Foulkes? I think we need to have a little chat, don't you?'

Guns turned in his direction. Half, he noted. The other half remained trained on a pair of double doors much larger than the ones he'd come through, which had an army Land Rover parked crookedly in front of them. The hands holding the guns were white-knuckled and trembling. Bobby didn't blame them.

Foulkes looked around; if he was surprised, he didn't betray it. One hand held a detonator, and the other a pistol which he pointed at Bobby. 'A little chat? I hardly think so, Mr Caffrey. Corporal, shoot that...'

'Wait! I'm not Caffrey! I'm Jenkins! Robert Jenkins! I can tell you everything you want to know!'

Foulkes raised an eyebrow. 'Everything? That's quite a boast, Mr Jenkins.'

'Everything! Stray, the araka, what Jowett's up to – everything! Just let me go through into Tourmaline before you blow it up. Please, that's all I ask.'

For all that Foulkes had sounded as cool as a cucumber, Bobby could see that he was sweating. 'You make an interesting proposition, but I think right now is hardly the time to...'

A shadow fell over them, and they both looked up to see the hexagonal dome panel directly overhead shatter as a dark figure plummeted towards them. It was not falling uncontrollably, but wreathing itself in wing-like swathes of semi-physical shadow which billowed, catching the air and slowing its tumbling descent. Still, it was sudden enough for Bobby and Foulkes to be able to do nothing but shrink from the falling debris. At seven other points around the dome's circumference, the remainder of Lilivet's Brood smashed their way inwards, provoking fire from the soldiers who found themselves surrounded.

Toren landed between Bobby and Foulkes. 'All you had to do was share,' he said disdainfully, and with one human hand he slapped away the detonator, which flew, spinning, into the grass, whilst a shadowflesh limb seized Bobby by the throat. 'And as for *you!*' he snarled.

'Yeah, I get that a lot,' Bobby choked. As he pulled at the band of muscle, it contracted savagely, and the world dropped away into darkness.

CHAPTER 22

THE SHADOW

1

Bobby was standing, mired up to his knees in a stinking sludge which plucked at him with blunt, formless fingers as it tried to climb his legs. The place he was in had a dim, undersea quality, darkening to pitch blackness high overhead, and filled with the rumour of vast vegetable shapes moving ponderously in the gloom. The oneirocline; the dreaming space between worlds where the Aions slept. But whereas before he'd flown high above them in the bright shallows of dreaming, here he was trapped at their abyssal level, helpless and alone. Of Foulkes, or anything remotely human, there was no sign. He pulled at his legs, but they might as well have been set in concrete.

You.

That voice again – it was a mockery of human speech, assembled out of a cacophony of screams and sobs, and even though it was only one word, he winced at the sound. He thought he might very quickly go mad if he had to endure a longer conversation.

Something massive approached in the dimness, extruding and reclaiming pseudopods of its substance, as if feeding from the surroundings. It swarmed with araka; they crawled on its surface and clouded the water like flies around a corpse. *So many*, he thought, appalled. *How can so much evil come from us?* One of the pseudopods came to within touching distance, shaping itself into the facsimile of a human form attached at the back of its skull by thick umbilical tissue. It walked towards him lightly along the surface of the mire and took on

Toren's face, and Bobby realised that as powerful as Toren was individually, he was still only one of countless appendages of this Aion.

Yes, well, it said, seeing that it was recognised. *Just so we're clear, see yourself.*

Toren reached out a hand and stroked Bobby's cheek. It was like being touched by something long dead and eternally decayed. He recoiled and saw the truth of himself.

Every shameful thing he'd ever done: every lie, every petty theft, every wank, every drunken pass at a pretty girl, every argument, every time he'd given up, every time he'd made his mother cry, every bug he'd squashed, every copied piece of homework, every man he'd punched, every woman he'd fucked and abandoned. Adriana, who'd waited for him to make good his promise in Singapore; Allie, pregnant with his child, and his first reaction to run like hell; the men on the Spinner, dead by his actions; Sophie, dead; Berylin Hooper, dead; Marjorie Lachlan, dead; so many dead, never mind that he had been given no choice, because he was responsible. He was responsible for *everything*. He cringed as he remembered and felt the weight of every single one of them, simultaneously, because none of it had gone away or been forgiven or atoned for – it was all still there, as raw as the first moment, all in the Shadow, to be brought out and picked over and picked over and picked over like a scab on an infected wound which would never heal. Looking at all of the lives he'd ruined or blighted, he realised how much better off they'd all have been if he'd never existed, and how much better the world would still be if he simply didn't go back to it.

Oh, don't worry, said Toren, his voice screaming at the edges. *I'll let you take care of that in due course. But for the moment, you hurt my man, and I need to know how that was done.*

'My blood,' Bobby replied, numb with horror at himself.

Your blood? What the fuck's your blood got to do with it?

'The thing that spawned you, the araka, it woke up when it tasted my blood. Later, I gave it more, and that made it strong enough to exist in the Realt. I guess that also made it vulnerable to me, because when your man attacked me, I just took it back, and it killed him.' One more death to add to the list. At the same time a question wormed its way through the morass of his self-pity: how did Toren not know this? If he could read Bobby's mind, how did he not know?

Because his blood was in Toren too, of course, and the knowledge was so close to him that he couldn't see it – like when Allie had described the disease which had put her in a coma, she'd said that the shock had come from the fact that she was a doctor and the infection had struck so close to where she should have been strongest. She simply hadn't seen it coming.

Allie, who was having his child. His blood was responsible for so much, and this worst of all: that their son or daughter might have any kinship with the gloating thing in front of him.

'No,' he said.

Toren's laugh was dry, amused. *No?*

'Not my kid. Me, fine, whatever. I deserve it, probably. But not my kid, you bastard.' Bobby raised his head, and the look on his face made Toren falter backward a step – but not far enough. Toren had come too close when he'd touched Bobby to show him the truth of his own shadow; now Bobby's hand lashed out and gripped him by the wrist.

That grip burned as Bobby's blood reclaimed its own. Toren's araka flesh writhed out of his pores, shrieking as it bit and lashed with barbs, teeth, and talons. Although his abhorrence was just as strong as when he'd killed Voluschek, Bobby was simply too weak and traumatised to complete the same kind of exorcism and was forced to let Toren go.

2

The submarine darkness tattered like fog breaking apart in a high wind, and Bobby found himself back in the daylight of Foulkes' dome. He supported himself with his hands on his knees and retched onto the grass while Toren sprawled several yards away, bleeding from eyes, ears and nose. Rainy, his face stricken, was cradling Toren's head.

'What did you just do?' demanded Foulkes. 'How did you do that?'

Around them, the fighting had paused as the surviving soldiers regrouped, and the Brood, stunned at their leader's wounding, milled uncertainly.

'Told you,' coughed Bobby, wiping strings of puke from his mouth. 'Get me into Tourmaline. I'll tell you everything. I'll kill the rest of these things for you.'

Rainy gave a wordless howl of rage and launched himself at the two men, changing as he did so and brushing aside two bullets from Foulkes' pistol.

Then Carmen rippled into existence next to Bobby, armed with an assault rifle. She dropped him a wink, turned, and unloaded the full thirty-round magazine into Rainy at almost point-blank range. Strong as the Brood were, that amount of damage couldn't be ignored, and he was thrown back. She tossed the empty rifle aside and flung herself on him with a banshee scream, flashing in and out of corporeality as she shrugged off the limitations of a human shape and attacked from every direction, so that to the onlookers it seemed that a nest of serpents was wrestling with twisting ribbons of brightness. Out of the screaming storm her voice rang clear: 'Bobby! Get out! Get out now!'

Gunfire and screams hammered out once again as Foulkes supported a stumbling Bobby into the low arch of the Ketterley Oak, stooping to snatch up the detonator as he went.

'Wait!' said Bobby, at the shimmering curtain of the meniscus. 'What about Carmen? What about your men?'

'What about them?' replied Foulkes, dragging them both through as he pushed the button. Their passage was helped by a battering ram of concussive heat which flung them forward...

3

…and they fell, smoking and semi-conscious, onto the flagged stones of a wide and high-walled courtyard. Strong hands dragged them away from the roaring of a large tree which was on fire from root to crown, and dumped them at the feet of a man in a high-collared uniform with many brass buttons.

Legate Geiran, Regional Supervisor to the Interstitial Assembly for Elbaite and its Maritime Dominions, looked down at his colleague from the Realt and his strange companion.

'So, Martin,' he said. 'To which part of your carefully worked out schedule does this belong, exactly?'

4

Chandler slipped through the ruins of the Ketterley facility, having to sacrifice intel for speed. It made him twitchy, having to leave Joey back at the car babysitting Noben, but Runce was an acceptable substitute. Hegemony assets would be here soon to investigate; the only reason they weren't here already was because this place had obviously been kept totally off the books – so much so that they'd isolated themselves from reinforcements, the stupid, paranoid bastards. This only made it all the more interesting.

There was also the remote possibility of finding Jenkins. Even though he was more likely long dead, he had brought Chandler this far, and that was further than most. But the more wreckage Chandler saw, the more his optimism faded.

'Bloody hell,' said Runce, picking his way over the rubble after him. 'Something's literally torn this place apart.'

'Several very large and angry somethings, by the look,' Chandler replied.

There was plenty of damage from munitions – grenade blasts and the riddled pock-marks of automatic weapons fire – but also evidence of a much more disturbing style of combat. Metal beams which had been twisted like pipe-cleaners. Walls which were folded open like tin cans where the enemy had gone after their prey. Human remains: clawed, bitten, wrenched apart, in some cases so badly that Chandler couldn't be sure how many bodies he was looking at. He was sure that many of the victims had not been dead when the mutilation had happened. Whatever was responsible had lingered.

He even found one of them, at the bottom of a stairwell leading to some underground cells. The body was dressed as a civilian, and expensively so – nice dark suit, shiny shoes – and apparently uninjured. Just dead, next to piles of clotted black tissue lying around the body in stringy, deliquescing clumps like overcooked spaghetti. When he prodded one, it twitched and tried to crawl onto his shoe.

'What the hell is that?' asked Runce, disgusted.

'Your guess is as good as mine. One kind of Hegemony shit or another, I imagine.'

They climbed back into the open air. The dome was a saw-toothed ruin, with a wide crater at its centre. There was nothing to give a clue about what had been in here, but something about it prickled at Chandler's nerve endings all the same. He climbed down and stood at the very bottom and thought there was the faintest trembling of a rainbow shimmer at the edge of his vision, but it refused to resolve into anything more substantial.

The only thing he found which was of any interest was a single costume earring, shaped like a bunch of grapes.

'Mean anything to you?' he asked, tossing it to Runce.

Runce inspected it, and tossed it back. 'No. Should it?'

Chandler sighed and looked around. 'I don't know. Looks like whatever happened here, we missed it.'

CHAPTER 23

ELBAITE

1

As prisons went, thought Bobby, it gave some five-star hotels a run for their money.

It had been a monastery in a previous life, carved in straight, hard lines from the dark basalt of the columnar island on which it stood – one of hundreds which crowded the precipitous coast of southern Elbaite like the broken stubs of monolithic pier pilings. None of the others were inhabited, however. Bobby decided that this place must have been chosen by the heretical Symmetrists to plant the sister tree of the Ketterley Oak precisely because it was so isolated, but in the centuries since then, the monastery had become one of many mansions owned by House Geiran, who had eschewed monastic austerity for creature comfort. The thick basalt walls were perfect for protecting carpets, tapestries, silks, cushions and delicately carved furniture from the relentless battering of the ocean weather.

Luxurious though it was, and even though he and Foulkes hadn't been put in anything so vulgar as an actual cell with bars, it was still a prison.

He stood on the windswept balcony of his apartment, staring at the grey-green mass of ocean seething against the sheer rock face hundreds of feet below. From here he had a good view halfway round the walls to where a crew of navvies was lowering wooden crates down to a small steam vessel moored at the cliff base. Somewhere down there was a jetty, reached by a narrow stair carved into the cliff. Somewhere high above, there was also an aerostat spire. Both were guarded by

Elbaite soldiers armed with Foulkes' guns. Soon after their arrival, Foulkes had quickly disappeared somewhere with his Elbaite counterpart, leaving Bobby to stalk the monastery's hallways and chambers like a restless phantom, exploring as much as he could. It was one way to try and take his mind off the crushing black irony of his situation: he had made it back to Tourmaline, only to find himself on the far side of the world and behind enemy lines.

Foulkes found him on the balcony and watched him watching the men lowering their crates of guns.

'I suggest you don't bother even thinking about it,' Foulkes said. 'Even if you could somehow smuggle yourself into one, you'd starve to death before they opened it up. Why don't we talk about your more realistic options?'

'Why don't you go fuck yourself?' suggested Bobby quietly.

Foulkes laughed and leaned against the stone balustrade with his arms crossed, facing back into the room. 'You're thinking of the guns, aren't you?'

'You're damn right I am.'

'Well, fine. I have no intention of trying to explain or justify anything to you, so you go ahead and hold that thought. While you're there, why don't you tell me about Stray and Danae and the people you met there? Maybe I can convince Geiran to leave that particular little shit-splat of an island alone.'

Bobby's fingers tightened on the stone. Again, he saw the blunt shapes of airships pouring heavy automatic fire into Timini's market place and bodies floating in the harbour. 'You're too late. Oh, I get it, this war was always going to happen. Jowett sent his team to clear us out of the way in the first place. You and him are as bad as each other. But you didn't have to send them fucking *chain* guns.'

Foulkes shrugged. 'So now here you are, stuck between a pair of evil old men, able to make a small difference. Climb down off your moral high horse and get your hands dirty. Talk to me. You promised me answers if I brought you here.' He gestured around. 'Well, here we are.'

Bobby laughed bitterly. 'Yeah, on the other side of the world.'

'As they say, be careful what you wish for. But I'm sorry, I didn't realise that you had a specific destination in mind. On the other side of the world from where, exactly? To what or whom are you so eager to return? Someone on Danae? Someone from Stray? The woman in Runceforth's reports, perhaps? Oh you needn't look so surprised, Robert, you must know I have my agents everywhere. I'm going to need a lot more information from you now – and I will also need you to hold to that promise you made me.'

'Mate, I wouldn't piss on you if you were burning in the street.'

'Nothing has changed, you know. Your continued survival remains contingent on how useful you prove yourself to me. In an hour or so I will be returning to the real world, and if you are still here when that happens Geiran's men will put a bullet in your brain. It's that simple. If, on the other hand, you come back with me, I give you my solemn word that I will find you another way through to wherever it is you actually do want to be. There are always other ways through.'

Bobby stared at him. 'Your word. Are you kidding me?'

'What choice do you have? I know you can hurt them,' he added, with quiet intensity. 'Those araka-spawn. I saw that with my own eyes. This person, this *thing*, has proven to be quite…' his mouth twisted in disgust. 'Tenacious. At the very least, tell me what it is so that I can try to do something about it myself.'

'So that you can make him work for you, you mean?'

'You saw it – did it strike you as being an entity likely to be bribed or coerced?'

'Supervisor Foulkes,' Bobby began as calmly as he could, trying to keep a lid on his temper and failing. 'I'm not sure if you've got the wrong impression of me in the short time we've known each other, or whether you've been playing cloak and dagger for so long you've forgotten what a normal person looks like,' and he was shouting now, 'but *I am not a fucking assassin!*'

'Don't think of it as killing, then. Think of it as pest control. And I'm sorry, Mr Jenkins, but you are far from being normal.'

'All I want...'

'Does! Not! Matter!' Foulkes coloured and thrust his hands in his pockets as if ashamed of his outburst. 'You will come with me and track this monster down and kill him, or you will die here, regardless of what you do or do not think you are. I'll go one better: I'll find where your Sleeping Beauty lady friend lies and make sure she wakes up as a drooling moron...'

Bobby lashed out, grabbing Foulkes by his coat lapels and shoving him hard against the stone balustrade so that he was leaning backward over a hundred-foot drop. 'You fucking touch her,' he snarled.

Foulkes smiled as he choked. 'Of course that's what it would take. How depressingly predictable. Your heroic anger is all very impressive, but you're not so far gone as to doom yourself by killing me; you still have hope, you see. So, knowing that I will find and kill her, give me an alternative.'

With great reluctance, Bobby let him go and staggered away. His head felt stuffed and swollen. He took a deep breath and braced himself against the stone. 'I was harvesting kelp,' he said, 'when I cut my hand, and there was something strange about the blood that came out of it...'

He told Foulkes everything then – all that he needed in order to understand where the walking Shadow called Toren had come from, anyway. Despite Foulkes having intuited his relationship with Allie, he said as little about her as possible and absolutely nothing about her pregnancy. It took the better part of an hour for him to get to the events at the dome, and when he was done he felt hollowed out, empty of everything including his anger. The navvies had stopped loading, and the supply vessel was steaming away, towards the dark mainland.

Presently there were the sounds of a door opening in the room, heavy footsteps of soldiers, and the door to the balcony was opened by Legate Geiran. Behind him stood a squad of six riflemen carrying very modern-looking assault weapons. His own SA80s, Foulkes noticed. Seeing them pointed at him was particularly disquieting.

'My lord,' admonished Foulkes, 'there really is no need for an armed escort. My man here is quite docile.'

Bobby bit back a retort and edged closer to Foulkes. This didn't look much like an escort to him; six was far too many to guard against one man doing a runner, especially with so many sentries around.

Geiran stepped back so that the riflemen formed a neat line in front of him. 'It all depends on the destination to which you are being escorted,' he replied.

The riflemen took up firing positions.

'Geiran,' began Foulkes, 'listen to me…'

'I think not. Since you are unable to provide me with further armaments from the Realt, then you remain nothing more than a security risk. I cannot have the secrecy of this place compromised.'

'But murdering another member of the Assembly…'

'…happens all the time. I would like to thank you, however, for doing such a thorough job of scuttling your own side of things, in which I will suggest that your remains would surely be found if only the destruction were not so severe.'

'They'll never believe that.'

Geiran shrugged. 'They don't have to. They simply need a reason not to pursue the matter further, as we both well know. Men, on my command…'

Bobby grabbed Foulkes and pitched them both backwards over the stone balustrade.

2

There was a moment of tangled free-fall, and then the ocean rose up and smashed them. If Bobby hadn't spent most of his short life on Stray falling or diving into the water several times a day, he would certainly have been knocked unconscious and they'd both have drowned. As it was, the impact – not to mention the sudden, freezing cold – was enough to stun him, and he floundered weakly to the surface, coughing. Foulkes popped up next to him, face down and motionless. Bobby reached for him before the heaving coastal swell could separate them and dragged him onto his back.

Shouts from above, the rattle and crack of gunfire. Spits and spats in the water around him.

Oh, how I've missed this, he thought, beginning to tug Foulkes away with him.

The distances between the basalt pillars which rose out of the ocean in this region varied from a few dozen yards to over a mile; the nearest one to Bobby was the only thing he could possibly use for cover, and it wasn't all that far – probably only a hundred yards or so – but the combination of the heavy swell, the weight of his waterlogged clothes, and having to tow Foulkes' unconscious form made it exhausting within a few strokes. Meanwhile the firing continued from above. It was only a matter of time before one of them got lucky.

But they didn't. Maybe it was the unfamiliar guns; maybe it was the swell shifting their targets around. Bobby didn't care. He could only grip the back of Foulkes' collar as tightly as possible and grab for the nearest outcrop with his other hand as the sea rose up and threw him at the rock-clustered base of the neighbouring column. His chest struck a hard edge; savage pain flared there. The rock was slimed and sharp with mussels; his fingers skidded away, flesh tearing, salt-water stinging. He struck out again, and the pain when he gasped for breath was like being stabbed. He found a handhold and dragged himself closer, towing Foulkes, shoving him up against the rock so he didn't slide back in. Then he rested for a moment himself, arms clasped around a rock and his head bent against them, panting, every intake another stab. *Christ, I hope that's not a rib.*

Bullets ricocheted off the stone several feet above his head.

'Oi, sleeping beauty.' He slapped Foulkes. 'Wake up.'

Foulkes' head lolled.

Bobby slapped him again. 'Wake *up*, dozy bastard.'

Foulkes' head lolled in the other direction.

'Fucksake.'

Half-crawling, half-swimming, he hauled the unconscious man around and between the tumbled slabs, expecting at every moment to feel a bullet bite between his shoulder blades. The waves alternately shoved him against the stone and tried to drag him back out into the currents which seethed between the rock pillars, so that every action was a barely controlled lurch to maintain balance or grip. He managed to scramble enough of the way around the pillar to get out of the direct firing line, and then he collapsed again, but he knew it was only a respite. They'd send out boats soon.

Foulkes sputtered and writhed feebly.

'There ya go.' Bobby helped him along with another couple of slaps.

Foulkes retched up seawater and struggled to look around him. He twisted, cried out, and slid off the rock onto which he'd been dumped. Bobby grabbed him back again before he could be caught by a swell. This time he clung on by his own meagre strength, limp as a hank of seaweed.

'What...' he coughed.

'You're alive,' said Bobby. 'Fun, isn't it?'

Foulkes groaned. 'What. Do we do. Now.'

'We wait for them to send out a boat to finish us off.'

'Not. Funny.'

Foulkes' head thudded onto the stone beneath his arms and he began to shudder – whether from chill or shock, Bobby didn't know. Probably both. He tried to calm his breathing, to keep it shallow so that it didn't hurt so much, but the cold water was making him hyperventilate. He tried taking his shoes off, but his fingers were too clumsy for the job, so he settled for ditching the jacket. It wasn't going to keep him any warmer, and was only likely to drag him down. The gunfire persisted for a while and then stopped.

Presently there came the shouting of voices, a lot nearer.

Foulkes raised his head at the sound. 'They're...' he started, but all he saw was Jenkins diving into the water and disappearing. Too traumatised to even be properly angry at this additional abandonment, he lay and watched numbly as, around the pillar, a small rowboat appeared. It was crewed by two oarsmen and a marine, scanning the rocks as they fought to keep the small craft clear of the towering stone column. He was spotted quickly. The marine raised his rifle, obviously struggling to maintain a kneeling position in the pitching boat. Then Foulkes realised that its violent motion wasn't being caused just by the waves; Jenkins had surfaced on the other side of it, hands gripping the gunwale, and was rocking it hard from side to side. The marine swung his rifle around in a panic, overbalanced, and was the first to go over the side. One of the sailors raised his oar to use as a club, but that just gave Jenkins the opportunity to grab the blade of it and pull him in too. Jenkins moved around and hauled himself into the boat over its stern as the third Elbaite sailor pulled a knife and shuffled towards him; Foulkes couldn't see clearly what happened next except that there was a grimly contained struggle in the bed of the boat, and moments later Jenkins was tipping the sailor's limp body over the side.

'Foulkes!' he yelled. 'Get over here! Now!' He struck with the remaining oar at one of the thrashing figures in the water.

Foulkes looked at the surging waves. They were likely to dash him back onto the rocks and break every bone in his body, but they were also taking Jenkins and the boat further away.

No choice.

He took a deep breath and threw himself in, swimming with clumsy overhand strokes toward the boat. Immediately, the surge of water swept him off course; for every yard forward he gained, it dragged him three sideways. It was crushingly cold, and his arms soon lost what little strength they had. The boat was only a dozen yards away but it might as well have been in the Realt. A wave closed over his head, filling his mouth and nose with stinging brine, and as he coughed his way clear he knew that another one of those would finish him.

Then a rope hit him in the face.

'Grab it!' yelled Bobby.

Foulkes did as he was told and let himself get dragged towards the boat. He lacked the strength to get himself into it, however, and he was too heavy for Bobby to manage it unaided. He clung to the side, gasping.

'Look, you're just going to have to hang on, then,' said Bobby. 'I'll get us to shore as quickly as I can. Only got the one oar though, so who knows. If anything bites your feet just yell.'

Foulkes' teeth were chattering. 'Fuck. You. Jenkins.'

'That's the spirit.'

3

It took Geiran's search teams until the following morning to discover the splintered remains of the boat and the sailors' bodies, washed ashore far along the coast. By that time the tide had come in and gone out again, taking with it any tracks or scent which dogs might have been able to follow. To make matters worse, the coastline was precipitous and scored with innumerable ravines and gullies, any one of which the fugitives could have used to escape inland.

Squads were sent to scour every farm, homestead, and village for a league up and down the coast. Only two returned with anything resembling solid news: a solitary farmer who reported that his barn had been broken into during the night and food had been stolen from his kitchen, and in a nearby village small enough that a family's clothes disappearing off their washing line was a noteworthy event. In larger settlements, reports of petty crime were so common that it was impossible to sift out anything which might have indicated where the escapees had gone. So, in the railway sidings of a large industrial town several miles inland, nobody took any more notice of two raggedly-dressed men hopping aboard a slow-moving freight-train in the dead of night than if they had been ordinary tramps.

4

Bobby and Foulkes munched on cinnamon bread and dried fruit as the freight carriage's sway and rattle carried them along the coast in the pre-dawn gloom. They'd managed to get one of the big sliding doors open, because the chill was preferable to the claustrophobia, and they sat either side of it, watching the world slip past in translucent layers of slate blue and salmon pink. Bobby saw a wide, broken coastline of lagoons and salt-flats which the train curved around and cut over in a series of causeways and low bridges. Occasionally there were small, roughly built shacks stuck right out on the low-lying marshland, hemmed in on all sides by shining water – and once, a man prodding with a long pole at a dozen fat shapes which wallowed towards a crude pen built in the shallows. When he asked Foulkes what it was, Foulkes glanced up, grunted 'Oh, just a selk-herder,' and went back to staring morosely at the scenery.

'A what?'

'Selk-herder. Selks are big fat stupid creatures – a bit like manatees, but only the same way as cows are like buffalo. They're grazed on sea-grass; the milk makes a salty kind of cheese, if you like that sort of thing.'

'Right. Probably no good on a pizza, then.'

'Except a seafood pizza, one assumes. Do they make seafood pizzas?'

'I think so.'

They munched and stared while he train clattered its curving way through the labyrinth of coves, inlets, and marshes.

'It's a funny thing, the sea,' said Foulkes suddenly.

'Speaking as one who's had to live on it,' replied Bobby, 'I don't think I'd choose the word "funny".'

'Hmm,' he conceded. 'Possibly not. You see, the Schism which divided our worlds, so far as we understand it, separated the landmasses quite distinctly. But the sea… ah, the sea now. Much more fluid, of course. Pardon the pun. Much harder to say that much here or this much there. Impossible to delineate. Subornation events across water locations are often more dynamic, longer-lasting, unpredictable. You'd know, of course – Stray, and everything. If I were a poetic man, I might venture to suggest that there's something about the sea which remembers when the world was whole and wants it to be so again. Maybe that's why it terrifies me so much,' he added quietly.

'Are you sure you should be telling me all of this?'

'Oh, what can it possibly matter now?' His gaze out of the doorway was hollow. 'You still haven't explained why you saved my life in the first place.'

'The truth is, I don't know. I'd like to say it's because I'm such a wonderful guy who values life above everything else, no matter whose it is, but that's not true. I'd have let your pal shoot you and chalked it up to cosmic irony, except something made me grab you. I have no way to explain it. It's like I wasn't in control of my own actions.'

Foulkes thought about this for a moment. 'Well then here's another thing I shouldn't be telling you,' he said. 'There is a theory that human personality is indirectly shaped by the Aions in the womb.'

'That doesn't sound hugely comforting.'

'Brain activity begins at about eight weeks' gestation. Even towards birth, a fetus spends nearly ninety per cent of its time sleeping. That's over six months, right at the start of its existence, going in and out of the REM sleep which carries us all into the oneirocline. The theory holds that while there, the Aions reach out to a child's developing consciousness and affect it – giving it shape, texture, colour, however you want to describe it. We know that they do this to adult minds but to a much lesser extent; they exercise themselves in our dreams as figures of myth and legend. The personalities of unborn children, it is believed, are much more directly manipulated due to prolonged exposure, giving rise, as adults, to particular patterns of thought and behaviour. This is why primitive cultures believe that every man has a totem animal which expresses their spirit, and why so many people still believe that astrological signs control their fate and personality. I think it's a load of rubbish, myself, but then I'm a Scorpio, so I would, wouldn't I?'

As an attempt at humour, it fell flat; Bobby was miles away, considering Allie's unborn baby. Was that happening to his son or daughter's soul right now? Was it being shaped by the ghosts of dead gods? What if something like that Shadow which possessed Toren and his people got hold of his child? How on earth did you fight such a thing?

'So basically we're all just puppets – that's what you're saying.'

'No. They don't control our thoughts or actions any more than an alcoholic or a musical genius or a homosexual is controlled by whatever genetic markers predispose them towards those behaviours, but they do set the ground state for adult development. If you want an explanation for why you are the way you are, and some of the more bone-headed things you've done, it could be that while your personality was being reconstructed you were touched by the Aion of something stupidly heroic that sacrifices itself before others and refuses to give up even when things seem hopeless.'

'I think I like the sound of that.' *You have the soul of a gambler, I believe*, Chandler had told him.

'Yes, well, like I say, it's obviously total rubbish. Believe whatever gets you through the night, Mr Jenkins.'

'I'll tell you what I believe: I believe your plan sucks, that's what I believe.'

'No you don't. If you did, you wouldn't be on this train with me. You'd have stolen the first airship you could find, in the deluded belief that you could somehow cross a warzone and navigate eight thousand miles to Oraille without getting yourself killed.'

'Well maybe now that I know I'm the incarnation of a legendary hero, I can do just that.'

'It's not incar– oh, never mind.' Foulkes rubbed his brow wearily. 'I blame Joseph Campbell for this,' he muttered.

'Who?'

'It doesn't matter. Just so long as we get to Benst in one piece. My contact will be with us shortly; he can get us into the Admiralty building, and we will be able to find Geiran's door to the Assembly Chamber.'

'So you keep saying. And you think your idea for breaking into what must be one of the most closely guarded buildings in the whole of this country is not in any way deluded.'

'It is sometimes an appropriate response to reality to go insane, Mr Jenkins.'

'That's good. Very pithy. You should put it on a t-shirt.'

They sat in silence and watched the margins of the shoreline slip past.

5

Bobby tried to doze, but the pain in his rib cage made it impossible. The train was rattling through the outskirts of a large town, farmland giving way to reservoirs, canals, and factories. Soon it would be tenements, shops, and stations, and he and Foulkes would have to find a way to hide from the increasing attentions of railway workers. Everywhere, he saw the signs of military mobilisation. Troop trains passed them, heading for the coast, crammed with soldiers who sang and laughed, and flat-bed freight cars carried the canvas-shrouded shapes of artillery guns. Above them flew tidy formations of combat 'stats, while static lines of defensive barrage balloons cast shadows over fields and hedgerows.

'I bet you're loving all this,' said Bobby, waving at it.

Foulkes looked and sighed. 'Mr Jenkins, the problems that afflict this world stem from the fact that our two realities are massively imbalanced. They're like a pair of scales with one side so heavy that the whole set-up is liable to go crashing to the floor at any moment. So that leaves you one of two choices: either you trim the excess weight off one side, or you add some to the other. Now, trimming the excess weight off our reality, with its population of seven billion, is just a bit more drastic than anybody except the most fanatical in the Assembly are prepared to accept. Thus the consensus is to bring this world up to our level as quickly as possible. We only differ in our chosen methodology.'

'Methodology,' Bobby shook his head, laughing softly in disbelief.

'War is quite simply the single most efficient civilising catalyst we know. Put very crudely: no V2 rocket, therefore no moon landing and no satellites, no internet and no Sky TV. It doesn't even really matter what the outcome of this particular war is. The upshot will be to force Oraille to counter Elbaite expansionism by ramping up their own R&D, with all the technological spin-off that entails. All I'm doing is speeding the process up, getting the painful bit over and done with as quickly as possible.'

'Are you trying to say that you're doing these people a favour?'

'Answer this, then: if someone could have given the Americans the atomic bomb the day after Pearl Harbour, how much quicker might that war have been over? How many lives saved?'

Bobby remembered again the destruction of Singapore, and found that for once he had no defence against Foulkes. The notion that there might be anything upon which to agree with this man disturbed him profoundly, but all he could do was bite the inside of his cheek and glare out at the preparations for war which slipped past.

As the day progressed, and the train took them inland and ever closer to the Elbaite capital of Benst, Foulkes became increasingly restless and irritable, checking his watch and roaming about the cargo container, muttering to himself. Bobby ignored it for as long as he could, but in the end had to say something.

'Look, what is it? If you were any more on edge you'd cut yourself.'

'We should have heard something by now. There's contingency for the possibility of me being trapped here, but he's a good twelve hours overdue.'

'Who – your contact?'

'No, hero, the Easter Bunny. Who do you think?'

'You're expecting to get a message from him in a country with no wireless technology while on a moving train?'

'I'm expecting him to be here himself, actually. He's a lucid dreamer from our world; he should have keyed in on my location and been here by now.'

Bobby fingered the capsule with Allie's hair which remained hidden beneath his shirt. It hadn't glowed since his arrival, but then he wasn't expecting it to, since it was now physically in the same world as Allie and not here in a dream. It made perfect sense that someone like Foulkes would employ lucid dreaming agents to carry out his dirty work here. 'So your contact hasn't been able to make contact,' he mused. 'I think he should change his job title.'

Foulkes just growled and continued to pace. 'Joke about it all you like, but if he can't help us get into the Elbaite Admiralty building, we have a significant problem.'

'Oh. Yeah, right. I hadn't thought of that. Shit. So if your contact remains incommunicado, then surely the only thing left is that we have to find a different door in a different country – ideally controlled by someone on the Assembly you're still on speaking terms with. You know, who doesn't want to actually kill us on sight. Is there anybody who still fits that description, do you think?'

'There is no way I can possibly explain our existence here which will not end up with us being arrested by the Interstitial Assembly and executed.'

'Not without you owing somebody a massive favour. Come on, you're all as corrupt as each other – I'm sure you'll be able to find some way of making a deal. I'm not talking about going anywhere as far as Oraille – but Elbaite is part of the Tourmaline Archipelago, right? So find some reasonably neutral island and offer them iPads or antibiotics or something.'

'And how do you propose we get there? We have no papers and no money to bribe anybody to look the other way, never mind buy passage.'

Bobby smiled and emptied his trouser pockets. While he'd had the relative freedom of Geiran's mansion, he'd been able to steal a number of small but valuable items – a few pieces of silver cutlery, a pearl-encrusted candle holder, and a jade figurine of a naked sea-nymph. He had done so without any compunction whatsoever; at the back of his mind had been a vague idea of selling them and using the money to help the victims of Elbaite's aggression in the Archipelago. Now they had a much more immediate use.

Foulkes examined them with reluctant approval. 'We'll see,' was all he said. 'I think I might have to revise my opinion of you, Mr Jenkins.'

'Oh, for fuck's sake, don't say that you're starting to like me. I don't think I could handle that.'

'No, I wouldn't go that far. I was thinking that whatever Aion you have been touched by has more than a hint of the trickster about it.'

'Thanks. I think.'

6

They hopped off the freight train just as it was rolling into the centre of town and disappeared into the labyrinth of warehouses and sidings. They found a pawn shop run by a tiny old woman with three sets of spectacles on her head and the haggling skills of a rottweiler, from whom they got probably a quarter of what Bobby's loot was worth. It was still enough for them to approach the captain of an independent courier 'stat called the *Balthus,* who was prepared to offer them no-questions passage to the Schorle Group. His wife was

Dravanese, with no love for Elbaite, and as long as Bobby and Foulkes weren't carrying state secrets or anything which would get him into more trouble than he could bribe his way out of if they were found, he was fine with that. And so by midnight the two men found themselves bedding down exhaustedly in the cramped aft quarters of an airship, surrounded by bags and bundles not much different to the freight-car in which they'd started the day.

CHAPTER 24

Oceans Burning

1

The journey to Schorle was a slow, zig-zagging affair, as the *Balthus'* captain gave a wide berth to the palls of smoke which hung here and there over the Archipelago, flagging the conflict between the Elbaite and Amity forces as clearly as warning signs. On the 'stat's navigational charts, the Captain pointed out Sibbik, principal island of the Schorle Group, which so far had remained free of the fighting.

'That's because there's nothing to fight over,' he said. 'Not unless they start fighting with fish, at any rate. No timber, no coal, no metals. These people are traders.'

Schorle was not a single island but a chain – both figuratively and literally. A period of intense undersea volcanic activity half a millennia ago had ejected tens of thousands of cubic feet of pumice, which had accreted on the surface in huge rafts, caught in the strange currents of the Archipelago and stirred into ever-shifting fantastical loops and swirls as they were colonised by vegetation and animal life. Human migration followed and stabilised the rafts with earth and lime, forming a solid base for towns to grow, and as the small communities evolved into a nation, they made their political and cultural links a physical reality by connecting themselves together by huge chains, each link as big as a warship, and anchoring themselves to the sea bed against storms and tides. On paper, Sibbik looked like the spiralling foam on a cup of coffee dozens of miles across.

'My god,' breathed Bobby. 'And we thought we were so clever, on our little Stray.'

'There is nothing you can build that nature does not already have copyright on,' remarked Foulkes. Bobby couldn't tell whether he was agreeing with him or not.

Neither of them got the opportunity to see it from the air, because a few hours later, the *Balthus* began to descend towards the apparently empty ocean. Foulkes marched onto the bridge and demanded to know what was happening. In response, the Captain pointed to a line of dots in the air above the horizon. 'That's the Amity barrage,' he said. 'Big sentry 'stats tethered to warships. Not the front line yet, but it won't be long. They're going to stop me to check my papers, and if you're on board, they're going to arrest you for not having any. Passengers on 'stats are always checked. Them's on boats, almost never – especially if they're refugee boats.' He pointed down, where they could now see the shape of a large sailing vessel which they were approaching. She was riding low in the water, her decks crammed fore and aft with hundreds of human figures, many of whom had seen the *Balthus* and were pointing upwards and waving.

'Now wait just a moment,' protested Foulkes. 'We paid you to get us to Schorle, not foist us off on a bunch of pirates the moment things get a bit tricky!'

'Mister,' said the Captain, 'if the barrage guards find you and decide that you're Elbaite spies, they'll confiscate my papers, impound my ship and probably execute me along with you. That's a bit trickier than I'm comfortable with. You can come down nice and polite and let me pay those pirates to give you passage, or you can jump from here with my gun up your arse and hope that they do it out of the kindness of their hearts. Your choice.'

The *Balthus* moored to the top of the refugee vessel's main mast, and they climbed down towards the deck, where a circle of the ship's crew were keeping the foot of the mast clear of refugees with sticks and guns to prevent them from swarming back up it and mobbing the airship. The noise and stench of the mass of desperate humanity engulfed them; it was like climbing down into a third-world football stadium.

Bobby and Foulkes stood by mutely, feeling like cattle as the two captains discussed them and thick wads of currency changed hands. Then they parted, and the *Balthus* prepared to cast off. Several of the more desperate or brave refugees attempted to rush the mast anyway, but they were beaten back brutally by the crew and ended up being carried away by their friends, bleeding and moaning. The two newcomers watched the airship dwindle into the heavens, and then their new captain came swaggering towards them. He was lean-muscled and carried a long-handled bill hook slung over one shoulder.

'Sir...' began Foulkes.

Bobby cuffed him. 'Shut up!' he hissed. 'Keep your eyes down. Don't antagonise him.'

Foulkes shot him a poisonous look but did as he was told.

The captain regarded them with lazy contempt. 'You two are different,' he sneered. 'I don't like that.'

They kept their mouths shut and stared at the deck while he walked around them.

'I like this, though,' he added, and plucked the talisman out from Bobby's shirt.

'Hey! No! *No!*' Bobby yelled, trying to pull it away. His reward was the handle of the bill hook slamming into his guts, and it doubled him up, wheezing. The captain yanked the talisman free with a snap, and reversed the hook, aiming its point at the exposed nape of Bobby's neck.

'Wait!' Unbelievably, Foulkes was shielding him, one hand raised protectively, but also waving the wrist-watch he wore there. 'Take this! We're no trouble! No trouble! Take it!'

Scowling, the captain took the watch. 'I'd have taken this anyway,' he said, but he was turning away all the same. 'Make sure your friend behaves, or I'll see if you have any expensive fillings too.' He strolled away, examining his new trinkets, while Foulkes helped Bobby limp away to safety.

'Don't say it,' Bobby groaned.

'I wasn't going to. I think we should just find a patch of deck and settle down out of everybody's way.'

This was easier said than done. People sat or sprawled over every available square yard of deck; shade was fought over, as precious a commodity as water. Families huddled together protectively, the children staring around with wide eyes and crying for food which their exhausted parents didn't have; groups of young men sat in sullen circles, plotting impotent rebellion; elderly couples rocked together, fanning each others' faces. Almost everyone had some kind of injury – burns, bullet-wounds, broken limbs – not all of which were bandaged. As they stepped carefully between people, looking for a space, Bobby and Foulkes saw at least three corpses being thrown overboard. They ended up squashed head-to-tail between a father who was pleading with them for something in a language neither of them understood, and a scrawny girl who was keeping very tight hold of a squirming piglet which was obviously her family's last and most prized possession.

Bobby nudged Foulkes and gestured around. 'How's this for your efficient civilising catalyst, then?'

'Oh, shut up,' Foulkes muttered. 'That watch was given to me by the Duke of Westminster.'

2

The curving channels of open water between Sibbik's solid arms were busy with ships, most of them carrying refugees. As they arrived, Bobby saw fishing ketches, skiffs, scows, dinghies, and tramp steamers – all crammed from one rail to another with hollow-eyed humanity, faces tear-streaked through the soot from their burned homes, clutching pathetic armfuls of belongings. He also saw many war vessels flying Amity colours: stars against a blue field, topped with Schorle's triangle of three linked chains.

Before they'd departed, Foulkes had sent a clatter message to the Hegemony representative of this island state whom he claimed he could trust – insofar as he could trust anyone –

who met them at the landing spire and introduced herself as Chancellor Qavram. Bobby felt a familiar impotent sympathy when he saw the rifles with which her escorting soldiers were armed. They were going to be hopelessly outclassed by what Elbaite was bringing. It was only a matter of time.

Her exchange with Foulkes was terse; it was obvious that she had more than enough on her hands dealing with the influx of refugees and that two more from the Realt only added further complications. Bobby didn't know what it was that Foulkes offered her. He didn't care. He was content to play the part of Foulkes' prisoner just so long as it got him back into the Interstitial Assembly Chamber, and suffered being handcuffed, knowing that arguing would do him no good. It never had. The only thing that he'd ever been able to do which had made the slightest bit of difference was to fight, so he kept his temper and waited.

3

Bobby knew that he shouldn't have been surprised by the sight of Chancellor Qavram's door – there was no reason why they should all have looked as unassuming as Jowett's – but it took him aback for a moment all the same. It was at least eight foot high, reinforced by ornate metal bands like a pirate's chest and dozens of locks of every shape and configuration.

Qavram produced a large metal hoop bristling with dozens – possibly even hundreds – of keys, and selected one which was so ordinary looking as to be indistinguishable from the others. She unlocked the door. He suspected that it would do no good trying to remember which key opened which lock, as it was probably a different one every time. 'The Committee for Ontological Contiguity is currently in recess,' she said. 'You have a short time to cross the meniscus back to your own realm. Move swiftly and do not get caught. These soldiers are not just for your prisoner, Foulkes. Deal or not, you will die before I allow you to imperil my position.'

Foulkes bowed. 'Always a pleasure, my dear lady.' He turned to Bobby and pushed him towards the opening. 'Come on, hero. Let's get you home.'

He had imagined that it would be one thing to visit the Interstitial Assembly Chamber in his dream but quite another to see it with waking eyes, yet it looked exactly the same, and it brought home to him how little difference there really was between the two states of consciousness. The Chamber was just as empty as when Jowett had shown it to him and Allie, but it bore signs of recent occupation. In the tiered stalls of the Tourmaline side, jackets hung on the backs of chairs, and cardboard files and large leather-bound books were stacked on side-tables. The crumpled end of a freshly-stubbed out cigarette still smoked in a heavy glass ash tray. On the Realt side, a projector screen was scrolling through a screensaver slide-show of someone's holiday snaps from somewhere Nordic-looking. All mundane enough, were it not for the silently roaring rainbow wall which separated the two halves, and the circular stone altar which stood at the exact centre.

Again, none of this interested him; somewhere behind one of the many other doors curving to right and left of him was the one which led to Jowett's office, and Carden, and Allie.

There: he could even see which one it was.

'Move.' Foulkes pushed him again, and they started down the steps toward the Chamber floor while Qavram's soldiers stayed close to their door. He heard the dim murmuring of distant voices behind closed doors. A laugh, a clink of glass. The committee was in recess.

Plush carpet gave way to stone, and he was at the bottom, facing the barrier between worlds. Oneirocline, Jowett had called it. As thin as a thought and at the same time wide enough to imprison gods.

He stopped.

'I can't do this,' he said.

'Very funny,' replied Foulkes. 'Move.' He was shoved again.

Bobby spun to face him.

'A couple of weeks ago, a man asked me what I would be prepared to do to be with the woman I love again. I told him that I would tear apart the world with my bare hands and watch it burn, and I stand by that. I don't care about your Aions. I don't care about this Toren arsehole and what he may or may not be capable of. As far as I'm concerned, you're all welcome to each other.'

'You have a responsibility...'

'To her – yes. To *you*?' He laughed in Foulkes' face. 'To the world? Sorry, but I can't carry that. It's too big.' He pushed past Foulkes, who tried to grab hold of him. Bobby pistoned his elbow out as hard as his handcuffs would allow and connected with Foulkes' jaw – who cried out and fell on his backside, nursing a split lip. Bobby pursued, planted a foot in his chest and shoved him flat to the floor. Then he gave Foulkes another, much harder kick in the meat of his thigh. Foulkes screamed and twisted.

Bobby knelt down beside him. 'Uncuff me, or I'll just kick you unconscious right here and do it myself.'

With trembling fingers, Foulkes obeyed.

Bobby tossed the cuffs away. 'That's the last time I let any of you bastards do that to me. Now piss off and go run your little world.' He started back up the stairs towards Jowett's door and the Schorle soldiers, who raised their rifles at him in alarm.

'Don't be a fool!' Foulkes shouted. His chin and teeth were shiny with blood. 'I will find her! I will find her in the real world, and I will make her kill you herself!'

'Maybe,' said Bobby and carried on climbing until he was within a foot of the lead rifleman's gun.

'They will shoot you, you know!'

'Maybe,' he repeated. 'Maybe they're smarter than that. Because I don't think gun shots and Schorle troops violating the neutrality of the Interstitial Assembly Chamber would be a very good idea, do you? All those Committee people in recess, running to see what the fuss is about. You know what would happen then.' He wasn't talking to Foulkes now, but to the man in front of him: another human being, with human imperfections, like a scar over one eyebrow and a mole on one cheek. There was a wedding ring on the hand holding the rifle barrel. 'Every Hegemony state in both worlds would send troops through that door to punish the idiot who gave that order. Yes, alive I may be a security risk, that's true. But if you shoot me, the Hegemony will make war on your home, and what's happening in the Archipelago is going to look like a pub brawl in comparison. I'm no threat to you. All I want to do – all I've *ever* wanted to do – is just get home to my woman and my baby. Let me go. Please.'

The rifleman's eyes narrowed slightly. Bobby held his breath.

The rifle barrel twitched fractionally sideways: *Go*.

Bobby went.

4

He found the door to Jowett's office in Oraille and knocked. He had no way of knowing if there was anybody on the other side to hear, or if he could be heard at all, but he did it anyway.

Nothing.

He knocked again, louder. He expected the soldiers to change their minds at any moment; there were quieter ways of dealing with him. A knife was what he feared, and the skin between his shoulder-blades crawled. He looked back, but Foulkes had taken advantage of the distraction to hobble back into the Realt; all his bluffs called, all his lies spent.

Still nothing.

Bobby thumped, rattling the door in its frame. Further down the Chamber, a side door opened, out of which came a group of men and women, chatting in low tones as they moved to retake their seats. He saw the riflemen slip away quietly through their own door. Nobody had seen him for the moment, but moments were all he had. He pressed his forehead to the wood, not daring to knock again.

'Please,' he whispered. 'Somebody, for God's sake, please…'

The door opened, and he fell inward, catching himself at the last second. The young woman on the other side blinked in astonishment, and Bobby smiled weakly. 'Hello, Miss Fortescue,' he said. 'Is your boss in? I don't have an appointment, I'm afraid.' And he collapsed over the threshold.

CHAPTER 25

HOME

1

'Runce is safe,' said Jowett, hanging up his coat. 'I've just had word.'

'Oh, thank God for that,' said Allie, pouring tea for them both. 'So what do we do now?'

Another day, another home. She had refused to return to her rooms at Beldam, and there was no way Crowthorpe was going to allow her back under his roof, even with the threat of Foulkes' assassin removed. Jowett had pulled a few strings and found an apartment for her in the same building as Angela Fortescue, who had been only too happy to take Allie under her fiercely protective wing. It was small, but neat and clean, and a good start, she'd decided. And here she was, making tea for her very first visitor.

'We deal with Foulkes properly,' replied Jowett, sipping. 'Now that Runce has given us the information we need.'

'That would be the royal "we", I assume.'

'I'm sorry?'

'Me! What about me? What do I do now?'

'You?' he blinked in surprise. 'Well, after we've sorted out the Foulkes situation, you settle down here in Carden and receive the best hospitality and pre-natal care that a grateful Oraille can offer. This...' he waved around at the apartment. '...this is just temporary.'

'Yeah, it always seems to be,' she mused. 'I don't know, I quite like it here. Just so long as I agree to be poked and prodded by your Collegium pals so they can find out what makes me tick, right?'

'Your *voluntary* cooperation with the Department would certainly be most welcome in assisting us in finding new ways to combat subornation, yes, but it is not a prerequisite.'

'And I'm supposed to simply trust you on that.'

'Allie, I would have thought that by now every day of your continued existence in my world proves that you can trust me, when there could be all sorts of awkward questions raised about why I've let you stay so long.'

'You did tez me,' she pointed out. 'How did you know that it wouldn't send me back?'

'I didn't. I hoped.'

'But you took the chance anyway.'

He met her gaze squarely. 'Yes. Yes I did.'

'Hmm. Still think you're not a cold-blooded son of a bitch?'

He conceded the point with a rueful little nod and a sip of tea.

'I'll tell you what I'm not going to do,' she continued, leaning forward. 'I'm not going to be *cared for*. I'm not going to let you or anybody else shut me up in a five-star prison cell like some kind of VIP freak while you all wait to see what pops out of me in nine months.' She put her hand protectively to her belly. 'I'm certainly not going to sit around with my life on hold, waiting for Mr Robert Andrew Michael Jenkins to find his way back, if he ever does.

'I'm going to come and work for the DCS.'

She was rewarded with what she had come to realise was a very rare expression on Jowett's face: dumbstruck surprise.

'I'll start at the bottom, don't worry – making the coffee, fetching the mail, that kind of thing. I'll train; I'm not such an old dog that I can't learn a few new tricks. Those tez guns look pretty simple to me. Can you imagine how awesome I'd be as a lucid dreaming counter-subornation agent?'

'Are you…' Jowett swallowed. 'Is this a job interview?'

'I guess so. And before you mention the fact that I'm pregnant, I should warn you there are laws against that kind of discrimination.'

'Not in my world, there aren't.'

'Well maybe I might do something about that, too. Does the name Emily Pankhurst ring any bells?'

'Only alarm ones.'

'So do I get the job?'

He sighed and rubbed his face. 'I don't imagine that I have much option, do I? I think we can start you somewhere considerably higher than the mail room, however.'

She smiled. 'That will be most satisfactory, Director Jowett. Would you like a piece of cake?'

They ate in companionable silence for a while, until she asked 'So now that we know Runce is okay, what happens next?'

'The Hegemony has very strict laws and procedures, for obvious reasons,' Jowett explained. 'The most dangerous thing that an operative or, Reason forbid, a Regional Supervisor can do is to wilfully subvert those procedures. Clearly, Foulkes has been doing this on the most egregious scale, and with the evidence we have, I am confident that I can successfully pass a motion censuring him for gross procedural non-compliance.'

'Wow,' she deadpanned. 'I bet he's just wetting himself with terror.'

Jowett ignored this. 'He'll be physically executed, of course.'

'Oh, of course.'

'But obviously with the stakes so high, the punishments are that much more extreme. In this case, nothing short of a complete existential excommunication.'

'Okay, now *that* sounds bad.'

'It's something of an administrative chore, but it can be done. What makes it particularly unpleasant is that it involves redacting the condemned from the memories of anyone and everyone who might have known them. Some individuals are so powerful that they continue to exert a strong and dangerous fascination even after death, and those ripples can be very tiresome to deal with. Copycat killers, neo-Nazis, religious martyrs – you know the sort of thing.'

'So how do you do that?'

'After they are executed, we feed their blood to the Aions.'

She waited for him to crack a smile, wink, indicate in some way that it was just a joke. But he didn't.

'Shit,' she said.

'Indeed. You know of course that the Aions reach out in their ageless sleep and insinuate themselves into our dreams, briefly taking on the forms of the gods they once were?'

'Oh, yeah, that old chestnut. Who doesn't?'

'Well, with the rare taste of a living soul in their mouths, they will hunt down every trace and echo of that soul and devour it – every memory, every recollection, every dream, every piece of gossip, hearsay and rumour, every dim sense of vague recognition – like a starving dog licking the smell out of an empty bowl. Simple physical death is not enough, do you understand? He must also die in the minds and dreams of everyone who ever knew him – only that way can the damage he has wrought be prevented from worsening.'

'Not to mention that it is one hell of a deterrent.'

'There is also that, yes.'

'That's a really horrible punishment, on so many levels. So!' she clapped her hands and rubbed them together. 'Let's get that administrative ball rolling, shall we?'

2

Allie spent the most of the next day shadowing Miss Fortescue and learning the basics of how the DCS worked, while Jowett disappeared to make whatever arcane arrangements were required for an existential excommunication. As she was reading through a basic primer on Oraillean history, Miss Fortescue put her pen down, looked around with a conspiratorial air and leaned across.

'Miss Owens, can I ask you a question?'

'Of course – on one condition.'

'What's that?'

'For the love of God, drop the Miss Owens crap. It's Allie, or no answers for you.'

'Very well, then. Alison.'

'A fair compromise. You may continue with your question.'

Angela looked around again, plainly nervous, and dropped her voice so low that Allie could barely hear it. 'Working for Director Jowett, I see a lot of things pass across my desk that I am forbidden to discuss with normal people. But you're not, that is to say, I, um…'

'It's okay, no offence taken. I'm not normal. Normality is highly overrated, as far as I'm concerned.'

'Thank you. Once I saw a postcard picture of a building in your world, the Realt. It was most peculiar – not really a building, not with walls and rooms and windows – more of a structure. It had a very wide arched base and the sides, well, they curved inwards and upwards so that the top was very tall and thin, like an aerostat spire. It was so odd-looking, it seemed that it should be very well-known, and I wondered: have you heard of such a thing?'

Allie was grinning. 'The Eiffel Tower, yes, I've heard of it. It's in a city called Paris, in a country called France. I've never been there, though. It's supposed to be very romantic. And very expensive.'

'Paris,' said Angela thoughtfully, trying out the unfamiliar name. 'France. I should dearly love to see it. It seems a shame that such travel is impossible.'

'I wouldn't grieve over it too much. I've seen things in your world that top anything in mine. Still, the grass is always greener on the other side, as they say.'

'We say, the sky is always bluer from your lover's bedroom window.'

'Honey, with sayings like that, I think you'd love Paris.'

'I…' She stopped and cocked her head towards Jowett's office door. 'Did you hear something?'

'I hope not. I thought he was out.'

'He is.' Angela took her keys and listened at the door. 'It sounds like someone knocking.' She unlocked the door and opened it a crack, peering into the darkened office. Allie could hear the knocking now, coming from further inside. It sounded like someone was stuck inside a closet. Seeing that the office was empty, Angela opened the door wider. The knocking became a heavy thumping, and they could now both hear quite clearly that it was coming from the door to the Interstitial Assembly Chamber.

'Get the guard,' she whispered, and Allie ran to obey.

When she returned with two armed guardsmen, Angela was standing by the Chamber door, ready to open it. She looked back at Allie and raised her eyebrows questioningly. Allie nodded. The door opened.

A raggedly-dressed man fell inward and collapsed at her feet. 'Hello, Miss Fortescue,' he said. 'Is your boss in? I don't have an appointment, I'm afraid.'

Allie stared. *Bobby?!'*

He was dressed against the cold in a long coat and a woollen beanie hat pulled right down to his eyebrows, grinning like an idiot on Christmas Day.

She threw herself at him and wrapped her arms as tightly as she could around him, feeling him clutch her hard to himself in return. There were no kisses – kisses were for later, that and more besides. For the moment it was necessary for each to reassure themselves of the simply physical solidity of the other.

'Hang on…' She pulled back and examined his face. 'You're not dreaming yourself here again, are you? You are *all* here?'

'All here, ma'am, present and correct.'

But something hadn't felt right when she's had her face buried in his shoulder.

She yanked the hat off his head. 'Jesus Christ, Bobby, what have you done to your hair?'

Foulkes limped through the Chamber door and into his Whitehall Office, heading straight for his desk. He hurt in half a dozen places, and he was pretty sure that bastard Jenkins had knocked one of his teeth loose, but medical attention could come later. There were plenty of other things he should have done, too; tracks to be covered, traces to be kicked over, loose ends to be cut and cauterised. The biggest, of course, was Ketterley. The loss of the Typhoons could easily be attributed to a training flight accident, and the seismic trace of the explosions to a minor earthquake; the biggest headache was missing-persons contingencies which needed to be activated for dozens of dead personnel. Even tracking down and eliminating the araka-spawn responsible for it all was nothing compared to the imperative of maintaining his invisibility. Yes, there were many things which needed to be done. But as he licked the blood from his wobbling tooth, the only item on his personal to-do list was to track down Jenkins' lover, the woman from Stray, and make sure that she died in the most painful and humiliating manner possible.

The problems began when he logged on to his computer. His desktop was completely empty. With mounting disbelief and rage, he discovered that there were no files, not even empty folders, no shortcuts, no drive icons – nothing. He was shut out of online accounts for everything from Amazon to the govsys intranet, which refused his password three times and then froze him out permanently. Even his darknet accounts seemed to have been suspended, which was impossible. The only thing that still worked was his email, in which a single unread message sat, marked urgent. It was simple and stark:

IAC Regional Supervisor Martin Matthew Foulkes: access to resources suspended, pending investigation by the Office of Procedural Compliance, in response to a petition of grievance raised by Director Timothy Jowett, DCS. Failure to comply with the requirements of the Office will result in immediate existential excommunication.

The details of Jowett's petition were appended in an attachment, of which he read no further than the first paragraph before hurling his monitor across the room with a shriek of fury.

'*Resources?!*' he screamed at it. 'You want to see resources do you, you officious little prick?'

He snatched up the desk phone and punched numbers as if he could stab through its plastic casing.

It was answered with a cautious 'Hello?'

'Croft!' he snapped. 'It's Foulkes. Get your arse in here now!'

'Sorry to have to disappoint you, Mr Foulkes,' said Croft's voice, 'but Croft isn't currently available to take your call. I'm Officer Runceforth, Carden DCS, and I'd be only too happy to take a message for you, with Director Jowett's compliments.'

This time, Foulkes' scream of rage was loud enough to rattle the windows. He slammed the phone down and sent it in the same direction as the monitor, followed by the lamp, his in-trays – whose contents flew everywhere – and the chair, then stood in the ruins of his office, panting and staring around with wild eyes like a pursued animal finally at bay.

'Not on your terms,' he growled, his voice hoarse. '*Never* on your terms.'

Cut off from every resource and abandoned by every ally, Foulkes knew who he could finally, ultimately turn to.

4

She had him. Allie had her man inside her again, in her bed, in her home, and everything was well. The first time was quick, overwhelming them both with the simple need for flesh to know flesh. Later, she stroked the fuzzy stubble on his scalp while he kissed the bruises on her throat, and she counted his wounds and made him tell her how he'd come by each one, and then he did the same with her, and all the while they moved in slowly spiralling circles around and inside each other, until the time came when their stories were told and the only things left to say came in gasps of heated breath, and they lay together again.

'You know what?' Bobby said, looking around. 'I think this is the first time we've done it in an actual bed.'

'Ah, the sweet romance of it all,' Allie answered. 'Tell me, does the sky look bluer than normal to you out that window?'

'What?'

'Never mind,' she said and snuggled closer.

'How is... everything else?' he asked, stroking her stomach.

'Fine, as far as I can tell. It's still very early. But that's not what you're asking, is it? You want to know whether or not I've decided to keep it.'

She heard him swallow hard. 'Have you?'

'Here's the truth of things, Bobby. Doctors reckon that up to a fifth of pregnancies spontaneously miscarry in the best of circumstances, and that goes double for women over forty, so this whole thing is just a big lottery to begin with. I might not get any say in the matter anyway. When Jowett tezzed me and I was nearly sent back, someone in here hung on, so I've decided to leave it up to him or her to decide how badly they want to be here, and take it from there.'

'Oh-kay,' he said cautiously. 'Sounds reasonable.'

'No, it's a big cop-out!' she laughed. 'But it's a cop-out I'm comfortable with, so it'll have to do. I'm making a place for myself here, Bobby. What will you do, now that you're back?'

It was his turn to laugh. 'Bloody hell! I've only just got here, and that was difficult enough. The furthest I can see at the moment is where my next cup of tea is coming from.'

'It's right over there, in the kettle,' she said. 'Go on!' And started to push him out of bed.

CHAPTER 26

THE ADMINISTRATOR

1

There was activity at the centre of the Interstitial Assembly Chamber. Three grey-smocked technicians were installing a large mechanical device on the circular altar, moving back and forth through the meniscus as if it wasn't there while they tightened bolts and installed components. It was a wide hoop of brass approximately a yard in height, fashioned in the form of a dragon swallowing its own tail at the apex. A complex system of gears and counterweights governed its rotation both vertically and horizontally, which the technicians were adjusting, calibrating, oiling and spinning through the range of its movement. At rest, it was bisected exactly by the meniscus.

Their work was overseen by a woman – or that was Bobby's first impression, because as she spotted them and came closer and he saw the flat chest and boyish features, he became less sure. Yet he, or she, or whatever they were, moved with a grace which would have shamed a male ballet dancer.

Jowett bowed. 'Administrator.'

The Administrator of Procedural Compliance bowed in return. 'Director Jowett. I received your somewhat hastily composed petition.' The voice wasn't giving Bobby any clues either, pitched somewhere between a teenage boy and a female newsreader. 'You level serious accusations against Supervisor Foulkes.'

'Yes, Administrator, I do.'

'Yet only recently you yourself were found to be principally culpable for the breach caused by the demon Lilivet, who was one of your agents – a finding due in no small part to Supervisor Foulkes' report into the matter. One might consider your petition to be simply a bit of vexatious tit-for-tat mud-slinging. Many in the Assembly might.'

'Administrator, I am not in the habit of risking my own life to call someone names,' responded Jowett a little stiffly. 'If I want to do that, I'll pick up the phone.'

Bobby nudged Allie and whispered, 'What's all this about risking his own life?'

She shrugged. 'Search me.'

'In addition to which,' the Administrator continued, 'you present as your principal witness this Alison Owens: a lucid, suborning dreamer who should have been returned to the Realt the moment she was discovered.'

Allie gave a little wave. 'Hello, actually in the room here.'

Jowett winced.

The Administrator ignored her. 'Frankly, I would dismiss this petition out of hand, were it not for the fact that what you have accused him of is so serious that the merest possibility of it being true demands investigation. Even if you are successful, you will still have to answer for her existence.'

Jowett smiled his wry smile. 'Be assured, Administrator, if I am not eaten body and soul by the Aions, I will gladly have my knuckles rapped for Ms Owens.'

'And I'm *still* in the room,' she muttered.

The Administrator turned and regarded her with cool, grey eyes. 'Forgive me for what must seem discourtesy to you. It is unusual enough for anyone not a member of the Assembly to be here, let alone someone in your condition.'

'Exactly which condition might that be?'

'Well, exactly.' The Administrator's gaze flicked down to her midriff and back. 'What has Director Jowett offered you in return for your testimony?'

'Amnesty,' replied Jowett.

'I was addressing Ms Owens,' said the Administrator casually, but Jowett fell silent and took a step backward as if slapped.

'What he said,' replied Allie. 'A home for myself, and my man here, and our child. Don't tell me you haven't done it before. I understand your whole policy of keeping the two worlds separate, and it's not as if I don't have ties in the Realt, but going back there in the state my body's in – frankly, I'd rather die than live like that again.'

'You understand that may happen soon enough in any event?' the Administrator pointed out. 'Your life is tied to that other body; you cannot expect it to survive much more than a few years, even with the Realt's best medical attention.'

Allie nodded. 'I understand that too. I guess what I'm looking for is a short-term residency visa rather than full citizenship.'

'Don't talk that way,' said Bobby, grimacing.

'Why not?' she said to him. 'It's the truth. Please don't be holding out for a happily-ever-after, Bobby, because I'm sorry, love, it's just not on the cards.' She turned back to the Administrator. 'So what about it then? Does my testimony get me a place on your cosmic witness relocation programme?'

The Administrator nodded. 'Of course.'

'And one more thing,' added Bobby.

The others turned to stare at him.

'The war,' he added. 'It stops now.'

One of the Administrator's eyebrows arched slightly. 'Which one?'

'Don't be bloody clever. You know exactly which one. In the Archipelago. Call off the Elbaite invasion of the islands.'

'Bobby…' began Jowett.

'Mr Jenkins,' said the Administrator coolly, 'as important as I'm sure you think you are, the political recalibration of that region cannot be simply "called off", as you put it, even if we wanted to. Far too many complex historical and cultural factors have been at play for far too long. The cultural heterogeneity of the Archipelago – with all its fragmented languages, beliefs and customs, all rubbing up against each other and fraying holes in the fabric of the meniscus – is a fundamental threat to the successful propagation of Hegemony. It is no coincidence that when Stray appeared it did so just there. The uniformity conferred by becoming part of the Elbaite Maritime Protectorate is in itself nothing more than a stopgap measure – a darn in that fabric, if you will – until Oraille is in a position to take its place as a truly global influence and provide a more rational, secular framework.'

'Yeah,' said Bobby. 'Foulkes said something like that too. And in the meantime, thousands of innocent people have to die, do they?'

'Yes. If it's any consolation, exactly the same thing has been happening in the Realt for centuries too. You are aware of the stakes, I take it?'

'Oh, don't give me that end-justifying-the-means crap.'

'Mr Jenkins, shall I tell you what happened the last time such a view as yours held sway in the Assembly? World War One. All those little Balkan states squabbling with each other over ethnic and religious feuds which were allowed to fester by a weak laissez-faire Assembly too afraid to sacrifice the few for the many, dragging everybody else down with them. It took a Depression, six more years of war and two atomic bombs for your civilisation to claw itself back from the brink of another dark age. It will not be permitted to happen again.

'I am given to understand from Director Jowett that you have something of a talent for playing one side off against another, Mr Jenkins. Please understand, however, that in this matter you have nothing with which to play. You are being offered amnesty and nothing more. See to your nearest and dearest and leave the governance of reality to those who are better qualified.'

As Bobby opened his mouth, Allie clenched her hand around his tight enough to make the bones creak, and his retort emerged as a squeak of pain.

'For once in your life,' she hissed out of the corner of her mouth, 'just keep it zipped, okay honey?'

The Administrator regarded the three of them. 'If we are in agreement, then?'

Nobody said a thing.

'Good.'

One of the technicians approached, carrying two locked wooden boxes. The Administrator produced a key, opened them both, revealing in each one a faceted glass vial filled with red liquid.

'Is that what I think it is?', asked Bobby.

Jowett took one of the vials and held it up to the light as if inspecting a glass of wine. 'Everyone elected to the Interstitial Assembly must supply a sample of their blood,' he explained. 'So that the Aions will recognise them. This one is mine. The other belongs to Foulkes. They will both be held in the balance of the Assembly's judgement when my petition is heard, and whichever of us the Assembly finds against will have his blood fed to the Aions.'

The dragon's fore and hind claws formed receptacles at two o'clock and ten o'clock on the circle of its body, into each of which the Administrator set one of the vials. 'On this side, Jowett. On the other, Foulkes. The scales of the ourobouros are weighted, and detachable. When the Assembly has heard each man's case, they will vote for who they believe to be guilty by removing a scale from that side of the device. The imbalance will cause the accused's blood to rotate higher and higher until, if enough scales are removed, it sits fully in the meniscus. Once that happens, and the Aions acquire the taste of that blood, it is only a matter of time before they locate the condemned and remove him from the circles of the world.'

In response to Bobby's and Allie's expressions of disbelief, the Administrator gave a tiny apologetic shrug. 'As I say, we normally prefer to do this kind of thing by committee.'

'Wait,' protested Allie, 'so, if the Assembly finds in favour of Foulkes, Jowett takes the punishment? That's insane!'

'It is one of the oldest of laws,' said the Administrator. 'That the justice you deal be the justice you face.'

'It's barbaric!'

The Administrator's demeanour turned cold. 'Since it is also the means by which you hope to secure safety for yourself and your loved ones, I suggest that you make an effort to accommodate yourself to its ancient wisdom.'

'In other words,' Bobby whispered in her ear, as the Administrator stalked away, 'keep it zipped, honey.'

3

The ventilation shaft's iron cover spun to the ground with a heavy clang. Foulkes put his crowbar to one side and peered down into the square black hole he'd just revealed. Nearly two hundred feet below the streets of Birmingham lay the warren of tunnels and chambers that was called simply the Anchor Exchange, built during the height of fifties Cold War paranoia – a combined nuclear bunker and hardened telephone exchange which had already been obsolete by the time it was finished. Those of its entrances which had not been bricked over in the following decades were securely watched, but there were still half a dozen ventilation shafts which rose above ground level like squat towers in alleyways, parks, patches of waste ground and the backs of delivery yards, protected by their very ubiquity. The invisibility of the bland had always been the Hegemony's first and best line of defence, but in this case it was going to be their own undoing, because there was nobody to stop Foulkes from gaining access now.

Rungs of an access ladder disappeared into darkness. After one final look around, he climbed in and began his long descent.

Unaccustomed to physical exercise and fatigued by his adventures in the Archipelago, his arms and legs were trembling by the time he reached the bottom. He kicked the grating out from beneath his feet and dropped into the service tunnel below, landing clumsily in a pool of frigid water. His torch picked out curving concrete walls lined deeply on both sides with giant cables, conduits and pipes; these upper levels of the complex were still used for the city's communications infrastructure. The araka-spawn wouldn't be here. They would be deeper, having crawled in from the tunnels which connected to the Mailbox and gone to ground like the wounded animals they were. He set off in the direction of the city centre, where he hoped that the lower levels were still accessible.

He whistled the theme from 'Dad's Army' cheerily as he went; there was no point in pretending to hide from them. *Who do you think you are kidding, Mr Hitler, if you think we're on the run?* Ah, there was wisdom in the classics.

He passed through wide, echoing chambers where banks of ancient telephone exchanges sat in the dark, rusting away quietly; others where stacks of cardboard boxes, their contents long forgotten, mouldered into each other. He walked along balconies which looked out onto lightless abysses, down metal staircases and past heavy pressure doors like the ones in submarines, and finally found a shaft leading even deeper. Below, he could hear the sound of rushing water. Heavy industry, with its thirst for water, had declined in the decades since this complex had been built, and the lower levels had been left to flood.

That image came back to him again: a constellation of little black stars, floating in the canal around Maddox's hollowed-out corpse.

'We are the boys who will stop your little game,' he sang softly, and began to climb down. 'We are the boys who will make you think again.'

He made it four rungs before something grabbed his ankle and dragged him into the night.

4

'How did you find us?' spat Toren. His face was inches from Foulkes' own, twisted with rage.

'If you break into a man's greenhouse, you'd better not try to hide in his cellar,' answered Foulkes. 'It was obvious. I don't need their computers to find people. I think sometimes they forget that.'

His torch lay some distance away, under three inches of water, but it still cast enough light for him to see the five araka-spawn around him – the rest having either perished at Ketterley or been cannibalised by their stronger brethren. They didn't bother wearing their human shapes any more; the barbed shadows of their limbs coiled and uncoiled around him sinuously like razor wire given life. Only Toren looked remotely normal, but the hand which gripped Foulkes' throat terminated in talons.

'You say "they",' Toren observed.

Foulkes smiled and gave him the key to the Interstitial Assembly Chamber. 'I'm ready to share now.'

CHAPTER 27

EXISTENTIAL EXCOMMUNICATION

1

Bobby watched the delegates of the Interstitial Assembly trickle into the Chamber over the course of an hour and found himself thinking, not for the first time, that this must all be some kind of joke. If someone hadn't told him he was looking at representatives of every conceivable race and culture across two realities he'd have sworn that he was looking at a crowd of middle-ranking Eurocrats enjoying drinks during the interval at an opera.

They mingled and chatted, shaking hands, kissing cheeks, greeting old friends and renewing old jokes, the complacent motorway murmur of easy small-talk between people utterly secure in their power. These couldn't be the people responsible for every major war since the Dark Ages, surely? The ones who dictated the life-spans of religions? They looked like the sort of people who would use calculators to settle the cheque after a restaurant meal.

He didn't see the moment when Foulkes appeared. One moment there was a knot of people in suits laughing over something on the Realt side, and then he was ambling out from them to take his seat by the ourobouros, hands in pockets as if he hadn't a care in the world. He caught Bobby's eye through the meniscus and, unbelievably, winked.

He crooked a finger at Bobby, beckoning. Bobby threw a look of query at the Administrator, who simply shrugged, so he approached Foulkes across the open floor of the Chamber. They stood on other side of the meniscus, with only a metre and yet all of existence between them. Foulkes pitched his voice low, under the hubbub of the settling delegates.

'I know who she is,' he said, indicating Allie.

'It's no use threatening me. I'm not the one putting you on trial.'

'Oh, this isn't a threat. At least, not directly. More a question. You see, I know she's in a coma in the Realt, so I can appreciate why she wants to stay that way.'

'Is there a point hovering anywhere nearby?'

'Only this.' Foulkes reached out to the meniscus and stroked it with his fingertips. It responded in shivering rainbow whorls spreading out from each point of contact like a soap bubble. 'What do you think would happen if this weren't here?'

'You know exactly what would happen. The Aions would...'

'Never mind the Aions!' snapped Foulkes. 'Focus, boy. They are less than nothing to you right now. What would happen to your *lady* if this wasn't here?'

'She'd wake up. She'd die. As you damn well know.'

Foulkes pursed his lips and did a little so-so dance. 'Maybe. Maybe not. Maybe with this gone and no artificial barrier between the two worlds, there would be two of her. Maybe she'd be freed.' Before Bobby could retort, he grinned. 'I'm just putting that out there. You know, to chew over.' And he strolled back to his seat.

2

'Ah, now I think this is someone you both need to meet,' said Jowett, and led Bobby and Allie towards a man and a woman who approached from the Realt side. Bobby didn't recognise either of them. If he'd been the sort of person to read the business papers he might have been able to identify her as the CEO of a multi-billion-dollar corporation with arms into everything from the baby formula to uranium mining.

'Stephanie, my thanks,' said Jowett.

'Thank me later,' she said, and there was something terse in her tone which rang alarm bells. 'When you've dealt with your messenger boy here and his little band of hangers-on.'

'Is something wrong?' asked Bobby.

But Allie was deaf to all of this. Her eyes were locked on the businesswoman's companion: dark-browed and wide-mouthed, with the wiry physique of a long-distance runner or a Hollywood vegan. She rubbed her throat and glared at him. 'You better be who I think you are,' she told him. 'Because meniscus or not, if you're the other guy I'll kill you with my bare hands. It's freaking me out just looking at you.'

He made a face and plucked at his clothes. 'I know, lass,' he growled with distaste. 'Try *being* me.' He nodded at Bobby. 'Jenkins. I never did get my sword back from you.'

Bobby stared. '*Runce?!*'

'In the flesh. So to speak.' His voice dropped with urgency. 'We have to talk.'

'Not yet, you don't,' said a new voice, and Bobby finally saw somebody he *did* recognise.

'Chandler!'

The other man nodded a brief greeting. 'Jenkins. Good to see you're not dead or mad or trapped in someone else. Makes a change in this place. Director Jowett,' he continued, turning his attention away, 'I have in my possession here an employee of yours, by the name of Bill Runce, who I believe has information you want rather badly.' He clapped a proprietary hand on Runce's shoulder. 'I further understand that you have offered me amnesty and a trip home in return for getting this man to you, for which I'm grateful. Nay, touched.'

'That's true,' answered Jowett, who could tell that more was coming. 'Your point being…?'

'It's not enough.'

'Not enough.'

'Not by any means. I also have, under my wing, so to speak, a large number of Passengers who have been pursued, exploited, enslaved, and in some cases deliberately exiled to the Realt by your Hegemony – not to mention the innocent vessels from that world themselves. I want amnesty and return for *all* of them.'

'*All of them?*'

'Every single blessed one of them. This Chamber will be made permanently and irrevocably accessible for free passage to all who find themselves trapped in either world, or you have no witness.'

Jowett turned to Runce. 'Well I rather think that depends on what he has to say about it, doesn't it?'

Runce glared at Jowett through Croft's eyes with such an expression of distaste that for a moment Bobby thought he was going to leap through the meniscus and attack Jowett then and there. 'It was my idea,' he growled.

'But this is madness!' laughed Jowett in disbelief. 'I don't have that kind of authority!'

'You have the authority to put it to your Assembly,' said Chandler. 'That's all we're asking. For now. Oh, and if you're thinking that you can fob me off with some hollow promises or even, God help you, try to detain me in this place, you should know that when we found your little back-channel set-up in Wales I also found a laptop belonging to one of your agents who had very helpfully left it unencrypted.' The easy smile vanished. 'When you say yes to me, you mean it, or I will do damage to the Hegemony that you will not walk away from.'

'Jowett!' snapped Stephanie the CEO. 'Say yes. We can negotiate later. They've already cost me a quarter of a million.'

The expression on the Director's face suggested that the answer was being dug out of his flesh with knives. 'Yes.'

Chandler's face was wreathed in smiles again. 'Great!' He clapped his hands together and rubbed them. 'Right, where can a fellow get a decent drink around here?' He wandered off, slapping backs and shaking hands with Hegemony representatives who stared after the strange little Asian man in the camouflage trousers, mystified.

Runce turned back to Allie and Bobby. 'There's something the pair of you need to know,' he said in a low voice. 'About you, lass. Now.'

Bobby and Allie exchanged fearful glances. 'What is it?' she asked.

Runce shook his head and gestured at himself. 'Not like this.' He stepped back a little, surveying the haze of the meniscus in front of him and taking deep breaths, as if he were a free-diver preparing himself for a world record attempt. 'I don't like this,' he muttered and took a slow step forward. 'It's alright for you bloody half-dream freaks – I've got a pension, you know…' He took another step forward and into the meniscus. There was a moment of distortion, when through the refracted reality of the oneirocline it seemed that he had doubled, and then the old, craggy-headed Runce was stumbling into their arms while the dark-browed man collapsed to the floor on the other side, dispossessed.

Runce gasped in pain. 'Mind the shoulder, dammit!' He turned wondering eyes to Bobby. 'What were those… those *things*? Were they…?'

'Tell you later. Come on, soldier.'

They helped him to a chair, and Allie brought him water. 'So,' she said. 'What is it? What do I need to know?'

Runce sipped and looked at her, and they were shocked to see tears in his eyes. 'Oh, lass,' he whispered and stroked her cheek. 'I'm sorry. Truth to tell in this place, I don't know if this is good news or bad, but all the same I'm sorry. The fact is, my girl, you're dead.'

3

Dead.

She must have misheard. Or it was a threat, and somehow he really was still the assassin or had switched sides. That kind of betrayal would have been preferable.

The questions formed themselves speechlessly on her lips.

'It was Chandler that told me,' he explained. 'I got him to find out where you were – you know, in hospital like you're always saying – so that I could keep an eye on you in case Foulkes tried anything funny. He said that, ah, you died in that world. Four months ago. Peacefully, it seems. No single major cause. Your body just… gave up. Cremated and interred in

Lakewood Cemetery. We checked, double checked, triple checked, but there's no mistake. I'm sorry.'

The chamber, which had been so busy and full of noise a moment ago, was empty to her – vast and echoing. Two words struggled free from her throat and died in the wasteland around her: 'That's impossible.'

But she knew that wasn't true.

'I don't care how many times you checked,' Bobby insisted. 'You're wrong. I mean, she's here! She's fucking right here in front of you! Why would you come back and say such a thing?'

Allie calculated backwards. Four months would put it at the time when she'd accidentally fallen into a worldpool during an ordinary supply run from Stray, woken up, and found herself tied by tubes and machines to the broken shell of her body. The time when she had tried so hard – *so hard*, nobody could comprehend how hard she'd willed her body – to get better, but it just wouldn't, and so she'd given up and come back.

'I killed myself,' she realised. 'But... I didn't.' She turned to Bobby. 'So what am I now? How am I still here? What...?'

What about the baby?

Bobby could only shake his head helplessly.

'You're here,' said Runce. 'Isn't that enough?'

The noise in the chamber increased as consternation erupted at the discovery of Foulkes' assassin lying unconscious in the middle of the Chamber. Then Jowett was there, demanding to know what in Reason's name was going on. She let herself be led numbly as he got them up and drove them out, back into his office in Oraille.

4

'Did you know?' she demanded, advancing on Jowett. 'Oh, of course you knew,' she continued, without waiting for him to answer. 'You got your contacts in the Realt to check me out as soon as you knew what my name was, didn't you? You've known for weeks.'

At least he didn't insult her by trying to lie about it. 'Yes.'

'Then why in God's name *didn't you tell me?*'

'Because there was no need to. I didn't want to upset you; I couldn't *afford* to upset you. There was every possibility that *had* I told you, the trauma would have made you unable to exercise your unique ability to suppress subornation.'

'And you needed that so very fucking much,' she retorted in disgust.

'Yes! Without you we'd never have caught Foulkes' assassin, and he wouldn't be standing trial for his crimes right now!'

'Without me and Runce,' she corrected. 'You used us both.'

'He's an officer in the DCS; it's his job.'

'Aye, but it's not hers,' said Runce. 'You put a civilian woman in harm's way.'

'Don't you start with that,' she threw at him. 'I have no problem putting myself in harm's way. But I will not be lied to, not about something like this. I can't believe that I was going to work for you! I have a family over there, and they've had to watch me die, and I never knew! How could you do that? Don't you have any kind of human feeling left? Come on,' she said to Bobby and headed for the door. 'I've had enough of these people.'

'You can't leave,' Jowett pointed out. 'We made an agreement, remember? Amnesty in return for your evidence.'

'You've got Runce,' she said. 'It's his *job*, remember?'

'And your child?'

She rounded on him, and the force of her fury made objects in the room tremble. 'I would rather give birth in the middle of the fucking ocean than let my child have anything to do with any of you!' she snarled.

'So you were lied to. Welcome to the world.' Jowett's tone was heavy with scornful disappointment. 'Stop acting like a child yourself and take some damned responsibility for what you've seen. That man out there,' he jabbed a finger in the direction of the Chamber, 'puts monsters in children. He used a hradix in a twelve-year old boy as nothing better than a *guard dog*. He infested Sophie Marchant's parents with an araka *just to see what would happen.*'

'You're just part of the same system,' she countered. 'You're no better.'

'*I never said I was!*' he shouted. It was the first time she had ever truly seen him lose his temper, and it dashed cold water on her anger. 'I claim no moral high ground here! I know exactly what I am and I look myself in the mirror every morning and I stand by that! Gods, woman, do you think I actually care whether or not you *like* me? Do you think you are in any position to *judge* me? You are both witnesses to crimes against the innocent, and if you want to accuse me of being complicit in them, then you go ahead and good luck to you, but you *will* stand there and you *will* tell the Assembly what you have seen. You ran away from your own life once, and that was your decision, but you will not run from this. You will not leave him unchallenged and call your precious morality anything other than the selfish wounded pride that it is!'

Jowett finished, scarlet-faced, his chest heaving. Allie stood with her fists clenched by her sides as if she couldn't make up her mind whether or not to tear his head from his shoulders. 'Bobby?' she whispered, her voice hoarse.

'Your call,' he said. 'I'm with you either way.'

Slowly, like pieces of rusted machinery being prised apart, her hands unclenched.

'I'm doing this for Sophie, not for you,' she said to Jowett. 'You and I are done.'

She stalked back into the Chamber, followed by Bobby and Runce. Jowett took a moment to compose himself before he followed. It was a long, long moment.

5

Gradually, like the tapering off of rain, the murmuring of the Assembly ceased. The brass armatures of the Ourobouros gleamed in the lights of the Chamber. The Chief Administrator of Procedural Compliance stood and began.

'Representatives of the Interstitial Assembly. A petition has been raised by Director Timothy Jowett of the Oraillean Department for Counter Subornation against…'

'Excuse me?' interrupted a voice.

It was Foulkes.

He had his hand up.

The Administrator arched an eyebrow at him as fresh murmurs of surprise arose.

'Sorry,' Foulkes continued, 'I'm sure that was going to be a wonderful speech, but no.'

'No? What precisely do you mean by no?'

Foulkes stood and surveyed the Assembly with a smile which was lazy and openly contemptuous. 'What I precisely mean is that if you think we're all going to sit here for weeks and months while this farce of a petition plays itself out then you are all precisely out of your tiny, bureaucratic little minds.'

The murmurs arose to a swell of astonishment and anger.

Bobby nudged Jowett. 'What's he doing?'

'I have no idea,' Jowett replied, his face set with anxiety.

Foulkes' voice rose above the hubbub. 'But I shall make it easier for you all. I confess!' He spread his arms wide in mock surrender and smirked at the room. 'See? All done. I freely confess to all charges laid by Director Jowett, annoying little cocksucker that he is.'

'My god,' whispered Allie to Bobby. 'I think he's drunk.'

'Yes,' Foulkes continued. 'I have maintained an illicit breach of the meniscus through which I have been arming the Elbaite forces with Realt weapons.' He paused and cupped a hand behind his ear. 'What? No howls of protest from Legate Geiran? Wait – he isn't even here? How truly astonishing. But yes, I provided them with overwhelming military superiority in order to shorten a costly and inefficient conflict and get the job done. Yes, I have been employing Passengers in the Realt and taking advantage of their backwash abilities – again, *to get the job done*. The job, ladies and gentlemen, as if you needed reminding, of keeping this thing nice and big and strong.' He gestured at the meniscus – then, to gasps of astonishment and horror, formed a fist and punched straight through it. He waggled his fingers on the other side at Jowett in a sarcastic greeting.

'But it's *not* strong, is it? I mean, look at it. I could take a piss through this thing and nothing would happen. And what good does it do, exactly? Tell me, any of you from Oraille, Jassit, the Amity: have our efforts to shore up this barrier against the tide of subornations – the wars we foster, and the monsters we make – made any difference at all? Let's be truthful to ourselves here, it's just getting worse, isn't it? It's getting worse because it's not the meniscus which needs strengthening, it's the human souls on either side of it. We have become weak. Dependent. Convinced that our dreams will save us and hiding from the power of our own divinity in pathetic little bubbles of fake reality. You say that if this fell, then the Aions would be set free?

I say let them come.'

From their hiding places in the Realt side of the Chamber, the Brood of Lilivet threw off their cloaks of darkness and stepped forth.

CHAPTER 28

THE UNWORLDING

1

Only a madman or someone with nothing to lose would attack the Interstitial Assembly Chamber, Jowett had said. *How about one of each?* thought Bobby, as chaos erupted on both sides.

The attacking Brood were ragged things, barely able to cling to the remnants of their human shapes, but still immensely strong for all that. Four of them swept around the Chamber's highest tier, talons gouging the stone, scything into those Hegemony delegates who attempted to flee through their doors and driving the rest in a stumbling, screaming mob down towards the Chamber floor. Some carried on and plunged through the meniscus, but most stopped at it, unwilling to break this greatest of taboos even in their terror, and milled like cornered sheep as their unfortunate colleagues who had been caught higher up were shredded apart in showers of blood and flesh.

The retaliation was immediate and overwhelming, as Toren and Foulkes had known it would be: armed guards from behind almost every door in the Realt appeared and opened fire. The Brood, half-wreathed in shadow, flitted in and out of sight; they plucked guards away at random and dashed them against the stone columns, and scuttled over the high-domed ceiling to draw fire down on the soldiers on the other side of the chamber. With enemies in all directions around a large semi-circle, the crossfire resulted in worse carnage than the creatures could have caused alone. Some of it passed through the meniscus, wounding and killing delegates on the other side, and the holes which were made did not close. Forces on the other side were only slightly slower to respond. A squad of DCS agents grabbed Jowett, Runce, Allie and Bobby and started bundling them back up through the tiers of seating towards Jowett's office.

The confusion of screaming, weapons fire, smoke and blood-letting made it very easy for Toren to reach the Chamber floor unhindered, in more or less his original human form.

'You done monologuing?' he said to Foulkes as he passed.

Foulkes waved him on. 'She's all yours now.'

'Good.' He caught Foulkes by the throat, his fingers becoming tendrils which thinned into needle-tipped filaments and bored through skin, muscle and cervical vertebrae to the spinal cord inside. It took less than a second for his shadowflesh to infiltrate Foulkes' brain, like tree roots spreading in time-lapse. It was disappointing; Toren had wanted this to be slow. He'd wanted the time to savour this man's self-destructive loathing – his petulant, masturbatory glee at destroying something which he had dedicated his life to building. Instead Toren had to satisfy himself with swallowing his soul in a single, swift draft.

'Oh, don't look so surprised,' he said to the corpse as it collapsed.

He used it to strengthen himself so that when he approached the meniscus he was able to show his true nature in its full, multi-limbed glory, the Shadow made flesh. Those of the Hegemony who had fled down here a moment ago saw him and either ran back up to take their chances between the bullets and the claws of his Brood, or else dived through into the other world. He ignored them, and with talons like the teeth of dragons he began to rip great swaths out of the barrier between the worlds.

Yes, let them come. Let them all come, and I shall put angels in your brains.

'Stop him!' yelled Jowett to Bobby.

'Me? Why me?'

'What do you mean "why"? Look at it!'

Down in the centre of the Chamber, surrounded by bodies, Toren was howling with laughter as he tore jagged rents in the meniscus. Just as at the dome, Bobby wanted nothing more than to leap down there and destroy with his bare hands the creature that he had helped to spawn, but this time he checked the urge.

'No. Like Allie said, I'm done.'

'But you must! That's your blood at work down there! The meniscus must not be allowed to fall!'

'Why? So that you can keep your control over the rest of us? I don't think so. Looks like your cosmic chickens have come home to roost, Timothy, old bean.'

'You bloody fool!' Jowett wailed. 'You have no comprehension of what will happen if that barrier falls!'

'What, ancient gods reawakening to destroy all of humanity? Do you seriously expect any of us to still believe that? Oh, I know the Aions exist, of course. I've seen them. But I think your apocalypse stories are just more of the same old fear-mongering. I think if the Aions do wake up, it's going to be much stranger than *any* of us can imagine.'

Jowett turned in panic to Allie. 'Make him see sense,' he pleaded. 'What about your child?'

'I'm dead there, remember? That barrier's doing nothing for me any more.'

Some of the rips were now so large that they were lengthening of their own accord, and through them Bobby could see the murky light of the oneirocline bulging at the fabric of reality on both sides. The Chamber, itself constructed mid-way between the two worlds with the meniscus as its keystone, began to shudder. Columns cracked, and fragments of stone fell from overhead. He and Allie grabbed each other's hands and ran for the door to Oraille.

Jowett let them go and screamed at his men to fire at the abomination below. Four tezlar bolts raved through the meniscus and into Toren, doing just as much damage to both. Toren accepted it as his due; his was the work only of a High Priest, to prepare the way and sacrifice himself if necessary. Besides, nothing was truly lost in the Shadow. For a moment he was illuminated from the inside out by purple fire, and then it burst from him in a hundred places, burning him to ash.

The meniscus had suffered too much abuse, however. The rips and holes elongated, joined, became chasms running from floor to ceiling, and as they did so the convulsions of the chamber increased. Its supporting columns collapsed completely, and huge blocks of masonry, millennia old, tumbled from the ceiling to smash chairs and desks where for generations the Hegemony had steered the course of two worlds. With them went the last surviving Brood and any unfortunate human souls unable to escape. The Ourobouros was crushed into scrap, its delicate mechanisms pulverised. Too late, Jowett realised his peril and threw himself up the heaving stairs towards his office as the men behind him were buried in the wreckage.

Bobby saw, and despite Allie's protests he ducked out of the door and tried to catch the other man's hand, but the rain of stonework beat him back, and he could do nothing but watch Jowett's expression of terrified pleading disappear under the rubble.

Then Allie slammed the door behind him, and the noise cut off like somebody throwing a switch.

3

Chandler watched, speechless, as the meniscus ruptured in the air above London. He'd escaped the Chamber early on, when it became apparent that Foulkes was embarking on some kind of self-destructive rant which was never going to end well, sidling through the door quietly and out of the office in the Shard which housed it. The security guards –

who less than a minute later would be dying under the claws of Lilivet's Brood – couldn't wait to get rid of him quickly enough, even summoning him an express elevator to speed him on his way. When he got to street level, the first warning he had that something strange was happening were the many passers-by who had stopped and were gazing, open-mouthed, at the top of the Shard's eighty-seven-storey height.

The oneirocline was emptying into the world.

Later, from speaking to other survivors of what became known as the Unworlding, he learned that similar eruptions had occurred from every single one of the Chamber's doors in both worlds; it had been both cornerstone and seal, and with its destruction, there was nothing to prevent the pressure of millennia's worth of human dreaming from pouring forth. It could only be seen from the iridescent diffraction it created as it mingled with the normal atmosphere, like heat-haze, and where it did so it caused meteorological chaos. Cloud bands and tempestuous winds formed along a front which was initially circular but quickly distorted as it spread, obeying laws which were only partly physical. In the weeks and months to come, they would join and form massive storm cells: great walls of cloud wracked with rainbow lightning sweeping across the earth, the hurricane winds which accompanied them altering the reality over which they swept so that, when they passed, parts of Tourmaline and the Realt lay tumbled together like torn-up scraps of paper. It was in this unworlded landscape that the Aions would awaken.

All of that lay in the future. For now, he stared up at the storm clouds gathering, and listened to the sirens begin.

EPILOGUE

Months after the worst of the reality storms had abated, Allie took her man, her daughter, and a few trusted companions, and made the journey that she had put off for so long. It was by no means simple. She was told that to attempt such a journey with a baby was suicidal, to which her ironic smile and response of 'been there, done that, got the t-shirt' didn't leave the naysayers any the wiser.

Much of the geography of both worlds had changed – indeed, some experts weren't even sure whether there *were* two worlds any more, or one, or something in between. Surface travel was dangerous enough, and foolhardy in the extreme beyond the enclaves of civilisation where the Unworlding had caused anarchy. Trans-oceanic air flight was slightly safer, but only by 'stat, since coal was always easier to find than aviation fuel, and electromagnetic interference made Realt technology notoriously unreliable. Navigation was by a combination of dead reckoning and payment in alcohol for the knowledge of local pilots in bars. They found passing places between parts of reality which seemed to be mostly Tourmaline, and parts which were mostly Realt, bartering for passage with the creatures who guarded them. They fled pirates and bribed officials, and once they had to kill a man. And of all the things, they found that the most reliable tool was the little plastic Christmas cracker compass which she'd kept from her days on Stray.

At the end, in a city locked in snow, they found a long-abandoned graveyard, where they searched for a day amongst the cremation niches whose brass plaques were black with tarnish, before they found what they were looking for.

Alison Jean Owens
Beloved Mother, Taken Too Soon
b. 8/13/1973 – d. 2/19/2014

Allie looked at it for a long time.

'So that's me,' she said.

'No,' said Bobby, and kissed her. 'This is you. The better part of you.'

They turned and went back into the warmth of their RV, because little Sophie had started grizzling, and it was time for her dinner.

ACKNOWLEDGEMENTS:

Steve Jones for proof-reading and general tactical and weapons advice; Gustavo Ruiz, Alberta Hill and Ada Veen for checking my Spanish vulgarity; Andrea Swinsco and everyone at Showmasters for so many new readers; Kelly Wright for Stateside PR; Anna and Emma at Snowbooks; Owen Matthews and Steve Broadbent for helping me build Project Tezlar; Iain Grant, Heide Goody, and all the other Birmingham Writers for encouragement and pointing out to me the weirdness on my own doorstep; TheThem for sanity-preserving D&D sessions; Hope for giving me the gender of Allie's child and Eden for the name, when I was too cowardly to make up either; and TC, who never lets me forget what really matters: love, family, and home.

Please Enjoy a Sneak Peek of...

The Aions

Tourmaline: Book Three

CHAPTER 1

THE SQUALL

1

The last of the Exiles urged his tired horse along a broken highway, fleeing from the reality squall which bruised the sky at his back and stomped the earth with rainbow lightning.

The highway was a graveyard of decades-old abandoned vehicles, fossilised by their own rust. They'd been driving on the left – that and the licence plates were his only indications that he was still somewhere analogous to the British Isles. Or possibly it was New Zealand. These days, it was hard to say. Of course, there no longer were any such places, but he was old and stubborn enough to persist in thinking of the world in Realt terms.

The tarmac was broken into uneven slabs by countless fissures and crevasses, the result of the tectonic torture which had been inflicted on the land. Often they were too wide for his horse, and he had to make long detours while the squall muttered behind. When he slowed too much, he felt the outriders of its wind pluck at his hair and clothes, and he pushed the poor animal harder in his fear. It was exhausted, starving, limping, and unlikely to survive much more of this.

At some point in the forgotten past, in the days just after the Unworlding, when people still thought they could impose order on the chaos, someone had made a stab at clearing a lane through the middle, and before long he saw it: a big army SUV stripped down to the axles, probably by the same people, once they'd realised that clearing the highway was futile, because after another mile it didn't exist at all.

The highway stopped, as abruptly as if cut with a colossal knife, though the traffic had continued to spill out onto the marshy terrain which replaced it and spread out in a scattered fan, as if the sheer momentum of the queue behind had made them unable to stop and they'd ended here, drowned up to their wheel arches. He stopped at the brink and looked down over them. What had these people done when they'd found that the road suddenly disappeared? he wondered. Probably the same thing a lot of people had done in response to their changed world: died.

'Just like you're going to die if you don't get a move on, Chandler, old boy,' he muttered to himself. It was a long time since he'd called himself that. Even longer since he'd been spooked enough to talk to himself.

The squall had been following him for eleven days.

There had been a hill village, no different from any of the hundreds at which he'd traded: a miserable cluster of crude huts enclosed by a palisade wall, overlooking a valley where farmers tried to coax crops out of a reluctant earth. Funny how less than two decades from the collapse of its technological golden age, humanity had fallen back on subsistence patterns two thousand years old. A baby had been born in the night, its cries heralding a wild show of rainbow lightning across the hilltop, indicating that an Aion had been made flesh. He left that same night, not wanting to witness the inevitable: the Hegemony's Godkillers would come, having seen the lightning from miles away, and if the parents didn't have the sense to run they would be forced to offer the child up to them on pain of the entire village being put to the sword. The last thing he had expected was for the storm to follow him.

That it was following him, he was certain. Something about him was attracting it, as if he were a human lightning rod; something in his dual nature as an Exile. He'd watched as, one by one, the others of his kind had been caught up in the big storms of the Unworlding's first days – some of them had been friends and allies for many years – getting struck by iridescent lightning and being prised apart, back into their original selves: the exiled soul from Tourmaline and the person from the Realt within whose body they had been trapped. For the vast majority of them, this had been their dearest wish come true. For him, on the other hand, it was liable to be a death sentence.

He babied his horse over the broken lip of the tarmac's edge and down onto the bog, which was a mistake, because his mount immediately went in up to its knees and lurched to a halt, snorting and quivering. He lashed at it with the reins and kicked at it with his heels, more harshly than the poor beast deserved, before giving up. Even if he could get it to move, having to continually chivvy it would take longer than just walking. Plus, he'd be lighter on two feet and able to find firmer ground more easily.

'Hah. Keep telling yourself that. Oh, and shut up.'

He dismounted, slung the saddle bags over his shoulder and gave the horse a slap on the rump to let it know it was free to go anywhere it liked. As a single-natured creature, the squall wouldn't bother it – it wasn't the one about to be torn in two.

A light pattering of rain began to fall.

'Bugger. Buggity-buggering wank. I said shut up!'

He scrambled back up the rubble slope to the highway verge, which was bordered by a high chain-link fence. Where it met the slope it was torn like cobweb and its rusted supporting poles lay toppled. He seized the end of one and hauled it after him back down into the bog. It was about ten feet long, bloody heavy, and dragged like an anchor. Not for the first time, he mourned the loss of his backwash powers. They too had been lost with the Unworlding.

'Christ, I hate being mortal. If you don't shut up I'll... All right! Keep your knickers on!'

With long, awkward strides, Chandler made his zigzagging way out into the grey-green desolation, angling vaguely towards one of the tor-like granite outcrops which thrust their knuckled fists out of the bog, as if giants were struggling to free themselves from the grave. The squall fretted behind, strobing the terrain ahead of him with its hungry lightning.

'Not,' he panted. 'That. Easy. Pal.'

By the time he reached the nearest outcrop he was caked in mud up to the knees and exhausted. It was also raining steadily; the squall was minutes behind him, if that. He manoeuvred the clattering pole as high as he could, and even though there was no way he could stick it in the ground he still managed to wedge it on a steep diagonal so that a good yard of its length stuck into the air above the highest of the rocks. It was the best he could do, he decided, and slithered down the lee side where he collapsed against the stone, gasping.

And then the reality squall was upon him.

Jags of iridescent lightning lashed and detonated like gunshots as they earthed themselves through the fence pole and away from their human prey. It juddered and rattled with each strike, and all Chandler could do was huddle against the driving rain and hope that it would stay upright. The worst of the squall was passing directly overhead now, and his nostrils were full of the mingled stink of ozone and his own terror.

But in the end it was simply too powerful for such a makeshift arrangement to last.

With a hollow crash, the pole slipped to one side and bounced down the rocky side of the tor, and the lightning, freed from its leash, raved around the outcrop, looking for him.

Run! Chandler raged at himself. Do not sit here and let it take you like an animal! Don't you dare! But he simply wrapped his arms around his sodden knees and buried his face in his lap, and waited. He'd seen it happen to other Exiles, this decoupling of souls. Most of them had gone to it willingly enough – some even actively seeking out the reality storms so that they could be freed from their Realt bodies – but all the same, it had seemed to him like one of the worst kinds of pain imaginable. Then the rainbow lightning hit him, and he knew he'd been wrong.

It was far, far worse.

The bolt hit him square in the back of the head and tore its earth-bound path down through every fibre of his central nervous system. He spasmed and jack-knifed as its light enfolded him in incandescence, darting prismatic shards of nacreous fire from every pore so that it seemed he was being consumed by an inferno of mother-of-pearl while his mind sang a wordless hymn of agony with two voices. Then the light grew, and spread, and split, and died, and there were two men lying on the bare stone where before there had been just one.

2

The young Asian man whose body Chandler had worn for so many years, having now returned to himself, stared around in open-mouthed confusion. At his feet was an old man – too old to be rightfully still alive. His long hair was white, his cheeks sunken, and his limbs skeletal.

Chandler, staring back at him, felt a sudden searing pain in his ancient chest which had nothing to do with the lightning strike. He was paying the inevitable price for having used the backwash to keep time at bay for so long, and his body was reminding him that he didn't have much of it left.

'Come... here, boy,' he croaked, beckoning with one claw of a hand – then saw it, and brought it closer to his nearly-blind eyes. His fingers looked like knotted twigs, his knuckles swollen with arthritis. 'Christ, no,' he groaned.

'Who are you?' the young man whimpered. 'What is this place?'

'Your grave if you don't shut up and listen to me. I'm dying. Listen.'

Recognition flared in the young man's eyes. 'I know you! You're the voice in my head!'

'That's rich, that is,' said Chandler, and began to laugh, though it quickly became a tearing, bloodstained cough. He brought his sleeve away from his mouth and stared at it, too. These were the same clothes he'd been wearing when he'd been Exiled; he hadn't seen them in all that time. He suddenly, desperately wished that he had a mirror so that he could see his own face again, as hideously geriatric as it was bound to be. Impossible. 'Please,' he gasped. 'Get me to shelter. I'm...' but his body completed the sentence for him, shuddering violently in the cold.

The young man – Nawal, that was his name, remembered Chandler – looked around helplessly at the desolate landscape. 'I can't see anywhere.'

'The c-cars. Back there. Inside one of... them...'

Nawal helped the old man to his feet; it wasn't hard, as he weighed next to nothing, and tried to help him walk down, but in the end it was easier to simply pick him up and carry him. Finding a vehicle which didn't have gaping holes in the roof was harder, but soon Chandler was lying on a back seat of disintegrating cushion foam, in a derelict hatchback which smelled like generations of rodents had lived and died in it. Rain made white noise on the roof.

'Great,' he snorted. 'You get the clothes and I get left with my old bony arse. Typical divorce, I suppose. Still. Tell me,' he added. 'What do you remember?'

Nawal frowned, concentrating. Everything was fuzzy and scattered, like the clots of cushion foam spilling everywhere, but some of them formed partial shapes, and some of those shapes were names, and some were faces.

'Ula, my home,' he said. 'Then the tap fever comes – "malaria", the soldiers call it. All the villagers are dead or have run away, and I'm so sick, my head feels like someone has lit a fire inside it. I have strange dreams, and I know that I'm dying and seeing jannah...'

Chandler shook his head. 'No. Not heaven. Not remotely. My world. My city. Carden.'

Nawal's eyes widened as the memory grew clearer. 'And then you... you were in me! In my soul!'

'Yes, sorry about that, old boy. Though in my defence, there really wasn't a lot I could do about it.'

'You are a jinn!' Nawal backed away in terror.

'Of course I'm not a bloody jinn,' Chandler wheezed. 'I'm a bootmaker. Still, rub my tummy and I'll grant you a wish.' He chuckled, but it quickly became another apocalyptic coughing spasm. When it subsided, he realised with disgust that he'd soiled himself. He didn't want to see his old body now; he wanted to rage at it and beat it with its own bony fists for betraying him like this. It took all that remained of his fading strength to turn his head and fix Nawal with a single glittering eye. It held the younger man, who saw in it the strength of will which was all that was keeping him alive.

'Listen!' the old man's voice was the raven's croak of his own death. 'The gods have returned. They are being born into the souls of this new world's first generation. They are still young and don't know themselves or the scope of their power, but once they do, once they do,' with a titanic effort he struggled up into a sitting position and glared at Nawal with eyes that demanded he listen even if he did not understand. 'Even this blasted world will be a paradise compared to what follows. It must not – not! – be allowed. Here.' He reached into his jacket and brought out a slim leather object: a hip flask.

'I'd almost forgotten this was here,' he murmured, turning it over in his hands and feeling the heavy slosh of liquid.

'What is it?'

'Eh, what?' Chandler squinted up at him. 'Stian, is that you? Who are you? Oh Christ,' he groaned. 'Not this. Please not this.' With a visible effort, he collected his rapidly scattering thoughts. 'For a moment I thought you were... it doesn't matter. This? This is a trace, nothing more. But traces can be followed. To things that have power. Things that can help.'

Nawal squirmed with helplessness. 'I don't understand!'

'Of course you don't. You will, once you start to remember the details of your – my – our life, but that's ...' he waved it away. 'There was a man who knew how to follow such traces. Jenkins, his name was. Robert Jenkins. In Carden. Find him. Give this to him.'

'But I don't know where that is!'

Chandler propelled himself upwards and grabbed Nawal by the coat lapels, hauling himself to within spitting distance of the terrified young man's face. 'Then you'd best get a fucking move on, hadn't you!' he rasped. Nawal could smell the stink of the old man's death on his words. 'Do you think darkness is all there is? Do you think that the araka were the only things out there in the oneirocline? They all walk the earth now – gods, araka, and the lamdesh too – but if you don't get this to someone who can do something with it, then all that there will be is darkness, don't you understand?'

His voice abruptly softened, and his eyes grew wet and wandering. 'Don't you understand, Stian? I did everything I could, I truly did. I'm so sorry it wasn't enough. But you have to go now, baby brother. They'll have seen the storm, and they'll be coming to find out who made it.'

'Who will?'

'The Godkillers, Stian! The Godkillers! You can't be here when they arrive. You can't let this fall into their hands!' Chandler folded Nawal's fingers around the flask and pushed it close to his chest. 'They'll destroy it too, and it's all there is. It's all I have left of you! You and the lamdesh...'

Exhausted, he fell back. His breathing was so slight that for a moment Nawal feared it wasn't there at all. Rain drummed on the hollow shell of the car, dripping incontinently through the sieve of rust, lost to the earth.

In time, the old man's eyes fluttered open. 'What was I saying?' he whispered.

'Nothing which made sense.'

'Oh.' The faintest of smiles. 'No change there, then. Do you think...' he started, choked, and tried again. 'Do you think that new baby and its parents managed to get away?'

'I don't know.'

'I think they did,' said Chandler with the ghost of a smile. 'I would very much like to think so.'

And with that, he died.

3

There was no way of burying the old man's body, which left Nawal no choice but to abandon him where he was – though he took comfort from the fact that Chandler had professed no sort of faith, and thus it seemed fitting that his remains be left to the elements and creatures of the wild. Nawal spent as long as he dared scavenging through the derelict traffic for what precious little he could find, mindful of Chandler's warning about the Godkillers, whatever they were. He was sure it would all come back to him eventually. Mostly he searched for any clothing which wasn't completely rotted away, in old suitcases from the trunks of cars. Wherever this strange land was, it was chilly almost beyond endurance, compared to the heat of Bengal.

He reclaimed the horse, which had not wandered very far, and gave it a name: Buraq, after the heavenly steed which the Prophet had been given by the angel Gabriel. It was skittish at first, fearing that he would mistreat it again – it could not know that the man it smelled was not the same as before. But he had nothing to run from now and was patient with the animal, leading it carefully out of the bog, and so it came slowly to trust him.

A stranger watching him leave that dead highway would not have been able to tell any outward difference from the man who had fled along it before the squall, except possibly that he was burdened by more layers of clothing. He was, however, lighter by the measure of one human soul.

CHAPTER TWO

CAULDRON STREET

1

Sophie Owens' journey home from the Collegium didn't have to take her through Cauldron Street Market, but she went that way all the same. The broad span of Esquay Bridge would have got her home quicker, and through a classier part of town – all marble-dressed town houses and bay windows – which would have made her mother happier, but the route off the Hythe onto the Tara's East Bank was much more interesting. There was a rattling pedestrian walkway under the rail bridge to Peddlars Court, which bounced alarmingly every time a train went overhead and sifted rust and coal smuts onto the heads of the people hurrying below. Then there were the cobbled ramps that switchbacked up from New Wharf, where navvies yelled, laughed, and cursed at each other in a dozen different languages as they shouldered bags and bales and sacks and crates from river craft to carts to warehouses to the market itself – goods from the lands outside the city which she'd never seen.

She knew it worried her parents, that a girl like herself in the tidy, multipocketed coveralls of a Collegium 'proby' would attract unwelcome attention, but Sophie felt the opposite: in the tide of so many faces, she felt safely invisible and anonymous.

Lanes and alleyways scrawled up from the wharf in a warren of narrow terraced houses – made from the ruins of the more orderly tenements which had been here before but collapsed in the Unworlding – which leaned together, so closely packed that it seemed that this was the only thing keeping them upright. And then there was the market itself.

Tiers of multicoloured awnings filled the crater of a great sink hole which had opened up in the middle of the city, at the centre of which was the steaming pool of an upwelling hot spring fed by some geothermal fault far underground. Heavily riveted pipes the width of a human body drank deeply of it, transporting heat to the city's generators and major centres of industry and power, although how much of it actually got there after being tapped off illegally on the way was anybody's guess. There was more than enough left for the market's lowest tier to be perpetually aswarm with laundry gangs, and Sophie loved their raucousness and colour and occasionally violent territorial disputes. She could lose herself in the babble of other languages and pretend that she was out in the world beyond Carden's walls.

Her earliest memories were of travelling; an infant's dim recollection of movement, the rumbling of 'stat engines, and of being surrounded by wider spaces than these. She knew that shortly after the Unworlding they had made a great journey, but she'd never been able to coax from her parents any concrete details about where or why. All she got from her father was a firm but vague promise that once she'd graduated from her peripherae studies, he'd start taking her with him on his survey expeditions for the Collegium, but as a fully paid-up member of the crew rather than a 'useless, snot-faced piece of ballast', as he put it.

'Oi! Owens! Boff-girl!' yelled a male voice.

Speaking of which, there was Howie.

She wandered over to his stall, only swaggering just a little. It was a family-run concern selling tools, kitchenware, and odds and sods of ironmongery. Howie's Pa had put him straight to work in the market once he'd finished his Core schooling, aged twelve. He was lanky, spotty, and by his own admission had been suffering a hopeless crush on her for years, which quite conveniently coincided with the end of Core and her suddenly becoming out of his reach. Boys were so predictably stupid.

'Hi Howie,' she said. 'Howie's business going?'

'That never gets old,' he grinned. 'Did you think of that one your Owen?'

'Ooh, nice one. How long have you been brewing that?'

'Only all day. But in answer to your question: completely shithouse.'

'Sorry to hear that. I feel like I should buy a spoon or something to help.'

He bristled in mock indignation. 'I don't need your high-town charity, thank you very much! How about you, anyway? Mastered any secrets of the universe recently, Probationer-Savant Owens?'

'The universe doesn't hide any secrets, boy,' she replied, lowering her voice into a parody of the grave intonations of Savant Warshak, their universally loathed Core teacher. 'It's all out there in plain sight...'

'...we just need to learn how to see it properly,' Howie finished, and they laughed.

'Well,' she sighed, 'I'd better be getting on. Say hi to your sisters for me.'

She was moving away when he caught her arm and said 'Wait.' His voice was low and urgent, and there was a strangely intense look in his eye which she'd never seen before. It made her a little afraid, and she shook free. 'What?'

He looked around as if afraid of being overheard, and his voice dropped even lower. 'Do you want to see something amazing?'

'Jeez, Howie! We're a little old for "you show me yours and I'll show you mine", aren't we?'

'What? No! Ew! I'm not like that!' She gave him a Look. 'Alright, I am like that. But not this time! Sophie Carmen Owens, do you want to see one of the secrets of the universe up close and personal – and no, I do not mean my penis.'

Joking aside, it was the way he'd used her full name that clinched it – she hadn't been aware that he even knew her full name.

'Okay,' she replied cautiously. 'But what is it, first?'

'Oh no, that'll spoil the surprise.'

'Howie. This is me. How do I react to surprises?'

'Badly,' he admitted. 'Sometimes violently.'

'Well then.'

'But if I tell you, you'll either think I'm lying or you'll call the plod!'

'All the more reason for me to know what I'm letting myself in for.'

'Fine,' he sulked, but the power of his secret couldn't keep the glee out of his voice for long. 'It's an araka.'

'Bullshit!' she snorted.

'See?'

'No, but seriously, you are such a bullshitter.'

He didn't reply, merely stood back with his arms folded and that strange small smile on his face, daring her to prove it.

'You cannot possibly have an araka. That's like telling me you've got a... a tiger shark at home in your bath.'

And still he wore that expression – the one she'd never seen before, even though they'd been friends since they were in nappies.

'Oh, I have got to see this,' she said, and he led the way without another word.

2

It was dead, there was at least that.

The act of catastrophic subsidence which had created Cauldron Street had severed the drains and sewers in the area, and though they'd been diverted and bricked up, a few of the old tunnels were wide enough and poorly secured enough for adventurous children to explore, play dungeons, and build bandit hideouts. She squeezed after Howie behind an iron grill and into a brick-lined tunnel so low that they had to crawl, and followed him as it twisted below the city streets, past junctions and through cistern chambers where every so often she could see slanted bars of daylight coming through other grills high above at the ends of air shafts. Then there was a small, domed room littered with cushions, blankets, stubs of candles and broken toys.

'This was my place,' he explained. 'When we were kids.'

'How come I've never seen it?'

'Because you're a girl, of course,' he answered, in the same kind of tone he might have used if she'd just asked what that big, burny ball of fire in the sky was. She was learning all kinds of new things about her old friend today, it seemed. 'It used to be a coal cellar for a big house. Coal got shovelled in there –' he pointed to a wooden hatch in the ceiling, ' – and shovelled out there, in the basement.' He pointed to another smaller hatch set low down in one of the walls. 'Then the house fell down and a lot of smaller houses got built where it stood, including mine, but the old basement was still here. My Pa uses it to keep stock and... well, you'll see.'

He went to the hatch in the wall, listened for a moment, and then opened it – first a crack, then all the way. It opened silently, and Sophie could well imagine how carefully he kept that oiled so that nobody would hear him sneaking away to his secret lair.

'One of his mates works on the river gate,' Howie continued. 'You know, clearing away the crud which comes downstream? Well four days ago this fetched up against it.'

He motioned her to look, and so she did.

The basement was cluttered with the sort of junk she'd expected to see – crates and barrels and dim shapes shrouded in dust sheets – except at one end where it had been cleared and a crude platform constructed at an angle against the wall, like a large display board in the Collegium's museum, except without the glass case. Nailed to the board, with its limbs carefully positioned and coiled, was a creature which, even slumped and pale in death, made her bowels clench in terror. She wanted to claw her way bare-handed through the brick ceiling to get back into the open air and escape the sight of it.

'They're charging a shilling a time for people to see it. Pa's raking it in!'

She'd thought that, at worst, they'd found something like a squid or a giant land-crab and were using it to con the gullible. Freak shows weren't uncommon in Carden, with the world being the way it was these days. And although she'd never seen an araka directly, she'd heard enough about them from eavesdropping on her parents' late-night conversations, and she'd lain awake listening to her mother soothing her father after screaming nightmares.

No squid had tentacles tipped with talons like that. No crab had that tooth-lined, concentric maw.

'Sweet Reason...' she breathed, aghast.

Howie was grinning. 'Do you want to touch it?'

'Do I want...?' She stared at him. 'Are you fucking kidding me? Do you know what that is?'

'I told you,' he said proudly. 'And you said I was bullshitting you.'

'Well no, I definitely take that back. You're not lying. I admit it. You're just completely fucking batshit insane, that's what you are!' She kept her voice pitched low, but the venom in it filled the small room like a scream.

'What? I don't...'

'When there were two worlds and the dreaming space between, those things...' she jabbed a finger at the monstrous corpse '...lived there. In our nightmares. The worst possible things we could ever imagine doing or being, do you get that?' She was ranting at him in a sing-song nursery voice, as if he were a child. 'Then, when the worlds went "Hello!", it emptied, and they all came here. On earth. With us. That's why we have the walls and the river gates in the first place, remember? And now you've got one in your basement like it's the world's best Show-and-Tell?'

His face closed. She'd pissed him off, and she couldn't say it bothered her much. 'I don't care what things were like before,' he said. 'I care what things are like now. Now, we're poor and hungry half the time, and this thing has put food on the table. Not that I'd expect someone like you to understand that.'

She folded her arms and her own face closed in return. 'Well that was fast. Did you get that from your Pa, too? Look,' she continued, as he opened his mouth to retort. 'I don't care what you think about me, really I don't. But those things are lethal, even when they're dead. You have got to get rid of it. Please. I won't tell anyone, I promise!'

But she did. After they made their silent, frosty return to the surface and she hurried away from Cauldron Street without even saying goodbye, she went straight to a constable and told him about the araka. For the next few days she went straight home by the Esquay Bridge, and after what she thought might be a decent length of time to let tempers cool down she stopped by the market – but of Howie's family ironmongery stall there was no sign. A sausage seller was in their place, and the iron grill over the broken drain was fixed with many bright new rivets. Their narrow little house was shut up and dark, and one gossipping old codger of a neighbour was only too happy to tell her that the father and mother had been arrested and the children had been taken away by relatives to some distant and foreign part of the city.

Sophie went home and tried to feel sorry for herself over betraying her childhood friend, but when she remembered that pale, many-limbed shape with its circle of dead teeth she found that she simply couldn't.